SOUND OFF!

SOUND OFF!

American Military Women Speak Out

Dorothy and Carl J. Schneider

E. P. DUTTON • NEW YORK

Published in the United States by E. P. Dutton,
a division of NAL Penguin Inc.,
2 Park Avenue, New York, N.Y. 10016.

Published simultaneously in Canada by
Fitzhenry and Whiteside, Limited, Toronto.

Library of Congress Cataloging-in-Publication Data
Schneider, Dorothy.
Sound off!: American military women speak out / Dorothy and Carl J. Schneider.
p. cm.
Bibliography: p.
ISBN 0-525-24589-8
1. United States—Armed Forces—Women. I. Schneider, Carl J.
II. Title.
UB418.W65S36 1988 87-19988
355′.0088042—dc19 CIP

COBE

DESIGNED BY MARK O'CONNOR

10 9 8 7 6 5 4 3 2 1

First Edition

For the women who talked with us, whose book this is

Contents

Acknowledgments

Besides our interviewees and the other people we talk about in our introduction, we are indebted:

To our friend and former colleague, Colonel Donald Bletz (Ret. USA), who opened the doors of the military to us with the help of Lieutenant Colonel Nick Hawthorne; and to Lieutenant Commander Elizabeth Calhoun, who introduced us to the Coast Guard.

To the public affairs officers in all five services who arranged interviews for us, but especially to Mary Farris at Hanscom Air Force Base, whose help soared above and beyond; to Major Pete Clark, who gave us pictures; and to Chief Petty Officer J. C. Mowery, who set up outstanding interviews with Naval enlisted women.

To military specialists Charles Moskos and Arthur Hadley, who generously shared their information; and to Carolyn Becraft of the Women's Equity Action League, whose expertise, gained from personal military service and professional advocacy of military women, deepened our understanding.

To our favorite people, librarians, but especially to Bohdan I. Kohutiak of the Army War College Library; to Ben Frank, an expert on Marine Corps oral history; to Eva Moseley of the Schlesinger Library at Radcliffe College, where the tapes and transcripts of our interviews will be stored; and to Anne Penniman, of the Essex, Connecticut, public library, who continues to put up with our multitudinous requests for interlibrary loans.

To all our friends who listened to our stories; to our agent, Elizabeth Knappman, who helped shape the book; and to our editor, Caroline Press, who enabled it.

Neither of us needs thank a spouse—we both typed.

Insignia of the United States Armed Forces

OFFICERS

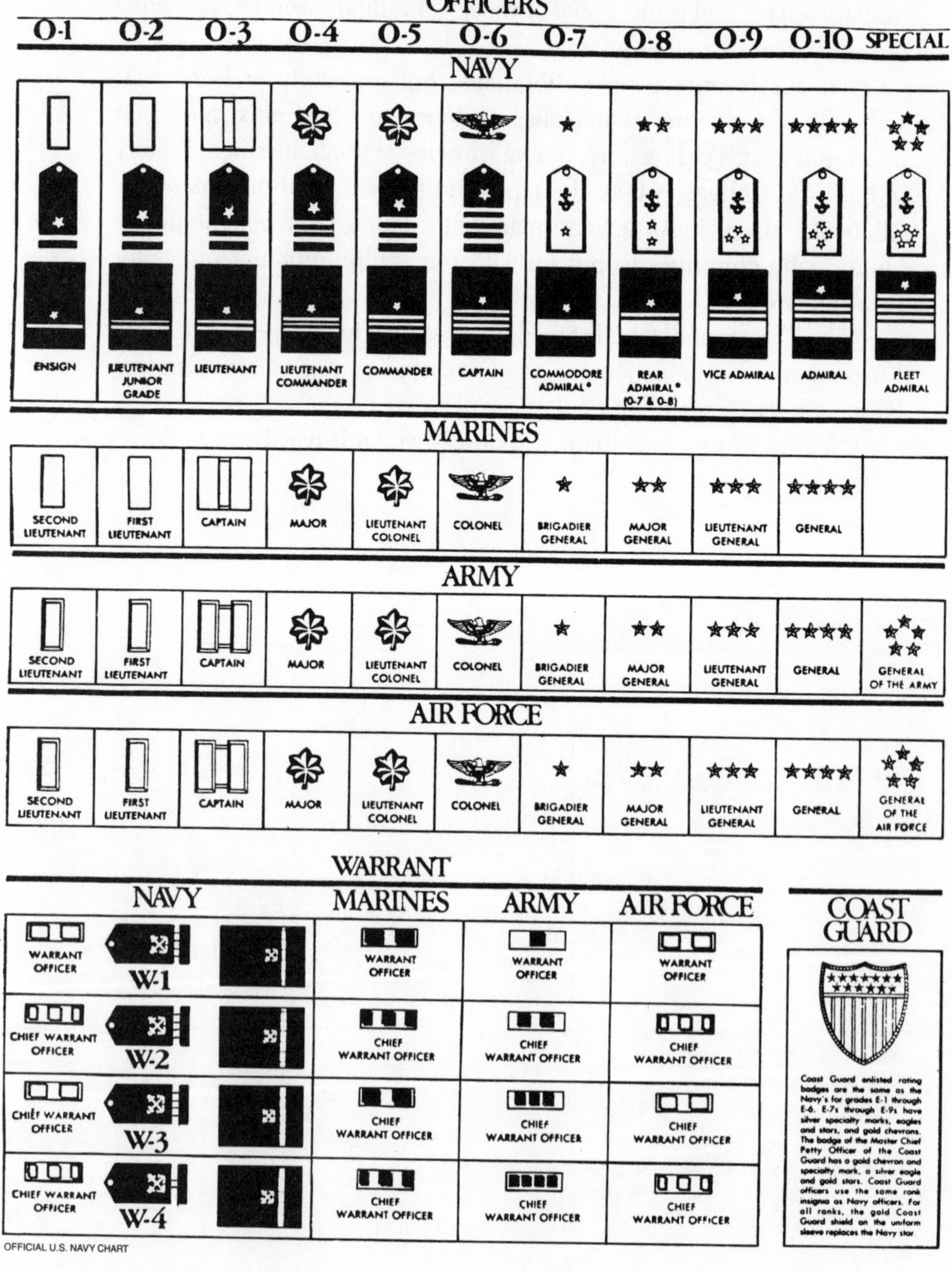

Insignia of the United States Armed Forces

ENLISTED

E-1 E-2 E-3 E-4 E-5 E-6 E-7 E-8 E-9

NAVY

E-1	E-2	E-3	E-4	E-5	E-6	E-7	E-8	E-9	
SEAMAN RECRUIT	SEAMAN APPRENTICE	SEAMAN	PETTY OFFICER THIRD CLASS	PETTY OFFICER SECOND CLASS	PETTY OFFICER FIRST CLASS	CHIEF PETTY OFFICER	SENIOR CHIEF PETTY OFFICER	MASTER CHIEF PETTY OFFICER	MASTER CHIEF PETTY OFFICER OF THE NAVY

MARINES

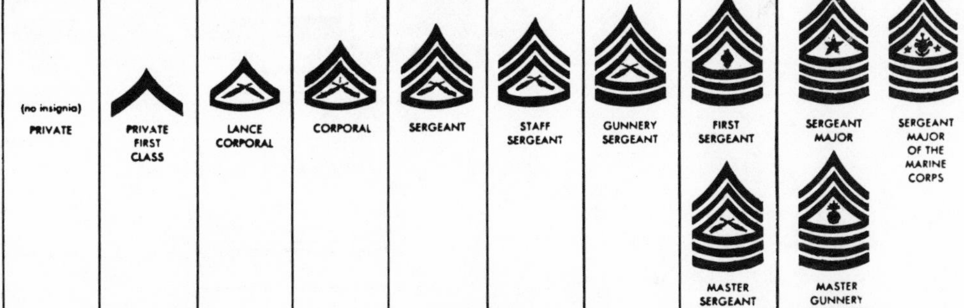

ARMY

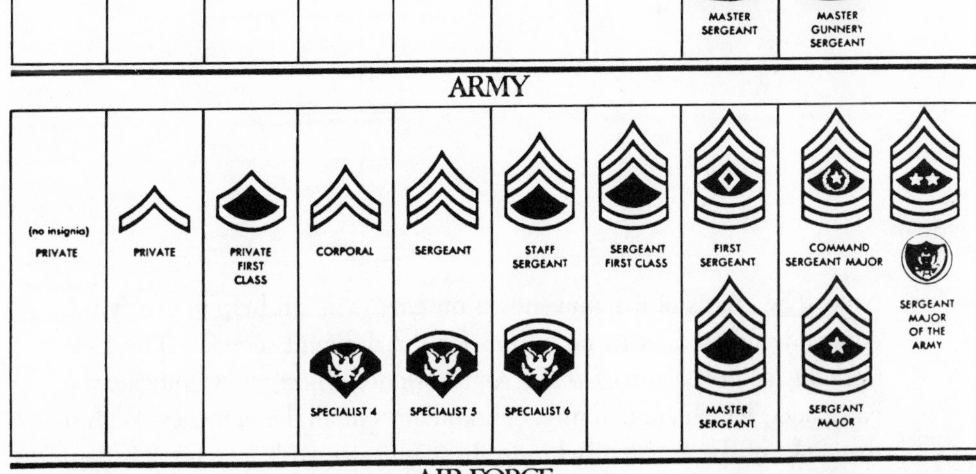

AIR FORCE

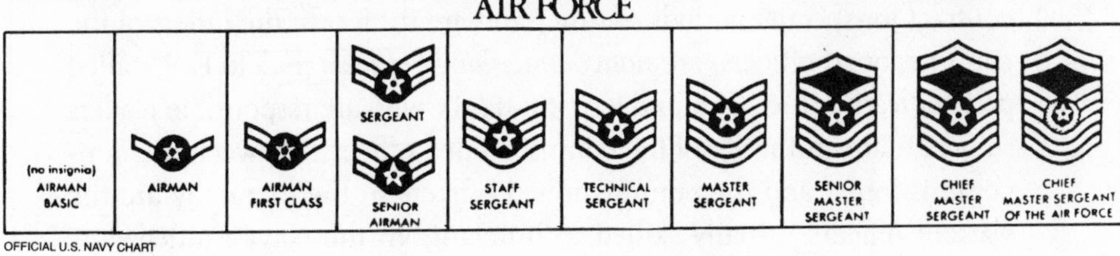

OFFICIAL U.S. NAVY CHART

Glossary

Note: The charts of insignia shown on pages xii–xiii help to clarify the confusing differences in rank titles for the different services. The E-# (for *enlisted* ranks) and O-# (for *commissioned officer* ranks) indicate the pay grades, which are common denominators in all the branches. Within the ranks of the enlisted (who do the hands-on work, receive less pay, contract for specific periods of time, and are subject to the orders of the commissioned officers) are *noncommissioned officers* (E-3 to E-9, called *petty officers* in the Navy and Coast Guard), who are responsible leaders subject to the authority of the commissioned officers. Between the noncommissioned and the commissioned officers in the hierarchy are the warrant officers, usually skilled technicians. In the Navy limited duty officers are commissioned, but restricted to certain ranks and single fields of specialization. Our interviewees talked a lot about being subject to the commands of *everyone* of superior rank, "above me on the totem pole."

AIT: Advanced individual training (in MOS)

APR: Airman's Performance Report

Article 15: Disciplinary action, as provided by regulation

ASVAB: Armed Services Vocational Aptitude Battery

AWOL: Absent without (official) leave

BTZ (below the zone): Basis for early promotion; deep selection

boot camp: Basic training in the seagoing services

bootstrap program: One of several programs by which the military prepares enlisted members for officer candidacy, usually by paying for their educations

BX: Base exchange, store

cammies: Camouflage uniforms

chain of command: Hierarchy of authority. To register complaints or seek help, the servicemember must work first through her own supervisor, then step by step to the next highest authority.

chaptered out: Involuntarily separated by regulation

CNO: Chief of Naval Operations

CO: Commanding officer

commissioned officer: An officer whose rank and power in active service is conferred by the President; ranks as second lieutenant or higher in the Army, Air Force, or Marine Corps, or as ensign or higher in the Navy or Coast Guard.

CONUS: Within the continental United States

counseling statement: Written reprimand

CQ: Charge of Quarters; responsibility for the order and safety of a barracks, office, and so on

cut-off score: Number of points required for promotion within a particular MOS

DACOWITS: Defense Advisory Committee on Women in the Services

deep selection: Basis for early promotion

detailer: Person who assigns servicemembers to particular positions and places

DI: Drill instructor

Dining In; Dining Out: Party for officers only; party for officers and their guests

DO: Deck Officer

DOD: Department of Defense

EO: Equal Opportunity Office, whose function is to protect the civil rights of minorities

first sergeant; first shirt: Senior NCO in charge of personnel problems. See Chapter 3, page 90, for explanation.

GS rate: General Services (civil service) rank

gunny: Gunnery sergeant, Marine Corps

Human Relations Council: Group designated to work out equal opportunity and similar problems

IG: Inspector General

Joint Domicile, Joint Household, Joint Spouse: Programs designed to assign military wife and military husband together

LDO: Limited duty officer, who functions within a single field of interest

lines: Ropes (seagoing services)

LORAN: Long-range navigation

MAC: Military Airlift Command

mast: A hearing, in the seagoing services. A *captain's mast* is a hearing before the captain; a *request mast* is by the request of the servicemember.

master-at-arms: Military police for Navy and Coast Guard

max: Attain a score established as the maximum, especially on a physical fitness test

medevac: Evacuation for medical reasons

meritorious promotion: Promotion before expected time, or without usual tests

MK: Mechanic MOS

monitor: Person who assigns servicemembers to particular positions and places; detailer

MOS: Military occupational specialty; a numerical code, for example, 76-Whiskey (petroleum specialist), 11-Bravo or 11-Bang-bang (infantryman)

MP: Military police

NBC: Nuclear/biological/chemical defense

NCO, noncom: Noncommissioned officer (in enlisted ranks)

NCOIC: Noncommissioned officer in charge at a given time and place

OCS: Officer Candidate School

OER: Officer Evaluation Report

OIC: Officer in charge at a given time and place

on profile: Restricted in physical activities

OTS: Officer Training School

OUTUS: Outside the United States

passed over: Not promoted at the usual time

PCS: Permanent change of station

petty officer: Noncommissioned officer, seagoing services

PFT: Physical fitness test

PT: Physical training

Ranger: Army infantryman, specially trained in hand-to-hand fighting, surprise raids on enemy posts, scout, and reconnaissance work

recycled: Compelled to repeat part of basic training

remote: An assignment, usually for a year, to a dangerous or primitive post, where the military does not send families

ROTC: Reserve Officer Training Corps

SAC: Strategic Air Command

Social Action: Office in charge of EO and drug and alcohol abuse

Specialist: Title indicating expertise in an MOS, followed by a number indicating enlisted rank, as in Spec-4

strike: Get on-the-job training in an MOS

tech school: A school that provides training in an MOS

tender: Ship responsible for maintenance and repair of a Navy combat vessel

TDY: Temporary duty

TI: Training instructor

troop: Enlisted servicemember

watch: Duty, period of responsibility

WAC: Women's Army Corps, dissolved when women were integrated into the service (1978)

WM: Woman Marine

WOPA: Women Officers' Professional Association (seagoing services)

XO: Executive officer

Preface

We first met American military women on U.S. military bases in Japan and Korea, where we spent two years teaching college courses for the University of Maryland to American troops. As we came to know the servicewomen among our students, we grew curious. What, we wondered, does their growing presence, *in peacetime*, in all branches of the armed forces mean for them, for the military, and for the country?

Few Americans comprehend what is involved; and many still think of servicewomen in stereotypical terms left over from World War II. We began to understand why as we read the literature: mostly statistical, institutional, and historical studies of military women. And their roles have provoked controversy. Some feminists treat them as victims of or collaborators in a patriarchal system; others hail them as victors in the struggle for equality. Peace groups argue that, for their own and humanity's sake, women should not emulate men but instead persuade them to reject war and its institutions. Absent from the disputes and most of the literature are the voices of the servicewomen themselves. (But see Sources for Women in the American Military.)

Servicewomen are not abstractions but real people whose military lives are not only intrinsically interesting but also important to the national security. To ignore their voices is to risk flawed judgments. We need their testimony to flesh out the quantitative studies and analyses, the opinion polls, and the disputes about women's roles in a changing society.

So, in 1984 and 1985, we asked over three hundred women of all ranks in all branches of the armed forces to talk to us about their work, their lives, their concerns, and their ideas. Listening to them was a delightful, demanding, and mind-stretching experience. What they said is the basis of this book.

Oral history—gathering and preserving information in spoken form—has obvious limitations. It requires articulate respondents with differing points of view and experiences. In proportion to the whole female military population, for instance, our sample overrepresents servicewomen in nontraditional occupations and women of longer service, because we needed their different viewpoints and their wide range of experience. More of them plan a service career than is typical among military women generally. But oral history, although a shaky base for generalizations, lends color and tone to the line drawings of existing surveys and statistics. When the samples are broadly based, when the narrators are many and diverse, the reliability of oral history increases.

The over three hundred women we interviewed differed in service branch, rank, age, occupation, experience, ethnic background, educational level, and personal circumstances. Most of them tried hard to be accurate and honest, even on matters that embarrassed them. Often they had hewn their ideas out of discussions with other military women: as a Navy master-at-arms remarked, "I've had some of these same questions thrown to me by my peers when we've had time to sit down and gab. So you're not only getting my views, but some that have been thrown at me as well, and I've incorporated."

With the cooperation of the Air Force, Army, Marine Corps, Navy, and Coast Guard, we interviewed servicewomen on sixteen Stateside military installations and at the Pentagon. As a rule their supervisors or the local public affairs officer chose women of promise or high achievement, or women with unusual responsibilities or experiences. In a few cases where we were regarded as something of a nuisance, or if last-minute substitutions had to be made, the supervisor simply grabbed the nearest available woman: "Here, I don't know what they're doing; I heard they're writers; but Public Affairs says it's DOD [Department of Defense]-approved, so go talk to them." At least one supervisor added: "Put on your dress uniform." Sometimes supervisors were amused: "Have I got a doozy for you—she went AWOL [absent without leave] the first week in basic training." And sometimes they were embarrassed: "I don't mind your talking to her, but you should know she's undergoing company punishment." Some outstanding interviews were set up by a senior male NCO who was intrigued by our request that he schedule only *enlisted* women (because we had already talked to a number of officers in his branch).

Once we began interviewing we learned of other good prospects. "Talk to so-and-so; she's the first woman to do this-or-that." "She went to Grenada." "She's a boomer on a KC-135." "Would you like to talk to a single parent with triplets?" Some women asked to be interviewed. (So did some men, who alleged that they knew more about servicewomen than the women themselves. We did not avail ourselves of their expertise.) Occasionally we spotted someone with a special qualification and requested an interview.

The Women Officers' Professional Association (WOPA) through its then president, Captain Louise C. Wilmot (USN), and Lieutenant Norma Anderton (USN), arranged interviews with some twenty-five Navy women, enlisted and officers, including two World War I veterans. We attended the spring 1985 meeting of the Defense Advisory Committee on Women in the Services (DACOWITS), where we interviewed several of its servicewomen advisers. We also interviewed a number of veterans—from World War I to Vietnam—met at reunions or located through veterans' associations, personal referrals, and references in publications.

Our selection process inevitably skewed toward the successful, although we certainly encountered women who vented frustrations and, occasionally, rage. We did not seek out irate or victimized women—

but some showed up, as did women whose satisfaction ranged from moderate to ecstatic. We did not, typically, see the "losers," although we talked to several women who wanted nothing so much as out.

We learned something from each interview. Some people express themselves more easily than others; some reflect more about the shape and meaning of their lives; some are more sensitive to nuances and trends. Some are natural survivors, while others suffer from real and imagined slings and arrows. Together they provide a composite picture, intricate in substance and personal in tone, of the lives and fortunes of American servicewomen.

Of course we encountered apprehensions and fears. Some military people were at first concerned about our good faith and reliability. A very few women feared that what they said might be reported to their military superiors; others looked for trick questions and implied criticisms. We were apprehensive that the military might send us only happy ringers and even tell the women what and what not to say. In time, their fears and ours diminished. No doubt our indomitable respectability reassured some doubting base commanders and some distrustful interviewees. No one in the military ever imposed conditions on our project or asked us to violate the confidentiality of the interview. Never were we denied appointments with any of the women we met casually on base and asked to interview. At no installation did we glean universally favorable reports. And most interviews reached a point where defenses were lowered as women became involved with their stories. We always began by explaining that participation was voluntary, no matter what the servicewoman's supervisor might have told her. To our knowledge only one public affairs person attempted to influence what the interviewees said: the women "did not appreciate" this effort, and told us so. Usually the public affairs officer "tasked" with helping us worked enthusiastically, perceptively, and efficiently.

The taped interviews, each lasting an hour to an hour and a half (or occasionally longer), were open-ended and loosely structured. One way or another we introduced certain topics into each interview, but our procedures were informal, designed to encourage each servicewoman to speak freely about her own concerns and experiences. We talked with each woman individually. Usually each of us interviewed separately, but now and then both of us shared the interview. Most bases gave us the privacy of separate rooms for interviews, but some could offer only office corners; occasionally we would arrange to meet a busy servicewoman at lunch at her club or dining facility or in the waiting room of an air terminal from which she was about to embark.

We found no typical "Ms. U.S. Servicewoman." Two youngsters we interviewed were just completing basic training (we went to their graduation the next day); a Navy chief in her mid-sixties was about to retire. Some women showed up in their class-A uniforms, some in fatigues or cammies (camouflage uniforms) or flight suits, a few in civilian clothes. An enlisted woman arrived spick-and-span after having spent a grueling twenty-four hours on duty on a submarine tender. A Naval officer arrived after an all-night session preparing a report for a congressional committee. A doctor showed up with her baby. Many women were mystified about why they were there but determined to do their best; others came prepared with résumés, couldn't wait to launch into their "war stories," and came back to tell us things they had omitted. A supremely confident career servicewoman breezed in and announced, "This base commander's a real asshole. . . ." Almost all of our interviewees, bless them, talked frankly and informatively about their military lives. (Some carefully monitored their language lest they discomfit us; their circumlocutions were masterpieces of creativity.)

The structure of the book developed from the interviews, as common issues and concerns emerged. In deciding what to include, we looked first for widely shared opinions; then, equally important, for a range of viewpoints and experiences. Finally, we chose to quote those who conveyed these ideas wittily or succinctly or with an imaginative turn of phrase. But we reluctantly had to omit as many wonderful stories and pungent observations as we include.

We have deliberately avoided examining all the problems that women experience, to concentrate on the problems significantly affected by or unique to being a woman in the American military. We identify our black respondents as black at their own request. We use the rank of each servicewoman at the time of her interview. Since then some have left the service, and many have been promoted. Finally, even though we adopt the servicewomen's own practice of referring to themselves as "airman" or "yeoman," the reader should remember that all persons identified solely by military rank or occupation are women; when we refer to a man we say so.

SOUND OFF!

1. "What's a Nice Girl Like You Doing in the Military?"

"Normal women do join the military. They're not all airheads. They're very intelligent individuals. People need to know that."

American military women have survived their identity crisis. The 220,000 women Marines, soldiers, airmen, sailors, and Coast Guardsmen now on active duty know who they are and what they're doing.[1]

Seventy years ago, in World War I, the American military first enlisted women as full-fledged members: 12,500 in the Navy, 300 in

[1] We follow the practice of our interviewees in speaking of servicewomen as "airmen," "seamen," "Coast Guardsmen." Males are identified as such. The Department of Defense (DOD) in September 1986 claimed 216,823 women; the Coast Guard enrolls about 2,300.

the Marines, and a handful in the Coast Guard.[2] But the American public still knows little of the history of its military women, is misinformed about their identity and motivation, and only dimly recognizes their growing presence and contribution. So servicewomen still hear the question: "What's a nice girl like you doing in the military?"

THE STEREOTYPES

> *"That's the first question: 'What is an attractive woman like you doing in the* Army*?' I say, 'Sir, probably for the same reasons that you are.' "*

What the question means depends on who asks it. Pacifists and traditionalists are implying: "Why did you, a well-intentioned, intelligent, gentle person, join an organization whose business is to fight?" Women are supposed to nurture! And feminists: "How can you let yourself be exploited by a militaristic, authoritarian, patriarchal organization?"[3]

Those who ask deny that joining the military, for women as for men, can be an act of patriotism, an opportunity for upward mobility, for adventure and travel and growing time. Yet many women, examining their options, see a military experience in just these terms. Would they be better off working for General Dynamics?

Surely no one, male or female, should join the military unless he or she believes its existence necessary and its purpose honorable. As John Keegan remarks, servicepeople have "declared by their choice of career where they stand over the ethics of violence and the role of force."[4] They have, that is, at least implied consent to the principle of the necessity or inevitability of war.

But equally women, like men, ought to be able to choose their

[2] The Nurse Corps, although established as an auxiliary as early as 1901, did not receive full military status until 1944. By the end of World War I, "34,000 women had served in the Army and Navy Nurse Corps, the Navy, the Marines, and the Coast Guard." Jeanne Holm, *Women in the Military: An Unfinished Revolution* (Novato, Calif.: Presidio Press, 1982), pp. 9–12.

[3] Pacifist authors like Birgit Brock-Utne in *Educating for Peace: A Feminist Perspective* (Elmsford, N.Y.: Pergamon Press, 1985) and radical feminist publications, like *Off Our Backs*, phrase the questions more vigorously.

[4] John Keegan, *The Face of Battle: A Study of Agincourt, Waterloo and the Somme* (New York: The Viking Press, 1976), p. 23.

own work. And it is hardly surprising that in a society where their civilian counterparts still make only about three-fifths of men's wages, women are choosing to join one of the few American organizations that they perceive as offering equal pay for equal work. For many women, it's a choice based on a realistic survey of their options. "I've had a chance to compare, because I was out of high school a year and a half before I came in," said a young black soldier. "I feel I have an equal opportunity in the Army. The opportunities on the outside are there, but it's harder. In here it's offered to you. Out there it's going to take some digging to find it."

> *"There's a lot of misconceptions on the outside about women in the military. It's either that the females go out with every single male on base, or they're gay. You can't win. I just wish that they would respect us for who we are and what we're trying to do."*

Other players of the "nice girl like you" gambit are really talking about sex: "Any woman who goes into the military is either a lesbian or a slut." In World War II this slander weakened recruiting, at a time when General Eisenhower was pleading for more women volunteers. President Roosevelt ordered an investigation, believing that German intelligence had concocted the idea; instead the FBI traced its origins to American barracks, where angry, defensive young men retaliated against the female invasion of a sacrosanct male bastion. But the myth still whispers in the public's ear.

Just as society generally includes some lesbians so, we must assume, does our American military. But in fact a more hostile environment for homosexuals, male or female, does not exist. Homosexuality is the most dreaded of charges, incurring social ostracism (for fear of guilt by association) and the threat of immediate discharge. As for women who are interested in heterosexual promiscuity, it's hard to see why they would choose the military, which works them long hours, dresses them in khaki, limits their use of makeup and jewelry, and sends them on bivouacs with no shower facilities.

"I'm like, 'Get out of my face,' " said a black lieutenant in the Air Force. "You do see women that are loose. And I've met women that I know are gay, and women that are in search of a husband. Well, all of us are not in here for that. You don't have to be any one of the above." And a tech sergeant sensibly commented, "You get all kinds. From all walks of life. You're taking people from all over everywhere and putting them into the military environment. You're going to get good ones and bad ones. But you get that anywhere, anywhere you go."

The military labors to educate the servicemen of the 1980s about equal opportunity and against sexism. What's more important, with women now integrated into all the branches of the military and into many more military occupational specialties (MOSs), today's servicemen work with servicewomen and necessarily depend on them as members of the same platoon or workshop or crew—the same team. Working together undermines the myth: "Boy, these men really don't want us here, but when you work beside them and you run beside them and you sweat beside them, they learn to accept you for what you are."

THE WOMEN AND THE BOOK

This is the book of the women who talked with us. They tell their stories, offer their opinions, advance their arguments, describe their work and experiences. They discuss the national policies that govern their careers. They confront their problems and relish their successes. In their own ways and words they tell what it's like to be an American servicewoman.

Most of them are on active duty. They range in age from seventeen to eighty-five—although the oldest on active duty is sixty-four. In rank they run from privates in basic training to brigadier general and rear admiral. Some of them are single, some married, some divorced, some widowed. Some are mothers; some are pregnant; most are neither. Their parents are white, black, Navajo, Sioux, Cuban, Haitian, Honduran, Puerto Rican, Filipino, English, Chinese, Japanese, Korean, Samoan.

How they resent the assumption that they're all alike! "The picture that people get of a woman in the Marine Corps is like a linebacker for the Green Bay Packers," says a staff sergeant. "You have to be this tank-looking person. Can't I be pretty and have a brain too?" They come in a variety of sizes and shapes. They vary as widely in personality as in physique. They defeat preconceptions.

Who are they? Everybody's daughters, sisters, mothers, cousins, wives, and aunts—though the rich and the privileged are rare among them and the poor are numerous. Recent high school graduates, college dropouts, holders of baccalaureate and advanced degrees, waitresses, engineers, beauticians, doctors, MBAs, lawyers, hospital administrators. Many of them come from blue-collar or farm families, but some from managerial, some from entrepreneurial, and a few from professional families. A significant minority belong to a subculture of military families, but others are the first in their families to join the military. Many come from families of more than three children; and only children are a rarity among them. Birth order doesn't seem to matter: some are oldest children, some in the middle, and some the babies of the family.

Like men who join the service, few women intend to make it a career. The overwhelming majority of servicemembers leave long before retirement. And women's retention rates are lower than men's—in no small part, our interviewees say, because so many of them find it difficult to combine military careers and family responsibilities.[5]

Military women usually like structure—or at least can tolerate it—but at the same time they enjoy the diversity of military life: frequent job changes, frequent moves, living in a variety of cultures, and a heterogeneous mix of colleagues. As military women, they take the less-trodden path, but they like the security that the military provides.

We encountered few ideologues, missionaries, or reformers. "One of the pleasures of mixing in military society," Keegan comments (p. 23), "is the certainty that one will meet there" no or few "zealots, monomaniacs, hypochondriacs, [or] . . . the compulsively argumentative." Most military women do not see themselves as pioneers. They are pragmatists, who enter the service not to change it or to prove what women can do but for their own practical purposes.

When they reminisced about joining the military, servicewomen talked about their early hopes and expectations, not the realities that they met. Before they joined most of them knew the military only by

[5] Servicemembers become eligible for retirement benefits only after twenty years. For military goals of retention and retention statistics, see in *The All-Volunteer Force After a Decade: Retrospect and Prospect*, ed. William Bowman, Roger Little, and G. Thomas Sicilia (Washington, D.C.: Pergamon-Brassey's, 1986): Maxwell R. Thurman, "Sustaining the All-Volunteer Force 1983–1992: The Second Decade," p. 267; and C. Robert Roll, Jr., and John T. Warner, "The Enlisted Career Manpower in the All-Volunteer Force," pp. 62–64. See also Glenda Y. Nogami, "Retention of Women in Non-Traditional Jobs," in *Women in the United States Armed Forces: Progress and Barriers in the 1980s*, ed. Nancy H. Loring (Chicago: Inter-University Seminar on Armed Forces and Society, 1984), pp. 72–79.

hearsay. Later they awakened to basic training and the actualities of military life.

WHY DO THEY JOIN?

> *"In 1972–73 the Vietnam War was winding down, and there were a lot of protests. I am very patriotic. It was a matter of putting my money where my mouth was: 'OK, I think we all have a responsibility to keep our country free. All right, the time for me to stop talking and start acting is now.' "*

Pride in America and a sense of obligation undergird most servicewomen's beliefs, actions, and intentions. Many of them allocate the responsibility for defending the country equally to women and to men. They join the service as a patriotic duty.

Some of the more gung-ho are John Wayne groupies. "I just looked up a recruiter in the phone book and asked him did they have women in the Marine Corps.—[I was] influenced by John Wayne movies," a sergeant of nineteen years' experience told us. And an Army helicopter pilot reminisced: "I had run away from home like when I was thirteen trying to join up, because I think when I was just a little girl I saw John Wayne on TV. 'Man, I'm going to join the Army.' "

Several women startled us by equating service in the Peace Corps with service in the military. "I was just going on nineteen. I thought I wanted to give my life to other people, and I tried to join the Peace Corps. I was wanting to go to Africa and help plant gardens. They said I needed a college degree—to help people plant gardens. I was so angry that day, I went down to Manchester and I picked out which uniform I liked best—and here I am, twenty years later." To such idealistic young women, the Peace Corps and the military alike represent opportunities to serve the country and humanity.

The decision to commit three or four years of one's young life to the service, or to make a career in it, though, seldom evolves from a single motive, even so strong a one as patriotism. Usually several factors combine.

An Air Force major tried to unravel the tangles of her motivation. She had been teaching and taking flying lessons when "A recruiting poster literally grabbed me: a gorgeous picture of a young woman officer and a young male officer, in their dress uniform, smiling. I was the youngest member of the faculty, and seeing nobody who was single. 'Hmmm, I can see a rut happening here.' And the idea of travel appealed to me. I was also brought up on a lot of World War II movies, in a time when there was a lot more obvious patriotism. I think the pomp and circumstance impressed me. I would see the Thunderbirds at the Air Force base in my home state. I had almost gone into the Peace Corps, but I didn't think that I probably was made to live away from electricity. Not just men should do something for the country. I really thought that women should do something besides stay home and make babies for their country. So many intangibles go together to get you to a decision."

> *"Well, my dad had it in his mind all along he wanted me to join the service, you know, 'cause it's a good way to grow up."*
>
> *"The most important thing that the military has given me thus far is time . . . time to think, to be able to sit back and analyze things, to know exactly who I am, what I'm made of, where do I want to go, what do I want out of life. I needed that."*

Many young women join the military as a first move away from the family and into independence and maturity. "I guess being young you want experiences," said a black intelligence analyst/interrogator, who left college to enlist. "Taking the plunge," a Marine staff sergeant called it. "I wanted to leave home and see what it's all about."

"A typical eighteen-year-old girl with growing pains"—and her parents—may see the military as a secure refuge for the "growing time" she needs. "I was young, dumb, and full of Pepsi," an airman first class put it. "I was going wild at one point," a black flight-plan processor admitted. "I couldn't get any more money to go to school. I kept getting laid off from every job. I told my father I needed a little bit more discipline than my parents could give me. He told me to join the military, so I did."

An Army warrant officer reminisced: "When I was seventeen, I ran away from home. I lived in the orange groves and I lived on the beach and I lived in the back of my car. When I turned eighteen, I walked in the house with these papers and said, 'Sign this. I'm going into the Army.' My father said, 'For a hundred years I'll sign. At least

I'll know where you are.' My mother goes, 'No, no, no. You can't take my little daughter.' My father says to her, 'Be smart. Sign that piece of paper. If she goes AWOL, they're going to put her in jail. If she runs away from home, there's nothing we can do. But the Army will take care of her.' "

Some young women look for a fresh start—a late twentieth-century version of joining the French Foreign Legion. "I thought one of the quickest ways to just get away from some of the problems I was having and make a new life," said a bandsman, "would be kind of like a radical change. I thought maybe the Army would provide that." "I joined the Marine Corps more or less running away from reality," a corporal reflected. "I was a mixed-up person. I was facing a lot of growing pains and a lot of pains altogether. I felt I cannot fail at this, like I've failed at everything else. Now I can walk around with my head high and proud of it." "This was another environment as secure as being at home. I was fed, I was housed, I was paid. People were taking care of me. They care that you're at work on time, that you're not lost or running around. I had a certain amount of restriction, but not half as much as at home."

If the recent high school graduate shudders at the idea of four more years of school and doesn't know what she wants to study anyway, she may resort to the military. "I did not honestly know what I wanted to do," said a black staff sergeant who walked away from a full scholarship at the University of Pennsylvania. "I wanted someplace to just take it easy for a little while. I could go through all the B.S. degree with the military. I just wanted a place to stay, food to eat, and a little pocket change. I enlisted in the Air Force."

"My father said, 'That's for men. It's too rough for you.' He honestly believed that they were going to send me home from boot camp because I wasn't going to make the physical part. I surprised a lot of people."

"Anything you want, go out for it. No half steppin'. Go all the way."

"It's a challenge!" our interviewees often repeated. No insoluble problems—only challenges. Women take the dare, meet the challenge, and join the service. A Marine captain recruited his wife into the Corps. How? "My husband said 'Go for it! Do it! Take a risk!' "

Often a young woman seriously accepts a challenge—however lightly made—from someone who suggests that she can't make it in the military. She grimly determines to prove herself, to show him. (All the challengers that we heard about were male—usually fathers.) "I was mean. I was determined that if my father said no, I was going to show him that I could."

"I am an Aries," said an Air Force lieutenant colonel. "My father is an Aries. I love my father dearly. But we butt heads. My father said, 'You're nuts! Going into the military, the way you hate authority? There is no way that you will ever make it!' I said, 'My stand on this, Dad, is that it's my chosen authority rather than that that is shoved down my throat.' "

A staff sergeant in avionics electrical maintenance: "I couldn't go saw down firewood with my boyfriend and his friends. At first the idea of the Air Force appealed to me out of spite: 'I'm going to go join the military and show them that I can do some of the things that they can do.' So I did." "I came in the Army on a bet in a way," said an Army corporal, "even though I was going to come in anyway. My brother got kicked out of the Air Force the day before graduation, and he said I couldn't do it. So we bet a hundred dollars. I won. Yes, he paid me. I made sure he did."

"I was afraid I would be washed out," said a senior airman. "The only thing that kept me going was that a guy I knew back home said that I wasn't smart enough to get into air traffic control. I was so down and out. I felt like 'Oh man, I'm never going to get this.' I was reaching way down to pull up my bootstrap, and that's where I was getting the strength from: 'I'm going to show him.' And I did."

> *"I have a second cousin who was in the Navy—oh God, in the early sixties. You know how so often it's the men in blue or the men in uniform? This was a woman in uniform; long before women's liberation ever was heard of, this woman was doing something that was not known for women. She was glamour in uniform."*

> *"My dad just asked me, 'So you think you could be a doggie?' Army, they call us dogs; Marines, jarheads. My dad was a Marine for twenty years. My father and me are the only ones out of our family that's been in any type of military."*

In many military families the tradition that the men join the armed forces has mutated into an expectation that sons and daughters alike will serve. Such families know full well the material benefits of the military, and the father who has heartily opposed women in the service in his own day becomes their advocate when his daughter joins.

Some women compete, covertly or openly, with their fathers. "I'd like to be a master sergeant," an Air Force staff sergeant with twelve years in told us. "That's, I think, what my dad was when he retired. I'd like to either be the same or beat him out. It's something to joke about: I'm going to go farther than he did! He was so set on wanting his kids to join. He couldn't talk my brother into it, so I guess I took up the slack, carried on the tradition."

Others live out their mother's dreams. A black Spec-4 (Specialist 4th class, E-4): "The day I took the oath, my mother started telling everybody, 'I'm so happy. I wanted to join the Army, but they wouldn't let me. Now my daughter's in.' " "My mom is really proud," reports a Marine lance corporal in the military police (MPs). "She's got all my little diplomas hanging up. She mentioned once that if she was a bit younger she wouldn't mind doing it herself for the travel."

Or a mother knows her daughter's dreams well enough to help her fulfill them. "I was a crazy fool and I wanted to jump out of planes. My mother? She's the one that picked it. The recruiter was at our house talking, and I left to get something to drink, and my mom was describing [that] I was outdoorsy, I liked sports, and the recruiter said something about being a paratrooper. My mom said, 'That's it! Tell her when she comes back. I bet that's what she'll take.' Sure enough. He told me and that's what I wanted."

> *"My entry into the Navy came out of the lack of anything better, a party atmosphere in college and a sorority house environment. I saw an ad on TV that said 'Join the Navy and see the world,' and said in front of about twenty-five people, 'That's what I'm going to do.' Lo and behold, the next morning the Navy recruiters were on campus."*

Now and then uncertainty about what she wants combines with impulse to lead a woman into the service. "I worked in a clothes boutique and in a restaurant—two jobs, but I wasn't really doing much of anything," a sailor told us. "I knew I didn't want to go to college. I didn't feel like staying at home. I went shopping, and there was the recruiting station, and I enlisted." "I came in on a total whim," said an Air Force tech sergeant. "Fifteen minutes before I walked into the recruiter's office, I had no prethought at all of going into the military."

A Marine was teaching in junior high school. "You get all involved with the students. With the same thing every day you can become stupid. I think you get burned out. I'd always thought of going into the service. I was going by the recruiting station and said, 'If there's a parking place open across the street, I'll go in.' Well, by golly, there was."

"Why did I join?" repeats a black engineman on a tug. "Curiosity. Curiosity."

"So I thought, 'God, I can still go to school, keep my mother happy, the Marine Corps will pay for it, and I'll be on my own.' "

Significant numbers of women join the service for its educational benefits. Many women take college courses, even complete their degrees, while on active duty, with hefty financial aid from the military. Many others build up funds (partly from their own contributions, mostly from those of the military) with which to pay for a college education after they leave. Still other educational payoffs—available to fewer people—take the form of ROTC (Reserve Officer Training Corps) scholarships; four-year educations at the service academies; and the bootstrap programs by which the services send enlisted members to college full-time to prepare them for officer candidacy.

"You know [my father], being an E-9 with five kids, you don't have a whole lot of money to send kids to college. So we were trying to figure out how I could go to school, and that was the only way I could do it, was to have a scholarship. [With ROTC] I could go to the school I wanted to," explained an Army lieutenant. Like the chosen few women who attend the service academies, ROTC graduates owe the military some years of service—though one Coast Guard Academy graduate preferred to describe this debt as "not really a five-year obligation; it's a guaranteed five-year job." High achievers in high school find themselves solicited by the service academies as well as by civilian colleges and universities. "I had been looking at colleges like Cornell, the University of Pennsylvania, Hofstra," a lieutenant told us. "I had gymnastic scholarships to a few schools. The academy sent a letter to my high school looking for women gymnasts, and so I figured I might as well just ask them to send me some information. What the heck, right? If they had wanted five dollars, I probably wouldn't have sent them the application, 'cause I just couldn't imagine myself in any military service. I just sent it in as a goof. When I was selected, it was like 'Uh, oh, now I have to make a decision.' Then really my mother gave me a good push: 'You have to at least try it.' "

All in all, many servicewomen take a lot of college and graduate courses. The enlisted woman most often is working toward an associate or baccalaureate degree, course by course, term by term. The officer may decide that she needs a master's degree to advance. And the military will help finance the costs. "As a civilian I was working many, many hours a week," said an Air Force vehicle operator/dispatcher, "and I was going to college at the same time. No time for play, it was all work. Barely had enough money to make ends meet. The main thing I was headed for in the military was education, and I knew that they could help me with that. It was an answer." A black Army PFC put it more succinctly: "If I join the military, they will pay for my education, and that would be a relief out of my pocketbook."

> *"I mean, my mother working at a company for twenty-three years, I was making more than her in the military after five. It crushed her when something like that happened."*
>
> *"When I first came in, my main purpose was to have a job. I didn't want my mother taking care of me any longer because I had been such a burden on her my last year in high school."*

Women, following the long-established practice of men, now are using the military for upward mobility and job training. Consider this young black woman, now a staff sergeant, whose father disappeared when she was five and whose mother is on welfare: "When I graduated from high school, I decided I really didn't want to stay and hang on the block and I really didn't want to put any more pressure on Mom. I couldn't see myself just laying around the house as some of my peer group and taking drugs and going downtown, no job, yet wearing good clothes, so you must be stealing 'em. I had been reading this *True Love* magazine. It said, 'Why not join the Air Force? Free education, free boarding, free travel.' So I said, 'Well, that sounds good.' "

For women in their twenties or early thirties, job-related motives predominate. Such a woman may find the jobs that the military offers more interesting, more promising, or better paid than the jobs she can get in the civilian world. Even women with presumably marketable skills and training may have trouble getting started or progressing as civilians. "Upon graduating from college I realized that having a degree in economics, I was qualified to do one of two things: either entry-level management or sales. I realized I didn't want a nine-to-five job: sit at a desk, work in a furniture store or restaurant or insurance company in Midwest, middle-class America. I wanted something different. I wanted something stimulating."

And what of the young biology major with an emphasis in microbiology, a minor in biochemistry, and a love for the sciences, who nonetheless could find no job in her field when she graduated? She seized eagerly on an Air Force promise of a year's training in meteorology, and finds her work in the weather service fascinating. She wants to complete a master's degree in yet another science before she leaves, thereby adding "another string to my bow."

A woman may be looking for experience to get the civilian job she wants. MPs often have their eyes on a job in civilian law enforcement.

Some women seek the security and stability of a military job. "The plant that I was working at closed, and I said, 'This is it. I'm going. I'm never going to have to worry about getting fired or not having something to do.' Before, my husband and I never wanted to buy anything on credit, because we didn't know we were going to have a job the next day to pay for it. Now we've really well-established credit. You know that you've got your feet planted in the ground and you're not going to fall. My mom said, 'You crazy? You going to leave your kids?' But I'm not going to leave 'em. I'm going to help them. My father worked three jobs at one time to give us everything we wanted. I told my husband, 'That's what I want for my kids. If the Army's going to give that, I'm going to go.' "

The famous military benefits also attract women. Much of a servicewoman's pay comes in the form of housing, food, the privileges of shopping at low-cost facilities, low-cost medical services, recreational opportunities, and social services. A lieutenant, formerly in the enlisted ranks, counted her blessings: "As enlisted members, I don't see how the life can be even compared to civilian. We have for the most part Saturdays and Sundays off. We have so many holidays during the year. We have thirty days' paid vacation. There are so many advantages that it outweighs those little nittin' annoyances that we have to work around."

"You get plenty of medical benefits," said a pregnant mother of two. "If you get injured, you go right away and get looked after. As a civilian I know for a fact, medical bills will kill you. If my little girls get sick, I can take 'em and not have to worry about . . . bills."

> *"While I was working at the hospital as a housekeeper, a friend of mine was getting ready to retire. Margy was sixty years old, and she was getting maybe a little more money than I was, not much. She was a good worker. She knew more about the hospital than anybody. I used to keep saying, 'I don't want to be her twenty, thirty years from now.' "*
>
> *"Now I got some place to go, as far as always striving for something. I got a purpose. I'm not just in the ho-hum, take each day as it goes. I make each day happen."*

When women compare military and civilian jobs, they weigh heavily three factors. First, the military is set up to train people for most of the jobs it wants them to do. Second, the military has adopted a policy of up or out, so women need not fear being kept indefinitely in entry-level jobs at the minimum wage (though they may in some MOSs find that promotions creep and lag). Third, as the military is an institution of young people, it must perforce give its women early responsibilities, for which they would have to wait years in civilian organizations.

All of this flashes "Opportunity!" to a woman like the Marine photographer/printer, a thirty-four-year-old single parent, who told us: "Here I am on the outside; I've been working for five years at the same place, checker in a supermarket, and in that five years I've gone from a dollar seventy-five and was making two seventy-five, which was no money. I came into the military. It gave me a learned skill. It learned me a lot about life. It gave me a steady job—which I had on the outside, but here, the longer I stay in, the more I can advance. Seems like I wasted the years before I came into the military. I wasn't going anywhere in my job. I wasn't going anywhere in life really."

An Air Force lieutenant colonel left her teaching job to build a military career when she assessed her possible futures: "In the high school, you can teach, you can be the department chairman, you can be the assistant principal or principal, or you can go into counseling. There's only one principal, two assistant principals, about five counselors, only one department chairman for whatever your specialty is. And there's a whole slew of teachers. There's no progression. In the military, there's progression. I took a pay cut to come into the Air Force, but all of a sudden I had passed what I would have gotten in teaching. I had more visibility."

Women also give high marks to the opportunities for increased responsibility that the military offers. As a nurse, an Army major, told us, "After I'd been in the military and then I went to being a civilian, I wasn't used to being bottom of the totem pole. Even though I would be junior member, by rank, in the military, I still had lots of responsibility and authority. Lots more independence and reliance on my own ability to assess and make decisions."

Often enlisted women as well as officers enjoy greater responsibilities than they might expect as civilians. The twenty-three-year-old corporal, a high school graduate, who supervises fifteen people in her office, is by no means unique. As a Coast Guard lieutenant commented, "One night I was up there on the bridge of the *Chase*, and it was the midwatch, from midnight until four in the morning; it was sort of slow, and I figured out the mean age of the people on the bridge. I was twenty-one, and the qualified DO [deck officer] was twenty-two, and we came up with some incredible age. I said, 'This is almost a four hundred-foot ship, we're responsible for a hundred and eighty lives, and here we are. In some states you're not even allowed to drink at this age.' "

On the other hand: "They give you the responsibility but don't necessarily give you the training to go along with it," an Army officer observes. "I mean, it's a dichotomy. In the civilian world, you get all the training you need, and think, 'C'mon, give it to me, give it to me,' but here they're saying 'Here, take it, and learn it as you go.' It's training by fire. You see a lot of good soldiers, enlisted and officers, getting burned because they didn't have the training to prepare themselves for that job."

As more American women plan their futures on the assumption that they will earn their own living, as more of them must single-handedly support their children, they value more highly the financial security and career potential of the military. "This other lady had like three kids, including a seventeen-year-old son. She'd always been at home. But when her husband developed this heart problem, she had to get out and get a job, so she joined the military as a clerk, made her way up to E-5, and then found out about flight school and says, 'Well, I can become a warrant officer and make more money and take better care of my husband and my kids,' so she put in to go through flight school. Her husband cleaned house and took care of things, and she went through the program. I really admire that woman. She's still flying and doing her thing and trying to get twenty years in the military so she can retire and continue to take care of her family."

> *"I know women that have been literally told in their civilian jobs that they gave the promotion to the guy because he's got a family. In the service you can promote through the ranks just like a guy."*
>
> *"I know I'm making the same amount of money as a male in my rank. That's not to say that I won't be the first one picked to make coffee, but at least I know it's going to be equal pay."*
>
> *"I am not going to take a cut in pay just to become a civilian again."*

The military, a Marine noncom says, is "one of the few occupations right now that women can become involved in where there is definitely equal pay for equal work, there is definitely the same promotional opportunities that men have and the same kinds of consideration that your male counterpart has. That is one of the main selling points for me to stay in. Besides, I've been in this company now for a little bit less than twelve years, and I'm already in the middle-management phase with responsibility that I probably would not have in a major corporation on the outside."

Women in the military talk a lot about equal pay for equal work. "We already have that," they say proudly. True? Yes—if it means equal pay for equal rank. Often—if it means equal opportunity for advancement in the lower ranks, officer and enlisted. Sometimes—if it means equal opportunity for advancement in the higher ranks.

"The higher the rank, the fewer and farther between women get," a West Point graduate acknowledged. "It's not that they're not as capable. It's that they get out, number one. And number two, twenty years ago when the sergeant majors that are here now were getting into the Army, women weren't getting in. The other reason is . . . the fields that women are in traditionally have a higher promotion score [it's harder to get promoted] than the ones the men are in." Senior Navy women answered questions about the dearth of women in the highest echelons more optimistically: "We're growing 'em."

All the same, servicewomen compare favorably the military's practices on equal pay and equal opportunity with that of most employers in Hometown, USA. Or even in a national market. "I'm probably right now the highest-paid female band director in the United States. I can't imagine that a college is paying a band director, at least a female band director, as much money as a captain in the Army makes. And public schools sure don't. The benefits are just so good, and I really feel like there is an equal opportunity for me here, with my peers." A third-class petty officer described her seventeen frustrating years of trying to build a career in a major New York bank: "In my civilian life, it was harder to get ahead. I really had to prove myself more than a man would have. In the Coast Guard Reserve, I feel sort of equal. I think we all have the same opportunities. I've never been slighted in any way and I haven't been given any special favors because I'm a woman, which is fine with me because I don't want that. I feel better about myself here, and I just feel better about the whole situation."

REACTIONS TO JOINING

> *"Oh, boy, yes, Dad is proud of me. Dad has me and my brother's pictures on the mantel, our military pictures, and he salutes us as he goes to work."*
>
> *"I went home and said, 'Mom, I want to join the Marines.' She fell apart. 'What, what . . . ? Please wait for a year. If you still want to go at age nineteen, I'll talk Dad into it.' But when I finally came back from boot camp, they were prouder than me! It was somethin' else, yeah."*

For her family, a captain alleged, her joining the Marine Corps was "deviant behavior! My not going to college right off the bat was a real shock. Now it's 'My daughter the Marine!' " Recruiters meet resistance: "I said, 'Mom, please, let the recruiting sergeant come up here and talk to you.' 'No, no, no, no, no.' The first time he came up my mom threw him out of the house. The second time he came my mom sat down, she listened to him and then threw him out."

"My father said: 'No daughter of mine is going to join the military,' and all this kind of old-father routine," said a Mexican-American corporal. "I never had the nerve to do it till after my father passed away. I'll never forget that when I came home from boot camp, my mom said, 'Your father would have been very proud of you.' It made me feel like, I can tackle the world with this, y'know." "My father said, 'It's basically over my dead body that you'll join the Marine Corps.' Fourteen years later I think he is still shocked that I've survived." "My mother just didn't think that that's the kind of thing a girl should do. But my father kind of liked the idea. I think it kind of highered his esteem of me."

A young black woman, now a staff sergeant in the Air Force, confronted an indomitable mother: "She said, 'Well, you go to school.' I says, 'Ma, I barely made it out of high school.' 'No, I want you to go to school. You're not just gonna get a job.' So I went down and saw the recruiter, and I came home and says, 'Ma, I'm goin' in the Air Force.' She goes, 'Right' [*skeptically*]. The recruiter came to my house, four o'clock in the morning, to take me to my physical. I was looking out the window waiting for him to come, because I didn't want him to ring the doorbell. Well, I missed him. He rang the doorbell. My mother woke up: 'What's he comin' here for? What does he want?' I said, 'Ma, I'm goin' in the Air Force.' She goes, 'That's what you think.' She gave my recruiter the third degree: 'Where will she be goin'? What will she be doin'?' The sleeping arrangements—she wanted to know everything. She wouldn't let me go to the physical alone. I was the only one there with my mother. Before I got on the plane to go to basic training, my mother looked at this other girl and said, 'Now, you take care of my baby. You take care of her.' We went to basic training together, we went to tech school together, but when we graduated from tech school, I went to Arizona, she went to Guam. Before we left, she called my mom and says, 'We've graduated from tech school. Is it all right if I stop taking care of her now?' "

Some extremely conventional parents, though, approve their daughters' departure from the paths of traditional femininity because it accords with their patriotism. "My dad really liked my coming into the service," says an Air Force captain, "because he's extremely patriotic. He's so far to the right he would fall off."

Siblings may protest. "My sister and I had a big fight when I decided to join. My parents were backing me up. But she had heard stories from people that had either gotten discharged dishonorably or gotten out of the service on their own. She said, 'Oh, you're going to become a lesbian or a drug addict. You're going to lose your femininity. You're going to become tough and hard.' That's where I said, 'If that's really the way it is, it's not going to happen to me. You have to stand for something, or you'll fall for anything.' You don't have to change for anybody, whether you're in the military, whether you're in the civilian world. A lot of people get in trouble in college dormitories, y'know. It's just life. And I'm not saying there's a bunch of lesbians and drug addicts in the military. That was her own prejudice that she heard."

A husband, sure that his wife would hate the military, may try to discourage her. "He had just gotten out of the Navy, and he said, 'No way. You're not going to like it.' But he finally said okay. He didn't want everyone to think that he wasn't letting me do what I wanted to do." "The only reason my husband's in the military," said an Air Force captain, "is because he went down to the recruiter so he could find out information to talk me out of it. He got pulled right on into it."

Even when families approve, friends may criticize. "Some of my friends just laughed. Or they really were concerned about my mental health!" "My boyfriend hated it. In fact, he took me to see a movie called *Apocalypse Now*. He was hoping that that would deter me from going in the military. Boy, was he wrong! I was even more interested when that movie was over." Poor fellow! You never can tell.

Despite the resistance of families and friends, more and more young women of the 1980s look at joining the military differently from people of their parents' generation: not as a revolutionary action but simply as one more option. Along with their male high school classmates, they take the Armed Services Vocational Aptitude Battery (ASVAB). On college campuses they hear about military opportunities. Gradually they are learning that even the Marines are looking for a few good women.

SIGNING UP: OPTIONS

> *"I knew absolutely nothing of the Coast Guard. I thought that it was something similar to the Peace Corps. My first serious question to the recruiter was 'If I join, do I have to cut my hair?' All of my life, up until two years ago, I sat on four inches of my hair. He said no.' The other services, you did. So I chose the Coast Guard."*

Which service to join? Young women choose in the same ways as young men. The Army's door was the first in line at the recruiting center. Her father or mother or aunt or uncle was in the Navy. The Coast Guard doesn't just train for war; it has a real peacetime mission. She applied to the Navy and the Marines, and the Marines came through first. Rumor has it that the Air Force really cares about its people, offers fewer restrictions and "more of a corporation-type job." "When I went to the Army, they had a wide variety of open fields, and with the scores that I'd gotten I could have my choice of jobs. So I picked the Army." "I had processed to enlist in the Army, and on the day I was to raise my hand and go in, I overslept. God must have been looking out for me. I was too embarrassed to go back to my recruiter. I'm so happy now that I went to the Air Force."

Often a particular recruiter sways the recruit's decision. "I distinctly remember the Army recruiter looking like a bag of worms." "I went in to the recruiting station, still thinking of Navy. The Navy, for some reason that day, [had] 'Out to lunch' on the door. The Marine recruiter came out in the hall all squared away and said 'Hey, come on in and let's talk.' " "I called the Army for some information, and there was this rather aggressive and eager first lieutenant who was a recruiter. She was really bubbly and excited." "I called back to talk to the Army recruiter. They have extension phones, and I happened to get the Air Force recruiter. He says, 'You don't want to talk to an Army recruiter. Come down and talk to me and if you don't do well on the test, *then* we'll take you over to the Army. No problem.' "

All too often the recruit depends unquestioningly on the information the recruiter gives her. In her eyes, the recruiter knows all about the military, and she knows little or nothing. But the recruiter, after all, works for the military and has a quota to meet; he or she does not automatically place the needs of the recruit first, any more than a real estate agent necessarily thinks of the needs of a purchaser first. Moreover, because women constitute such a minority of the military, a male recruiter may know little about opportunities for them.

Stories about recruiters range from the legendary to the abusive. "I was lucky; my recruiter didn't lie to me." "He did tell me a few lies, but they weren't major type things. Partially it was a misunderstanding on my part. Like there *are* bases like Camp Pendleton that have horseback riding, sailboating, skeet shooting. I thought, 'I'm going to be able to do all this stuff in boot camp.' Wrong-o!" "I'm not going to say he lied, but he kind of twisted the truth a little bit. He told me that for women each service is basically the same. This was kind of a little bit of a lie, because the other services are easier, even for the women. I haven't regretted being in the Marine Corps, though—even though the first two months in boot camp, I literally cried; I wrote my recruiter and asked him to get me out. I asked him why was I lied to. I asked him why was I told it was going to be a charm school." "I'm still hunting for the recruiter who recruited me. I'm going to kill him if I find him. The man lied to me. Well, not really. These recruiters can't paint the real picture. I won't say no one, but certainly a great many people would not enlist."

We have interviewed outstanding recruiters, deeply concerned about the futures of their recruits. Recruiters who advise some applicants to seek out other services for which they are better fitted, or to reconsider the advantages of civilian life. Recruiters who strive valiantly to prevent or repair recruiting errors. Lucky indeed are their recruits.

Knowledgeable recruits insist on getting all the recruiter's promises in writing. The services pay as little attention to what the trainee alleges that the recruiter promised orally as the IRS pays to the aggrieved taxpayer who foolishly relies on the oral advice of an IRS agent. "The recruiter promised me that I would be a physical therapist: 'Oh, yes, oh, yes. You're going to be a therapist. You sign the paper and raise your hand.' Which I did. When I got to basic training, they laughed at me. 'Where's your paper with your guaranteed job?' " But the services respect the written word. If the recruit can show them "where it says" *x* in the regulations or on a contract, *x* it will be. Probably. (See pp. 158, 159.)

Many a young woman rushes headlong and pell-mell into the service, only to repent at leisure. If she hurries, she must seize whatever immediately offers. If she waits, she can search for better opportunities, comparison-shop among the various branches, bargain for a guaranteed school, post, or job—or even, occasionally, for rank. But repeatedly women told us of choosing service or job because it was instantly available.

Like the black E-5 in the Army who really wanted to do paperwork, but "I wanted to leave right away, because my mom's house had burned down, and she lost everything, and I wasn't making enough money and

I wanted to go somewhere where I could just hurry and send her some money. They were telling me that there wasn't no slots open in the MOS that I wanted to come into. I was going to have to wait like a year. So I'm a 76-Whiskey, a petroleum specialist. The recruiter did tell me, 'It's almost like a clerk-typist. All you're ever going to do is paperwork.' I really didn't know what that MOS meant until on the bus going to our units everybody was asking the bus driver, 'Well, what does my MOS do?' And when I asked [*laughs*], he told me that 'Petroleum specialists pump gas.' Oh, I could have just died. And now it's kind of hard to get out of, because they're short of people in that MOS. I'm kind of like stuck."

Normally the college graduate applies for an officer's commission. But sometimes a recruiter persuades her to join as an enlisted member, usually on the grounds that she can later become an officer and her enlisted experience will make her a better one. If she agrees, she gives up a lot. Higher status—in an organization where almost everything depends on rank, and the oldest and highest-ranking enlisted member is subject to the orders of the youngest commissioned officer. Higher pay and other benefits. The opportunity for more interesting and challenging work, and more power. The company of the people whose interests and background and even age are most likely to approximate hers. And the military saves for its enlisted members a number of disagreeable tasks, like the famous G.I. parties (intensive cleaning hours).

"If you have to be a woman in the service, it behooves you to be an officer, because you don't have to tote the barge. The heaviest thing officers pick up is a pencil, really, even on a ship. The enlisted women on the deck force on our Coast Guard cutter had some trouble. One must have weighed no more than eighty-five pounds. She was the cutest little thing . . . looked about twelve, you know. It was just sort of hysterical sometimes to see her do some of the things that she was asked to do. The guys would help her out, but to call her an able-bodied seaman was really stretching it."

The enlisted college graduate watches officers getting the chances for which her own abilities and achievements qualify her, but which are denied her by rank. "Now that I know about recruiting and quotas, I know I could have come in as an officer. The recruiter failed to tell me that. That kind of stings a little bit when you find out later on." Although she values the experience of being enlisted, "because the backbone of the Marine Corps I think really is the enlisted people, if I were to stay in I would go officer."

Almost all the enlisted college graduates that we talked to agree that they have learned a lot *but* they would never go enlisted again. Exceptions occur mostly in the Air Force, where college graduates in the enlisted force are relatively numerous and where insistence on constant educational upward mobility is intense. Or in the service bands, where highly educated musicians, by a quirk of custom, are in the enlisted ranks.

"When I entered the military," says a Spec-4, "I was teaching college. I was in pursuit of my doctorate in physical education. Why, with a master's degree, didn't I become an officer? My recruiter told me that it would be more beneficial to myself and everyone else if I joined in the enlisted ranks. If I found out that I enjoyed the Army, then I could stay in and proceed on to Officer Candidate School. I came in enlisted, and now I'm having a difficult time trying to become an officer. Many of the officers say I should not even be in the enlisted ranks. All you need is a two-year education to become an Army officer. I have more education than many, many of the military officers right now."

INITIATION: BASIC TRAINING

> *"It takes a special kind of woman to, number one, enlist in the service, and then to stay."*
>
> *"Were there times when I was about ready to resign? Cry, yes. Resign, no."*

That rite of passage known as basic training introduces the recruit to military life. Dreams end and reality begins. The military woman fatefully signs on the dotted line, raises her hand, and takes her oath. She has still to undergo the much mythologized initiation, tales of which arouse something between mild apprehension and acute panic.

How traumatic or cataclysmic it is depends on the woman herself and on the service she chooses. Each service designs the first eight weeks or so of military life to suit its own purpose. Sailors understand the

Navy's purpose, for instance, as mainly to teach them to live together at close quarters. But Marines report that the Corps structures boot camp to teach them to be "lean, mean, and green," in top condition physically, and fiercely loyal to the Corps. Marine Corps boot camp and Army basic training certainly get women's attention much more than their equivalents in the other services.

All the services aim to separate the recruit from her civilian past and to school her in the military life, a process often described by military women as a "mind game" or "head game." If the process succeeds, the recruit develops a new self-image, a concept of herself as a soldier, a sailor, a Marine, or an airman.

Some of our interviewees went through basic training with men, some in women's groups parallel with men's, and others in isolated groups. Shifts of policy on whether or how much to integrate women's and men's training have recurred ever since the abolition of the separate women's corps.

> *"You know all the stories you hear about boot camp, like the toothbrush in the latrines. On television, they make it look funny and cute. It's really humiliating and embarrassing. You look back on it and you do find it funny then, but not when it's happening to you, you don't."*
>
> *"Boot camp was definitely a challenge. You really have to reflect upon yourself. Your standards, how disciplined you're going to make yourself and how far you're going to push yourself. You really find out who you are in eight weeks, or who you've been and knew you were, or who you were and never knew."*

Deliberately, the DIs (drill instructors, known in some services as TIs, training instructors) strip away possessions, personality, past. The trainees, deprived of their makeup, their mementoes, and their talismans, are to start a new life on an equal footing in an environment distinct from the civilian world. Privacy, individuality, and status fall prey to the demands of the group. Sleeping, eating, running, talking, smoking only on command, in a rhythm not their own, they live in open squad bays, forty or more to a space, with their new uniforms arranged in their lockers in militarily ordained ranks, subject to the seemingly mindless vagaries of the all-powerful DIs. "With a lot of the orders they just play with you. To teach you. The DI would say, 'Okay. Put on your PT [physical training] things. You have a heartbeat to do it in.' So we'd hurry up. Then she goes, 'I changed my mind. You're not going to PT. Put back your cammies.' Cammies are the worst things to put on, because you wear boots with them and you've got to lace them up. Then she'd say, 'I changed my mind. Get back into your PT gear.' "

The process is painful, for most recruits miss their old selves and familiar paraphernalia. Homesick youngsters sob in their "racks"—as Marines call their beds. They are punished for smiling, for saying the wrong thing. They are rigidly scheduled to shower, eat, sleep, and work with other women whose like they have never seen. They are stretched physically, mentally, socially. A former teacher analyzed the process: "I think what they do is try to get everybody to the same level whether you are seventeen, eighteen, twenty-four, twenty-eight. You are all cow manure or less. It was like starting at first grade. When I'd say I had a college degree, they'd say, 'Wrong, you have nothing. You are nothing.' That takes a while to assimilate after you've felt like you're something and helped others."

Above all, trainees are haunted by a fear of failing, which could occasion recycling (repeating a week or more of training) and prolong the whole horrible affair. "I would rather have gotten out altogether than to be recycled."

For the older recruits, better able to analyze gamesmanship and more steeled to humiliation and rejection, the physical demands usually present the most severe challenges. "I turned thirty in basic training," said an Arabic language specialist, "so it was probably a little harder for me, because I wasn't in that great a shape. But my determination, I think, was stronger than some of the other kids' that went through it. A lot of 'em tried to get out. I just wasn't going to go back home and lose face."

"I found myself older than most. I was twenty," said an "embassy brat" who had lived all over the world. "I found myself with girls that had never left the same town they had grown up in. I had a much easier time at accepting the regimen, because I was much more lighthearted about the whole thing. They lock us up in this building and I can't go for a walk and I share a bathroom with a lot of other girls. They fuss about the way I fold my underwear [*laughs*]. I thought this is, you know, just crazy. I can't believe this. I was the clown of the group."

Younger recruits more often protest the invasion of privacy and personality, the nit-picking. "I had a problem with saying 'ma'am,' because to me 'ma'ams' were grandmothers. They said, 'Yes, what?' I says, 'Yes, I agree.' So I had to go to the latrine. I had to go in each stall and say 'Yes, ma'am' ten times. After that I said 'ma'am' after everything."

> *"When I got to basic training, everybody was hollering and screaming. 'You're not ignorant. Why are you hollering like that?' In my house, you don't talk loud. The physical things we had to do, the obstacle course, I loved that. But all that screaming!"*

Gentle, soft-spoken women shudder at the noise and quail before the put-downs. Street-smart women accustomed to shouts and quarrels loathe and resist the demands for punctuality and precision. "I had had a very very easy life. Some of these women who had had a very hard life were just a lot tougher and didn't let things get to them. Me, I was really upset. 'Oh, my God, please get me through this.' " "The way those people talked to me in boot camp! I was a little house girl, and I wasn't used to anything harsh. They didn't think of you individually, so they didn't think of you as an individual as nice."

Some women, though, enjoy even the fabled Marine boot camp. Advance warning helps. "I was a real skinny, real scrawny little thing. But I didn't have any trouble at all with boot camp. My recruiter gave me this overview of the program. Other girls, their recruiters didn't tell them anything. They get there and it's really a shock. When I got off the bus, I expected someone real awful was going to come up and tear us apart. Instead the sergeant came up and said, 'Okay, ladies, take these cards and fill them out.' The next morning everything changed. They woke us up at four-thirty banging on trash cans. And the Marines who took us around, got us our uniforms, kept saying, 'Wait till you see your DIs. You're going to beg to go home.' When we saw our DIs, one of them was about as short as me. I got to feel that my senior DI was like my second mom. She was strict and she was hard, but she was fair.

"A lot of times it was hard work. You think you did a good job, and they'll say, 'This is the worst thing I've ever seen in my life. How dare you even bring it up to me?' You think, 'God, this is the best I've ever done.' But you try harder, and you find out you do better. You think, 'I'm not going to be able to stand this for two months.' But day after day after day goes by. And it's graduating day. You made it. It's a good feeling."

For some women, though, basic training is catastrophe. "We had one girl that didn't talk to anybody, all the time through boot camp. You're so busy. You worry about the person who bunks with you and about the person next to you, but for some reason nobody noticed this girl. One day in the mess hall she sat in front of me, and I say, 'God, this tastes awful, right?' She didn't say anything; she didn't nod to me. My bunkie said, 'No, she won't talk to anybody.' We noticed that, and we tried to help her. Right before we graduated she tried to commit suicide. During mail call she tried to bang her wrists on the clasps of the foot locker until they made cuts. She was taken away and we never saw her again."

The gurus of basic training are the DIs—male or female—who combine the roles of coach and mistress of novices. Their opinions loom as overwhelmingly important to the recruit. They have developed their own techniques to cope with their mind-boggling task. They may not strike a recruit; they may not curse her. But they may and do scream at her. They invade her body space, their noses a quarter of an inch from hers. They "drop" her to do push-ups or mountain-climbers (a body-wrenching exercise on all-fours) and order her to her feet for countless jumping jacks. They create the unreal, disorienting atmosphere of a nightmare.

Most often they alternate two techniques: derogation and encouragement. "The drill instructors: on the one hand, they make you feel like you're a nonhacker and you're not going to make it; on the other hand, they're encouraging you to make it, because it's going to be an honor. They're playing it both ways. You don't like anyone telling you 'I can look at you and tell you're not going to make it.' You've got to prove them wrong, because this is a person you don't even know telling you something about yourself, and you do the exact opposite just to make them look bad."

A Marine corporal of Hispanic-Mexican descent: "I'll tell you a little story. When I was at boot camp, I got recycled. Those [extra] twenty days were a lot. When I got out of the extra instruction platoon [designed to provide more individualized instruction], and I went to a new platoon, eight days before graduation, I walked up to my drill instructor, whom I did not know really. I said, 'Ma'am, I do not want to be a Marine.' I told her that I lacked self-confidence and I didn't know if I had the mental capacity to finish my exam. I said, 'No, I'm not going to be a good Marine, y'know.' I told her, 'I have shin splints.'

"She just stood there. She says, 'No. I'm not going to take none of this at all. You're going to graduate. You're going to be a good Marine.' In those few days afterwards, we had our emblem ceremony, and my drill instructor put the emblem on my cover [hat]. Again she told me, 'No matter what, don't let anyone ever put you down. If you have that self-confidence, you can do whatever you want.' I'll never forget that. I'm sure a drill instructor has that faith in every one of her recruits, but I thought that was just for me."

Successful trainees, much as they may have complained, often look back in amusement and affection, professing a new understanding of the DIs' efforts to develop precision, self-control, and teamwork. "I didn't like the pickiness," says an avionics electrical maintenance airman. "Now that I'm out, I realize they had to weed out the people that don't have enough patience. If you didn't do things exactly by the book, you could cause an airplane to have an accident, cause death or an injury."

A black staff sergeant valued the self-control she learned. "I've had training instructors to yell in my face. I'd say, 'Yes, ma'am.' I went back and beat on that closet and I'd cry but when I went to give her whatever demerit [accept any punishment] she wanted, I'd stand tall." "I've had people yell, and I've had bosses yell at me, and I can really deal with it," said an airman who once had managed a Kentucky Fried Chicken franchise, "but I didn't have the opportunity to walk away from the training instructors. They teach you how to control yourself and your situations. You need the security of knowing how to handle yourself."

What most astonished our interviewees was the transformation of a motley group of women into a working team. "As the weeks grew shorter, the girls in the flight started working together. In the last couple of weeks we all turned to each other. One example: we had to run a mile and a half in order to pass. I had been out of the physical conditioning because I came down with pneumonia, and I didn't know if I was going to make it. About ten of the girls ran with me, even though they didn't have to. It was an overwhelming feeling to see fifty girls from all different backgrounds put aside any harsh feelings and work together. We had girls that were brought up in the rough parts of town and wanted to fight: they figured fighting was their way up. They just set that aside and decided that teamwork was what it was all about."

Servicewomen even recall appreciatively the PT universally used as punishment. "My company commander knew we had problems passing some of the physical tests. One of the problems was sit-ups. So if the platoon messed up, it was like 'Down,' and we all had to do sit-ups. He was working to get us through. He wasn't out there to scare us to death and make us feel small. He respected us as women. There was no name-calling. It can get pretty gritty, the female nasty names. He called us 'Ladies' and made us feel good."

But DIs don't always succeed, and trainees don't always learn. "In our case, no support system built up in boot camp. I think we had too many bad apples that weren't recycled or let out. We had some who had come from a tough life. A girl from New York had a switchblade taken from her when they went through her suitcase. I think it's harder for people like that to take anything; they had to take enough in the city. They're 'not takin' nothin' from nobody,' they tell you. We were supposed to be a team, but the recruits just didn't have that discipline and respect. The kids were getting into trouble. An individual would zip one off, and you'd all get punished. The drill instructors tried to get peer pressure to work, but the recruits just weren't mature."

Sometimes, that is, recruiters' errors become trainers' failures and recruits' defeats. A Coast Guard E-6, a college graduate who personally found basic training "boring, just boring," felt an empathy with the other women. "We started out with fifty-five, and we dropped down to I think it was forty-three. We lost most of our people because they couldn't swim. I felt very badly because I think that's something a recruiter could have told them: 'Take two months, learn to swim, and then come and enlist.' "

What keeps the trainee alive and functioning through put-downs, misery, and boredom? A curious amalgam of her own force of character, her own motivation, and the DIs' skill. "We had a lot of majority members who had never been around blacks, and never even seen blacks, except in the newspaper and on television," said a black staff sergeant. "I'd always stand tall. I wasn't belligerent, and I wasn't even angry, but I knew that some things weren't quite right. But I felt that if there was something in life, I had to go for it and I had to be positive."

"Why did I stay?" responded a Marine sergeant. "Well, I thought that it could not have been as hard as I thought it was, because all the other girls were going through what I was going through, and they were staying and hacking it. I cried a lot of times, but I tried. Even though I felt that it was cruel and unusual treatment. Then the first thing you know you're actually laughing and having a good time and meeting new people. I guess that was what motivated me to keep going, seeing other people round me make it, and having my recruiter write me, 'If I'd told you exactly what it was going to be, you would not have gone.' My mother's encouragement also. I shocked myself to make it through there."

"I went to basic training with the enlisted people. They knew I was going to OCS, so I was immediately put in a leadership position. Everytime I had a couple of minutes to myself, whether it was in the bathroom, or trying to change socks, it was always 'Carrington, Carrington.' There was absolutely no time for me. Everything was devoted to my troops. But then from there I went to OCS and gained a new appreciation for basic training, because OCS made it seem like a Sunday School picnic."

"I went to the infantry school OCS at Fort Benning. It's very physically and mentally stressful."

Initial military training for both enlisted members and officers aims to teach military customs, history and physical conditioning. But while enlisted schools indoctrinate recruits in group values and teamwork, officers' training emphasizes the ability to plan, to command, to lead. "We go through Officer Candidate School for ten weeks, and they determine if you are Marine Corps officer quality. If so, you're commissioned and you go to the basic school, where you learn tactics, weapons, the legal aspects of being a Marine Corps officer, all the rules and regulations.

"About three years before I came in, they started an integrated basic school, having the women in with the men and doing everything that the men did. By the time I got through it they had cut out some of the things: we were not allowed to do offensive tactics. It was pretty boring, walking around behind. We used to make hand grenades out of snow. But on the hikes we went the same distance, carried the same weight in our packs, carried our weapons, carried the extra machine gun. We would set up defensive perimeters, digging holes and laying out mines and concertina wire.

"We had six women in our platoon and about thirty men. Probably half of the women who went through that program wish that it had stayed integrated and half of them think it's better now. I wish it was the way I went through. Unless the men actuallv see you doing those things, they don't believe it. If you start off on a hike ahead of them, they don't believe you took the same route. But if they see you standing next to them, they have a hard time believing that you aren't capable of doing that. And I think it's important for the women to see the men. After I completed that twenty-mile hike, with blisters, miserable, in pain, I thought, 'I'm pretty special to do this.' Then I went to get some Band-Aids. There were some men over there, and I thought, 'Gosh, they hurt just as much. I'm no better than they are. Rats!' It made me see them as a little bit more human. They're vulnerable. They hurt. They get hot. They get hungry. They get tired. And I know how miserable they are when they're out in the field, because I was there."

Let a black Army PFC sum up the experience of basic training: "I was afraid. Yes, ma'am. That was my first time leaving my grandmother [who raised her], and she cried and I cried. I called home often. I just missed her so much. I was on bended knees most of the time. Me and the Lord grew close, that eight weeks away. I think I made it harder on myself than it really was, being so worried. But I was afraid to shoot a weapon. When I got to Fort Jackson, I could not do one correct push-up. When I left, I could do thirty-two. I'm only required to do sixteen. I doubled it there. Yes, ma'am. Running everywhere. Running from lunch, running from breakfast, running from dinner, running for physical training. Which was good for us.

"I grew up a lot while in basic training, 'cause I knew I was on my own. Every decision that had to be made, I had to make it by myself. I could pray about it and ask the Lord to give me the right answer, but I still had to talk with myself. Also I realized that my grandmother wouldn't be there all the time for me, and [it was] time to grow up now. It just made me respect myself as well as others much more, and it's just made me a woman."

2. Woman's Place in a Man's World

" . . . this male-dominated institution, this job that's created for men."

"I feel that our male counterparts are beginning to accept us as people they can really truly depend on and work with. It's in the first stages of its . . . I don't know what the word is. It's metamorphosis."

Its 220,000 women comprise about the same proportion of the American military—10 to 11 percent—as black people comprise in American society at large. In this traditionally male stronghold, military women confront the problems of being a minority. Without safety in numbers, often lonely or even isolated, they know that everything they do is highly visible—and therefore highly vulnerable to criticism. They are excluded by law or tradition from the military's most prestigious occupations—just as black and Oriental men were in the past. And they are the objects of antagonism from some of the male majority.

MINORITY STATUS

> *"That was one of the hardest things for me to get used to, that I was in a fishbowl. Just the minute that I would do something, someone was always around saying 'I knew it. They shouldn't have women in the Marine Corps. They're more problems than they're worth.' "*

> *"A man can fall out every time or whine on field problems [training exercises] and it's not as big a deal. It's so much more obvious when a woman does something wrong."*

Women are scarce to nonexistent in some segments of the military world: in the infantry and the artillery, on fighters and bombers, and on most Navy ships.[1] Many a woman finds herself the only woman in the unit in which she works and lives—a lonely and sometimes a desperate life, requiring radical adaptations.

Their scarcity and the rapid changes of the past decades have made military women willy-nilly collectors of "firsts," for which they pay a high price in isolation and exposure to criticism. Every senior woman we talked to, enlisted or officer, had her experiences as first woman in her unit, first in her rank, first in her MOS, first to attend a war college, in the first class at a service academy. We'd guess that fully 60 percent of all the women we talked to had chalked up at least one "first."

Even a woman in such a traditionally female MOS as personnel administration says, "After a while you want to just talk to a female. I get tired of looking at men, listening to their conversation. I don't mind talking about sports and cars—well [conversations about] girls I can do without. But it'd be nice every now and then to have a conversation with a female. Or come in to work and see something else than these guys."

"If I could change one thing in the military," says a senior airman, "I would put more women in it. We're trying to get all the girls on one crew, because that way we will have a little bit of power. There'll be more women to take the comments. It would make attitudes different, the guys' attitudes toward women. I think it would help the morale of

[1] Women's exclusion from these segments and the interservice discrepancies are due to the peculiarities of the "combat-exclusion" legislation *and* its interpretation. See Chapter 5. Women do serve on Navy tankers and repair vessels, Army ships, and Coast Guard vessels.

the guys too. I'm not saying that in a weird way; don't take me wrong. But back in school, where there's usually a pretty even number of men to women, it seems like it was a lot happier."

Being one among many causes all kinds of problems, an Army staff sergeant on a field exercise in Hawaii discovered: the twenty-five men in her unit slept in the tent in which they worked, but she had to walk a half mile to sleep in a "woman's tent." "Finally I made me a corner in the men's tent, and I put rope up on both sides and put my camouflage blankets on them and I said, 'I'm sleeping here. I came with you guys and I'm not goin' cross-country here every day to the other tent.' The girls in that tent worked night shift, so I had to sleep there by myself at nighttime. It was more dangerous for me than it was sleepin' with all the boys. I went to my commander: 'Sir,' I says, 'I think it's unfair that I have to stay away from my unit, just for me being female. I already asked all these guys if they could handle a woman sleepin' next to 'em, and they said fine, and I said well, I can handle the men.' Boy, did I find out that night the sergeant major snored terrible!"

But sharing a tent with the guys doesn't appeal to everyone: "It's sort of hard, you know, to sleep. You be wondering, anybody coming over here? And then it's hard to get dressed in the morning with a male that you're not even fond of just looking at you."

Women who pioneer in nontraditional MOSs experience isolation particularly keenly. "The marine field [in the Army] is really special," said a Spec-5, "because we have only three female warrant officers, and that's just been within the last year. I was getting really disgusted, because I didn't want to be the first one. The marine field is a clique of redneck warrant officers that sit around and drink beer and talk about how the last one didn't dock his boat right, right? Then to have that one female go up there and make it. Everybody just really looked at her: 'Well, she doesn't know what she's doing. She hasn't been in long enough.' And yet they can take a guy in that's been in less than her and may have had less experience, and they don't even notice him."

"When a woman fails in a nontraditional career field," an Air Force tech sergeant observed, "she stands out like a sore thumb. If you take a maintenance unit, where you might get thirty new people a year, maybe one or two are going to be women. If she fails, you've got a 100 percent failure rate among women. And they use those statistics. They're distorted, but they use 'em. I've seen it happen in schools that have a notoriously high failure rate. Out of five classes of twenty people you might have one woman. If she fails, it stands out. There are women that don't make it over in Personnel every day, but because there are so many of them over there it doesn't show as much."

SECOND-CLASS CITIZENSHIP

> *"The hardest thing in the military? Getting people to overlook the fact that I was a female. When new people come in to the unit they go, 'Do we have any females?' I always tell 'em, 'It's not the fact that it's a female. It's still a troop. And we still gotta train 'em, just like they were just anybody.' "*

Their minority status combines with the "combat-exclusion policy" to deny women full citizenship in the military world. As Naval Captain Patricia Gormley remembered her earlier service in the Marine Corps, "We were called Women Marines. But the 'Women' was always in front. You just wanted to be 'a Marine.' They said you were, but we weren't sure if we always believed it, because when push came to shove, the Marines went, we stayed. As long as we can't do everything that the men do, there's always going to be that door that you can't step through."

Not being eligible to do everything that servicemen can do means exclusion from combat MOSs—where promotions come fastest and bonuses run biggest. It means not getting to fly fighters and bombers or drive tanks; not going to sea on aircraft carriers and destroyers and submarines; not being allowed to serve as Marine guards at U.S. embassies abroad.

This second-class citizenship, say many servicewomen, makes for second-class careers: women seldom reach the high ranks attained by men of equal ability. Yes, the Air Force has promoted a woman as high as major general; the Navy has had a rear admiral; the Army and the Marine Corps have their brigadier generals. (In the Coast Guard, which readmitted women as regulars only in 1973, no woman has yet reached a rank above commander.) But no woman officer has ever attained the highest rank in her service; no woman has ever achieved the top-rated enlisted rank in any of the services. The higher the rank, officer or enlisted, the smaller the proportion of women. Until 1967 the rank that a woman could attain was limited by law.[2] Now, many servicewomen believe, the combat-exclusion policy stunts women's career growth.

ANTAGONISM

> *"I think we have a lot of gentlemen in the Army that work hard, and they don't want that tagged on 'em, that they're a bunch of animals, 'cause there are a lot of nice people in the Army."*
>
> *"Some of them still think, 'Women didn't go out and get their asses shot off to do this. We did. Why should women be allowed in the Corps?' "*

The responses of military men to military women, say our interviewees, range all the way from support and protection to assault. One extreme: a supportive and pragmatic male supervisor, extolled by an Army E-4. "This Spec-4 used to harass me. He used to make his odd little comments. He was just being perverted. Finally I told my sergeant, 'Sergeant Mack, this guy's really getting to bother me.' Sergeant Mack says, 'Hit him.' I said, 'I can't hit him. He'll kill me.' And Sergeant Mack taught me—every day, after work, he'd teach me a karate move. He says, 'He's not going to mess with you.' So next time this guy said something to me, I hit him right smack in the chest. He never ever said nothing to me again. Sergeant Mack says, "I could tell him to stop, but you have to make him stop. You can take it to your chain of command, but they're going to put him in jail, just for being obnoxious. If you can handle it yourself, handle it.' " Bless Sergeant Mack.

And the other extreme, a young male rampant: "In basic you go to church on Sunday, boy, just to get away from your TI, whether you believed in God or not. I met this fellow at church. We were walking around the church grounds, broad daylight, and he pushes me in the bushes. I'm not thinking about what this guy is going to do to me. I'm thinking, 'My stockings are ripped. My uniform is dirty. I'm going to get in trouble with my TI.' And he jumps on top of me. I said, '*What*

[2] Jeanne Holm, *Women in the Military: An Unfinished Revolution* (Novato, Calif.: Presidio Press, 1982), p. 192.

are you doing?' He said, 'Isn't that what WAFs [Women in the Air Force] are for?' Ohhhh. I was livid. I slapped him. Yeah, he backed off."

As a Marine staff sergeant puts it, "It's a learning process for a lot of guys. Even now there are guys at this command, staff NCOs, male Marines, this is the first place they've ever dealt with women on a professional basis. They think we shouldn't have gotten in World War I as Marinettes, much less have our Women Marine companies and then, God forbid, become a part of the regular Marine Corps."

> *"The big hassle we get out in the fleet is 'Oh, you're just a little girl. You're not going to be able to pick me up and carry me out of a hole if I get knocked out and there's a fire down there.' My answer to that is 'I may not be big enough, but I'm smart enough to figure out a way to get you out.' "*

Male resentment shows up in all sorts of grievances, some with a modicum of justification, some not. Some servicemen dislike the servicewoman's intrusion into the male group. She may protest a serviceman's use of foul language or his sexual braggadocio—or the other men may tell him to clean up his act in her presence. Where is his freedom to be a man among men? How can he and his buddies be a band of brothers when she is forever around? How is he supposed to treat her? Women have such bizarre needs: not only bras and pantyhose, which Supply never had to bother with before, but who can remember to order tampons when the unit is going to the field?

If some servicemen protest women's presence, others protest their absence: some servicemen, that is, feel aggrieved because the combat-exclusion policy shuts women out of ("lets them off") the infantry, an assignment that few males crave. The same policy (or the Navy's interpretation of it) keeps women in shore billets, necessitating more sea duty for men, a major cause of complaint among male sailors. If women don't brave the same dangers, don't do the same dirty work, don't take the same unwanted assignments, what are they doing in the military anyway? In vain women protest that they would if they could. All the "grunt" [infantryman] knows is that he's out there training to do something dirty and dangerous, and she isn't. (Neither are most other military men, but their absence is not so conspicuous.)

"Women are now issued seabags in the Coast Guard. My time, we had lockers. What does it mean? Equality! The men hated that we had a locker. They had to fold everything up and put it in their seabag. Now women get their seabags and baseball caps. The Coast Guard has finally recognized that women are not a passing fancy. The future is now."

Some servicemen allege that women are always "getting over," not doing their share of the work, because they're given special treatment, because they're not strong enough, or because they're lazy. When someone has to carry a heavy load, the supervisor always calls for a man. The supervisor lets a woman lie down because she is suffering menstrual cramps or morning sickness. Some male is always carrying the hundred-pound tool box for the woman mechanic, or helping her change the big tire or hold the heavy spare part in place for welding. She gets to ride in the front of the truck. And so on.

Beyond a doubt, as most military supervisors are still male, women sometimes do get special treatment. Some women do strain and stagger under the heavy materials that they must move, and servicemen often help them—though not always. And some women do use feminine wiles to escape work or to avoid getting dirty. An Army second lieutenant struggled to understand why: "I work very hard to do what I do well. I know what's expected of me as a soldier, and that's what I'm going to do. I don't see that same feeling in most of the women, and I think part of that is because they're not pressured to do that. You know, if someone's not going to push you to your highest achievements, then you're going to sort of slack off." But, as a Navy E-7 observed, sloth is not confined to one sex: "The guys are usually always saying that the females don't want to do this; they won't want to do that. They got guys just like that. You can't say it's just females doing it."

"It threatened his masculinity. People would make comparisons: 'Look at his wife. She's a drill sergeant, and look what he's doing.' "

Competition fuels male resentment. Historically the services have set higher enlistment requirements for women than for men.[3] In the

[3] See, for example, in *The All-Volunteer Force After a Decade*, ed. William Bowman, Roger Little, and G. Thomas Sicilia (Washington, D.C.: Pergamon-Bressey's, 1986): C. Robert Roll, Jr., and John T. Warner, "The Enlisted Career Manpower in the All-Volunteer Force," pp. 58–59; and Martin Binkin and Mark J. Eitelberg, "Women and Minorities in the All-Volunteer Force," p. 98; n. 36, p. 100; and n. 65, p. 102.

enlisted ranks the military relies heavily for promotion on written tests, in which women's verbal skills give them an advantage. Women's conscientiousness in handling details helps them to master clerical and managerial jobs. And women present fewer disciplinary problems than men. "The quality of the women as compared to that of the men?" responded an Army lieutenant, a platoon leader. "Much higher. Organizational skills are much higher. When they're put in a situation of responsibility, they tend to do much better. They're more mature than their peers at certain levels, especially E-1s through E-4s. I think that you'll see soldier-of-the-month awards are traditionally won by women, eight, nine times out of twelve."

Even in physical training some servicewomen challenge the men. It doesn't help that drill instructors sometimes use the women's performance as an incentive: The "C'mon, are you going to let a girl beat you?" approach does nothing to warm the welcome extended to servicewomen. Some women do relish it, though, like the Marine who told us: "At the staff school when we ran I was in front of the guys. They said, 'You're in great shape. What do you do? Run marathons?' It made the guys want to not fall out, because they see me up front and they're embarrassed. They need that once in a while." "It wasn't fun, making me drop for push-ups in front of the whole platoon at airborne school," a West Point graduate mused. "The women were made to go first in everything. Jumping off the two hundred sixty–foot tower, I was the first one. Women were the first ones to go out [of] the plane to show the men, 'The women can do it. So can you.' "

Some servicemen who enjoy competing with other males can't deal with women as competitors. "When I was at the [ROTC] detachment my freshman and sophomore years, we never had any troubles with males and females being together. It wasn't until I got to summer camp with cadets who attended military schools only for men; for some it was the first time that they had ever seen a woman in uniform. At first they were like 'Wow, she's really doing well. This is great.' After a while they felt really threatened, and they almost started not liking me, because I knew my stuff."

"I was chosen to lead a night patrol," a Marine lieutenant reminisced about her basic school. "I took this seriously. Easter weekend everybody went away. I went out and I combed my area, made sure I knew where everything was, so when they dropped us off from the helicopter I could lead everybody. They recommend that you do a terrain model. I had these little American flags, and we got bubble gum and like Juicy Fruit wrappers to indicate water, certain things for the landing zones. The next day in the classroom the instructor said, 'I want everyone to give Lieutenant Smith a round of applause. I have never seen a better-led patrol, a better terrain model in my entire career, even out in the fleet.' But the only ones that gave any applause were, of course, the Women Marines—I could not have done it without them—and one male officer. Later he said he went back to his platoon and said, 'You bunch of jerks. Are you that insecure that you cannot support a fellow Marine?' "

Sometimes a serviceman having trouble at home vents his wrath at his wife on the nearest servicewoman. "You come in and take all the crap you shouldn't have to take. I'll take it a little bit, and then I'll just go, 'Hey, get off my case. If you've got a problem with women, go home and talk it out with your wife. I don't need to hear your crap.' If they have a problem with their wives at home, they come in and they look for the first female: 'Huh, there's another one, man. Huh.' "

Servicemen may be taken aback by servicewomen's independence. Women earning the same money as men for the same work don't respond in the expected ways, as a black Army E-4 reported. "A lot of the guys in the service, they be trying to tell you what to do. But like if you own a car, if you rent an apartment, if you tell them, 'Well, I'm here too, and I'm making my own money,' they don't like that. I guess they think they've taken over the world so they can take over you too, but it don't work like that."

> *"A lot of old crusty sergeants just have this straight, narrow thinking, and it's really funny. They always say, 'In* my *Army, I wouldn't have any women.' I tell 'em, 'Well, it's not your Army.' "*

> *"I have found that Marines one-on-one usually are pretty nice people. But as a young enlisted Marine I also found that when you got several of them together they could be very—what should I say?—less than nice."*

Two kinds of servicemen, our interviewees say, have the most trouble dealing with servicewomen. First, men nearing retirement who have worked only with men, now forced to reconstruct their image of the military *and* their images of women. "A lot of them are clumsy," a Marine corporal observed, "not used to being around women at work.

It takes a while for them to change. Their language. Some of them change their clothes in the office, and then they find out they can't. The jokes—they don't want to say the wrong things. What do I do with her now that she's here?"

Second, men with macho self-images, often young and unsure of themselves, brought up to believe that women are made only for men's pleasure and convenience. If an eighteen-year-old woman is sent for her first assignment to an isolated Coast Guard small-boat station, where she is the only woman or one of two among a group of servicemen like these, she's in for a testing and racking experience. They will vie for dates with her and proposition her, making it a point of honor not to take no for an answer. Her male peers and her supervisor can make her life and work a torment. Only by presenting herself "professionally" from the beginning can she survive—quite a lot to ask of an eighteen-year-old in a strange and hostile environment.

The problem is exacerbated when the military tells men in a particular unit that they are special. As an Army lawyer observed, "We have a lot of problems with those guys, because they've been pumped up to believe that they are elite, they're infantry soldiers, they're tough, they're manly, they can handle drink, they can handle women. We have a lot of guys beating up their wives, alcoholics, on drugs, and half the time the command doesn't want to hear about it, because by God this guy's a good troop. He's just great in ceremonies. You know, wonderful."

A Marine captain analyzed what happens: "I went down to the basic school and talked to some women second lieutenants. One gal said, 'Ma'am, what would you do if one of your contemporaries said, "What are you doing in my Marine Corps?" and he was not drunk, he was deadly serious?' I told her, 'Well, one of my contemporaries, I'd probably turn around, dial Bethesda [Hospital], and tell them to come down and bring a big net: "You've got one." He's still at the maturity level, like subzero.' I told them, 'What they're doing to you here is getting you all fired up, motivated to go out and take the fleet by the tail and just tear it up. They've got these guys pumped up, just like you get pumped up. Those young men are scared to death. They don't know if they can compete against the men. And here you come, a woman. They have statistics that the women in the Marine Corps, enlisted or officer, are all a notch above. He's scared to death of you, so he's going to come off with this Mickey Mouse trash. If he gets too outrageous, swat him down. But otherwise just be you.' "

With 220,000 women in the military, even the old curmudgeons and the young bulls have to deal with them (though we heard stories of men who would request a transfer to another unit to avoid having to work with or for women). As a Panamanian Marine staff sergeant said, "Some of them are more macho-fied: 'Oh, a woman shouldn't be here. She should stay home.' But at the end it was like 'Well, they're here, so now we'll live with them.' "

HARASSMENT

> *"He says, 'Well, you want people to think you're attractive, right?' I said, 'Yeah. After five o'clock. But from nine to five I'm a sailor. Just like you're a sailor.' "*
>
> *"I'm six years into the military, and these guys still see me as their little sister. I am not your little sister. I am a sergeant E-5, just like this man sitting right next to me, who I happen to outrank in time in grade, but he's in charge of me, so he thinks, because he's a man."*

Sexual harassment is hard to define, servicewomen recognize, and even harder to prove. "I had one case where a female seaman wanted to book her chief," reported a lieutenant who functions as an investigating officer. "She happens to be black, and he was a Filipino, and she wanted to say that he was discriminating against her. The supervisor tells you that she is not doing the job, she doesn't show up, problems like that, which are very easy to prove. The various booking chits [records of infringements] on this seaman are all real and well founded. The seaman says 'What about So-and-so that did the same thing? You didn't book that person.' 'Well, these booking chits are the results of five other times that you've done this.' It's really hard to prove sexual harassment."

Servicewomen also acknowledge the vulnerability of men to false accusations of sexual harassment, as well as the vulnerability of women to its actuality. A black Human Relations NCO reported: "This female said the NCO she was working for was harassing her because she wouldn't go to bed with him. So I asked a lot of people, male and female, that she worked with. Everyone was telling me that she had a bad attitude and she just wouldn't do as she was told. Finally I confronted the NCO that she accused—he was like in a state of shock. I went back to her, and she took back her story. She said she *felt* that was why he was harassing her because she wouldn't go to bed with him, but he never said it. And I showed her how serious that was that she almost made him lose his career behind that. I really don't like being the one to jump, take someone's career away from 'em or take their rank or money, but I will stand beside whoever is right, regardless if you're male or female."

Servicewomen also acknowledge the existence of reverse harassment. "I'm not going to call any names, but I have seen some women talk pretty strong to the men," said a black soldier. "So I figure it can go both ways. Right, women making sexual suggestions to the men." A Marine captain also warned that "Men can be harassed that way too. It's like a double-edged sword. You can very well have an enlisted woman—or an officer, I guess; I've never heard of an officer doing it—come up to her OIC [officer-in-charge] and, you know, put . . . moves on him. He says no, and she goes over to *his* OIC and says, 'Well, Lieutenant So-and-So puts moves on me.' And they'll be more inclined to believe her, because of the climate now."

In short, servicewomen know the complexities and the hazards of the charge of sexual harassment—though, like the rest of us, they don't always know how to cope with them. But we continually heard complaints about men sexually harassing women—sometimes merely irritating them, sometimes crippling them in their work, occasionally ending a promising career.

"I get called 'Miss Goody Two-Shoes.' But then if I turn around and I just go along with them, I'm a slut. I'm a bitch. It's a Catch-22 situation."

Many servicewomen hear the foul language and sexual bragging that make up so much of servicemen's conversation as sexual harassment.[4] "I've gone through the military with my own little personal crusade, I call it, just as a joke. There's a lot of cursing that goes on,

[4] Barbara A. Gutek reports that an environment characterized by swearing and obscene language encourages sexual behavior. *Sex and the Workplace: The Impact of Sexual Behavior and Harassment on Women, Men, and Organizations* (San Francisco: Jossey-Bass, 1985), p. 108.

a lot of foul language, dirty jokes, sexual innuendos. I make it known that I don't want to hear this. A lot of the guys feel that because of ERA and it's a work environment, I should have to listen to it. I disagree."

Men also harass women by name-calling, heavy-duty teasing, and "joking." They accuse women of being pushy, mouthy, sexually unattractive, or lesbian. Contrariwise, they allege that women get ahead by using sex. "I get highly upset," says a Marine corporal, "when you hear people talking, and they find out, 'Oh, she's an E-5 or an E-6, so where are her kneepads?' " An Army MP investigator told how "about a month ago, we had a E-8 female come in our office and when she walked out I said, 'Boy, that's something you don't see every day—a female master sergeant.' And he [a serviceman] says, 'Yeah, she's either really got her ducks in order or she's come up on her back.' "

"I'm getting to feel bottlenecked with what I can't do. It always comes out to the fact that I'm a female. I see no other reason why I'm not given the positions, like platoon sergeant, that I should be. I'm always the assistant platoon sergeant, even though I have more experience and more rank than the person I'm supposed to be working for."

Even more damaging are the male actions that endanger the servicewoman's career. Men ignore women, assign them meaningless tasks, refuse to teach them the skills of their MOSs, refuse to serve with them, refuse to obey their orders. When she was still a second lieutenant, an Army captain recalled, she talked to her superior about her marriage plans. "He was real snotty, and I almost detected a hint of jealousy. He basically was the cat's meow on the prowl, and here was one of his lieutenants, a female at that, getting married. Believe it or not, I didn't get selected a lot of times, most of the time, to go out and support an exercise. He would send the other platoon leader, a male. Oh, yes, I was being kept from doing my job. That was obvious."

An Army helicopter pilot told us of her amazement when an infantry company commander's hang-ups threatened her performance. Although she had formerly served in the almost entirely male artillery, this was "The only time I have ever encountered any discrimination, and I tried to put it out of my mind because it was such a shock to me. He would refuse . . . I mean he would talk to me, but he would talk to everybody else more so. He would talk to my [male] senior warrant officers even though he was really addressing me. He refused to see me as a platoon leader who could get his mission accomplished. He refused to accept that a female could be a pilot and an aviator. I just dealt with it the best I could. Talked my frustrations out a lot with the warrant officers—they were very helpful. It was just the particular individual's problem and not mine."

"Once we get to the scene [of the crime]," said an Army MP investigator in plain clothes, "we have to direct the military police as to where we want them to go, what they're to protect, what to collect in the way of evidence. You don't have trouble with young privates, because they don't think 'Well, she's a female.' They think, 'She's a sergeant, and I'm going to get it if I don't do it.' But another NCO, they'll deal with a partner who is younger than me, or less experienced, or he's still in uniform more readily than they'll deal with me. That's when I have to come off as Attila the Hun and say, 'Hey, look, I will be the one calling the shots here.' Then you're thought of as a mouthy chick."

Men's refusal to obey a woman's orders is a particularly damaging ploy, for if supervisors cannot enforce their authority, their performance evaluations suffer. "A lot of people will not follow a female officer," observed a black E-7. " 'Aw, she's just a female officer.' They turn right around and they say, 'Well, we're gonna do what we wanta do anyway.' They get away with it, because they all cover for each other, and she never really understands what they're doing. She'll say, 'Did we get this done?' First sergeant says, 'Yeah, we got that done.' And she thinks it's done her way, when actually they didn't do it her way."

An Army captain gratefully recalls her commander's help in such a situation when she was a young second lieutenant: "The commander finally sat on one of my platoon sergeants who was being—boy, if I had him now, I would have court-martialed him, I think."

Supervisors too play games. "I stayed an E-2 for fourteen months. E-3 is supposed to be automatic after six months. But I had a slight gender problem—I wasn't a guy. I hadn't done anything wrong. I had never been late to work. I won Post Soldier of the Month, got a five-day pass to go to Berlin. But that squadron leader got mad at me 'cause I was getting too many passes [rewards for outstanding performance]. I couldn't win for losing—like walking up a down escalator. Luckily one [male] E-5 stood up for me. E-5 they tried to hold up on me too. I went to a primary leadership course and got the Douglas A. MacArthur award. So when I came back, they kind of couldn't turn their heads the other way. Took 'em more than a year from when they started my paperwork—it should only take a couple of weeks. What did I do? Kept my nose clean. I'd go to my section supervisor, who treats women great, but not women in his career field. I'd go to the NCOIC [noncommissioned officer in charge], the OIC [officer in charge]. Finally I got to the promotion board. (Even though I had to borrow maternity uniforms off another lady, because mine were on order for eleven months!)"

Given that so many military women live as well as work with their units, social and professional relationships can get tangled. An NCO described a desperate experience during her assignment in Korea as a young troop straight out of basic: "When my boyfriend left, all of the other guys made a list as to who was next in line to inherit me, and I told 'em, 'None of you will.' They were married or they had girlfriends already. They were nice enough to work with, but I didn't want anything more. They sabotaged me. They said terrible things to me. I finally got up enough guts to fight back, and [later] every one of 'em apologized to me. I said, 'Fine, you want to treat me this way. I got this little letter poised here that's going to your wife to let her know that you've got your own little yobo [Korean girlfriend] over here and I've got this other little note going to your yobo telling her you're leaving and not taking her with you.'

"I'm not proud of what I did. I didn't send anybody any letters. But the threat was there and it was the only way I could think to handle it. And to this day, I want you to know that the person who instigated that hatred towards me, he and I are friends and we correspond. But it took me months, seven months to win that battle. It hurt a lot. I spent a lot of nights crying."

Such male behavior as these servicewomen describe disconcerts women, shakes their self-confidence, and interferes with their ability to do their jobs. We heard enough incidents of it to conclude that Freud underestimated the importance of sex.

Beyond obscenity, verbal assaults, and career blocks lie the direct attacks: sexual blackmail and rape. As several supervisors commented, young recruits are particularly vulnerable to sexual blackmail, overt or subtle, in that they are taught to obey the orders of their superiors. "That's hard for the young female Marine, who works for some staff

NCOs who see that she's young and impressionable and naïve and away from Mom and Dad," said a lieutenant. "It's easier to hit on her or to do something to her that she may not tell somebody about, touching her, saying let's go for a ride. She doesn't know any better. It's a harshness for someone to be thrown into that kind of situation. As a result, you have Marines who become very bitter, because they think the gunny [gunnery sergeant] is supposed to do this with them all the time. You have to make sure that the gunny gets prosecuted or gets handled in the correct way, and that she's pulled out of it."

If the young servicewoman does resist, the supervisor may use his powers against her in mean and petty ways. "As a young airman I had trouble with sexual harassment. I had a supervisor who told me all about his pregnant wife, he felt like he was living with a nun, why don't we go down to the . . . y'know. I flat out told him no, I wasn't interested in that type of thing. I spent the next three and a half years on midshift [at undesirable hours, instead of the normal rotation from shift to shift]."

Even older, more experienced women must exercise ingenuity when they're confronted with demands uttered in private, where the situation comes down to his word against hers. "I had a problem where I was at odds with one particular supervisor," said an MP NCO. "The end result was, I moved to a different station, because it was that or my career would be ended by this one person. I felt sexual harassment was underneath, but I didn't feel that the people in my chain of command would have listened and been sympathetic, so I didn't bother using it. I just found a way to get out of there, and I've been very happy ever since." And a Navy chief told us about a "time when even my job was threatened. I was between a rock and a hard spot. I didn't know whether to say something about this person, because, especially an officer, they can ruin your career. I didn't want my career ruined, but I wasn't giving in to this person either. I handled it on my own, because I didn't want their career ruined, and more importantly I didn't want them to get into trouble to where my career would be ruined."

Usually the physical assaults servicewomen told us about were reported but handled semiofficially, at as low a level as possible, by people who wished to quiet the troubled waters or swim out of them.

One woman, separated by a continent from her husband and child, confused and lonely, sobbed as she told us about her involvement with a serviceman. When she tried to end the affair, he stripped her, beat her, took nude pictures of her, raped her, and put her in fear of her life. She was full of guilt because she had been a "bad girl" and of praise for her "good-heart captain": "She saw my problem, she no hesitate, and she just . . . she's great. She makes me feel like I'm not alone in this world. She makes me feel that I'm one that belongs under her hand." The interviewee believed that she had narrowly escaped being thrown out of her service.

Only one victim of a physical assault who talked to us about her experience had pressed formal charges. A highly intelligent young woman, she had established a brilliant service record. The sexual assault occurred at sea. "I was asleep, and someone came into the berthing area, and I woke to certain touches, and the fact that I was asleep meant that within a certain margin of error I had no idea what was actually done to me. I booked him. It went to captain's mast [a hearing before the captain], and the captain felt that it was a serious enough charge and that there was enough evidence, so he sent it up for a court martial." She fought in vain for a transfer off the cutter. "I spent hours in a little minihell. This man, where he slept was not fifty feet from where I slept. I saw him many times. While the captain felt that the charges were serious enough to bring to court martial, he didn't feel it was serious enough to separate the two of us, i.e., put him in a locked room somewhere, in a cell.

"I will say in rape and assault cases military law is a lot more fair than civil law—civil law is hell on a woman. And I had close friends I could talk to about it. I had all the women on the ship standing behind me a hundred percent. I had men on the ship standing behind me a hundred percent. Except for this one man, they were all my brothers. I had people coming up to me and saying 'You say the word and he'll be dog meat in an hour; I can guarantee you.' In a way I wish I'd taken them up on their offer. I don't think I'll ever find that anyplace else in the world, that sense of camaraderie, that sense of brotherhood.

"They let the man walk. I still . . . I would like to hurt him, and hurt him badly. I was obviously disappointed that he wasn't going to have a Marine with him twenty-four hours a day while he made big ones into little ones. I have seen him, and it affects me. But I'm able to control the urge to pick him up and throw him in the river at the very least." Despite the strenuous efforts of many people at her current station, who praised her in the highest terms, the effects of the assault and the way it was handled have severely limited her ability to do her job and may indeed cause her to cut short her promising career.

> *"I've had a lot more problems with the wives than I have with the men. They really frown upon you: 'I wouldn't want you on a ship with my husband.' Think I want to be on a ship any more than your husband does?"*

> *"We spend a lot of time with the men. We go to the field, from here to California. We know them better than their wives know them, just about."*

Civilian wives of servicemen sometimes inflict another kind of harassment on servicewomen. Often newly married, inexperienced, and away from home for the first time in their young lives, many of them are terrified.

For years civilian wives' suspicion of military women was cited in framing public policy, particularly in keeping servicewomen off ships. A sixty-four-year-old Navy chief recalled: "When they brought out the U.S.S. *Sanctuary* [a hospital ship], they took women aboard. We had a hundred eighty women, and all we heard was that was the worst thing the Navy could do. The wives won't stand for it. They were afraid because their husbands would be having affairs with the women; we'd bring back a hundred eighty pregnant women. The *Sanctuary* went out for two years, and it came back. The wives said, 'Now we'll show you we were right.' Only the *Sanctuary* and the Navy Department proved them wrong. We had two women pregnant. Both were married to enlisted men on board ship. So from then on, we heard very little from the Navy wives." Now the force of civilian wives' suspicions of military women has shifted from the public arena to the private.

"Wives don't like me," an MP plainclothes investigator told us. "I've even gone so far as to avoid social functions because of the compromising situations they put me in. Not just for me, but for their husbands, who are my partners in crime! My first trainer thought, 'I'm going to have to be spending long nights with this woman. I know my wife, and I'm going to get this situation rectified.' He took me home, introduced me to his wife, who just happened to be pregnant, and she wouldn't speak to me. We went through a long period where we were working constantly, twenty-four, forty-eight, seventy-two hours in a row. I saw her one day and she just broke down, told me that she was afraid that her husband was having an affair with me, because he hadn't been home. I said, 'Honey, none of us have been home. We're working. Don't you believe him?' You can't get them to understand it. If you're halfway decent looking, it goes against you completely."

Problems are exacerbated by the different interests of the military women and the civilian wives. A black chief petty officer spoke of the "real close friendship" that develops among servicemembers "when you work together every day. A lot of wives, when you go to parties, seem to think something else. It's a threat that they don't know you. You guys work together and you talk the same language, and they don't know what you're talking about, so that's another threat to them. You be talking to the guys, and the wife is kind of left out and they're like 'Wait a minute. He came with me, not her.' "

"You know, I never thought about that," remarked a Navy woman who before her divorce had spent twelve years as a civilian wife. "But there was very little contact between me as a wife and the military women. When my husband would invite his friends home, I'm not sure how I would have felt if one had been a woman. There's that thing of jealousy. I can understand it, because it's more likely that that military woman's going to see more of your husband than you are. And at parties instead of talking brownies and babies, she's over talking crypto gear and radar."

Changes in the numbers and status of military women have reversed the long-standing situation in which civilian wives felt that they "belonged" in the military world into which military women were intruding. Now civilian wives confront the fact that military women are servicemembers, as they themselves are not. "Our company had a basketball team," says a black Army E-4, "and they were right good, so we went down to Fort Stewart to play there. The military females could ride the bus if they wanted to, with the basketball players. And their wives, which were civilians, they got mad at us because they couldn't get on the bus. But it was not ours, it was Army's saying they can't ride on the bus."

The civilian wife's feeling of being an outsider may even be partnered with a wish to become a servicemember, an Air Force staff sergeant remarked: "Matter of fact, the other day I was talking to a Navy wife, standing in line at the BX [base exchange]. She said, 'You know something? I wish I had joined. But I'm too old now. I'm thirty and I have two kids.' I said, 'Well, maybe you can get a waiver.' She said, 'I don't think my husband would let me.' I said, 'Try it. Bring it up to his attention. Ask him.' A lot of them kind of look at you with a bit of envy that they didn't do the same thing."

Although most military women, however unhappily, simply shrug off the difficulties of their relationships with civilian wives, some try to improve matters. An Army Spec-5 reported that the women in her unit "are in pretty good relations with most of the wives. A couple don't get along with us very well, but that's just 'cause they're insecure about their relationship with their husband. We're trying really hard. They throw Tupperware parties and all that goofy little stuff, you know, and we try and show up for it. Really! I've been to six since I've been here, and I don't like the stuff anymore. I've got so much Tupperware it's coming out my ears."

And sometimes the woman-to-woman bond proves tighter than other loyalties. "They accept me pretty good," said a yeoman second class, "because they ask questions that probably the men would say, 'Oh, shut up, you don't know what you're talkin' about.' Like I met one woman, she doesn't even know how much her husband makes. Your Leave and Earnings Statement, she doesn't know anything about it. I sat down one night and explained every block." A black E-5 chuckled. "If we become real close friends, I let them know their rights. I tell them: 'If you and your husband are having a problem, or he's not coming home, you have the right to call the commander and tell him about it.' I don't know if their husbands like it or not, but I like doing that, because I wouldn't want to be like that."

Even though she has more in common with her husband's fellow officers than with their wives, an Army captain says, she "straddled both lines. I would go to their Wives' Club, and I participated in their volunteer work. My husband always teases me, says, 'You don't have to do that. You're an Army officer.' But I didn't mind it, and I think they've received some exposure from a female officer. They've heard all the myths about us and all the crappy gossip, and I think that probably helped alleviate their fears. God, who wants their husbands? I have to deal with them all day. I certainly don't want 'em at night!"

"This was really a small base and I would have died for lack of anything to do if I hadn't gotten comfortable with wives," said a soldier. "My husband has always gone to everybody's house and he started taking me. Then the guys my age started getting married and bringing their wives and of course that was a lot easier: 'Oh, that's Cathy. You've got to meet her. She's crazy.' Once I'd been down to Honduras with these guys and they'd all come home and talked their wives' ears off about me and Susie. When they met us, they were all so proud of us, because you know their husbands always bragged about us!"

COPING

> *"I just determined that you had to develop selective hearing and somewhat of a tough skin. Then you had to decide was it too big a price to pay? Could you do that without becoming callous and hard? And if you couldn't, was it worth it?"*

The servicewoman's experience as a minority member in the military world depends partly on which service she enters, partly on her own personality and upbringing—whether she grew up with brothers and how her father treated her. In any case she's almost bound to go through a period of trial and error, while she gropes for comfortable and effective coping devices.

Some women protest that they have never experienced any difficulties—but usually add "but I know others who have," and often later in the interview reveal problems of their own. Sometimes these problems have been resolved; sometimes they seem to the woman so commonplace or trivial as not to count; and sometimes they are so bitter as to take a while to emerge. In its most extreme form this coping mechanism denies that the military world is a man's world: "I just don't see this as a male environment anymore. I mean it is, if you're talking combat or something. . . . But women have been a part of the military mostly ever since it began, whether it was being a secretary or the women in the Navy during World War I. I can't really say that it's all male-oriented."

But most servicewomen see themselves as a minority in a man's world. Feeling that if they can't beat the majority they might as well join them, some try to be accepted as "one of the guys." This technique has its dangers, for it may reinforce men's feelings that "their" premises are no place for women, but sometimes it works. A black Army E-5, for instance, has "found that if you act like one of the guys, you'll get along with them well. Anything they talk about, I can talk about. I used to read a lot, so I could fit in there. I wanted to be able to talk about football, or basketball. After they found out that I wasn't going to cry if they called me names, that I was going to get up and call them names back, they started leaving me alone. I really feel I have a lot more respect than some of the male NCOs in the unit."

"If you're not a man you're not in it, it seems like," says an Army Spec-5. "The reason that I'm where I'm at now is that I can run as fast as all the guys, okay; I'm as tall as them, so I can look at 'em at eye level; I can lift almost anything that they can—if not, I know how to move it and get it to where it needs to go; and I've learned to reason like them, how to communicate like them, how to swear like them."

But a captain, a graduate of a woman's college with a degree in classics (not, she says, the best preparation for the big bad world of the Marines), "started out trying to act like a man. I found out real quick that was not the best way to do it, because they'd laugh at you behind your back—or in front of your face. As time went on I found out that trying to act like who I am and what I look like, I'd have much more success."

And an E-7 described the difficulties the new women recruits in her auto-repair classes were likely to face. "We have one female in a class. Sixty men, and when they say 'Hey, you're part of the platoon. Let's go out and have a drink and have a good time,' naturally she goes; she feels protected, because she works with those guys, she eats with those guys; she's with them twenty-four hours a day. When you get a weekend pass, who else does she know? She goes out; they have a good time, and she comes back, and it's always rape. The Army says, 'Well, she shouldn't have been out there,' but you put one female with sixty males and you talk about cohesion. Whose fault is it?"

Not socializing also has its price, but pays off. "Men always went out and drank and chased the women whenever we'd pull into port. I could handle that for the first few years, just sitting on the boat and reading a book or something while they went out and had their own social clique. Now I can go out and have a good time with the guys and still be just their friend and not looked at—'cause I'm older and I'm married."

Should the servicewoman fall back on stereotypical wiles, flaunting her femininity? "When you want something, if you want to pass an inspection, [do] you wear a skirt?" a Navy petty officer speculated. "It's not really very smart, I don't think, because you're not accomplishing anything for the long run."

Some women simply adopt a "woman's" role already familiar and acceptable to men, that of the nurturer—mother or big sister. They sew on buttons and insignia. They act as confidantes. In this way they avoid being cast as either sex object or competitor. "I'm always like the peace-keeper on the crew, the den mother they call me sometimes," said a twenty-two-year-old senior airman. And a thirty-six-year-old lieutenant: "They're just not all that much older than my own children now, and some of them, this is the first time they've been away from home."

"One male actually flat out said to me, 'You were not put in the Marine Corps to be a leader.' But the bottom line is that they work for me. If they don't like working for a female, I always figure it's their personal problem, not mine. They don't have really the choice."

Other women shrug the whole thing off as "his problem." "When I was at OCS," said a black lieutenant, "every time we'd fall up [fall in for] a formation, about ten male Marines that lived upstairs from us would make catcalls. They think of the military as a man's world. Knowing that—not saying that I agree with it—I expect the male Marines to try to belittle me. But I know who I am. I know what my job is. As long as I'm doing it, they can pretty much—go their own way." A Navy yeoman pities a man who "doesn't mean to, but he just can't quit staring at my legs. I don't really take offense. It's like, 'Have you never seen a woman before? What rock did you come off of?' I'm sorry for them, that their minds are so narrow. I think men—no offense [to male interviewer]—have a tendency to just be this way, to look down on women and look at women as sexual playthings."

"His problem!" concluded an Army staff sergeant who missed getting a job she wanted. "Rumor control had it the reason I didn't get it was because there was already a female working there and the head boss didn't want two women working in the same spot. It really made me mad at first. I just thought, 'Forget it! I'm getting out and going to let these guys have the Army.' Then I thought, 'Wait a minute. I know I'm good. I've got reports on paper showing it, not from the same person all the time. Well, he don't know what he's missing! If a guy don't want me because of my sex, well, he don't know what he's missing.' "

> *"I like showing my Navy off. Yeah, the only thing wrong with my Navy is men! The guys in my shop, we'll be working on something, and something will go wrong. I'll go, 'Boy, men in my Navy!' "*

> *"I learned to dish it out as much as people gave it to me. 'Well, don't mess with her, 'cause you're going to get an earful back.' "*

Other women give as good as they get. "I don't see men as a threat anymore," a Marine staff sergeant told us. "I used to. I have grown into this, learning how to deal with men. One of the gunnery sergeants kept making sexual suggestions. For a long time I just ignored it. But one day when he called across the room for me to come sit in his lap, I just said, 'Shit, Gunny, if I did you wouldn't know what to do with it!'

Then there's the Coast Guard seaman out running with another woman. As they passed a barracks, men leaned from an upper-story window to catcall. Fixing the location of the window in their minds, the women dashed upstairs, explained the commandant's policy against sexual harassment to the startled men, and left to finish their run. Right is right!

"When I first come in," said an electrical systems installer, "I was really embarrassed, you know, embarrassed that I would cry. Or else I'd just run. Now I'll talk them down. I've said, 'I'm a lady and I don't appreciate it. You should show me more respect, 'cause you're a soldier.' He was like a representative to the United States, and he shouldn't talk like this."

"Some of the military guys!" said a black senior airman, in disgust. "One guy told me, 'I wouldn't date a military woman, because especially if she done be in a while she done been to bed with a lot of guys.' I say, 'I don't know where you're gettin' your information from, but it's not true.' I speak out, 'cause that just really ticks me off. Then they start thinkin' twice about what they be sayin'." Clearly it doesn't take her long to straighten out recalcitrant males: "I was standin' by the dayroom and a guy said, 'Yeah, man. Y'know, the new girl? I'm gonna go to bed with that girl.' So I walked in there and I said, 'What is this about goin' with this airman?' 'Oh, no, no, no, no.' I said, 'All of you are a bunch of babies. You don't know what your ass is. If you don't know what your ass is, you don't know nothing.' That was my mom's term. They just went [*gapes*]. All of 'em became my friends. If anybody said anything wrong about me, they'd say, 'No, man. Not Airman Smith. Not her. You got her wrong.' "

Professional situations also provoke counterattacks. A black staff sergeant advises, "Your superiors may give a guy certain projects where normally it should go to you, I guess because he's a guy and he's smarter than you are, or something. If you're an aggressive person, like I am, you go in and you say, 'Look, if you don't utilize me, I'm going to die here, and everything that you assign to me is sort of going to go down. Now if you're going to utilize me, give me what I'm supposed to have."

Some servicewomen take male put-downs as challenges. "Yeah, I have problems," says a Mormon Marine Corps corporal. "If you're a strong person, sometimes they're jealous and envious, and they want to cut you down or burn you with a lot of work. If your moral standards are high, sometimes they try to tear them down too. What do I do about that? Get grouchy. [*Laughs.*] You just guff it off. Women are going for it, man! Just work harder and show them. That's my little personal thing, getting perfect scores on PFTs [physical fitness tests], because it just feels good to me inside. A lot of guys can't do it, so in a way I've got an attitude!"

An electronics systems installer who must climb telephone poles and trees told us how, when she gets "big splinters in my face and my neck, and then in my arms, you just pick 'em out and drive on, because them guys are out there doing it. You just got to do it, you know, because the guys can make you look bad sometimes, so it will make you actually try harder. We have to work twice as hard, but it gives us a lot of determination when you see a guy up there and you're, like, afraid. He's going to treat you like a girl, and we don't want to be treated like girls in our work situation. After work the guy'll open the door for you on the way home. That's nice, but I don't expect a man to carry my weight."

Servicewomen like these struggle valiantly to compensate for the damage done their reputations by rumor, stigma, and the behavior of their sisters who trade on their sex. "The classic thing is women sliding through the Army on their back, you know," an Army E-5 said sadly. "They're messing around with their boss or something. I so badly wanted to disprove that. I know it happens, somewhere, some people, but I hate that the other people that are trying to do their job the right way get the flak for it. So I want to be one of the people that's proving it the other way."

> *"When I went to Leader School, a guy the very first day came up to my face, about an inch away from my nose, and said, 'I don't like women,' and walked away. I was at attention. I couldn't do anything, say anything. That man was my friend when I left. Excuse me, but I busted my butt to prove to him. . . ."*
>
> *"First of all, just let it roll off, okay? They'll give it to you. You just have to let it roll, all the punches, until you can see what you're doing, and then just take yourself seriously."*
>
> *"I try not to be a person that has to prove something to somebody all the time. I have a motto: As you go through life, try to improve yourself, not prove yourself. But I do find times that I do have to prove something. You have to prove that I can do this job just as well as you can, if not better. Now that you've seen me do it, okay. Let's cut the bullshit and just do it."*

Whatever techniques the servicewoman develops for combating harassment and disparagement, the women we talked to who have survived for any length of time agree that she must "prove" herself, repeatedly and constantly. A Coast Guard seaman with four years' previous service in a nontraditional Air Force job underlined the importance of competence: "On a small-boat station it's different than any other place in the world. I wondered, 'How can they live like this?' That's why I had so much respect for the girls. They knew their job. The top engineer was a female. She was just a seaman, but even the guys had to admit that she was the best. The other female, a young girl, was just on the deck force, I suppose. But she was good when it came to Search and Rescue, so she had the respect of the crew members." "You've got to act equal," says an Air Force staff sergeant. "I don't mean be a man—you can be as feminine as you want. But you have to do a good job. If you come in under the impression that as a female you can wink your eyeballs and get somebody else to carry your load, you're wrong. Dead wrong."

So also says a staff sergeant: "If you act professionally when you walk in the door, not giggly and sweet and cuddly, ninety percent of the time sexual harassment is not going to happen. Oh, [with] some old diehards out there, it does sometimes. But for the most part if I act professional, they'll act professional with me. Like I want to be treated. If I turn the tears on, they're going to treat me like 'a woman.' "

No tears? By this time, one would suppose, with athletes and male movie stars sobbing on screen and with all the rhetoric about tears as an appropriate release, people should have come to accept them. But many in the military still regard them suspiciously. "That's one of my downfalls. I cry at the drop of a hat. A lot of guys say, 'I like it when you cry because we know exactly what you're thinking.' But I've had that held against me—'Oh, you're too emotional.' Tears come out of my eyes, but that's not important to me. When I get frustrated, tears come out of my eyes. Guys get frustrated, they hit the wall. If I hit the wall the guys say 'Hey! Getting violent on us!' I don't understand why tears are such a no-no."

Difficult and demanding as the repeated "proving oneself" is, it works. Servicewomen weary of it but cannot escape its necessity. "I make myself recognize the fact that, okay, this is what society consists of," says a black staff sergeant. "Basically on top who's running the country is white males. If you just look at the majority of the people that we have in the military, which are those guys—they don't really want to work for you, and you have to prove something to them."

> *"When I was an executive officer a few foolish souls told me that they had never worked for a woman before. I said, well, that was too bad. What did they want? I decided that I was now in a position where I didn't have to hold their hand. They worked for me, and they'd like it or lump it, but the Navy way was that they'd better work."*

Besides competence, the military woman also needs confidence. "The uniform does give you the image," said an officer. "They see you as a captain. It's your turn after that, to prove that in fact you are. If you're not confident, then anyone who's stronger is going to overwhelm you."

A lieutenant told us how directly she handles challenges to her authority. "Every now and then I have to say, 'You don't tell *me* what to do. I tell you.' I had a master gunnery sergeant who didn't hesitate to tell me when he thought I was wrong. At the same time I could tell him, 'No, Top.' 'Well, I've got twenty-four years in; you're going to tell me this is wrong?' 'Yes, I am. I don't want to do it that way.' Then he would shut up. You just have to be assertive and let them know who's the boss. Even though they've got more years in than your age, probably. There's one younger male Marine, a sergeant: I don't think he cares too much for women. That just makes me all the more firm with him: 'Sergeant, this is the way it's going to be; get out of here.' 'Well, ma'am . . . .' 'Get out of here.' I hate to have to resort to something like that, but he's really the only one that I've ever had any problem with. One thing I think a woman has to overcome is that it's so easy to be easy. It's so easy to say 'Okay. Go ahead and do that.' "

Supervising helps build confidence. "I had a driver who had just gotten his license," said an E-5 Arabic language specialist, "and he wrecked a whole vehicle. Everybody was getting mad at him, but I told them it was their fault, because they gave him a license, and they had him drive this humongous piece of equipment. You get strong and you get mad. If you're a weak person when you come in, you have to learn to put your foot down. You get a lot of people that just because they're higher than you think they can walk all over you. If you're a supervisor you've got to look out for your people. I felt afraid. I didn't think I could do it. But I felt real good after the whole exercise, 'cause I didn't do such a bad job after all."

Clever supervisors salt their self-confidence with wit and ingenuity, as a Navy old-timer reminisced: "Hey, my first job as a chief, I had a hundred fifty women in that office and fifteen men. And the fifteen men worked with me. But this one E-6, he was an old-timer—I swear, he was in World War I. He said, 'Far as I'm concerned, you're just a greenhorn young 'un. If you think I'm going to work for you, you've got another thought coming.' I said, 'Whatever turns you off or on or in between.' So I divided up all of the pay records. I said, 'Okay, we have to have these done by a certain time today. Read my lips, shipmates.' 'You got it, Chief.' This guy's not doing nothing. Well, one day went by. Second day. Eight hours of doing nothing can get pretty boring. So third day he said, 'Uh, Chief, can I go over to the Navy Exchange?' I said, 'You can go over to the Exchange at ten-thirty. And come back after lunch.' Well, ten-thirty came, he gets out, and this other little third-class says, 'Chief, did you know that the Exchange is closed from ten to twelve?' [I] said, 'I know it, you know it, but he doesn't.' About an hour went by, right? He comes in and he threw his hat on the table. 'You're a pretty smart little chick, aren't you? You knew damn well that Exchange was closed from ten to twelve.' I said, 'Is it? I'm glad you told me, 'cause I won't go during those times.' Next thing I know, he said, 'Give me a couple of those records.' I said, 'Well, I'll start you out with one. I don't want to overtire you.' Later he was transferred, okay? Before he left, I had a box of chocolates and a single red rose on my desk."

Most of the women we interviewed try first to handle difficulties themselves, by whatever means they've developed or can think up. Many of the small unpleasantnesses they treat casually: "Every now and then," says a Cuban Spec-5, 'it's like the guys don't see you for a few minutes, and they'll start talking. You've got to remind them that you're sitting there, that you don't want to hear some of the stuff they're going to say, and they nine out of ten times will stop."

A Marine captain talked about how she treats "a senior officer that constantly makes kind of suggestive remarks. My initial reaction is to play along with it and tease, but if it gets to a point that you feel that maybe he's getting the wrong idea, then: 'Sir, I really just don't appreciate these types of comments.' That's the end of it. My husband used to say, 'You can get away with things. A male lieutenant would have never made that comment.' But I'm not a male lieutenant. I'm a woman."

Even with more serious offenses most servicewomen prefer to "go one-on-one," to tell the man how they feel and to warn him. A Navy petty officer advised that, if they decide to register a formal complaint, women ought first to "say something to them. Tell 'em one time. One time only. And if it comes again, put the report in. At least give them notice that you are going to do something. And if they do it again, no more chances."

INSTITUTIONAL AIDS

"I have a place to go and I have a support system out there. My sister works in a civilian company; she's run into a few situations, and there was really nowhere to go. Most of the supervisors are men, and she doesn't feel that she'd get the kind of support that she would need. We have that here. I haven't hesitated to use that to my advantage in terms of warning people."

If all her other coping mechanisms fail, the servicewoman can resort to formal complaints. Clearly established channels exist in the form of Social Actions offices and Human Relations Councils. The services give classes to tell her about them and, equally important, to inform men on the issues and the recourse. She does not have to wonder where to turn when the boss "comes on" to her and she cannot deflect his advances by ignoring him, joking with him, or threatening to call his wife. What's more, she has a choice: instead of using the Social Actions office or its equivalent, she may go up the chain of command. That has its difficulties, of course, when the offender is her supervisor, but means exist to circumvent him.

The very existence of an official system for complaint changes the atmosphere. It has cowed generals: "I had some general I was escorting around when I was in Protocol. I was a first lieutenant at the time, and it was sort of like 'Oh, wow, we've got a cute girl to take us around! Herup herup herup. Not bad legs!' So I just turned and I said, 'Sir, I think that's an inappropriate comment,' exactly like that, and let me tell you I had no trouble the rest of the time."

But no institutional effort to stop sexual harassment will work unless women have confidence in it. Ironically, of those we interviewed, the officers more than the enlisted women feared a backlash if they used the system. Fortunately officers are also in a better—but by no means perfect—position to protect themselves individually, "because an enlisted Marine doesn't have the firepower that an officer does."

A black Air Force officer would hesitate to use the system because "When you start talking sexual harassment, sexism, racism, everybody scatters. Social Actions, I guess, like any other program in the military, is controlled by the military. People would hesitate. That would be their last resort. The program is there. Whether it is fully utilized, or whether people actually have faith in that program, believing it's going to work, that's another question. I think most females would be very very hesitant. Like, for example, me."

"We've never had an officer request mast [a hearing before a superior officer] here," said a Marine lieutenant, who doesn't "think enlisted Marines worry about the effect on their careers of requesting a mast. I would have to have an awful big complaint to request mast with the commanding general. I feel like it would harm my career, which [my feeling that way] is terrible. I think the commanding officer would like to think 'Well, if you have a complaint, you come to me. We'll be adults and we'll try to talk it out.' Which we've done several times. I had a very good friend stationed overseas. Her commanding officer belittled her and just was the meanest thing to her the entire time. She says, 'He would cut me down. He used foul language against me in front of the troops, in front of the senior enlisted Marine, the sergeant major.' She kept a notebook of when, why, who was around, what happened, everything, every time he ever said anything to her. I spoke with her when she came back Stateside. 'Why didn't you go to the commanding general? You don't have to put up with that.' 'That would have made my life even more miserable,' she said. 'And I would have gotten the reputation, because the CO [commanding officer] would never do such a thing and it's all in my mind.' In her shoes I might have done the same thing."

But a Marine Corps captain, troubled by a bothersome major, eventually resorted to the system: "He was making comments in the office, like he'd come in and [say] 'Hi, sweet thing. What are you up to? How'd you like to go on up?' I took with a grain of salt some of his comments. But when he put his arm around my waist, that's where he had taken off the cloak of professionalism, let it drop in the dust. He was just some jerk. That's where you don't have to say 'Sir, I'm sorry, but . . .' I told him right off. Then I went and told my boss, he told his boss, and the major was talked to."

"The atmosphere is really good here. The battalion commander lets it be known that there won't be any sexual harassment. See, that kind of guidance and that kind of leadership has to come from the top."

"If some guy whistles at me, I know he's from off base, because no one on base would dare!"

The services differ in the protection they afford women—at least in the perceptions of the women who talked to us. Of them all, Air Force women rely most confidently on the system: "Nobody should have to live with something like that. Even if it's just a pat on the rear end. We don't take any of it . . . if you take it the first time, then when you go to press charges the second time they're going to ask you, 'Well, you took it the first time.' I strongly suggest you print that: if it happens the first time, just stop it right then. Oh, yes, we were warned about this in basic training. They tell you exactly how to go about it if you have a problem, who to contact. They explain to you all kinds of sexual acts, and the smallest, that you would never think of, you've put up with for so long, that can get a person in trouble. Like they had a poster, and one woman felt that it was just too sexual, and they just had the poster destroyed. You try to give me a civilian job that will do the same thing."

One reason for the efficiency of the Air Force system may be the frequency and quality of the classes designed to prevent discrimination and harassment, which are given, some Air Force women protest, ad nauseam. As an Air Force loadmaster remarked, "The Air Force is a real forerunner in the move toward equal opportunity and equal treatment, not only in the variety of ethnic groups that we have but in terms of men and women. The powers that be really shove it down our throats, equal opportunity and sexual harassment and you will not do this and you will not do that. For the guys it's traumatic: '*What* can I say to you that I'm not going to get in trouble for? . . . that you're not going to bite my head off for?' "

Whether or not these arduous educational efforts have succeeded in changing male attitudes, in combination with the prompt and thorough investigations of complaints they have changed male behavior on many bases. They transmit an implicit message: the Air Force really dislikes sexual harassment. Witness a male officer's concern to project the right image: he told us about a male NCO whom he suspected of harassing an enlisted woman "who in her uniform looks like Miss America and in civilian clothes looks like Miss Universe." The officer said that he told the offending NCO: "If I ever again hear of you bothering her, I'm going to take you out in back and beat the shit out of you. *Then* I'm going to take you upstairs and prefer charges. And if you ever tell anybody about this conversation, I'll kill you!" Whether or not any of this ever happened is immaterial—what matters is that the acceptable stance for an Air Force male officer is strong opposition to sexual harassment.

The Navy too gets good marks from our interviewees. A senior airman told us about her sister's experience in the Navy, where "she worked for an officer, very high-ranking officer; he lost his rank completely. That's because he was so high and in the political limelight. She got moved to a base of her preference to get away from all the rumors and gossip. Mmm-hmmm, he was just coming on to her—'Wanta go out? I know your husband's at sea; you must be lonely.' Oh, yes, she filed a complaint with Social Actions. It took about three weeks for the whole thing to end and her to get orders to where she wanted to go. They wiped the slate clean."

"You don't really hear any remarks about being a woman in the Navy, because there's just too many of 'em right now," a petty officer assured us. "You hear enlisted make their little comments about, what is it, 'Join the Navy and ride the WAVES,' " said an E-5. "I'll tell 'em right there: 'Don't say that, because I'm not that type of person. I don't want to hear that. I have a brain.' But usually you don't hear that where I'm at. Because they will be down on you real quick. They don't allow it." A young sailor of Korean descent disagreed, feeling that women "just kind of have to put up with things like that. You know, we have to make some sacrifice, I guess. Really, there isn't anything done about that. I've seen some of 'em who fought for it just ended up getting more trouble. Getting bad conduct discharge or something. Especially if it was toward your supervisor. It just looks back on the ones who is in lower rank."

Navy women did not report the same degree of educational effort that we heard so much about in the Air Force. But a Navy woman's remarks forcefully illustrated the impact of such attempts to change attitudes—as well as the unreconstructed nature of some servicemen. "I know there's a lot of cases where there's sexual harassment, and they have a whole committee working on that now where you have to go and see different movies and briefs on sexual harassment, so you're aware when it's happening, and the men also go so they can see what it does to the women. I had one boss that would come in on Monday morning, and . . . he's a riot case. Real funny. Typical things that he would say kind of offended me. He'd come in and say, 'Damn, I didn't get it again this weekend.' The first time I was, like, 'Oh, my God! This is what I've got to work with?' But it was just typically him. Then he went to one of the sexual harassment courses. When he came back, he says, "Does that really offend you?' Because he had no idea that it would. It was just his way of expressing himself, I guess."

Another Navy story underlines the overwhelming importance of the attitude of the service, which functions like a Freudian superego. "One of my bosses . . . I can't remember what he did. It's so long ago.

But I almost reported him. I told him, and he apologized and kept apologizing. 'Oh, no, no, no. Don't go up [the chain of command]. Don't go up.' I don't think he knew even what I was going to tell. He was all paranoid, thought he was going to lose his job and everything, and he apologized and apologized."

The women who talked to us in services other than the Navy and the Air Force showed more uncertainty about institutional efforts to combat sexual harassment. Their systems for recourse don't seem to function as smoothly, and their indoctrination efforts are not perceived as fervent.

The Coast Guard, for example, has established Human Relations Councils "responsible for helping each division realize what the commandant's policies are concerning sexual harassment, human relations, civil rights," but our interviews suggest that these councils are not yet up to speed. As an officer observed, "I think that even if there was a case, it would take like two years to get it through the courts. I just don't see it ever really happening, even though the commandant has a policy."

The stories of harassment that Army women told us, compared to those of women in the Air Force and Navy, struck us as particularly ugly and frequent; on one base they seemed to depict an environment laden with obscenity, sexual put-downs, and threats. Few of our interviewees placed real reliance on the Army's system for investigating charges of sexual harassment. "I talked with a major in Equal Opportunity, and found out the battalion never had an EO meeting," said a soldier of one of her bases. "They didn't have an EO representative. Round there they hate me for that." In her perception, that is, the Army was not swinging its weight behind efforts to reduce sexual harassment. We met many happy, well-adjusted, successful servicewomen in the Army, Marines, and Coast Guard, but by and large women in these services seemed by comparison to Air Force and Navy women hesitant to use the official systems, or to avoid them altogether. An Army lawyer described their system as not having "a lot of teeth to it. It's basically an informal resolution. If it's justified, then most likely judicial action will be taken against somebody, but I don't think it's perceived to have a lot of impact."

All the same, some Army women resort to the established system. "Yes, I'd report real sexual harassment," an E-4 told us. She expected none, because she has established herself as a sister to the men she works with. But "I feel if it could happen to me, it could happen to somebody else that doesn't know enough to go through your chain of command, and I'll make an example out of the guy. You have to go through your chain of command, tell your first sergeant, but a lot of women don't like to, because most men'll stick up for each other. But if you get a good first sergeant, they'll do something about it. If not, you just keep going up the chain of command. And you don't have to do it that way if you don't think they can help you. You go to EO; they have to do something about it. 'Cause you can go right up to your congressman and farther."[5]

Even if it works imperfectly, or hardly at all, it's better to have a system than not to have it. With a system in place, once a servicewoman becomes experienced and resourceful enough to warn offenders, "All you have to do is tell 'em that 'Listen, you're bothering me. I don't like it. If you bother me anymore, I'm going to report you.' Then they'll be gone."

And a Marine captain believes that their system is starting to take hold. "I've heard more incidents where people have come forward and said, 'The gunny told me if I didn't sleep with him that he was going to mark me down, or he was going to recommend that I not get promoted. So I told him, "Too bad!" ' Then they [the enlisted women] go and report [the harassment]." A lance corporal supported this view, saying that getting sexually harassed is rare: "People think it happens all the time. It doesn't, 'cause you get burnt too bad. Those guys don't need that."

Common sense and some experts suggest that as men and women get used to working with each other not only in the same work environments but in the same jobs, they develop new ways of interacting as colleagues. The military world encourages this by dressing women and men similarly or identically, by housing women and men in the same barracks or bachelor officers' quarters, by insisting that females

[5] The services maintain offices in Washington, D.C., to investigate and reply to complaints from servicemembers or their families forwarded by members of Congress. A servicewoman who works in one told us of a wide range of complaints, from the plea of a girlfriend to give her serviceman a pass for her prom, through a complaint from a servicewoman that she had been ordered to lose weight ("Here's my picture—do you think I'm too fat?"), to grievances of real substance.

are soldiers or officers before they are women, by putting more women to work in traditionally male jobs, by paying women the same as men of their rank, by placing women in positions where they supervise men, and by formally instructing their members about what constitutes sexual harassment and discrimination and punishing it. As a result, the services have probably moved further toward the reduction of overt and open sexual harassment than most civilian employers.

They still have a way to go. How far they will get in the near future is an open question. The Department of Defense has announced a major reorganization of its equal-opportunity policy-making, which, department officials say, represents an elevation of equal-opportunity concerns in the Pentagon. Critics see the action, however, as another step in a process of downgrading or phasing out equal-opportunity programs, prompted by a "Reagan administration belief that equal opportunity has already been achieved and therefore 'what is required is an executive council to simply monitor and fine-tune the system.' "[6]

An important advocate for servicewomen is the Defense Advisory Committee on Women in the Services (DACOWITS), formed in 1951: a group of thirty-two civilians, mostly women, of varied backgrounds, each appointed for a term of three years by the president of the United States. The DACOWITS meets twice a year to get answers and hear reports on the status and progress of military women. Between these meetings each DACOWITS member is asked to visit military establishments, to meet with the women there, and to listen to their concerns. The high-ranking women officers who work most closely with the DACOWITS value its influence.

These colonels and Navy captains and brigadier generals and commodores themselves comprise the best resource for the services on women's issues. They are survivors: highly intelligent, politically knowledgeable, pragmatically sophisticated. They are now making their voices heard on admirals' and generals' staffs. That's where it matters.

The attitude of the top command makes the critical difference for the quality of life of servicewomen. "In 1977 the Coast Guard made this great announcement," said Captain Louise Wilmot (USN), "that they were going to send women to sea. We were very excited when

[6] *Minerva: Quarterly Report on Women and the Military* 4, no. 2 (Summer 1986), pp. 51–54.

their commandant came to the Navy War College. I put up my hand, and I said, 'We're studying decision making, and I'd like to know how the decision was made.' He hemmed and hawed and gave us a statement about 'Well, the men when they first graduate can't go do this, but they're going to let all the women go do it, and I don't know how I'm going to explain that to the men.' I said, 'Well, very simple, sir. You tell them to do it and they'll do it. You tell them you think it's a good idea, and they'll think it's a good idea.' "

WOMEN HELPING WOMEN

> *"A Woman Marine gunnery sergeant taught me so much. She walked into a room, 'Hey, Gunny, how are ya doin'?'—from a male staff NCO. They respected her opinion. They respected what she was doing. They didn't treat her differently. I looked at her and I said, 'I want that.' "*

> *"I felt so good because I was around professional women. Military professional women. I just felt like, God's in heaven."*

> *"Like I told the girls, we're making the change. We're laying the stones down for the females to come."*

In their struggles to adjust, military women look for female role models and mentors. "It takes a lot of pressure off, to see somebody higher up there," says a Spec-5 who drives a boat. "Skippers are very domineering. When I was in the mate's position, I felt like 'Well, I can't get my point across, because I'm a female.' It's kind of like going up against your dad! A double-do pressure, because I feel like I'm letting my crew down. The crew's all men, and they look at me and say, 'I could go down and drink a beer with him and get more out of him than she is.' Now there's two female warrants [warrant officers], and I can sit down and talk to them. It makes me learn how to rationalize with somebody that's ranks above me, so that I just don't think, 'Oh, I'm hopeless, I'll never be able to talk to these people.' "

But senior women are hard to find. "You don't have many females up into the ranks, especially in the enlisted force," says a black Air Force staff sergeant. "I really don't know that many female master sergeants that I could say, 'Wow, I can't wait to make master sergeant so I can be like her!' The ones that you do see are very very sharp, so they're put into different places, working in the Pentagon, not at base level. The role models are not in the barracks; they're living in off-base housing, because they have the rank, or they're married."

> *"After I finished my college, I still hadn't decided to be an officer. I had almost fifteen years in, and I said, 'Do I stay in, make master [sergeant] the next time around, or do I go in a different area and try to break ground and make it easier for the women that were coming in behind me?' Because I was interested in that."*

Almost all the women we interviewed had a strong sense of obligation to other servicewomen. Even the very young and very new often had begun to develop this sense through the teamwork instilled in basic training. They felt responsible to other women for their own performance: "I've always been mindful that how I perform will have a lot to do with how the next person gets treated. It tends to color people's perceptions." "I feel the obligation to other women to be the best that I can be," said a reflective Air Force staff sergeant. "I was from one of those one hundred percent black schools. When I was in high school, the teacher asked, 'What obligations do you feel you owe black people?' At that time I gave him an answer like 'I'm going to get married. I'm going to raise my children the best way I know how so that they won't become a burden on the rest of society.' Since then I've reevaluated. I think about the question that you asked, How am I going to help women? I'm not going to say I'm going to give a million dollars to this fund or I'm going to do that. I'm going to be the best that I can be, because in doing that I will have paved the way for somebody somewhere. Just be a success."

Captain Wilmot appraises her selection for captain two years ahead of time as "a huge boost in the arm—not just for me, but for the rest of the women. You have to have people who are willing to be point women [scouts, forward patrols]. The third day I was at the Naval War College, I was in my little cubicle reading the management book, which said 'Women are not good managers. Women are terrible managers,' and gave all these reasons why women shouldn't be managers, and then as I went through the book, whenever there was an example of good management it was always a man, and if there was an example of bad management, it was always a woman. Well, I could feel my blood pressure going up. I thought, 'Ahhhhhhh.' So I found the department head, a senior civilian, and I said, 'I want to talk to you.' I know he didn't want to talk to me. Here I am at the school three days. He doesn't know who I am. He's a very busy man. He said, 'Well, what do you want to talk about?' I said, 'I want to talk about how you're going to withdraw this book from the course, how you're going to get us a book that meets our requirements.' I gave him the twenty-minute lecture, and he said, 'Well, I'm not going to do anything about that.' I said, 'Well, I just came from working in Washington, D.C., and if you can't get it accomplished, I know some people who can. So either you do it or I'll do it.' I was furious.

"I wrote a letter off to Prentice-Hall, the publisher, reamed them up one end and down the other end. Those people from Prentice-Hall beat a fast move to the Naval War College and they sat down with this department head and they gave him the contract to edit the author's rewrite! He had all my notes, and every time this man strayed off the path, the department head would bring him back, and finally he produced a book which was acceptable and which the War College used. Months later I was standing talking to the Dean of Studies, a Navy captain. He said, 'You know, you're the department head's favorite person.' I said, 'Why?' He said, 'Because of you he got paid from Prentice-Hall to edit that management book.' I said, 'Well, listen. Are we going to get a good management book for the course? That's what's important.'

"So when it was over some people were saying, 'Oh, that Wilmot. She's a holy terror. Who does she think she is?' And this very smart civilian woman in our class said, 'Well, you know, anytime that there's change, someone has to be the point woman. And Louise is just being the point woman this year at the Naval War College, and when she leaves, the other women won't have to be point women.' "

"The enlisted women knew they could come to me. Lot of times I couldn't really help 'em, but at least they knew that someone in the officer ranks was willing to listen, and if they did have a legitimate problem, talk to the commander for them if they didn't feel comfortable about it. It helped me too, you know."

Women feel a special responsibility for the young and immature who "start hanging around with the wrong crowd, the wrong guys, and then they mess up their life. If they don't have their morals set or have a goal really is what it is, what they want to accomplish out of the Army, it hurts 'em." "The new ones, they just get themselves in the worst predicaments," said a Navy yeoman second class. "And you have boys coming in the office all the time. It's fun, because I look back: 'Was I . . . did I do that?' I don't want to make them bitter; I want to make 'em want to stay in, want to do good. Right now their minds, I don't think, are all on the Navy! Their uniforms are sort of messed up, and they come in with bright-red nail polish on and two earrings in their ear. You got to tell 'em, 'Go in the bathroom and. . . .' Call and make sure they're out of bed when they don't show up. 'My God! She's just naggin' me!'—that's what they think probably. But someday they're going to understand when they have some seaman working for them that they've got to go find 'cause she's not at work."

A black master sergeant testified to the influence of a first sergeant on her Air Force adolescence: "If she hadn't been there, maybe I would have been out of the service now. She kind of kept me straight. I used to go to her office for fun—you know, like the little kid that do little bad things to get the attention of the old mom. She was the old mother of the dormitory. First sergeant, female."

"We try to take some of the younger ones under our wing and raise 'em right, I guess, is the expression—much as I hate that," said a master-at-arms [MP] E-6. "They're away from home, they're in love for the first time, and they're not sure what they're supposed to be thinking. A legal man and a religious person and I, we like to take them in hand and say, 'This is what you can and cannot do. If you need any help, let us know.' Believe it or not, the women on my ship are starting an old-girl network: we go to each other and we say, 'Hey, I need help in this area. Can you interfere?' It's like politics: you have to learn to do it."

"You come out of OCS; you have no network. You build it from scratch. And it's not just women-to-women; it's women-to-men; it's just having somebody that you know that you can talk to about a given situation."

Only one formal women's network now exists: the Women Officers' Professional Association (WOPA), for officers of the seagoing services.

With the sanction of the Navy, senior officers carefully and tactfully created this organization to help junior officers with their careers. Despite some doubts about whether or not a formal organization can fulfill the purposes served by the traditional old boys' networks, WOPA's members are using the organization to support one another and to solve some of the problems that military women face. Gradually they are increasing its range. We heard stirrings for the creation of other such organizations, particularly among enlisted women.

Even here, though, military women are wary. "It disappoints me that we're separating ourselves from the males," said an Army second lieutenant. "'Specially in the military, where we're supposed to be a team, and there's this really important need to work together. But I hope the network works. You need at least somebody to talk to."

Meanwhile many career-oriented women have developed private networks, with other servicewomen and with servicemen. This is an easier process for officers than for enlisted women—perhaps in part because in college they have learned more about how organizations work. In our observation the DACOWITS, with its members visiting bases and posts to invite women to come together and talk about their problems, is also showing them ways in which they can help one another.

A personnel staff officer in the National Guard Bureau described the first state women's conference for the Army and Air Guard: "About two hundred seventy women that were Army, Air, and then civilian employees of the Guard got together for the weekend. I did a briefing for them on the Combat Probability policy,[7] and they had workshops. It was a well-thought-out program, and it touched on a lot of different areas—fraternization problems, stress management, how to further your career, what you can do to help yourself—the nitty-gritty issues. I just hope that the idea will catch on."

"*It's good to have some type of* esprit de corps *with the women, but there's a danger to that too, because then people think you're cliquish and clannish.*"

[7] This controversial Army policy attempted to assign a coefficient of combat probability to each MOS, and on that basis closed several MOSs to women—a decision later partially rescinded.

"One female told me that she heard that I didn't like females. I said, 'How can I not like females, when I'm a female?' She say, 'Well, they say you're always hollerin' at the females.' I say, 'That's because I would like for all of 'em to be like me, but I know I can't make all of 'em like me. I just try to get the females to speak up for their rights and just because someone tell you "No, you can't do it," don't accept that answer.' "

Servicewomen must constantly balance their concern for other women against their need to perform well, to fulfill their obligations to the organization, and to deal justly with all the servicemembers for and to whom they are responsible. This divided duty puts them into uncomfortable situations. Will their actions further segregate women? Will consulting with other women violate the chain of command? In their eagerness for women's success, are they requiring more of women than of men? Or in their sympathy for women's special problems, are they letting women off too easily?

A helicopter pilot had to think out the implications of her command sergeant major's request "that I as the female officer in the brigade talk to the enlisted women on—I can't remember now—basically being sanitary and cleanliness in the field, using tampons and how to dispose of them. I'm like 'Gee! That is something that needs to come through the chain of command, because there is no WAC Corps anymore.' I refused. He was a very good sergeant major normally, and he was very upset. I just said, 'I'm sorry, but I don't believe in that. I think that it needs to be an integrated team, and that's your responsibility, Sergeant Major. Do it.' He and his supervisors, who at that time were all men, needed to address that."

Or, within the rigid hierarchy of the military, how much can senior women help junior women? The fixed rank structure, the fraternization policies, and the junior woman's awe of the senior woman may impede communication. As an Air Force officer said ruefully, "I am a role model, but I'm not approachable. Where I have gotten to know junior officers they will ask me questions. But for those who don't know me, I made lieutenant colonel; I'm not somebody that they're supposed to just go to and talk to. I would like to have a better relationship, but I really honestly don't know how to do it without causing all sorts of difficulties with the system, so I just have to work it on a one-by-one basis."

"It gets under my skin when a female says, 'I can't do that. I might break my fingernail.' You know, you want to strangle 'em. What the hell are you doing here to begin with?"

"I think the women that work will change them who don't. It's like the strong birds will push the weak birds out of the nest. It'll happen, right? We don't want anybody getting over [not doing her part]."

Servicewomen admit to sometimes being hard on other women, because it's so important to them for women to do well. "I'm known where I work as . . . pardon me, as being a hard-ass," says a Navy yeoman, "but I can't tolerate a woman that's not in proper uniform. There aren't enough men that know women's uniform regulations, so the women just get away with murder. I can't tolerate women that flutter their eyelashes and cry 'cause they can't carry the load. If they're not strong enough, they ought not to be here. There are plenty of women that are smart enough and strong enough and capable enough. I don't want you to think that I just shut them out, but it's just like a firm parent. I have to be harder than the male counterparts, because women get away with it for so long and with so many other people. One of the worst things that happens to women in the Navy is they allow that to happen to themselves. They just destroy themselves."

Competent and hardworking women resent lazy women bitterly. A Navy yeoman spoke of her anger at women who go into nontraditional jobs and don't perform well: "That may be because they're just physically too small to carry the parts. And that doesn't say anything less about them, because they can't. But it angers me that they come into these fields and then flutter their eyelashes to get Joe Sailor to carry the machinery for 'em, because that gives us all a bad name."

"I know I'm harder on the female MPs than the male MPs," says an Army sergeant. "If the guys do the same thing, I'll just think, 'Typical guy. It figures. Some jerky guy would do that.' But if I see some female do it, it bothers me, because I feel like it reflects on me: 'Gee, eight years I've dragged and dragged and dragged myself to get as far as I have, and now she's making everything look like less, because she's not acting right.' I remember trying to kick in a door of a patrol car one night to this female MP who had locked herself in there, because she was afraid to get out to go on a call. I tell you, if I could have got that door open, I would have killed her. She disgraced me. She disgraced me."

MEN HELPING WOMEN

> *"Some of my best friends have been male."*

> *"I'd work for him in a heartbeat again. He knew his job really well and taught me a lot. I still call him and say, 'Help me. What is the answer to this?' and he still helps me out."*

Luckily, military women need not and do not depend exclusively on other women for help. When we asked "Who's your mentor? Who's your role model? Whom do you want to be like? If you had a really bad personal problem, whom would you go to?" we heard over and over about supportive and protective men, men who had gone out of their way to teach and help women, men who genuinely wanted women to succeed. Lots of them were supervisors.

"My role models were my very first supervisor and my very first NCOIC," an Air Force tech sergeant reported. "I was wild. I was partying all the time. I worked hard, but I was very irresponsible as far as getting the things done that you have to do: your appointments, being to work on time, military-type way of life. I was bucking. They took me under their wing. 'If this is where you want to go . . . ,' and at that time no, it wasn't! I was just going to do my time. Four years, I wanted out, and that was it. But they told me, 'While you're here, to survive, this is what you have to do. You're not at home anymore, and nobody's taking care of you.' They showed me if you want to go far as you can possibly go, what you have to do to get there. How you have to discipline yourself and not only care about yourself, but care about the people around you, that you live with, work with, and that work for you. I have the utmost respect for those two people. They are both men."

"I got a good role model," says a white Army Spec-5. "Our acting commander right now is black and he's a warrant officer—to be a black warrant officer is a rarity. And he came in years ago when there was still a lot of prejudice. He was one of the most tactful persons I've ever known. He was a first sergeant for a long time and had to deal with people, and that's probably one of the most complicated skills there is, 'cause there's no manual you can pick up to learn it. I look at him and say, 'He's black and he made it.' I really had to learn not to blow my cool. Guys can go around and yell at somebody and get them to move out, but if a woman does that the guys just yell back and get hostile. I learned that this skipper always got his respect by treating a person with respect, and that's the way I was going to have to work. Anyway, he's more like my model and I have to say, 'Yeah, I have to be better than him.' "

Supervisors like these transform lives. "As a young airman without support in a man's job," a black Air Force master sergeant remembered, "I was kind of rebellious. You know, rebellious against the system. I had a lot of pressure on me. I worked with some civilians, and they didn't like the way I was, the way I did things, and my constant complaining. My mom was going through a hard time at home. I was working seven days a week. This is not what that recruiter told me, the way it was going to be. I almost got out about a year after I came in. The good Lord, I guess, must have been looking after me. I got a new job. I had a very good supervisor, a fabulous supervisor. That's probably what I needed from the beginning, somebody to stand behind me, to give me that little initiative, 'You can do it.' I think if I'd had another bad supervisor, you know, 'Women ain't this' and 'Woman ain't that' and 'Women don't belong here,' I probably would have hung it up."

"My husband's a lot of push behind what I've decided to do."

"Who's helped me most? I'm going to have to say my husband. Believe it or not. Especially when I was ready to throw it all away and give up, when I screamed, 'I quit. I can't stand it anymore.' "

Not all the supportive men are supervisors—a lot are husbands. "I think my husband has helped me most," said an Air Force captain, a navigator on a tanker that refuels other planes in flight. "I've learned a lot from him. When I first got here, he went out with me to the airplane. He was very sharp when he was a boom [hose] operator, and I knew I could learn a lot from him about the airplane. And not just in that area. There's a chain of command, and you have to get used to dealing with your immediate supervisor and kind of working up the chain when you have a problem, and that's not always something that you're used to doing when you've been a civilian your whole life."

"My husband, he's a real big help," says a black soldier. "He was in the military, but he got out. Now he's doing construction work here on post. He has, like, set hours, whereas I don't, so he gets to do a lot for the baby when I'm not there. He kind of encouraged me to do a lot of things, like to keep going to school. At first he wanted me to get out of the Army and we'd go home, but then we talked about it, and he said, 'Well, no, if that's what you want to do, then I'll support you all the way.' He was in the Army himself, so he knows exactly how it is. Sometimes when I go home, he'll tell me, 'Don't worry about it.' He cooks and everything. He's really good."

And many helpful men are colleagues, peers. "I have been pleasantly surprised," comments an Air Force captain, "by the welcome that I as a woman attorney have had from the other members of the community. In the civilian world the club is a lot more closed. The individuals in the Air Force, I've found, are concerned about an issue and need an answer and don't particularly care what you look like if you've got the answer or the facility to assist them. My boss's position is to have input on the decisions that are made—from everyone, not just the men. I was the newest person on the block last year, and I started right out with a major court martial."

Though the American military woman dwells a far piece from heaven, she too rejoices over the conversion of the heathen. Hear a Navy pilot: "One of the other helicopters went out to recover a target. It was sinking, but the recovery harness was still sticking up, and they thought sure that they could snag it. Unfortunately they remained in a hover too low and too long. That causes a salt encrustation to build up on the turbine blades in the back and the engine to stall out. Helicopters don't have enough power to hover on only one engine. So the aircraft settled into the water. The pilot tried to make a single-engine takeoff, was eminently unsuccessful, and shut down the rotor blades. The helicopter rolled over and sank almost immediately. We watched the whole thing. Then we picked them all out of the water and took them back to the ship. I was on my way down to sick bay to make sure the pilots were okay. A sailor jumped out of the corridor at me, comes to attention, gives me this salute—that just doesn't happen on a ship—and says, 'I owe you an apology, ma'am.' 'My goodness, I don't even know you! Why do you owe me an apology?' He says, 'Well, I was up on the signal bridge when the helicopter went into the water.' He said, 'We were all taking bets that *you*'d done it.' "

In the recital of military women's problems, it's important to remember that despite all their woes, many of them get along famously with male colleagues. Women form friendships with men as well as romantic and sexual relationships. Time and again they speak of the men in their units as brothers. Sometimes in our interviews the background to the narration of a deplorable injustice was the sound of women and men happily bantering at work in the next office.

They play as well as work together. "Now I'm coaching the guys," said a black Marine lance corporal. "I have a good team. All male. Some of 'em in my office were talking about getting a basketball team together. They said they needed a coach, and I said, 'I'll coach you.' It's something nice. They listen to me, and we practice really hard. I've turned down quite a few people; I'm not going to have anybody come on to our team, a stranger, and tear our team apart."

"I treat 'em as brothers," said a married enlisted woman. "In the crew's quarters, a small room with fourteen people, the racks are right next to each other. They weren't made for men and women: there's an opening at each end. Some women pasted paper boards [over the openings]. I never did; I just went to sleep. One night I had my pillow stolen through the crack, and I got up and went around to get my pillow, came back, and laid down. He took my blanket, and I got up and went around to get it. By the time I got back he got my whole mattress through the crack. It was just a riot."

A black staff sergeant commented on surviving the rigors of the National Training Center. "Out in the desert we got a guy that got stuck in the Portapotty, so [at the farewell party] we gave him a key to the Portapotty. I'm one of these people when I go to the latrine, I got to have something to read. So they give me a *Playgirl* magazine. If you can sit back and laugh about the whole ordeal after it's over with, after all the crying and the blood and the sweat and the tears and the stink and the funk's cleaned up, they're going to have a different outlook about going next time."

Servicewomen and servicemen work together, they socialize together, and sometimes they live in the same barracks or quarters. They have a lot in common and often enjoy each other's company. Not always. For some women the military is a disastrous experience, a place of harassment and unhappiness, which violates their ideals and principles, where they dread going to work, where no one effectively helps or understands. Many of these women leave before their terms are up. Some go mad.

Some commit suicide, or try to. Some get pregnant in order to get out. And some grimly count the days until their time is over.

But every woman faces the problem of having to earn as a privilege the place in the military that men claim—or reject—as a birthright. If, as Dr. Johnson remarked, "Every man thinks meanly of himself for not having been a soldier," the servicewoman confronts the fact that many think meanly of her for being a soldier. She must waste the energy that men can save for their jobs or their pleasures in proving herself, in smashing stereotypes and overcoming prejudice, in coping with men's questions and problems about her sexual identity and her gender roles. She must fritter away time and vigor in dealing with the question, spoken or unspoken: "Why won't you go to bed with me?" She must think about how to make men comfortable in working with her. All of these activities consume a lot of energy and a lot of time. Whatever she has left over the servicewoman can direct toward building her career.

3. Military Occupation: Job or Career?

CAREER FIELD CHOICE

> *"The military can be outstanding if you get into a career field that you're really interested in."*
>
> *"For women it's critical that they get in the right career field."*
>
> *"My recruiter was a boiler tender, and so he didn't have the slightest notion about anything about women in the Navy."*

Most recruits plan a military interlude, not a military career. For great numbers of young people the services furnish the first job—or at least the first job after McDonald's or Burger King. Many of these youngsters lightheartedly sign up for adventure, travel, escape, growing time, or more seriously for training and education—usually with the idea of a return to civilian life beckoning in the future.

Yet at the point of entry the recruit, often knowing next to nothing about possibilities or consequences, must make the crucial choice of a career field. "Yes, my choice of career fields made a very large difference," said a lieutenant colonel in the Air Force. "I did not know when I went into the Public Affairs career field that it was going to benefit me. Then I found out 'Well, hey, this is a good deal.' You're an extremely visible person. You work directly for at worst the vice-commander on base, at best, the commander. The commander is your rating official and your endorsing official is his boss; if you keep your nose clean you can do very well." (The higher the rank, the more impressive the endorsement.)

For the officer, making an early choice of career field may work pretty well. She is usually older than the enlisted woman when she joins; she has developed her interests in college; she may have skills or knowledge to use as bargaining chips. Even if she does not, the nature of officers' work, the time allowed them in some cases before they begin to specialize, and their greater ease in moving from one field to another alleviate the consequences of the original choice.

For many an enlisted woman, though, the "choice" comes at a time when she is ill-prepared. Her options are limited by military needs at the given moment—just as in a civilian job. The trouble is, for many recruits the choice of job is a second and secondary decision. In effect the recruit has chosen a company to work for; now she must decide what job to do within it. But often she focuses only on the company, overlooking the importance of the job choice.

After she has taken her tests, the recruiter will call up on the computer the available jobs for which she qualifies and offer the recruit a choice among them. Or, particularly if she has high scores, the recruiter may hand her a printed list of MOSs, with brief descriptions. The job titles, bred by euphemism out of technology, often confuse the recruit more than they help her.

Sophisticated recruits bargain with their recruiters: for rank, if they have needed skills or experience to offer; for location; for a guaranteed school or MOS. Most of them, though, naïvely rely on the recruiter, the local expert on the military. What the recruit learns depends on the recruiter's ignorance or knowledgeability about the hundreds of occupational specialties, his or her understanding of and sympathy for women's situation in the military, and the severity of his conflict of interest—concerned though he may be for the welfare of the recruit, his first consideration must be the needs of the services, and their current policies.

In the late 1970s, for example, social pressures and lack of qualified men caused the services to urge women into nontraditional fields, regardless of the women's wishes, abilities, or temperaments. "When I came in the service in 1978," a black staff sergeant told us, "they were trying to get as many females as possible into nontraditional career fields—jet engine mechanics, civil engineering. The Air Force put a lot of females into career fields just to balance them out, which I guess you could say was both negative and positive. Positive, yes, you have females in there. Negative, do you have females who really want to be in there? Sure, there are a lot of men doing work they don't want to do too. That's one of the problems." To restate the obvious, in recruiting, institutional needs outweigh individual needs.

If cross-training (retraining for another MOS) were easy, the original choice would matter less. Often it isn't. The service recruited people for a specific career field in the first place because it needed them there. It invested money in training them. If it retrains them, they will take months or years to gain expertise and experience commensurate with the ranks they have earned in the original fields. So a lateral move may prove more difficult than upward progression.

But few recruits are informed enough to make a sensible choice. A woman, for example, may not know enough at enlistment to weigh the pros and cons of entering a nontraditional field, which automatically increases her visibility. If she succeeds, she collects extra kudos and may be promoted more quickly. "If you can make it in a male-dominated career field," says an academy graduate, "I don't think there's any question that your effectiveness reports are going to go higher for endorsement, you're going to be eligible for more awards, because you've proven that you can survive and you can excel in a male-dominated world." But does she really want to go through the hassles of working with men who don't want her there, or of doing work that doesn't interest her? "When I walked through that gate, I was the first female they had ever had, 'cause I was the third female out of the missile career field. And I was the only black person—not just the only female—and we're talking about a shop of fifty or sixty people. We had everything there from rednecks to the guy that just doesn't know what to do with me because I'm a female, or he's afraid to say the wrong thing. We had several conflicts, until I was able to go out there and do what I was supposed to be doing. Once being out there, I ran into the people who were, 'Well, if I can do it, you can do it.' The weight of a missile ranges from a hundred fifty pounds to two thousand, three thousand pounds. You know the basic macho jock that's out there. Rather than using the hoists, he wants to lift them himself, him and his buddy. They expected me to do things like that. In the beginning, I tried it. But somewhere along the way, I said, 'Well, I don't have to prove anything to anybody.' Had little conflicts here and there. Eventually it sort of calmed down."

THE UPWARD PATH

One way or another the recruit chooses her career field. Her graduation from basic training is often followed by advanced individual training (AIT), a school to teach her the rudiments of her MOS. Then she is off to her first permanent duty station, where she confronts the expectations of the military—some of which may come as a shock.

For the services now expect their members not merely to do their jobs, to work long hours, and to be available and mobile twenty-four hours a day, but also to study and prepare themselves for more difficult tasks and greater responsibilities. In many ways, the services treat all their members as if they were building careers. The armed forces, like the fast-food industry, expect a high labor turnover, *but* they demand full-time availability. They immediately give their people extensive benefits, and they dangle before them the prospect of upward mobility.

"If there's a chance of making E-5, I'll stay in; if not, I'll get out."

The various branches differ in the rapidity with which they move their people up and in their tables of organization and their budgets, which limit the slots available for promotion. Many an interviewee mourned at receiving after her promotion tests the bad news "Passed but not advanced." "I'm not a dud by no means," said an Army staff sergeant, "but I just can't make the points to meet that 989—that cutoff score [accumulation of points below which no promotion is permitted] hasn't dropped in seven years. For 67-Goff [MOS for airplane mechanic] they have two [promotion] zones. I looked at the scores: primary zone, 289 people on the list, none promoted—zero; secondary zone, 78 people on the list, none promoted—zero. So it's about 350 E-5s in the United States Army who are not making E-6 in 67-Goff."

A soul-deadening experience, especially when it is repeated several times, especially when she must watch servicemembers in other MOSs advancing rapidly. Again and again, particularly in the Army, an interviewee told us that the points necessary for promotion in her MOS were set so high as to be literally unattainable, unless she won the Congressional Medal of Honor. She could max (receive the highest score in) all her physical fitness tests, get a college degree, take all the professional military courses available, spend all her off-duty time in community service, win awards for outstanding performance, and still end up a couple of points shy. "You're tired of being a certain rank for four years. I've been this rank for almost three years. The cutoff scores . . . this is the points you need. Mine's one of the highest: 998, and at the time I got 789, so within two years I can make it. But that doesn't help me now. That doesn't help me with my warrant officer school."

On the whole, though, the services labor—with mixed results—to encourage or even force their people to think seriously about their work lives. Early on, whether they are enlisted or officers, the services begin feeding them information about how to advance and develop a career. Drill instructors begin teaching and encouraging recruits, and supervisors continue the process. Because the military grades them on how well their people perform and progress, supervisors are powerfully motivated to insist that the new soldiers and sailors try for awards, take correspondence courses, study nights and weekends. To their horror, young women who couldn't wait to graduate from high school and have turned down family offers to send them to college confront new demands to buckle down and learn.

"Advice to a young woman coming into the Air Force?" reflects a black staff sergeant. "It depends upon her personality, but she can basically be whatever she wants to be. Pick your career field carefully. And go to school. That's number one. That will open a lot of doors. I have won different awards: three commendation medals; I got one of the highest awards for enlisted persons—the Military Service Award. I felt good! A lot of it hinged on education."

The Coast Guard delivers the message a little differently. Unless a young enlisted woman enters with a guaranteed school or job, she is apt to find herself sent to a small-boat station or put on a work force mowing lawns, cleaning latrines, and picking up cigarette butts. Sooner or later she must figure out that the only escape is upward and begin to study for her promotional tests, strike (get on-the-job training) to learn the necessary skills for a rating, or maneuver to be sent to school.

Evaluations, critically important for promotion, are given regularly in all the services. Injustices occur, of course, but at least raters must grade by known standards, and the servicewoman may object to evaluations with which she disagrees. The system functions not only as fair warning but also as motivation: "When I receive some type of negative result, a bad performance report, I'm motivated," says a black master sergeant in the Air Force. "I was kind of upset with my supervisor, and test time was coming in about a month or two. So I really got down and I really studied. I was going to show them that I was competent through my testing, my discipline, reading, and getting all this information I needed to take the test. Well, I was the last one to leave out of the test room that day. It takes several months before you can find out [how you did], but I went back to my job and the person that gave me the report that I did not like. I told him, 'Why don't you just shake hands with Staff Sergeant Jones?' He said, 'You think you made it?' I said, 'I know I did.' Positive. Oh, so positive. So he shook my hand. And it came out. I made it!"

But with the moral equivalent of grade inflation prevailing in most efficiency and performance reports (though the Coast Guard women we talked to deny its existence in their branch), a less than perfect report from an angry, prejudiced, or jealous supervisor may be fatal. (Servicemen also of course experience such injustices; servicewomen run the extra risk of discrimination against women.) One such evaluation dogged the career of an officer we interviewed. A woman with a great love of her service and an impeccable record, she had the misfortune to work for a former prisoner of war who strongly disapproved of women in the service. She was pregnant, working in a busy office, studying for her master's degree, and taking the next level of professional military education at night. "Then because of the pregnancy they said at the hospital 'Work no more than eight hours,' which was not the norm at my office. When some of my work was late, he started saying such things as 'Sounds like you're putting your personal life ahead of the Air Force. Didn't you ever hear of the Pill?' I wasn't the only person that had problems with him, but mine were all related to this woman kind of thing. Some people thought that I probably ought to go to the IG [Inspector General]. I said, 'Sure, an ex-POW? I don't care how right

I am, I'm going to be perceived wrong.' Plus my own personal thing, all this patriotism: 'God, this guy has suffered six years in prison. Who am I to cause him this kind of trouble?' If I had it to do over again, I would never allow that to be a stumbling block in protecting myself."

Although this kind of experience was rare among the women we interviewed, it was not unique. We have talked to able young officers whose careers were almost wrecked at their first assignments by men who disapproved of women in the service and, more tragically, to an older officer with a well-established career whose conscientious and principled service in the cause of women ended in the refusal of a promotion that her colleagues had confidently expected.

As further encouragement to think in career terms, in all the services the first few promotions come easy. In the words of a Signal Corps PFC: "All the Army asks of you is to keep your nose clean and keep your room clean." Or, as a black master sergeant put it, "If you could shine your shoes, had halfway decent intelligence, you could make sergeant. Real easy. There are certain ranks that you are going to make unless you go and hit a general up side the head." Not only do these early promotions bring additional pay; they also establish the new sailor or soldier as a full-fledged military member and move her up from the loathed position at the bottom of the totem pole, where *everyone* can tell her what to do. Officers similarly find the first few promotions almost automatic: "For us, up through lieutenant, we're fairly assured of getting our promotions. It's about a 90-percent chance—and one hundred percent at lieutenant j.g. [junior grade]. You really have to foul up not to be. Basically at that level they put the mirror to your nose and make sure that you're still breathing."

Early successes tell servicewomen that they really can advance, that they have moved into a world that recognizes and rewards ability and effort. Witness a meritoriously promoted (promoted before the normal time has elapsed) E-4 in the Air Force: "I'm on the right track. If you're striving to be the best of what you do, you've got to be noticed. I had won 'Airman of the Quarter' and then the new base commander had endorsed my APR [Airman's Performance Report], so that was a plus. An airman had never been put in charge of postal service before; they had to write headquarters for permission. So yes, there's ways. You definitely can work towards it."

And successes breed ambition. "I consider myself a career woman," says a twenty-nine-year-old tech sergeant. "My squadron has put me up for a lot of recognition. Two years running, I was the candidate for the Supply Squadron for Female Military Employee of the Year. I was also selected to represent the squadron as the Outstanding NCO—this includes the males and the females—of the Year. Last year I got the Outstanding Senior Supply Technician for the base, the Twenty-first Air Force, and the whole Military Airlift Command. Everything is just starting to kick in line for me. I tell my husband, to get you got to give. We're looking toward the future and the children. I bust my buns. I never had when I was a child. My kids have the best. I have managed to do it, and do it well."

As this servicewoman notes, the military inventively offers a myriad of awards. Usually the servicemember must study and prepare to go before a board, there to answer questions on current events or military courtesy and history or her job, in hopes of winning the title of "Airman of the Month," "Sailor of the Year," first for her/his own unit, then moving up competitively through progressively larger units. Just to be asked to compete, to represent one's unit, is an honor (and of course an experience that demands study and teaches poise). The military also makes the effort worthwhile in other ways: to the winner, a couple of extra days off, a trip, a guaranteed parking place for three months, a general's congratulations, a picture taken with him, and perhaps his endorsement on one's next efficiency rating—all reported to the hometown paper.

Sometimes, of course, things go wrong in the competitions the commanding officer or his PR person dreams up. An interviewee told us in some bewilderment about her experience as "Ms. Air Force Base X." A beautiful and bright senior airman, she competed on the understanding that the winner would represent the base at community functions: "My goal was to represent women and to show people that women in the military weren't so bad after all." But after some servicemembers boycotted the pageant as sexist, occasions to appear dwindled. Usually, though, these competitions do what they are designed to do, raise morale and ambitions.

The responsibilities thrust early on military members also reward and motivate them in their careers. The relative youth of the military population necessitates the use of younger people for greater responsibility than in the civilian sector. It is heady stuff for a young captain to control a budget of millions of dollars, or to negotiate contracts on behalf of the United States government with the senior vice-presidents of civilian corporations, often twice her age. Many a young woman, comparing her duties with those of the peers she left at home, revels in her opportunities. And the rank structure of the military requires that even E-3s and E-4s begin to supervise. Her "staff" may consist of one E-2, but the young corporal begins to think about leadership styles and problem solving.

"My bosses always had the confidence in me," said a black thirty-year-old personnel chief in the Navy, "but I didn't ever think I could do it. It took a long time for me to finally build up the confidence to 'Hey, I can do the job.' On my ship, I had an E-8, and he was retiring. I was an E-6, the leading petty officer [NCO] in the department. I expected another E-7 or E-8 to come in, and they said, 'Guess what? You're it.' My supervisors threw me in and they said, 'It's yours.' I learned a lot, 'cause I go on researching and finding out everything I need to know. They really make you use your own head, try to find how to solve problems on your own."

The services, like colleges, are peopled by young women and men as they grow from adolescents into adults (or plateau in some indeterminate stage of arrested development in between). In the services, as in colleges, many only drift to and fro, but some young Americans come alive and discover what they want to do with their lives.

A senior airman, just awakening to her opportunities, mulled over what happens: "The first four years, I knew I didn't want to go to school, but if I'm going to reenlist, what I would do is put myself through school. I would like to get my degree and go through officer training. After all, if you're going to make a career out of it, why not go for it? The Air Force will pay seventy-five percent, which is really excellent. I don't read much. But it seems like if it really advances me in my career, I'm going to study and read it. You know why you're doing it. And you know where it's leading to, where in high school you know you've got to get your diploma, but where're you headed after that?"

A legal clerk described her metamorphosis. "I went to an advanced school for my MOS, and the legal chief of the Marine Corps started telling us, the sergeants there, what they look for to become E-6. That's what did it. The number-one thing that he mentioned was off-duty education. I started with two courses; I was going four nights a week.

That was hard on me. I was used to watching TV, going to bed at eight o'clock. But I liked going to school. I was going because I wanted to. No one had pressured me. I was going to prepare myself to become a drill instructor, but I have decided that instead I would like to try to get my B.A. and apply for the warrant officer program. Being an officer will benefit me more, and also head me toward my goal." The sergeant now talks of going on for her master's, to prepare herself for civilian life after a full military career. "I'm twenty-four years old," she concluded, "and I feel like time is running out. At least you have to get your goals and patterns set."

WHAT THEY WANT

As they grow, some young servicemembers begin to find out what really matters to them. A black single mother of a nine-year-old has found in the Army both financial security for her family and pride in herself. "My mom says, 'Girl, you need to get married. Get somebody to take care of you.' Now, *she* made it that way. But *I* like to take care of myself. It makes me feel really good that I've done it by myself without being dependent on anybody. I like that. I like that a lot."

A black staff sergeant, a wife and mother, who completed her B.S. in three and a half years on the job and now intends to start work on her master's, said, "My goal right now is, I would like to make Senior [master sergeant] before I retire out of the military. I have eight years left. I have focused a lot upon my educational goals, and I haven't really focused as much as far as promotional goals as I possibly should. This article I had read about five years ago seemed to somehow fit in there, about fear of success. I like to go to my job, I enjoy what I'm doing, but when I start moving up into rank I think I have that blockage. I don't try so hard, and I'm pretty satisfied. But when my peer group starts to move up, then I get sick! Then I try hard! I guess it's somewhat that old mentality: I equate a lot of responsibility, a lot of rank, with getting old. At one time I said, 'Well, I'll be a staff sergeant and then the airmen won't talk to me. I'll have more responsibility, and I won't be able to really be with them like I am now.' And now that I've made staff, I say, 'Well, if I'm a tech sergeant, then I'll be called a battleax, and they really won't talk to me then.' [*Laughs.*] I guess it's just a cop-out, basically."

"If I'm not putting something in there that's really challenging, I get bored," said a black staff sergeant. "So I do change jobs. This particular job I'm committed to for six years, so I found out about a special-duty assignment [where] it's still the same career field, but the view of the job is different. After that I will have one more enlistment, and I plan to be a first sergeant. I have to make two more stripes, because a first sergeant is a particular billet for master sergeant or above. You work directly for the commander; you're like his right-hand man—or right-hand person—and you deal with the personnel—everything from disciplinary problems to morale builders, health and welfare. My last challenge with the military. As far as I know, there are no active-duty female first sergeants on this base. You could probably count 'em on your ten fingers, how many are in the Air Force. There are no black women ones. [*Laughs.*] None."

> *"I want to be a chief. I'm not going to spend twenty years in the war for nothing."*
>
> *"I'd like to go as high as I can. General, if that's in the making, if I don't step on my toes here in the process."*
>
> *"In ten years? I see myself still riding around the streets of Los Angeles [in the police department]. Well, maybe in the detective division, which is what I eventually want to work up to."*

If her ambition focuses on a civilian career, the servicewoman usually enrolls for college courses (mostly paid for by the military, provided that she earns a grade of C or better) or seeks experience and skills in the military that can translate into a good job "outside." With the right background, her civilian options can be attractive, even after relatively few years' service. As the military hires more civilians and turns over more of its work to civilian organizations on a contract basis, the servicewoman may even look forward to doing the same work as a civilian that she has done in the military. "Civilian contracts are taking over the LORAN [long-range navigation] stations, they're saying end of '87 to '89. It'll be '90 when I get out: with all the experience—specially the teaching, and I will have been probably at three or four LORAN stations by then—it's almost like guaranteeing a job in the civilian world, and good pay. It's a specialty that there aren't a lot of people trained in, because it's strictly Coast Guard now."

"What I really plan to do is become a civil servant in the same field I'm in now," said an Army Spec-5. "For instance, take over the editor job that's opening up at Fort X, which is a GS-9 position. When I get out of service, I'll have seven and a half years, and I'll be working on my bachelor's degree, and with all the experience, you know, I could go right into a job like that. A lot of the editor slots on Army newspapers are going civilian."

Or the servicewoman's experience may qualify her for a related field. A lieutenant commander leaving the Navy told us about her plans to market her "ten healthy years of intelligence experience. Around Washington, D.C., that's a marketable background. So I'll be working with a defense contractor on Navy issues initially and then transition into other things. Hopefully someday to get out of the intelligence business and get more into the business aspects of things."

> *"If you have calculus and physics and a certain amount of credits, they will send you to college to get your engineering degree. I'll come back as an electrical engineer and I'll be an officer."*
>
> *"Rank to me is like, well, I figure officers put their britches on the same way I do."*
>
> *"Don't you like me as an NCO? What's wrong with being an NCO? Someone's got to keep the officers in line!"*

Of the enlisted women who elect a military career, some try to become officers. Others, equally ambitious and high-achieving, seek instead the highest enlisted ranks. Why?

Some of them prefer the closeness to the troops, the hands-on jobs, rather than the remote planning that they see as the officer's function: they take pride in being the people who actually get things done, rather than just ordering them done. Often, of course, enlisted women argue this way on the basis of limited observations—and perhaps with a touch of fear of the unknown atmosphere of officer country.

"That's my cop-out," says a black staff sergeant in the Air Force. "They've often told me and they still tell me, 'Why don't you go for

OTS [Officer Training School]? Why don't you go and test?' I feel like I can do more where I am. I can relate to people more. And that seems to be my incentive. It's not money. It's people and having peace of mind. If I'm put into the situation where that's going to be compromised, I'm going to lose out big. People have a difficult time understanding, respecting that. But I'm comfortable with it." "I would never go commissioned," said a parachute rigger. "I'd love to be a warrant, but not commissioned. There's too much 'You'll do it this way. Your husband will do this.' I could not be regimented like that. I'm not conventional enough. If I want to go crazy, I want to go crazy."

No one gets to be a high-ranking NCO without learning the byways of the military, the possibilities for accomplishing what one wants by devious routes. Becoming an officer, particularly for a woman, often means walking the straight and narrow, because her every step is exposed. A black E-7 in the Army observed: "I even went as far as getting the paperwork. But I like to be in charge, and I like to do things my way. As it is here, I can make mistakes and recover. Female officers, black, cannot make mistakes and recover. They have a black female officer on post here. Everyone knows when she makes a mistake. I don't want any parts of it."

Other enlisted women point out the need to avoid a brain drain from the enlisted ranks. Most of all, enlisted women don't want to start over in a new and more political ballgame, as the rookie on the squad. "I feel like I have too many years in to start all over again. I've put enough work into being the rank I am now that I'd hate to have to go through all the officer schools just to get promoted. And not only that, I'd never make it to the top there. Giving up tech stripes to be a lieutenant—it just doesn't turn me on that much."

The enlisted woman who does aspire to be an officer may not make it. The "bootstrap" programs are highly competitive. A lot depends on understanding the system, help with composing the complicated application "package," access to the right endorsers—sponsorship by someone with clout—and always the current needs of the service. A Navy petty officer, a single parent, recognizing the odds, is hedging her bets. "I've recently applied for the enlisted commissioning program, which is very very competitive. I applied last year and was very junior and didn't have all the requirements that they needed. I've upgraded my application this year, but still . . . they told me they had a hundred billets to offer and eight of 'em were available for women. I'll have to pay my own tuition, but I can use my veteran's benefits to do that. But that will be my duty, will be to go to school full-time, and when I finish, then I'll have a four-year obligation in a commissioned status. Because it is so competitive, you sure can't put all your eggs in one basket. My enlistment is up in June. If I don't get picked up then [for the commissioning program], I will be leaving the service long enough to go home and finish my degree. I figure if I can get myself in a good position by the time I'm out, if I carry eighteen hours and go through the summer, then I can be out of school in a year. One way or another, I'll be back in the service in a commissioned status."

CAREER MANAGEMENT

> *"I fully and totally engineered my career. There were squares to fill and I knew what they were. I went out and got my master's degree and I filled that square. Professional military education squares, and I filled those."*
>
> *"Things such as performance reports, awards that you should receive. If you don't write it, you won't get it. If you're not bold enough to say, 'Well, I think I deserve this, and here's the paperwork that you need to do it.' Or 'I've already typed everything up and here it is. You can read it and sign.' "*

Manuals spell out what the servicewoman must do to get ahead. Officers talk about filling squares by taking advanced degrees, by holding command positions, by gaining operational experience. Enlisted women talk about accumulating points by "maxing" physical training tests, earning educational credits, winning awards, attending military schools, and taking professional correspondence courses. "They have this thing called the Performance Fitness Exam. I call it the Air Force Bible, because it's all about the Air Force and what they want, what they expect, and we're tested on that material to make our next grade. But I also look at that as a guide to move up, progress. I use that to try to see where I'm going or where I'm at; am I doing it the right way? Do I have management abilities? What do they want in a leader? It's all in the book."

An Air Force lieutenant colonel talked about building her career. "A lot of people will get incited to riot when they're asked to give input for their own OERs [Officer Evaluation Reports] or their APRs. I relished the opportunity. Not only did I give input, but I wrote out the whole thing and had it in final form. If he doesn't like what I provide, the wing commander can change it. I was sensitive to it to begin with: 'Well, he is my boss and he ought to know what I'm doing.' One has to get over the sense of modesty. I wouldn't be where I am today if I did not take advantage of the opportunities that were really given to me, and I would recommend that to anyone."

"I was selected the first time I submitted my application [to OTS]," said a lieutenant with fifteen years' enlisted service. "I had good endorsements. I submitted the letter from the squadron commander, even though he said 'For a woman she did exceedingly well,' because I knew that would give them a picture about what type of pressures I was working under. I had letters of endorsement from generals. They had been in charge of Recruiting Services during the time period that I was a recruiter, and I had met 'em—maybe only one time—but I'm not bashful now about asking somebody for help. I wrote off to 'em, I told them what I was doing, I sent them copies of my transcripts, I sent them copies of a résumé that I wrote up on myself. And I asked them, 'Please endorse my application.' Quite a few did respond. I thank those generals for doing that for me."

Career-managing servicewomen learn to take advantage of the systems the institution offers for advancement and for redress. A black master sergeant told us about twice receiving reports that she thought were unfair. The first time, not really caring, she did nothing. But the second time, having tasted success and formulated goals, "I wrote the board down at Air Force Manpower Personnel Center the whole scenario about what I had done versus what I had got rated, and I didn't think it was fair. About this time, being a staff sergeant, I thought I was something. [*Laughs.*] Making it in the military. I wrote the board a long letter, about four pages thick, and they corrected my performance report. Then I became a fighter."

Both the enlisted servicewoman and the officer can formulate a pretty good idea of their chances for promotion. They know when promotion boards meet and what they do. Sophisticated military women know down to the decimal point what percentage of eligible lieutenants make captain. We asked a captain to calculate her chances: "Oh, geez. I have all the squares filled right now except I don't have wings. I'm not a pilot or a navigator. And I'm not an Academy grad. Probably just about as good as anybody else's. I try my very best to do a good job. I started out in a very good area. You have lots of visibility. I think you have to be able to accept the responsibility for going after that visibility—it can backfire on you, especially being a woman. The other thing is that I try my very best not to say no. I've been accused of being a yes person. I'm in the middle of a source selection [choosing a corporate supplier for military purchases]. I have many other additional duties, and when the Dining Out [a party for officers and their guests] came along, I knew it was going to be a lot of work, but I said yes anyway. I have to prove to myself that I can juggle all that and still have come out intact and still have done a very, very good job at all my responsibilities. I guess that's really the key, is to show the higher-ranking people that guide your career that you can do it and that you know how to manage your time without coming unglued at the seams."

"If they don't have salt [go to sea], they're not going to get promoted and picked up like the men."

The career-managing servicewoman also considers how to position herself within her chosen career field. Women in nontraditional career fields repeatedly fight off efforts to confine them to office jobs; if they prefer hands-on work, if they like to work outdoors, or if they fear losing their skills in their MOSs, they may have to scramble just to work in the jobs for which they have been trained. Again and again we heard stories about men who resisted letting women do their own jobs: "The boss was hurting the women, because even though they were qualified to drive the forklift, he wouldn't let them do it. Do you know what? It was hurting the guys too, because they were getting double loads. The women were mad because they couldn't do their jobs, and then when the women go to take the promotion tests, they don't have the experience, hands-on."

"I got two new women in, like the beginning of last month," said a black staff sergeant, "and they wanted to put one in the office job. I had to fight and fight and fight to get her out. I told 'em, 'That's why the females don't know their jobs,' because they want 'em to do all the clerical work or make the coffee. I told 'em, 'If a female works under me, I will not allow her to go have a office job until she learns enough to satisfy me that she can go out and do her job in the motor pool with me.' Soon as they put the one in the office job, I heard the guys—they would walk around me and say their little comments: 'Well, I knew the women was startin' shammin' as soon as they got here and I knew they were startin' gettin' over. They don't have to go to work like we have to go to work.' I went to the first sergeant and I told him, 'This is what I was talking about was going to happen. Some of the guys have been to typing class and they can type better than some of the females. Why don't you give some of them the job?' But he wouldn't do it, so I told him, 'Well, she's my female, and I want her back out of the office.' He told me, 'Well, you have to put somebody else in.' I say, 'You can have one of my guys, but you can't have a female.' They said, 'Well, how about if she worked for you in the morning and she worked for us in the afternoon?' I said, 'Okay, I'll go for that, but she's not going to sit behind a typewriter all day long.' "

"I've been in, like I say, for eight years," a black crane operator told us, "and I've just got my license last year, because when I came in, they didn't want females operating equipment. I fought and I fought, and they kept saying no females will operate the crane. Right now I believe it's only two females in the unit that has a license for cranes. Me and a Spec-4. I operate the hundred forty–ton crane. It's pretty easy. I thought it would be hard too, the way they kept fighting for us not to operate 'em. They say now I'm an E-6 I'm in a leadership position, so I'm not supposed to operate equipment now. But if I get a chance I will get up there and operate it. That's what I told 'em: They waited till I got the rank to give me the license, so I wouldn't have to operate."

"I'm a tech sergeant, and I'm in maintenance, and I don't have a lot of experience on the job. When I first came in the job—this was ten years ago—they found a little place for me to work, instead of with the dangerous engines. Being ignorant, I didn't realize it was going to hurt me in the future. Now by virtue of my rank I am in a supervisory role, and I cannot relate to the problems that the folks are telling me, because I didn't even work on it myself. When my records eventually go before a board, they won't make me a senior master sergeant, because I don't have enough experience."

On the other hand, some women see advantages in moving quickly toward management—and they too meet opposition. "In missiles we had various sections: dispatchers and record keeping, which were basically office jobs. I voluntarily went into those sections," a black staff sergeant told us. "I am not an outside-worker type person. I don't like standing out there in the cold or working with my hands all the time. I'm basically an office person. I can take anything and organize it or create anything. They were very skeptical about putting me in the office, because it did draw a lot of attention. 'Why are you putting that female in an office? Why aren't you going to have her out there doing her job?' I spent seven years in missiles. I was in and out, because I had to keep my proficiency training together, but I was basically an office-type person. I learned more. When you're out there on the maintenance floor, you just don't know what the hell is going on. You don't know about the colonel or the general that sent the order down, or you don't know about the mission itself. Being in the office, you're aware of all of that. You do a lot of scheduling yourself, because you know what has to be done. And you know where the mistakes are coming from."

As they work to position themselves advantageously, some Navy women struggle for sea duty. "Women don't really have sea duty," explained an ambitious yeoman second-class. "We have tours of what they call OUTUS [outside United States] and CONUS [continental United States], and OUTUS satisfies both sea and overseas [duty requirements]. But there's an awful lot of women who want to go to sea. And there's still a limited number of ships that women can go on. The women that are career are cutting each other's throats trying to get the ships, because they see that it is a career path. If a woman has spent any time on board a ship, promotions come easier."

Should the career servicewoman take the job she would love to do or the job that will enhance her career? An Air Force captain weighed a choice between a headquarters job and an assignment in Greece: "My boss keeps telling me, 'You need to get those squares filled to get promoted. The Athens job sounds great, but remember it's a two-year assignment—right when you come up for major. All you would have had when you come up for the majors' board are wing/squadron-level jobs.' I cringe a little bit when they tell me to go to a headquarters job. But I know sooner or later I'm going to have to do it. I'm beginning to accept that more and more."

Of course, many young women are not that goal-oriented. "I am somebody who floats a little bit with the flow of the opportunity," says a Coast Guard lieutenant. "Yes, I was watching those opportunities. Very carefully? How carefully does somebody that's twenty-one watch opportunities? Here was a chance to do something different. 'Gee, it might be possible for me to get command of a ninety-five-footer.' I worked to do a good job, one, because I wanted to most of all, and I was having fun, and two, because I thought, 'Gee, you know, I'd like to give that a shot. I'd really like to have command, at least once in my life.' I didn't look at command as a stepping-stone to greater and better things."

What's more, Brigadier General Gail Reals of the Marines issued an impressive warning against becoming absorbed in gamesmanship. "Those people who are telling you they know all the right moves are the ones who probably in a few years from now are going to find they miscalculated and didn't keep their eye on the ball. I told a young lieutenant at Quantico not long ago: 'Well, Lieutenant, I really think that if you start worrying about trying to beat the system this early in the game, you're going to have problems, because you've got to realize one thing: there ain't no system.'

"You know people who calculate—'Well, I've gotta have a master's degree.' So they go to a school, and all they're concerned about is getting more credits for umpity-ump. Next thing you know, they're not on the promotion list when they should have been. And somebody will say, 'Well, hell, he was so worried about getting his master's degree I never saw him.' So he had his master's degree all right, but he didn't have the record to go along with it. I've seen that happen over and over and over again. I got an honorary degree from a college not long ago, but I don't have a credit toward a college degree. And I've served with people who have had master's and everything else and are dead in the water. They outfoxed themselves.

"Or they get upset 'cause they don't get promoted or get the jobs they wanted. Well, they thought they had it all figured, and they'd move from here to there and they'd be at headquarters and then Quantico and the promotion board looks at it and says, 'Gee, he's never been out in the real Marine Corps!' It jumps up and bites you. So sometimes you have to go with the flow. And do the best job you possibly can. The thing that sends people into orbit around here is talking about challenging and career-enhancing jobs. But the general who I work for says he's had two or three jobs that many people in the Marine Corps will tell you will be career stoppers. I mean, you will never go anywhere if you have those jobs. Obviously it's the end of the road, and you should have realized when you were there that you had been taken off the fast track. Well, he's got a whole bunch of those, and he's a lieutenant general.

"There just isn't any way to figure it out. If you're reasonably professional and you do your job the best you can, your chances are pretty good. If you forget to do that first and foremost, your chances are nil."

Despite all the mechanisms for upward mobility the military offers, getting promoted to its higher ranks, enlisted or officer, is far from easy—for anyone, man or woman. The pyramids narrow at the top. And the higher the rank, the greater the differences between men and women. "For women as you go up in rank, there's a lot less slots you can hold," says an Army first lieutenant. "A man as a major or whatever, captain, can go anywhere. He can take a job that a woman could take and jobs that women can't. The Army has been going back and forth and back and forth on what jobs are open to women and which ones aren't. So it's just going to depend on how many [women] they need down the road, I guess. Yes, the difference is combat. Right, and how far forward you can be slotted."

CAREER BARRIERS AND PITFALLS

As in any other job we know about, the military woman also needs luck—being in the right place at the right time, avoiding resentful or prejudiced supervisors. Women open up opportunities when they break into a career field hitherto reserved for men, but just getting in may require overcoming obstacles. A loadmaster on a C-5, the world's biggest airplane, told us how she managed it. "At the time there were no women in the C-5 program. I went over here to the people in the flying squadron. They were really excited about having a woman recruit in the career field. I wanted to be a flight engineer, but they won't let you do that unless you have a maintenance background. So I went to the personnel office, and they said, 'No women in the program. Sorry.' I said, 'Show me where it says that they prohibit women.' I was really curious as to what was keeping women from being involved. I think it was just a lot of guys that had been in for a long time in the flying career field, and they just didn't like the idea of women coming in.

Well, that just made me all the more determined I was going to do this. Like it or not, I was going to show them that, hey, that's not fair. So I applied for the C-5 program and it came through."

An E-5's description of getting the job she wanted offers a paradigm of tact and persistence: "They had me in the MA [maintenance] gang; I was cleaning decks, buffing floors. I said, 'Well, can I get on Security?' They said, 'Naw, they don't put girls on Security, 'cause they've screwed up too much in the past.' I said, 'Is this written down anywhere?' They said, 'No, no. They just don't do it.' So I went to my boss and he just said, 'Don't mess with it.' I said okay, but when you go to a new station you have an interview with the commander, like four or five days after you get there. So when I went in for my interview I said, 'Is it true they don't put girls on Security? Is there a reason for that?' 'Oh, no, that would be sexual discrimination.' A few days later they came up to me with a chit and said, 'If you want to be in Security, fill this out.' "

Military women walk a rocky road also if a guaranteed job does not develop as promised, or a job is phased out (like the job of navigator on many military aircraft), or if an MOS is suddenly closed to women (as when the Army's Direct Combat Probability Code closed numerous MOSs and units to women).

The first two of these roadblocks stop or detour the careers of male servicemembers too, but the last is for women only. "Now, there have been some ratings, like gunner's mate, that have all of a sudden closed to females, and you got females in 'em. What they do is tell 'em that they can stay in it until they come to the end of their enlistment, and at that time they need to find another rate to get into. If you're a second-class, that does hinder your career." "I was in college, majoring in physics and math, and I wanted to go into nuclear physics. I saw this little ad in the paper saying 'Nuclear Power Program,' so I looked into it, and it was the Navy. When I enlisted, that was what I was supposed to go into. Then when I got into the boot camp they closed it to women."

But the greatest problems for servicewomen who want to develop careers in the military remain those of sexual harassment and discrimination (see Chapter 2), the denial to women of career-enhancing assignments and career fields by the combat-exclusion policy (see Chapter 5), and the conflict between family responsibilities and military responsibilities (see Chapter 8).

4. Working Lives

WHAT JOBS DOES SHE DO?

More than half of all military women type, file, run word processors, work in hospitals and clinics, keep accounts and personnel and supply records—that is, they do traditionally female jobs. Many build responsible, satisfying, and often exciting careers in these fields, with expanding powers and wider opportunities as they rise in rank.

But more and more women are moving into other MOSs. From 1972 to 1983 the proportion of military women in traditionally female jobs dropped from 90 to 55 percent. Although the Army recently has swung back and forth, the services have moved strongly toward opening more MOSs to women, and they continue in that direction.

Servicewoman after servicewoman—whether in a traditional or in a nontraditional job—enthralled us by talking about her jobs, her achievements, her problems at work, by telling us her "war stories" or "sea stories." How best to convey that wide range and that flavor? Perhaps service by service, with one woman representing each.

THE COAST GUARD: LIEUTENANT SUSAN MORITZ

"The Coast Guard has a peacetime as well as a military mission," many of our interviewees said proudly. In peacetime the Coast Guard works under the Department of Transportation (now headed by a woman) to enforce immigration, drug, and fisheries laws; to conduct search-and-rescue missions for people in trouble at sea; to regulate port traffic and protect the coastal environment; and to enforce safe practices and provide aids to navigation. It functions on American inland waters as well as on the coasts. In wartime the Coast Guard is under the command of the Navy, with whom it regularly plays war games. Coast Guard women may do any job in the Coast Guard.

What does a woman do for fun and adventure after she has commanded a Coast Guard cutter? Lieutenant Susan Moritz reminisced about her past and speculated about her future.

"My senior year at the University of Massachusetts I went to Woods Hole Oceanographic on a work-study program, went on an oceanographic cruise, and fell in love. I'd grown up on Lake Winnipesaukee, and I just thought it was the neatest thing in the world to be on the ocean. I had a boat from the time I was ten or eleven till the time I grew up and joined the Coast Guard, when I got bigger boats! Some people call 'em ships! The Coast Guard had just been opened up to women, and they also were getting involved in the Fisheries Conservation Management Act—that was 1975. As I had a degree in fisheries, I thought that they might be able to use my talents.

"Right out of OCS I worked for a very gung-ho boss. I was very fortunate, because I was sent to the Federal Law Enforcement Training Center, where you send Customs people. I have been as close to a person who has specialized in the law-enforcement field as you can really get in the Coast Guard. Our tracks of learning and experience are not quite as rigid as the Navy. It's not uncommon for someone to start in a given area, lateral over to another, and shift back later on. We're a very broad experience-based outfit, because of our multimission emphasis.

"My first job in the Coast Guard, I was an intelligence officer and fisheries officer, and what I did was to board foreign fishing vessels. In one case a Bulgarian factory ship entered port. [I] boarded the Bulgarian along with my boss, a captain. I was only an ensign. He was very good to say, 'I want you to realize I'm not going along 'cause I don't trust you. It's just that I think I ought to take a look around.' I'm afraid that was before we changed our enforcement tenets, so they served vodka with lemons and sugar, and I drank too much. Ensigns do that, when you're only twenty-one, and I barely remember coming back.

"The Coast Guard opened up sea duty to women in 1977. I volunteered, said 'Me, please,' and they said, 'Okay, you're going to be a lieutenant j.g.; we'll send you to the *Gallatin*' [a cutter]. There we did mostly fisheries enforcement, although we did some drug-related cases. And we had a number of search-and-rescue cases, including a volcano eruption down in the Leeward Islands. One of our other missions was antisubmarine warfare. We have a live sonar watch on our high-endurance cutters.

"When you boarded a foreign fishing vessel, you were encumbered with a wet suit, which never fit. That's your lot in life afloat. You get cold and you get wet. You'd go out in the ship's boat, alongside this fishing vessel, and climb up a rickety Jacob's ladder, and there's always one or two rungs missing, always. You look like the devil. There's just no way you can look calm and professional when you're in a red wet suit and booties that don't fit. You'd meet the master. You inspect the books and then you get to go down into the lower hold to count fish—the fun part. You'd have to ride a cargo net or go down a conveyor belt to get to the lower hold, and then pick up boxes of fish and spot-check them and figure out whether the weight of fish in the hold agreed with the logs. Then you'd go to the fish-processing facility on the boat: you would see an enormous difference between the different nations with regards to how they processed the fish and how they fished for them. Of course, after a while you start to smell like a fish. You'd come back on board ship, and *nobody* would stand near you. It's like you have this five-foot bubble that followed you everywhere.

"One law-enforcement case that I remember, the *Sea Crust*, where we actually fired at her. Not into her—we fired in front of her to get her to stop. Oh, yeah, she stopped. She didn't have any choice. Tried to ram us too. They do that. We came up on *Sea Crust* from behind her, and in order to stop them [or any vessel], you have to come up alongside to get their attention, make sure you've gotten their attention, and hail them. Well, unfortunately, 'specially with a big ship, that puts you in danger, because of your position laterally with regards to the other vessel, so he tried to turn into us, using the rules of the road—we were the overtaking vessel and required to stay out of his way—and said, 'Don't cross my bow, Captain. Don't cross my bow.' Well, the executive officer had the conn [was in charge], so he put both engines all ahead full and kicked it into a right full rudder, which of course [with] a big ship like that, the stern kicks out. He just missed us. Came around and then we ended up going to general quarters and using the twenty-millimeter gun to fire across their bow, to get them to stop. And of course our boarding party went aboard and they were loaded with marijuana.

"Getting command became possible when they opened sea duty to women. One or two of the other skippers said, 'Well, what are you going to do next after your tour in the *Gallatin*?' I said, 'Oh, I'd like to have command of a ninety-five-footer.' They looked at me and said, 'You're dreaming!' I said, 'No, I'm not dreaming. I betcha it comes about. They'll open it up. They've got to.' And they did. I was still too young to say 'Well, there might be reasons why I can't do something.' I was only twenty-three, twenty-four, and as far as I was concerned, the world was open. I got command of the *Cape Current*.

"To a junior officer aboard a ship, it appears that the Coast Guard gives you every little nitpicky job in the world that they can, to prepare you for the wide range of problems that you're going to have in command. I had been to leadership school for junior officers. I had been to Search and Rescue school. On *Gallatin* I'd been to Guantanamo Bay [U.S. Navy—Fleet Training Group] to refresher training. We had had law enforcement. I'd been a boarding officer. We had put out a shipboard fire in St. Thomas.

"But sometimes I wished I hadn't taken command! [*Laughs.*] Oh, gosh, by the time I left that boat, I was really frazzled. The pace of operations and the personnel problems had just worn me out, completely. I started to feel badly about it, and then I remembered that my predecessor felt the same way when I relieved him. In retrospect it's an enjoyable experience. It's a trying experience. *Cape Current*'s mission was primarily law enforcement, primarily search and rescue, with a little bit of military readiness. I had been on board all of a week, and on July Fourth we had our first bust.

"I was twenty-five. Yes, the Coast Guard gives a lot of experience to its people early. We also try to have very experienced people, chief petty officers, assigned to the same units at the same time, to sort of cover the shortcomings every new commanding officer has, because every one of us thinks that we're the best in the world—we can't possibly make any mistakes. Of course we do.

"I initially had some personnel problems that were awful. The first week I got there, the second-class cook staged a protest and went on an unauthorized absence. The second-class bosun's mate got into a fight and was stabbed in the neck; he wasn't killed, but he was gone from my unit for the duration. The first-class machinery technician was on extended medical leave, because he had heart trouble. I had a chief MK [machinery technician] who was getting ready to retire, a chief quartermaster who was getting ready to be transferred. And I was two seamen short. I should have had a crew of fourteen. I ended up with a crew of nine, and it just wasn't enough.

"I had some problems with someone who did not believe women should go to sea. It undermines a person's confidence, when you work with that. And once your confidence gets undermined, your effectiveness drops drastically. I had a definite problem with that for probably four, five months. He finally did something that could not be tolerated and provided cause for a transfer. If I had recognized the symptoms sooner and seen what was coming, I would not have given him a second opportunity, which I did do. I was still believing that the world is nice, and you can help people along, and [if] you give a good person a second chance, they'll make use of it. But this particular individual did not. I really enjoyed a lot of people, and it's unfortunate that sometimes you run into a couple that tend to overshadow what was in general a very good tour.

"Some problems resolved themselves. I ended up with an absolutely super machinery technician, one of those people who can make things click. He's just enthusiastic and to him there's always a pony in there somewhere. I don't think quite that way, so I had a little harder time than I perhaps should have. In retrospect I would have done a lot of things differently. I think I would have passed some things on up the chain of command that I kept to myself. But things worked out in the long run.

"We had one case whereby a DC-3 had crashed off Grand Bahama Island, killing everybody on board. We were the first unit on scene, and we spent the next fourteen hours recovering bodies and particles [of bodies]—that's a very trying experience. I had one cook I really liked. We put two people in the small boat to recover the bodies. I didn't want to put people in the water, because I was afraid there might be sharks. And there were. This cook went out and tried to recover one person, and a shark came up, grabbed it, took it right out of his hands. Well, he backed up the boat, ran over the shark with the boat, and recovered the person. That's something the family will never know. I wrote him up, both him and the fireman in the boat with him, for medals, and they both got them. I was very proud of them and most of the crew, who did an absolutely super job. Yes, I was commanding only men. Myself and thirteen enlisted men.

"There is no feeling like it in the world to being under way, being in command, whether you've helped somebody who really needed assistance, or you have boarded a vessel and found it loaded with dope and you've seized it. There's no feeling like that, or a search-and-rescue case, a major one completed successfully. It's a very hard job. I have a little green book at home that I kept at the time, and I read through it, and I say, 'My God! Why did I even put up with that? How could I do that to myself?' But I'm glad I did. I grew a lot. I learned a lot. And I'd like to do it again.

"I have been the patrol boat facility manager here at headquarters for the last four years. They took my background, which is in patrol boats, and said, 'We want you to work on the long-term capability replacement program. It's time to replace these ninety-five- and eighty-two-footers.' To which I said, 'Hear, hear. I agree with you.' I worked on that. I'm sort of a medium between districts, patrol boats, and the headquarters bureaucracy. I read accident reports. I inspect vessels physically. I go with the engineers and we go all over them from one end to another, trying to see what sort of fitness the vessel is in. I am responsible for initiating the paperwork to request funds through the congressional budget process to support these units.

"One pleasant thing that can happen to you in headquarters is you can be assigned to a major acquisition. For the Island-Class patrol boats, we wanted the patrol boat proposed by a United States company to have been in service two or three years somewhere in the world—service that we could verify. As part of the verification process, myself and seven other men were split up into three groups and we went to different places to inspect the patrol boats that were proposed. One company had proposed the South Koreans' patrol boat, PKN, so I and another officer, an engineer, went to Korea to ride on it, and see if it would perform as advertised. We flew in to Seoul, and a few hours later I was on the boat, riding it and then inspecting it for the next two days before we left for Singapore, where we inspected another boat. The Korean officers we met were interested at first, or curious, as to how the Coast Guard could send this woman over to Korea. But they were very accepting, more so than even the people in Singapore. The Singapore officers were accepting too, but a lot of what I saw in both countries was more concern about how the United States would view their Navy [than about my being a woman]. Especially in South Korea, where appearances are ninety percent of it, and in Singapore we found the same problem. But it's a little easier for me to understand them in that most foreign navies are just like the Coast Guard.

"What I do and what I've done sounds really exciting. I hate to admit it, but at this point I'm bored. What I enjoy is being given a different challenge. After a while in the service the problems all seem to be the same. Their covering is a little bit different, but when you get beyond some of the surface layers, it's the same old problem. After a few years, you know how to find the solution and there's no challenge.

"If I stay in? I firmly believe that Coast Guard officers need to keep having operational tours. Too many people in this building and in government as a whole don't have operational experience, and it shows in the decision making. So I firmly believe that I need to go back to an operational tour. It's working out the mechanics that is extremely difficult. I was selected for command. I turned them down because at the time we weren't sure what my husband was going to do. He subsequently has retired from the Coast Guard. Now I'm faced with the choice of becoming a geographic bachelor to go afloat, or staying here and trying to go to graduate school. I'm up for selection for lieutenant commander. If I get picked up, I'd really like to have command of one of the one-hundred-ten-foot patrol boats. I don't think that's within the realm of possibility [because of a shortage of slots for lieutenant commanders]. Because of that I may end up having to go for graduate school, in which case I probably won't get back to sea again, which is not what I had in mind.

"I did a lot of job interviewing this last spring. I'm really not sure what I want to do. In my heart I still want to be an astronaut, but it's really not possible, not probable. I just haven't made up my mind yet. I don't know whether it's because I'm trying to match the interests of my husband and myself or whatever. I don't have children to worry about, but there's always the concern that bachelor marriages don't survive.

"Enticing me to stay in is the idea that I like to have fun and I like excitement and there's nothing as exciting as making life-and-death decisions on a vessel or a shore station. I have to weigh that against being part of a bureaucracy—and the Coast Guard is a bureaucracy."

THE AIR FORCE: TECHNICAL SERGEANT FRANCES CARDACI

The Air Force, responsible for war in and from the air, sets high standards of intelligence and education for its recruits because of its sophisticated technological needs. Many of its people are highly educated technicians in such glamorous areas as aerospace or fiber optics. Women can enter all but four of its MOSs—but those, of course, like fighter pilot and bomber pilot, are central to the mission. All the same, its atmosphere is one of promise, and our Air Force interviewees often spoke of opportunities present and to come.

Technical Sergeant Frances Cardaci, described by others in the Air Force as a "fast burner," displays the military woman's fondness for understatement.

"When I got out of high school I didn't want to go to college. I was eighteen, into a rebellious age. My father was kind of insisting and my guidance counselor was pushing. I had scholarships from the New York State Regents and from Mercy College. But I was working in the A&P, and I always had more fun at work than in school. I did go through one semester of college before I enlisted. I had a friend in Air Force ROTC, and she was seeing a guy in ROTC. They really enjoyed it, so I thought, 'Well, if the Air Force is all that good, maybe I'll give it a shot.'

"Everybody tried to talk me out of it. Because it was the military, not because I am a woman. My father never said 'You can't do that because you're a girl.' I don't think I ever ran across that, especially because the high school I went to was an all girls' school. Once when I was small, about four, I wanted a baseball glove. My mother said, 'Oh, no!' But my father said, 'Aw, come on. She doesn't ask for much. Give it to her.'

"I went to basic and to tech school, and they sent me to crew chief's school. 'Crew chief' is a job title: it doesn't necessarily mean that you're out there as a supervisor of a crew. A crew chief is an aircraft maintenance specialist or an airplane generalist. On fighters it's almost like a glorified gas station attendant for airplanes. You fuel 'em. You inspect 'em. You service the tires. You keep 'em clean. You tow 'em around.

"My first assignment was in England. That was when my father's attitude changed. He had been a weapons crew chief on P-47s in England during World War II, so he could relate. Then when I went to Mountain Home, Idaho, I did things like making Crew Chief of the Month or Crew Chief of the Quarter and Airman of the Month. He started thinking, 'Well, she's doing all right.' Then I started making rank, and he began thinking, 'Maybe this wasn't such a bad idea.' I was happy; that changed his mind too. I always have him come to these graduations; he just loves that stuff.

"I spent five years crewing fighters. I got very qualified on them when I was working on them. I was lucky. I made rank fairly fast. I went from being an airman to a staff sergeant. I never got to be a buck sergeant. You can test for staff sergeant as a senior airman. I made it my first time. But maintenance always seemed like it wasn't going to take me anywhere. I had my fourth stripe and seventh skill level my first four years, so after a while it just got to where I wasn't progressing anymore.

"I don't think I really knew what I was getting into when I first started thinking that I wanted to be a flight engineer. It started out almost on a whim. A guy from New York and I used to joke about becoming engineers and getting stationed close to home. In '78 they opened up a test program for women to get into flight engineer. I only had two stripes back then, and you had to have three. When I got my third stripe, I ran down to Personnel and told 'em, 'I want to apply.' 'Well, no, it was just a test program. It's closed now while they evaluate it.' In '81 they opened it again for women on a permanent basis. I went down and they said, 'Oh, you're a second-termer now; you've already reenlisted.' I said, 'Look, just put in the paperwork.' They gave it to me finally. I think they were tired of seeing me down there. 'Oh, she's back.'

"Yes, I had to learn how to make the military work for me. I preach this to my roommate, a brand-new three-striper. I kind of keep telling her that there's nobody more responsible for her career than she is. I have to try to remember that myself sometimes. If I really want something, to go for it. Like applying for engineering three times, until they were tired of seeing me.

"But I think I went to engineering school without really knowing exactly what I was getting into. I was a little apprehensive. Your losing unit [the unit that you're leaving] has to furnish your flying gear when you go to cross-train. The resource manager, some captain, told me to make sure I kept all that stuff in good condition, because it was a tough school and they wanted it back when I flunked out. I said, 'You're never going to see this stuff again.' There were times when I thought about it in survival school, when you think you can't take another five minutes of this, and then I'd say, 'I have to.'

"I went to survival school first. I was up there for three weeks. Physiological training in the altitude chamber. Basic survival, where they tell you a lot of stories about fliers that have ejected from airplanes, based on the experiences of fliers and ground controllers from Vietnam, Korea. While we were out there we didn't use tents; we used parachutes. You're trying to simulate that you ejected from an airplane. (Later, back at Mountain Home, I did jump once. I said I was going to do it and I did it, and I'll never do it again. I would wake up in a cold sweat sometimes afterwards. But when I was doing it, it had to be the most exciting thing I've ever done.) All you have is your parachute and whatever you have on your person. So they taught us to make little personal survival kits, make makeshift backpacks, use seat belts and harnesses from the airplane for shoulder straps for the backpacks. They kept us working at that stuff till ten or eleven o'clock at night. I was convinced it was just to wear you out. Then they take you up into the woods. We lived out there for five days. You learn an awful lot about how people react. Some people just weren't ready for it. After that there's a POW-type training, which is classified. Then parachute training: we didn't jump, but we did learn how to deal with rescue forces. After that I had to stay up there for water survival. It's to help you if a plane crashes. But the routes we fly to Europe, you don't really stand much of a chance anyway, because we fly across the North Atlantic. Once you're exposed to that kind of water, unless you're rescued right away there's not a whole lot of chance. If you're going to worry about that, you don't belong up there, you know. After everything else water survival was like a big letdown. We spent two days giggling.

"We were just so relieved. We had made it through the hard part. You learn a lot about yourself. You learn a lot about other people. It gave me a lot of respect for the guys that were in Vietnam, the POWs. One of the questions they asked us after we finished the POW camp was 'If you were in a situation where you were about to be overrun and there was just you and your thirty-eight, with your six bullets, would you take out five of them [the enemy] and save the last bullet for yourself?' I don't think I could do that; I'd have to take out six of them and hope that I got 'em mad enough to take me out too.

"Then I went to tech school in Oklahoma. At that time you went right through eight weeks of basic flight engineer course. I made honor graduate out of that. We were supposed to have about a week in between, then go to your systems course, which is your particular airplane. I was the third woman to go through the C-5 program down there, the only woman in my class. I enjoyed it. It was the most challenging Air Force school I'd ever been to. A lot of our training is on the ground, because it is so expensive to fly one of these things [C-5s]. We had a cockpit procedural trainer—just like a flight station, except that it doesn't have the navigator's station. You would 'fly' a mission from point A to point B in the simulator. They would throw in all the malfunctions, all the things that could happen to you. By the end of seven of those, you're convinced there's no way that this thing is going to get off the ground without something burning down.

"The first time I flew, I thought, 'God, this is really boring.' You fly five four-hours just doing touch-and-gos off the runway: you hit the runway and back up again. Nothing was happening, after all those simulators, where everything happened.

"I got here the end of October 1981. Our hours vary with the flying commitments. Sometimes you fly a lot, and other times it's like he [the scheduler] forgot your name. You call in and say, 'Remember me? Do you know I fly in planes?'

"Most of the places we fly to have maintenance [capable of repairing the C-5]. But you get places down in Saudi Arabia, maintenance isn't available. Then you rely on the crew chiefs who fly with us. Sometimes we fly without 'em, and then it's the engineer. What I can do in the air depends on what goes wrong. We're required to have a good system knowledge. We're the one the pilot relies on if something goes wrong with the airplane. The pilot is going to say 'What do you think?' Ultimately it's his decision, but ninety-nine percent of the time he's going to want your input. When you think of it, it is a lot of responsibility. Especially now, because we're phasing out the navigators, so we're getting more involved in fuel planning. They talk about our jobs as hours and hours of sheer boredom interspersed with moments of terror. I've been involved in a few emergencies. It'll get your attention. It's the not-routine stuff that separates how well you do your job, really.

"We are not allowed to leave the panel. If you need to leave the panel, there's two engineers. You can send somebody after the other one. There was a time when you could leave for a couple of minutes. But we had a few incidents where people were staying away a little longer than they should have. There were a couple of instances where they had some pressurization problems on the airplane, and because people weren't at the panel. . . . A pressurization problem at altitude can be extremely dangerous. We had one that I was involved in about a year ago, a rapid decompression. We had to hospitalize passengers, bleeding eardrums. We had to turn around and come back, but to another base because ours was having an ice storm.

"We do panel scans. We have paperwork throughout the flight. It keeps you involved. You do the paperwork and you do the panel, do the paperwork, do the panel. It's not like you're staring at every little gauge all the time. You have a lot of idiot lights on the panel too. A good panel is a dark panel.

"Two weeks out of every eight as a secondary job I edit airmen's performance reports and type 'em and route 'em. I think the reason I got the job is that I'm literate. I asked for it, because I enjoy writing. My chief engineer is patting himself on the back: 'That was a good idea I had putting you in there.' Yeah. Sure was.

"My squadron has always been really good. I was the first woman they had flying in the Third Squadron, but they never made a big deal about me. Of course I've run into some problems flying, as a woman. When you go overseas and have to stay in billeting, to get your own room you have to be a master sergeant. But if I am the only girl on the crew I have my own room. There were a couple of grumblings about it. I just tell 'em, 'Well, I don't go home and answer to anybody, and if you can say the same thing and you want to be a roomie, let's go for it. I don't have any problem with it.' If the situation came right down to where it had to be, 99.9 percent of the people I fly with over there, I don't think there'd be a problem. But there'd probably always be talk. On the airplane occasionally I'll be the NCOIC of the crew. Over in Ramstein one time, one of the guys, notorious for being a complainer anyway, said, 'Well, if we had a good NCOIC we'd all have single rooms.' I said, 'I got my own room. What's your problem?' It used to bother me when I was younger, newer at it, I guess, but I've learned what I can take seriously and what I don't have to.

"I had an incident out on a trip one time. I guess you could call it sexual harassment. This old major, a brownshoe type [formerly in the Army Air Corps], had been drinking. As a matter of fact, I don't think he even remembered it the next day, he was so drunk. The guys that saw it were very offended. They said that I should have slugged him. I'm not that type anyway, but can you just see me, hitting a major? You could kiss these stripes good-bye. Forget them. I was going to bring the incident back to the squadron, but we were always kind of taught if it happens out on a trip it stays out on a trip. So I let the poor aircraft commander, this young captain, handle it. And he did. He got an apology for me.

"Women in combat? I feel kind of strongly on that, because when I signed the paperwork saying that I wanted to be a flight engineer, I wanted to be a flight engineer, and I don't want to be a flight engineer conditionally. I don't want to be a flight engineer only if we're not at war. I don't want to be a flight engineer only if we're going to fly to nice places. I sit on what they call 'Bravo Alert.' It's a two-day telephone standby. You sit there with your bags packed. If they need you somewhere, they send you. If it happened to be a real war thing, then what? They continue to use me. As far as I'm concerned, that's fine. Pulling Bravo is part of the job.

"The problem, I guess, is that protection thing, where men are raised to protect women. I saw it in survival school. One day we had crawled up this hill with our backpacks and gotten to the top and just kind of fell out. One of the guys looked at me and said, 'You know, I give you a lot of credit for keeping up with us.' At my age? I was only about twenty-four and he had to be thirty-five, almost forty. I give you a lot of credit for keeping up with me!

"The future? I'm pretty well frozen on C-5s for the time being. I'm pretty content here. I want to keep flying. I think maybe in a few years I'll probably go up to Andrews and try to fly the Presidential Support Squadron. It depends a lot on what happens with the C-5s, the C-17, whenever it comes into production. As the laws stand right now, when the C-17 comes around, I'll be prohibited from it. You don't always have to make decisions right now. If you give it a little time, you're a little better off. You can deal with it more rationally.

"I couldn't fly if I was a commissioned officer because of my eyes. Now I'm too old to go to OTS anyway. But I'm pretty content. I'm doing all right. I think I'm doing a lot better than a lot of people I went to high school with that did finish college. I'll never get rich in the Air Force, but that wasn't my goal to begin with. I'm very comfortable. I bought a town house about a year ago. I've been all over the world. I'm going to Korea tomorrow. I've got friends all over the world. I can't complain about the time I've spent in.

"I've just about got my associate's degree, but right now I'm not taking any courses. The Air Force has schooled me to death recently. I went to Leadership School last year. Tomorrow I finish Human Communications—that was eight days. I just finished the NCO Academy at McGuire by correspondence. And I went to the Engineers' Instructor course for about six weeks this spring. It is something of an honor to be chosen. I'm kind of holding back a little on upgrading. I want to spend some time using the things I learned down there before teaching them. When I upgrade, I'll be teaching, but I'll also be responsible to stay proficient myself.

"I decided a long time ago that I wasn't going to get an ulcer from being in the service. You see some people just get so tense over everything. I think my first four years I was pretty what they call ate-up. I don't know how to describe it and keep it real genteel! If you tell somebody he's very ate-up, you're telling him—well, I guess to be polite you could call him an organizational man. Then after that I decided, 'No, I think I'll be in this for me for the rest of the time.' Not to say that I try to buck the system, 'cause I don't. A lot of my friends tell me I still am ate-up. But knowing myself from the first four years I know that I'm not as . . . Not that I'm not motivated. I'm just not as uptight. I can flow with it.

"One of my instructors at McGuire asked me, 'Got any aspirations toward being the Chief Master Sergeant of the Air Force?' I said, 'Yeah. Right behind you.' I don't know. It's the last thing you do before you retire. It'd probably be pretty interesting, but I don't know. It would be an awfully big precedent to set, because no woman's ever been in that position. I really don't know how much pull the Chief Master Sergeant of the Air Force would have. He's supposed to have quite a bit of pull policy-wise for enlisted people. Oh, yeah, it would be fascinating."

THE ARMY: SERGEANT FIRST CLASS MARY KYSER

The Army, the largest service and the most heterogeneous, is responsible for most land fighting but has its own ships and its own planes. Like the other DOD services, it excludes women from the most prestigious and career-enhancing MOSs, those most directly connected to its primary mission—combat. It employs women as, for example, nuclear weapons maintenance specialists, cargo specialists, tracked vehicle repairers, and Pershing missile crewmembers, but not as cannon fire direction specialists or combat engineers. Its women qualify on the M-16 and learn to throw grenades, but no woman can be a Ranger.

Mary L. Kyser, a black E-7, welcomed us, instructed her men that she wanted no interruptions, and sat back to tell us about her career.

"Yes, as far as I know right now I'm the only woman of my rank in my MOS. There's a lot of sergeants, staff sergeants. But as far as sergeant first class . . . once females reach the rank of E-4s, or they begin to reenlist, they get out of the MOS, because they don't really like it. A lot of 'em came in the Army because that was the only opportunity at the time, so they come in and be a mechanic for three years, and they change their MOS. But I didn't, and I don't regret it. It's a good field for females.

"Back in 1975, when I went to see my recruiter, he says, 'This is all that's available for you,' but I knew at the time that there was a shortage of women in this particular MOS, and recruiters will tell you anything to get you anywhere. So he buttered it up for me, and deep in my mind I knew I could handle anything anyway. So I came in first as a 63-Foxtrot, which was a related task for the 62-Bravo, which is mechanic. I went to AIT at Aberdeen Proving Grounds. The first unit I went to, at Fort Huachuca, Arizona, I was the only female 63-Foxtrot they had ever seen. Naturally they wanted to put me in the office, and for a couple of months I tolerated it. I did not yet know my jobs, so it was to my advantage. I would leave the office and say, 'Hey, I'm going out to work with the guys for a while,' and they'd say okay. I learned everything I needed to know.

"I like being outside. I like going. I'm not an office person. And 62-Bravo, being a mechanic, is really a lot of work. It takes a lot of dedication if you're really serious about it, because the Army depends on you. If they can't move, then you didn't do your job, and it makes you feel good when you know that you are part of something that is really important to them, and being a mechanic is very important. Once I got into it, I just loved it.

"Was I at a disadvantage compared to the men? I never looked at it that way. I might have been, but mentally I wasn't. And I think that was the most important thing.

"I stayed at Fort Huachuca for approximately two years, and it was great. I had a warrant officer who took very good care of me, showed me everything I needed to know. He even outlined my career for me, what I should do. He'd sit me down and he said, 'You should do this, this, and this. And when you become of rank of E-5 or E-6, you should do this and that.' He suggested that I go drill sergeant status, 'cause he said it was good for my career. And it was. It was a mooring for me as a person, but I know on my records it looks even better. I try to do the same thing with all my people now, because I know they don't know, and I just got lucky and got someone that really was dedicated to his job. A lot of people don't get that. 'Specially females. They just don't get that type of attention, without something else being there. It's always, 'Well, I did this for you, so you owe me.' But he was very good.

"I didn't have any problems with the guys, because I went in with the attitude that I'm a mechanic, so. . . . Once you give that attitude, you're a mechanic and that's it, no one bothers you. Couldn't afford to date the men I worked with, because there was always animosity. It's not really a hassle, but you always had to watch what you say and how you said it. Even now I have to watch how I present myself. If I slip up and say something that's meaningless, they always take it the wrong way, and they'll come back and say, 'Hey, you wanta go out?' I've been watching myself for so long now, it's natural. I always have that barrier there. It took me a long time to really understand why someone was always coming on to me when I didn't do anything, but it was there and I had to learn to deal with it. I decided I had to be strong and stand my ground. It's okay now.

"I was a sergeant when I left Fort Huachuca. I did my job, and I made my demands. The Army made demands on me, and I says, 'Fine. I'll do my job and yours too, but—what am I gonna get out of it?' They promoted me to sergeant in two years. I said, 'Well, let me do something different.' Because I'd been a mechanic. I knew what it was all about. I felt like I was at a standstill. Everybody says, 'Well, you've only been in the Army for two years.' I says, 'I still want to do something different.' So I applied for drill sergeant school. I never regretted it. I went to Fort Leavenworth, went to drill sergeant school. Completed three and a half years there as a drill sergeant, and loved every minute of it. Yes, that's a long time to be a drill sergeant, and it's something that you have to be mentally prepared for. The last six months was rough.

"Well, the Army wrote me a letter. They were very short of females in that MOS. They says, 'We're short of 62-Bravo senior NCOs. We'll send you to school at Aberdeen, and you'll go to Germany. We'll give you a bonus if you will come join us.' There was a lot of incentive there. Not only financial incentive, but the mental challenge of 'Can I do it?' I was an E-6 at the time, and I felt like that was a big challenge for me, because I had been out of my job for three years.

"I did everything possible to prepare myself. They sent me to school at Aberdeen for eleven weeks. Everything that I even thought I wanted to know was there, so I spent a lot of extra time, collecting a lot of books, talking to a lot of people outside of my normal class day. I was the only female in the class. We only had like three females in the whole building, out of, say, six classes. So I knew when I went to Germany, being a female, what I was going to be up against. Once you're a senior NCO, you have to lead by example, and you can't walk into a maintenance area and tell someone to do something if you're not sure what you're telling them to do. I spent a lot of extra time preparing myself. When I left Aberdeen, I had everything the way I wanted it: what I was going to say to my troops, how I was going to say it.

"In Germany I was the only female motor sergeant, and I loved it. You go in a maintenance area, and everybody says, 'Where's the motor sergeant?' You'll be sitting there, big sign on your desk, your name on it saying 'Motor Sergeant'—'Well, where's the motor sergeant?' They would call down on the phone and when I would answer they says, 'Well, let me speak to the motor sergeant.' It's great, because you get to say, 'Well, this is she speaking.' Then you have the attention on the other end, and they say, 'Well, is the maintenance officer there then?' I could go anywhere, do anything, and everyone was so helpful, because I would say, 'Hey, this is what's going on. I need some assistance.' Naturally they loved that. Over the years I've learned to identify males that are very egotistical. I try to stay away from those type people, but normally you know who will help you and who won't.

"When I went to the motor pool, there was a lot of changes going on. Two commanders had been previously relieved. An E-7 was the motor sergeant; he had like eighteen, nineteen years in the Army, and they were getting ready to relieve him. I says, 'Oh, God! What am I getting myself into? Am I next?' But what happened, I was under his supervision, and because I had never been a motor sergeant before, that was better for me. I could sit back and see all of his mistakes. Finally when they got a new commander, he says, 'This is who I want.' I says, 'Oh, no! It's my time now!' I worked a lot—weekends, nights, when nobody'd be there but me. I wanted to make a good impression, because I was the first female motor sergeant, and I wanted to leave a very good impression for females, okay? I know I might sound sexist, but somebody has to set the example.

"After Germany I reenlisted to come to Fort Dix, New Jersey. Sure did. And when I got here, they said, 'Wow! What are we gonna do with you?' They slotted me as an instructor [for mechanics] in the first module, and it was nice, because I had encountered training before, as a drill sergeant. I had a easygoing leader, and I saw things that needed to be changed. I'm a go-getter, you know. Regardless of what my job is, I'll do yours too. If you can give me a weak supervisor, I will sidestep him and do what's necessary to make things right. So I went in full force and made a lot of changes.

"Then they says, 'Well, we're going to send you to orientation, because we need a female at orientation,' and that really disturbed me—a lot. The only reason I was being moved was because I was a female, and I didn't particularly care for that. I'm not the type of person to scream 'harassment,' but I let them know I did not appreciate it. It really hurt me, but I would never let them know. I just let them know I didn't appreciate their move because I was a female—and that was the bottom line.

"Ten days later they told me, 'Well, we're doing this because you're good with the troops and all the troops like you. You should be in orientation when they first get here, so that they can see that females are mechanics.' Because they have a lot of problems with females coming in; they say, 'Oh, God, I don't wanta be a mechanic.' But if they see a female there, then it might distort their view a little bit, you know, to say 'Hey, this is all right' when really they would have a hard time. They do experience hard times.

"Then they talked about moving me again to another module, because they said, 'Well, we need a female over here to do this. If she can do it, then the other females will say, "Hey, it's okay." ' I said, 'No way. No way!' You have to put a stop to it somewhere. *Why* am I moving? I was here three months—I got moved because I was a female. Then you talk about moving me again, because they need *a* female here. Well, no. No. I had to stand my ground on that and let them know that I am an NCO. So they've more or less accepted the fact now that I can handle any situation, but I'm not going to be pushed around because I'm a female.

"When I came over here [to the first module], there was a lot of people that have gone now. Since we've all been over here, we've changed it a lot. We modified the classrooms, and we've done a lot of cleaning and throwing away, but we are always looking for new things for them to do, to keep the students busy, keep 'em interested. My instructors are beginning to get more comfortable with me now. 'Cause I wasn't in charge at first, and they were used to the same ho-hum every day. I can't deal with that.

"I got this thing about motivation. Did you hear 'em out there? [*The trainees are shouting in unison.*] We make all kinds of noise, because that's about the only thing that we have to motivate them here. When they come to class, if they don't motivate me and move me, move my instructors, then I get very upset. A lot of people don't agree with it. We don't care. We're always doing something crazy. We're always deviating from the norm. *But*—as long as no one comes down here and catches us, we're okay! We just raise hell all over the place, you know?

"Sitting in a hot classroom [all that the students do for the first two weeks] is very hard, but you have to show them that you care. You have to be calm. You have to be very easy with them. I don't like to yell at 'em, and I don't like my instructors to yell at 'em, because then not only are they bored and they're sleepy, but they've developed an attitude.

"I know where the students are coming from. I put myself in their situation: if I was in class all day, what would I want to do? What would make me feel good? The last day, we'll sit 'em down and we'll talk to 'em and say, 'What can we do to improve it? What can we do to not make you bored?' They come up with suggestions, and a lot of times we follow through. Sometimes we don't. Trial and error. We're almost where we want to be right now.

"They start here with the motto. Once they leave here they don't say it anymore. It makes me feel good, because every time you walk out the door, they. . . . They can see you twelve weeks down the road, they'll say, 'Motivated!' Or they'll say, 'Hey, Sergeant Kyser, we got a motto. You wanta hear our motto?' Because we are the only ones who say 'Hey, you are important!' And it makes 'em feel good, so they want to learn.

"You try to set an example for the entire school: Hey, this is what we are all about—not so much orientation, but *we*. We have to be sharp, and I demand that. They like that. They like telling jokes in class—they don't get that everywhere. They like being free. Now they come here and say, 'Oh, God, Sergeant Kyser, we don't want to go home! C'mon, can we stay here?' because we let them be themselves, and still maintain discipline.

"My ambition is to be Sergeant Major of the Army. I'm really working very hard at it, and I won't stop until I know for a fact that I can't get it. But I don't think it's possible to convince me that I can't. I set my goals in '75 when I came in the Army, and I have accomplished all my goals. They were very unrealistic. I said, 'If I don't make E-7 in eight years, I'm getting out.' I mean that's not realistic at all. Average time is eleven, twelve years. And I set that then, and eight years came along, and guess what happened? I was an E-7. I've completed my degree since I've been in the military. I wanted to be a drill sergeant; I've accomplished that. I wanted to be a female motor sergeant and accomplish a lot of things while I did that; I did that. I received the meritorious service award as an E-6, and that's very rare, for an E-6 in the Army, whether it's female, male, or whatever. And I did it because I did such an outstanding job as a motor sergeant. But I deserved it. Right now I'm at the stage of trying to set more goals for myself.

"Yes, sometimes I've had people who were jealous of me. But I have learned to ignore that. I do everything possible to keep myself in control and not give anyone opportunity to hurt my career or say something or do something derogatory toward me. I keep myself two steps ahead. I work harder than my counterparts. But if I don't, then I'm in the limelight. I have to stay out of that light, unless it's good for me.

"I'm at the point now where, where do I go? I have to really sit down and think about what else I want to accomplish, because when you get at this stage of the game, everybody likes to sit back: 'Oh, I'm an E-7 now.' That's not me. I really want to be Sergeant Major of the Army. Yes, I think I've got a good shot. There's no doubt in my mind.

"A lot of people say, 'Well, you're arrogant,' or 'You're cocky,' or whatever. I'm not. I just have a lot of confidence in me. If I don't have confidence in myself, keep myself motivated, who's going to do it for me?"

THE MARINE CORPS: BRIGADIER GENERAL GAIL REALS

The Marine Corps, which falls under the Department of the Navy, prides itself on being small and special—lean, mean, and green. Because its mission is primarily to fight in the most forward positions—taking the beaches, storming strongholds—it has traditionally recruited women "to free a man to fight." Now it is training its women in defensive combat, allowing them against precedent to wear dress swords and blood stripes [the red stripe down the pants leg], and moving them into non-traditional MOSs: for example, logistics, ordnance, motor transport, aircraft maintenance, and air traffic control.

When we interviewed her, Gail Reals had recently been promoted to the rank of brigadier general—the second woman in history to become a general officer in the Marine Corps.

"It's a difficult thing to come to grips with, being a general officer. You have to make some adjustments personally and to your management and leadership style, or things are going to come to a grinding, screeching halt. Got to learn to be very astute in determining who you are going to have working around and for you. Then pick and choose what you're going to spend time on. I have close to two hundred people that work just in the Manpower Plans and Policies Division. All I can do is kind of point them in a direction and hopefully try and keep them on track and monitor what they're doing and articulate what we need to higher authority. All of a sudden everybody wants to protect you. I guess there's a school for the care and feeding of general officers, because everybody wants to make decisions on what the general should hear, what she should see. There comes a point in time where you have to say, 'Listen, you can't control my life that much.' Beat people over the head occasionally, and tell 'em [*chuckle*] that it's not going to be their way. It's going to be your way.

"Oh, no. Oh, no. I'm not provided with any household help. Not at this level. Not at brigadier. My house is just a place where I keep my clothes and I get some sleep. It becomes a disaster area occasionally.

"My interest in personnel? Well, I joined the Marine Corps when I was nineteen years old and spent seven years as an enlisted Marine, before I decided that maybe I wanted to sign some things rather than just type them. I was a stenographer. When I became an officer in 1961, I spent a considerable amount of time as executive officer with a Marine company, and also in administrative jobs again. Then I was personnel officer on a couple of occasions. I commanded a couple of Women Marine companies and the recruit battalion at Parris Island on two occasions. My last couple of tours I was Assistant Chief of Staff for Manpower at the base at Quantico, and also in the Education Center involved with personnel. And in the First Marine Aircraft Wing on Okinawa, I was the Assistant Chief of Staff for G-1, which again is manpower, personnel, and those kinds of strange things.

"I enjoy that. I'm a great supporter of the women's movement in most respects, but sometimes in order to correct things, we have to overstate. We didn't overstate how many women were in the clerical side of the work force, but what we overstated perhaps was whether or not that was good or bad. In my experience in the military so far, being in administration has been a godsend, because it was one field from which they kind of picked people to be commanders. We tended to have more flexibility, more ability to move. If you were in some more specialized field, they didn't want people siphoned off. It was hard for them to get command and go off and do other things that we consider, quote, any officer can do, unquote.

"And I enjoy administration. I think women are good at it. So the thing we have to be assured of is that in our race to achieve more equity we don't shoot ourselves in the foot. Those of us who kind of enjoy that kind of work and are pretty good at it should not be forced to do other things. What we need is women being able to do what they're most capable of. I think we should always play to our strengths. If anybody comes along who is much better at mechanics or electronics, then she should have that opportunity, but we shouldn't just say 'Well, if it's clerical it's no good.' That's overkill.

"How do I account for the fact that I hung in there? Since I was selected and promoted I've had to do an awful lot of thinking about the past, and that's a question that's come up. If you look back at it over thirty-one years as a collective, you'd immediately throw up your hands and go screaming out the front door. Fortunately it came one day at a time.

"I joined the Marine Corps with the idea to do something different and to change. I joined for three years. Everybody was sure I was going to reenlist. The only person that wasn't sure was me. I'd taken some lumps along the way, and my first year in the Corps was not exactly what I expected. You worked here in the headquarters and while the civilians came in at eight and went home at four-thirty, you were in at six in the morning and you spent many a night here when big flaps were going on, staying until midnight or after. When I left I would have to go home and either participate in some training program or do something in the barracks, where I was a squad bay NCO. But I was working in the headquarters, it was interesting, I enjoyed the people I was working for and with, and I didn't think that I was going out in the civilian world with my skills and do as well. I didn't want to give up my sergeant's stripes. I said yes, I'll stay—for two years, though.

"Before that two years was up, I had an opportunity to go to Europe, and I almost turned that down. Just out of fright, I guess. Fortunately I had a sergeant major who said, 'That would be a mistake, Gail. On Monday morning I'm going to ask you again. Whatever answer you give, that holds.' On Monday morning I said, 'Yes, I'll go.' So I had a marvelous two years in Paris. While I was there, I made the decision to apply for the Officer Candidate course. I was not sure before I went whether I could make the jump, take on the added responsibilities of being an officer. I had gone into a different environment, something I was not sure I could do—something happened while I was in Europe. Probably it was [due to] all the wine I drank that I said, 'I think I can do it.' I came back and was private secretary to the assistant commandant. I was then a sergeant E-5. I looked down the road: 'If I stay in the Marine Corps, this is probably what I'm going to be doing for the rest of my career. I can be a first lieutenant before I could even make staff sergeant. I'm going to take a chance at this.'

"I was not sure whether my boss was going to let me go. General X had secretary after secretary, and they were getting a little tired of the fast turnover. The aide was concerned, but the general heard about it and said he'd always believed that the Marine Corps was much better off having people function and work at the highest level that they were capable of. Off I went.

"I guess that the time in which I decided that I was going to stick with the Marine Corps, come hell or high water, was probably after I was in Officer Candidate School. There were times along the way when I'd say 'There must be a better way to make a living,' but that usually only lasted a day or so. I guess when you make that kind of decision, you've made kind of a commitment in a career way. Then you have to handle the other problems that come up in that context.

"I got around the twenty-year mark, which was eleven years ago, I guess, now, and I was a major, and going to Command and Staff

College. The school really opened my eyes to the rest of the Marine Corps. It was kind of another turning point, in the sense of realizing that I had lived somewhat in a corner of the Marine Corps. There were about a hundred twenty–some male Marine officers, all majors and lieutenant colonels, and I don't know how many foreign officers, twenty-some, and I was the only woman. I'd worked around and with the men all the time, but in that environment I began to have for the first time that kind of collective experience. I began to realize the degree of isolation that I had experienced up until that time. I guess that I moved from what I would consider the old Marine Corps into the new Marine Corps as it pertained to women. That early part of my career where I came up as an enlisted Marine and then as an officer in command of women's units just doesn't exist anymore.

"I'd spent two years in Beirut, Lebanon, as personnel officer for the security guard company, and then had gone to Parris Island [South Carolina] and had an opportunity to be executive officer for the Woman Marine Training Battalion, so I went back to where I had gone through recruit training. Then came to headquarters as a major, was selected for lieutenant colonel, and was sent back to Parris Island to be the CO of the Woman Recruit Training Command. Some wonder what it is about command that people become almost lyrical about. There is no experience like having command and responsibility for people. It's one of the most onerous and yet worthwhile experiences you can have. And being in the recruit environment, where you can really see the change and what effect you're having on people, is absolutely exhilarating. Tiring and demanding, but also exhilarating.

"As a lieutenant colonel, in addition to being Assistant Branch Head in Human Resources, I was Special Assistant to the Deputy Chief of Staff for Manpower on Women's Matters. So then you say, 'Well, if you've stayed around all this time, perhaps built your credibility base or your professional standing to where you're going to have some influence on many things, but in particular women's issues and women's utilization in the Marine Corps, do you really want to hang it up now?'

"The organization itself too—I don't want to underplay this—has an addictive nature. I don't know of another word. Some people would want to call it brainwashed, but this organization can be very addictive. There's nothing in my experience nicer than being able to say you're a Marine.

"I was selected for colonel when I was here, which was a surprise to me. Every rank that I've made as an officer has been—'cause I started as a private. At any level, I could have not been selected and still be able to say 'I'm successful.' They couldn't take my success away.

"Then one day the person who was then director of this division walked in and he said, 'Congratulations, Gail. You've been selected for top-level school.' I came close to turning that down. I was wondering whether it wasn't time to take off the pack and do some things that I'd wanted to do for a long time. But women whose opinion I respected convinced me that that wasn't a good idea and I shouldn't do that to them. I went off to the Naval War College. There were twenty-six Marines in that year's class, and I was the senior one, of all the lieutenant colonels and colonels. It was a delightful experience, to a great extent because of the caliber of the people and the curriculum. But by doing that I had incurred an obligation for a certain period of time.

"Then they said, 'Well, you're going overseas.' They sent me to Okinawa, to the First Marine Aircraft Wing. I thought I didn't want to go to the school, and had a delightful year. I thought I didn't want to go to Okinawa, and I went to Okinawa and had a spectacular year. I was on the aviation side of the house, with which I had not really had much contact before, so there was a lot of learning to do, and the travel and the cultural experience were just marvelous. I came back to Quantico, I guess, with decisions to make.

"I think I had one more year left on my obligation. I guess it was the summer of '83, when I had met all my obligations. So I was back at that decision point again. Why stay longer? Well, I went to Quantico and I had a job, Assistant Chief of Staff, Personnel and Services in the Education Center. A lot of the women are more than willing to push me out on the end of the limb. I'm not sure all of 'em want to come out there with me, but they were really upset with my assignment. They thought it was not in keeping with what I had done . . . the schooling and the prior experience. I just told 'em to cool it. I would do what was assigned, and it would give me a chance to do some thinking about what I wanted to do.

"This was supposed to be not a challenging or career-enhancing job. The CG [commanding general] wasn't sure what to do with a Woman Marine colonel, or he thought he wasn't, and well, a good place for her was in the Education Center. Bottom line is I spent a very productive year there. Really got so involved that I was somewhat disappointed when the CG said that he thought that it was time that I came up and be his Assistant Chief of Staff for Manpower.

"So I became Manpower, and I was going my merry way for a few months, until one day the CG called me in and asked if I wanted to be the Chief of Staff. From a career point of view there was nothing that I could say except 'Yes.' But again, another obligation was incurred. You can't just take the job and then say a few months later, 'Well, gee, I think I'm going to retire, General.' There's always been a challenge or an opportunity around the corner.

"And you can't wipe out working with a lot of dedicated, smart professional people. The Marine Corps has gone through its trials and tribulations, like the other services did, when we grew for the Vietnam time and we had problems with quality. But there always has been that cadre of people that kept body and soul together and knew we would move out of those bad times and get it straightened out. The quality of the Corps has never, never been higher than it is right now.

"I saw an Army officer one day give a good lecture on his feeling about putting on his uniform jacket in the morning, which has all the paraphernalia that says to everybody 'I'm such and such in the Army, and you can see that I've done certain things over here, and you can see with certain patches that I'm associated with certain organizations within the Army. The other little things up here tell you what kind of business I'm in. Other people have to explain who they are. All I have to do is put on my jacket.' I've thought about that a long time, and I'm wondering how much is there, if I take off the green suit? What is left? How do you divide what is Colonel or General Reals from Gail Reals? And how much have you invested in the organization? It's difficult to walk away from it. I think I'm reasonably well prepared for it, but not prepared enough apparently over the last few years to want to do it before I had to.

"There are things I would have done differently and I could have done better, but I really don't believe that I ever would have had to back up to the pay table. I don't think that I've made the mistakes because of the lack of effort. It might have been the lack of intelligence or being able to analyze things, but I don't think it's been lack of effort. I think that's what I've been compensated for, or why I've moved up. I've always realized that I wasn't going to get there on my brains alone, and certainly not on my looks, so when others stayed for the normal eight hours, I was there for twelve or fourteen.

"I had my boss at Quantico tell me, 'You know this isn't what's really important, selection [for brigadier general]. The important thing is whether or not you're competitive to major general. That's what will be important for women.' That bothers me, because it's like the coach who thinks the next game that he's going to play is against a pushover, so he looks beyond to the next one and then gets clobbered by this quote unquote easy team. I could quickly have lost the ballgame by not paying attention to what I'm supposed to be paying attention to. I think the majority of the women that I'm reasonably close to understand that. They're not afraid to call or ask for advice, but they do it very judiciously, because they know that I can be spread kind of thin at times. At the same time I have to be careful about not seeming that I've said 'Well, I've got mine. The hell with you.' 'Cause that makes it a little hollow.

"You've got to attend to the business at hand. You've got to do that well and somebody's got to say you've done it well, and by so doing you'll retain your influence and you can do other things. If you don't realize that's your first concern and you can't rest on past laurels, all can be quickly lost."

THE NAVY: BOSUN'S MATE FIRST CLASS MARY LAROCHE

The Navy fulfills its mission at sea. Women confront career blocks because they cannot serve on its fighting ships—destroyers, aircraft carriers, and submarines. They do serve on hospital ships, research vessels, and tenders, and they do maintain and repair submarines and destroyers. They have recently made a major breakthrough with the successful screening of the first woman for aviation command. But many a woman, enlisted or officer, still struggles for sea duty, "haze gray and under way," which she needs in order to advance.

Bosun's Mate First Class Mary R. LaRoche is known on both coasts as "Mama Boat."

"I'd been to college and I'd interviewed in my field of studies. I wasn't satisfied with the offers I was getting, so I got a job at Penney's to bide my time. I really didn't see anything coming along the line in the interviews, so I walked into the recruiter office. The Navy recruiter took the most time and showed the most interest. I thought, 'Why not give it a go?' That was October of '77.

"In boot camp when the classifier interviewed me, I really had no idea. I just knew I was going in as an undesignated seaman. One-line job descriptions, you know. 'Okay. Whatever.' I didn't get any schools. Out of boot camp I was sent to the pier services on the tugboat. Learned my duties on the tugboat. I was a little bitter. My scores enabled me to qualify for any school open to women, and yet I was not able to get a school at boot camp. And when I went to my permanent duty station, two other people went with me, and I thought they had got preferred jobs. When you're checking in, it's just one person's decision. To me it seemed like a whatever-mood-you're-in-that-day decision. I said, 'Okay, I'll be a dumb bosun's mate.' Quote around the 'dumb.'

"On the tugs, I really liked it. We had a nice crew. I felt I should know what I was doing, handling my lines [ropes], so I don't create a safety hazard. Moving ships around can be dangerous. So I did this correspondence course for bosun's mate third and second [class]. I passed the exam but wasn't advanced, but I received the designation BMS [bosun's mate seaman]. In a couple of months I received orders to the USS *L. Y. Spear*. Submarine tender. I was upset, since I wasn't due to transfer for eight months. They said, "You got designated, and we're putting women on ships, bosun's mates on ships.' Well, bosun's mate rate, you're supposed to spend five years at sea. That's where the major need is for bosun's mates, on shipboard. I didn't find out until I had been on board about a year and a half that I was the first female bosun's mate on the ship.

"I think between sixty and eighty women originally reported on board. Back then in 1979 there were only about five ships with women. Now in 1985 I think there's over twenty: most all of your submarine tenders and destroyer tenders, floating drydocks, the oceanographic research ships. The first year was difficult. Women coming on board, the men had to move out of their berths, move in with somebody else. The men resented us taking over their berthing. There were men who did not resent us, who accepted us, but this is a pretty accurate generalization. The resentment was directed personally at us, the women, who, the men thought, volunteered for ships. I know for a fact I wasn't a volunteer. When they first started putting women on ships my chief warrant officer called me down and said, 'Do you want to go on any ships?' I said, 'What kind of ships?' They were tenders [which repair and maintain fighting ships]. I said, 'No, when they open up the destroyers and the aircraft carriers and the oilers, I'll be first in line to volunteer. But I don't want to go on a tender.' Took about six or eight months before some of the men started realizing that we were not volunteers; we were susceptible to orders just as the men were.

"Tenders don't go out to sea very much. When the submarines pull in, you tend to their needs. You can only fix them when they're in port. We were at Pier Twenty-two, and they called us Building Twenty-two, because we never got under way. About a month after I got on the *Spear* we went under way, had a liberty port [time off on land] in Fort Lauderdale. That fall we went down to Charleston for a month and a half.

"Then in March of 1980 we got under way. By the end of April we were in Diego Garcia in the Indian Ocean, where we spent several months. Went across the Atlantic and into the Mediterranean and stopped off at Alexandria for liberty port and through the Suez Canal and into the Indian Ocean. We came back the same way, stopped in Athens, Greece, and Malta, and made it back to Norfolk by that August. That was great. Just that the ship was able to get under way. We crossed the Atlantic. For twelve days you'd had your doubts that we were really crossing the Atlantic. Were we just making circles? As soon as we saw Gibraltar, 'We made it! My God! We made it!' Going through the Suez Canal was the highlight of the trip, as well as the liberty ports. Alexandria—I remember studying Egyptian history in school. I never in my life imagined I'd be able to stand right next to a pyramid and sphinx. I had been overseas prior to coming into the Navy, but most of the younger kids on the ship hadn't been outside the United States; it was an eye-opener for a lot of people. Of course we all became shellbacks crossing the equator, which you just never forget.

"Diego Garcia is just a coral reef, and there's not much there. It was a strategic point, because back in 1980 there was a lot of action in the Persian Gulf and the Indian Ocean. We were quite busy. We usually had four units out with us, two surface ships to starboard and two submarines to port. We were on port and starboard duty, which was arduous to say the least. If you put in a fourteen-hour day, that was a short day. Usually it was around sixteen to eighteen hours on my duty day, because I drove boats. We were anchored out. The only way to get to the island was to use the boat launch, and I had duty every other day, starting from six in the morning until the last boat run at night, which the earliest was usually eleven o'clock or midnight.

"At sea you're on water hours, because the ship makes its own water. The primary utilization of the fresh water is into the engine room, into the boilers, to keep the engines running so that the rest of the ship can function. Then the mess attendants, the mess decks, the cooks—water supply will go to them secondarily. Third status is the crew. If there's water, you get clean. You take a Hollywood shower, where you can wash your hair and shave the legs and just let the water run; or a Navy shower, a three-minute shower. The water came on as soon as the cooks started, about four-thirty in the morning, and went off at ten o'clock at night. It was hard coming in at midnight, caked with salt, sunburned, and there's nothing more you want than a shower. I had to wait until morning.

"In port at Norfolk I was in first division, your painting and preservation and line-handling division. You made sure your mooring lines were in good condition; if you needed new mooring lines you put in splices. You were the linehandlers for the submarines coming alongside. And we took care of our spaces in the hull. You scrape the rust down, get the rust off, prime the metal, and then get your paint spray over—that's a never-ending task. You rotate. Later I was in charge of the OPTAR—I have no idea what it stands for: your budget. Keeping track of things that some divisions hadn't bought that we think you might need. One year we got stuck without snow shovels—you have to shovel the snow off the ship—so the next August I went over to the supply sergeant and got a dozen. Later I was in the third division, where you maintain and upkeep the ship's boats—the captain's gig, the personnel boats; do various errands in port; make runs to the submarine squadron attached to us. Second divison is the crane division, so we learned to operate cranes.

"The ship sent me to several schools. Basic bosun's mate school for two weeks. Boat coxswain's school. A school to learn how to land a helicopter, using my hands for signaling. I got hooked on that on Diego Garcia. A lot of supplies, we could have carried them by boat, but when you have crate after crate after crate, it's a lot of work—

whereas another ship will pull into the lagoon and they just carry the supplies over by helicopter.

"When I was on the *Spear* I helped set up and worked with the weight-test quality control. Certain things that were carried on the submarines had to be weight-tested, to make sure they would hold the strain. Weight-testing is part of the knowledge of a bosun's mate, but I'd never before related it to a small piece of iron in terms of how that affected a torpedo in a torpedo tube in a submarine. I'm not familiar with submarines like a torpedoman is. I had to learn to read from blueprints. I was the first person that was not a torpedoman to qualify for nuclear weapons security watch. I made myself right at home in the weapons department. I didn't want to feel like an outcast. I insisted on learning their watches and standing their watches. I was Sailor of the Month in that department. I was really tickled: I was an outsider and I had won their world and fit right in and yet maintained my own identity and my own ways.

"I was on the *Spear* two and a half years. Then I reenlisted for orders to the *Norton Sound*. I liked that, a small ship, three hundred fifty people instead of about a thousand; it's more intimate. It's a missile test ship, the Ajax testing ship. We would go out to sea within fifty to one hundred miles of the coastline, and Point Mugu would launch a drone [an unmanned target]. It was just testing to see how the system was working and reading the computer printout and the data processing information that would help determine whether they were going to buy this project. We went out to sea every other week, just about. Had a lot of time under way. Went through the Panama Canal; went to Colombia; went to Jamaica.

"I was leading petty officer. I went there as a second-class bosun's mate, and I was in charge of everybody in the deck division in terms of determining the work that was going to be done, planning the work, projecting when it was going to be done, training the individuals. At sea your division is standing three-section watches. I had to get qualified people on the watches. Leading petty officer is usually a first-class petty officer job, and I was only an E-5. I did pretty good.

"Has it been difficult to be a woman in my rate? Well, when I started out, I was designated bosun's mate, and here's thirty men in the deck who think they know more about the rate than I do. Prove yourself, prove yourself, prove yourself. Not blatant, but so subtle. Well, they think they're being subtle. I've been in the Navy seven years, and six and a half of them has been in this nontraditional rate. I think I'm pretty aware of the methods that the men use to try and test me. That goes on all levels, inferiors, peers, superiors. Except for the officer ranks. Officers are your managers. They see what your weak areas are and your strong areas, and they work with you. They call me Mama Boat. A female officer told me recently that when she came aboard on the *Spear* another officer told her, 'Don't worry about the deck. Mama Boat's on duty today. She'll take care of everything that comes up. Call her. She'll tell you what she can do about it and she'll tell you what she can't do about it.'

"Mama Boat? Well, when you're a female in the Navy, the senior man that you work for is called your sea dad. When I got on the ship, being a bosun's mate, the guys asked me, 'Are you our sea mama?' Being the senior enlisted female rated, I said, 'No, I will not let you call me *sea mama*.' They said, 'Well, you're the only female bosun's mate we got.' Usually with the sea daddy and the female seaman, it's one for one. Here I was, one female with thirty men. I definitely didn't like this. So somehow it came about as Mama Boat. It's been that way since I've been in the Navy. A lot of people know me as Mama Boat. They don't even know my name sometimes. People will come to the ship and visit me. 'That bosun's mate, you know, they call Mama Boat?'

"How do I handle enlisted men who give me trouble? Well, various ways, according to the individual. When I had been on board the *Spear* about four weeks, we were moving a barge alongside, and I had one male and three females working for me line-handling. Each one of them has a line. These lines get wet and they're already very stiff and very heavy. I was telling the male, 'Tell these people how to take it around the cleat. The line's getting heavy. They don't have to sit there and hold it. They can tie it off on the cleat.' He wouldn't do it and he wouldn't do it. So I walked up to him and said, 'These folks just got out of boot camp. They've only been on board two weeks. They don't know what a cleat is or how to put the line on.' He said, 'You're so good. You tell them,' and started poking me in the chest. I saw red. I maybe twice in my life have done something like this. I grabbed him by the shoulders and picked him up—he was shorter than I was—looked him in the eye. He was between the bulkhead and me. I didn't even swear, but I let him know in very chosen words that he wasn't worth the clothes he was wearing on his back. I said, 'You work for me. This is the way it is. I told you about these women. They're getting stiff. Their arms are getting tired. I could take them off and let you take care of two lines.' We had words, you know.

"After that nobody on the ship messed in with me. From then on he and I were good friends. That was the type of incident that it took to get it across to him, and getting it across to him got it across to eighty-five percent of the parties in the department that when first-class says 'Mama Boat's in charge,' she's in charge.

"I was due to transfer in April of '84 from the *Norton Sound*. By then I would have had five years of sea duty, two ships, and before that a tug boat. All I wanted at this point was to get my shore duty, not live on a ship—you know, a rack where you look up and see pipes on the ceiling. You go into a bathroom and there's six stalls and they're all full. You have two showers and you've got to shower with fifty other people. I just wanted a place of my own. So I was looking forward to my shore duty in some kickback place, San Diego, where I could go in to work at eight o'clock, leave at three-thirty, four o'clock, have duty maybe once a month. Be nice to let someone else have a lot of responsibility.

"So I called my detailer [who makes her assignments] in September of '83 and said, 'I know this is early. What does it look like for shore duty?' 'Oh, Boats, you're being screened for a detailer job up here in D.C.' I said, 'You can't do that! I don't transfer until April. I want to stay out here. I reenlisted to get to the West Coast.' 'No, Boats, we screened seven hundred records, and you're the best candidate.' The problem was that more and more women are coming on as bosun's mates, and the detailers was an all-male shop. The women would call and say, 'You don't understand. You're not a woman. You don't know what it's like for us on a ship.' They were getting around the men. So the detailers were looking for a woman who had been on a ship. My policy is, when you become a bosun's mate, you are responsible for everything that rate entails, and that rate entails five years of sea duty.

"I didn't want to be a detailer. So, anyway, I'm a detailer. I'm responsible for about four thousand people. They don't all come up in the rotation at once. I work with at least one hundred a month. And that's just PCS [permanent change of station] orders. But people call you on other things too. You have to know what slots are available, get them filled. What's your fleet balance—making sure East and West Coast are balanced. Meeting the needs of the Navy as well as the individuals' needs. I have to make more decisions than ever, and more responsible decisions too. A lot of it is just to your own discretion. An individual may want to adjust his rotation date. You're the one to tell him 'Yes, you can' or 'No, you can't.' People call me from all over the world. I encourage everybody to call.

"Even though I get headaches and take aspirin and I get frustrated, I enjoy it. I went up for Sailor of the Year about two weeks ago, and that was one of the questions they asked me: 'What are the things that you dislike about detailing, and what are the things you like and find rewarding?' I can't put into words what it is. There's a lot of frustration from things you're not able to solve the same day they occur. You have to wait and follow on to crack them. You don't get the feedback of the individual saying thank you. Yet the rewards—the challenge of seeing what ships, where you need personnel, and the personnel calling you up. And you meeting their needs as well as your needs.

"I'll be doing this two more years. Then I'm going out to the West Coast! More than likely the Navy will be my career. But if I had a good job on the outside I would take it and join the Naval Reserves. No hesitation about if I got out and had a good lucrative job on the outside. I've known since I came in the Navy I would do my thirty years' active Reserves.

"The Navy is a very hard life. Where else do you go out to sea for six months? You don't see your family. You don't have any contact with the world. . . . They might post a news notice that's received in Radio Central, but that's not the same news notice that comes over the newswires. It's my personal opinion that it's edited for us on the ship so you won't get upset if you see something. It's a culture shock to come back. The countries we visited were poor countries. To come back to the United States . . . you went to a shopping center and you just looked.

"A commission? Coming in enlisted I had only a four-year commitment; as an officer it would be a minimum six-year commitment. I wanted to find out if I liked the Navy before I applied for an officer program. And I liked the opportunity to get into a school of training. At that time women officers were going into Supply as administrators in the offices. I'm kind of a maverick person. In college my major was poultry science. Not many women studied chickens, you know? And now I'm a bosun's mate, and that's also nontraditional. If I went into an officer program it would be I'm sure a nontraditional program again. And now that I'm in as a bosun's mate, I've come so far so fast, I want to make chief before I go into an officer program."

5. The Issues: Women at Risk

"They say they don't want us out in a war situation. They've hyped the public into picturing your mother out there bravely beating the Viet Cong with a rolling pin. They have women on the noncombatants that just happen to get caught in crossfire, and nobody ever talks about the WASPs that flew in World War II. It's not like we're not capable and it's not like we're not there. It's just that they don't make it legal for us or advantageous for us, yet."

"The thing that irks me, okay, is that we can put nurses in Vietnam, but we can't put females to work on ships. Why am I any more frail or liable to go off the handle than a nurse? They're just going to have to change. Write to your congressman, okay?"

Few Americans know how many servicewomen are in combat-related jobs and in combat training. That, for example, 200 American Army women went on the 1983 Grenada operation. That women served as aircraft commanders, copilots, navigators, fuel-boom operators on the tankers that refueled the bombers on the 1986 Libyan strike. That in 1987 248 women sailors, 12 of them officers, went to the Persian Gulf aboard the destroyer tender *Acadia* on a mission to repair the frigate *Stark*, damaged by Iraqi missiles.[1]

[1] *Newsweek* (November 11, 1985), pp. 36–38, and *Minerva: Quarterly Report on Women and the Military* 4, no. 2 (Summer 1986), pp. 26, 43; and 5, no. 2 (Summer 1987), p. 17.

Thousands of women served in Vietnam. Women soldiers have served on the crews of Army boats carrying supplies into El Salvador. Armed Coast Guard women board vessels suspected of smuggling illegal drugs or aliens. Servicewomen sit in Minuteman silos, ready on command to press the button that fires a missile.

Targets have changed since World War II. Women are in electronic warfare units, fighter-aircraft maintenance units at forward bases, and large rear headquarters—priority targets today. "If the United States is forced to fight in Europe or elsewhere, such as the Middle East," writes Arthur T. Hadley, "death will be an equal opportunity employer. More female soldiers, sailors, and airmen will die in the first five minutes in any next war we are forced to fight than were killed in World War II, Korea, and Vietnam combined. In fact, since females are clustered in the high-priority targets, initially women will die out of all proportion to their numbers in the armed services."[2]

Every day American servicewomen shiver or sweat on field exercises in Korea and the American desert, run miles beside their male colleagues on dusty Georgia or German roads, teach classes in nuclear/biological/chemical defense, shoot M-16s, throw grenades, and jump from airplanes. "We spent days on end in foxholes on sides of mountains, camouflaging everything," a Marine captain told us in describing her training. "You'd dig in deep. . . . Then we'd sit there while the men attacked us. Some instructors would try to let us charge up the side of the cliff with our M-16's going *butta butta butta*: 'Don't tell anybody I let you do this; I just want you to have that feel.' That's a feel of power."

All of this goes on legally, despite the much-cited congressional "combat-exclusion policy," which most civilians and many servicemembers assume would keep women out of danger. Closely examined, that "policy" amounts to less than most of us suppose. A jumble of a few laws, multiple interpretations, and thousands of administrative decisions, it invites disagreement and frequent changes of practice.

The laws on which the combat-exclusion policy is based are old, written in the context of World War II. (A hull maintenance technician's reference to "that old law back there in the 1800s" reflects her perception

[2] Arthur T. Hadley, *The Straw Giant: Triumph and Failure: America's Armed Forces* (New York: Random House, 1986), pp. 257–58.

of the law as antiquated.) In 1948, Congress passed Public Law 625, empowering the secretary of each of the services to define the military duty to which women may be assigned but specifying that in the Air Force women "may not be assigned to duty in aircraft while such aircraft are engaged in combat missions" and that women may not "be assigned to duty on vessels of the Navy except hospital ships and naval transports." In 1978, after Judge John J. Sirica had ruled that the law denied Navy women equal protection, Congress modified the law to allow women on noncombat vessels and even on combat ships for periods not longer than 180 days. That's it. Not a word about Coast Guard women. Not a word about Army women.

As these laws are currently interpreted, the issue is not *whether* women will be in combat areas, but how many? In what roles?[3] The issue is not *whether* they will be put at risk; they long have been, and will be again.

THE DILEMMA

> *"If Congress does not want women in the middle of a combat zone, for God's sake, they shouldn't station them in the European theater, the Pacific theater, et cetera, et cetera."*
>
> *"The services are straddling the fence [on combat], and they're put there by society. They can't say no and they can't say yes. To me, it's something that we deal with every single day. It confuses people. It confuses soldiers. It makes our jobs harder."*

The gyrations of the services under the combat-exclusion policy confound efficiency and confidence. Servicewomen are trained in an MOS and later removed from it. "Recently, concerned that women were being too exposed to danger, the Army closed off from them a previously open key occupational specialty, Fifty-four Echo, the nuclear, chemical, and biological warfare designation. This caused the Army's ability to handle

[3] In 1978 the Department of Defense told Congress: "Under current practices, a person is considered to be 'in combat' when he or she is in a geographic area designated as a combat/hostile fire zone by the Secretary of Defense. . . ." Jeanne Holm, *Women in the Military: An Unfinished Revolution* (Novato, Calif.: Presidio Press, 1982), pp. 337–38; see also p. 333.

nuclear weapons to break down, because there were not enough qualified men available to replace the female soldiers. Pressure from commanders in the field forced the order to be rescinded."[4]

Women cannot complete their jobs. "A woman officer combat engineer, she trains her platoon, and her platoon gets sent to Norway for NATO exercises. Number one, she can't go on the ship, so you have a transportation problem. Number two, when she gets over there, where are you going to put her? You're going to have to provide some kind of security and facilities."

Inconsistencies multiply when, "hiding behind the coattails of very old legislation," as Lieutenant Colonel Ruth Woidyla (USMC, Ret.) puts it, each of the services develops its own interpretations. Coast Guard vessels with women aboard play war games with Navy ships on which women may not serve. Marine women may not work with K-9 dogs, but Air Force women do. Army women train in Honduras while the Navy debates whether women nurses may work on aircraft carriers.

So ill-defined is policy on women in combat that, even within the same service, commands interpret it differently. "Grenada?" said an Army captain. "I've heard all kinds of stories out of there. They sent a planeload down there, some women on the plane, and then the commander down there shipped them back to Fort Bragg, and the commander at Fort Bragg sent 'em down there again. Didn't want 'em down there."

Seemingly conventional assignments result in mess and muddle. "I was Personnel Officer of the Seventh Comm Battalion. They provide communications for the division; go in right behind the infantry types. My battalion later deployed to the Philippines and they couldn't take me; they couldn't take the WMs [Women Marines] that did all the admin work. I was not only Personnel Officer; I was Adjutant. When they would take prisoners, the adjutant is responsible for controlling POWs, casualty reporting, and things like that. Nobody knew what to do. It was just horrendous."

The lack of a national policy endangers servicewomen and the national security. While the services report their conformity to the combat-exclusion policy, the Department of Defense waffles, the Con-

[4] Hadley, *The Straw Giant*, p. 258.

gress averts its eyes, and the nation ignores the central problem of the dangers that servicewomen will confront. The Congress has urged and ordered the armed forces to enlist more women, with the support even of conservatives who wish to avoid a draft. The armed forces, partly at the insistence of advocates for equal opportunity for women, have trained servicewomen as integral parts of combat support units. If war comes, they must either use these women in these positions, some of which are high-priority targets, or jeopardize the national defense by removing the women.

As a nation we have arrived at this situation without asking whether our medical personnel can make unisex judgments in triage, whether or not the numbers of combat fatigue cases will rise among both men and women as they see substantial numbers of women blown apart, and even whether we ourselves might react to seeing dead and dying servicewomen on our TV screens by demanding that women be removed, leaving no one trained to handle complex military equipment.[5]

SERVICEWOMEN'S VIEWS

> *"I am against war. That's not why I joined the Navy. It was the opportunity of learning, education, not to go to combat, fight for the country."*
>
> *"I don't want to be in combat. I don't want my* husband *to be in combat.* Who wants *to be in combat? But I don't have any problem with women in combat."*

In late twentieth-century "peacetime" America, few people join the military because they want to fight. Yes, many servicewomen are patriotic, sensitive to an obligation to serve their country. But most don't want to fight. Just like most military men.

Yet—should the servicewoman be excluded from combat, differ from the males, the "real" soldiers and sailors and airmen and Marines? Be denied full integration into her service? Face limitations on her military career because she can't go to sea, can't enter the specialties where promotions come fastest and reenlistment bonuses are biggest,

[5] Hadley, *The Straw Giant*, pp. 258–59, 282–83, *passim*.

can't get command experience? Be taunted by the males as being favored, protected, unable to do the real work of her service?

Servicewomen respond variously. The reaction we most often heard can be paraphrased as: "I don't want to be in combat, but lots of women do; if they can handle themselves they should be allowed to. And if I had to, I would." This answer emerges from barracks and club discussions as a kind of approved, safe response.

Individually, opinion among servicewomen runs the gamut from forthright fear to passionate indignation at being denied a citizen's responsibility. Most often these women are not theorizing but rather confronting real possibilities. They are talking about what they themselves should and would do, not prescribing behavior for someone else. An Army captain's remarks illustrate the struggle to confront the harsh actualities: "I almost want to say I'm really not sure about women in combat. I've seen how women perform out in the field, and they do their job. We sweat as much as the men, and we gripe just like the men. It's hard, just in a peacetime Army out in the field. A lot of lifting. The men have to help us out. But you know, you all pitch in. It's teamwork. I don't know. I think compared with men we'd probably perform the same mentally. I think that would be an equalizer across the board, stress. Now this is just observing women during peacetime environment. It probably would be a little different with incoming artillery. But everyone jumps at that.

"A lot of times we've talked about this very subject out in the field, between men and women, and I've talked with men who've been in combat in Vietnam. Sometimes the women, we bring up the subject, 'You guys would never be able to stand us; we're going to smell so bad,' and they say, 'You don't even notice that when you're in combat. Everyone smells bad.' I said, 'Well, you know women out there, when we menstruate, that'd be a problem.' And these men have said they won't even notice it. Everyone is so busy surviving. No one's going to bother to be embarrassed about that. That's probably true. I know when we're out in the field, 'specially during the summer months when it's just hellacious—people have been sweating and are soaked and everyone knows that they smell, but it's like you can overlook that. Everyone makes jokes, but no one takes offense, because when you come down to it we're all in the same boat. You'd be surprised what people can adapt to."

Of the women who went to Grenada, the few who have talked to us about it, all enlisted, were ambivalent: "You know, we all make the same pay, with the same rank, but as far as sending a female for straight-out fighting, I don't think so. But if you send a lot of guys without females, it sort of messes the guys' minds up. Sometimes they would come in and get about two gallons of gas, just so they could have conversation with a female, 'cause like I guess they missed their wives. But as far as sending women to combat, I don't think so. I think we should bring up the rear like they said." As for guard duty: "We had three grenades in our little bunkers and your M-16 and you had about two hundred forty rounds of bullets. They say if anybody walked past your post at night, you tell 'em 'Halt.' If they don't halt, you tell 'em 'Halt' again. You just take action then. But you know, I don't think I could shoot anybody just for walking. I explained this to this lieutenant, and he said, 'If they have one little boy over there and he has a grenade and if he walks up and pulls it then both of you are blown up. That's why you should tell 'em *Halt* twice and then shoot to kill, or shoot to wound.' I understood it more better, but it's still sort of hard just to shoot somebody for walking."

> *"I don't see where women in combat is particularly a problem for the seagoing services, as compared with the shore forces, simply because you're more remote."*

The servicewomen most apt to argue against the use of women in combat come from the enlisted ranks.[6] And differences of opinion show up from one service to another, developing in part from the jobs assigned women in the various services, but mainly from their divergent concepts of combat. The Women Marines who talked to us, for instance, were more likely to take a position against women in combat than women from the Air Force. The Marines think in terms of foxholes and hand-to-hand fighting; the Air Force women think about fighters and bombers and tankers and transports. The Marine Corps prizes its traditions; the Air Force, the youngest service, prides itself on its progressiveness. It's not surprising to hear more conservatism from Women Marines and more advocacy for change from Air Force women.

[6] Cf. Hadley, *The Straw Giant*, p. 257, and Charles C. Moskos, "Female GIs in the Field," *Society* 22, no. 6 (September/October 1985), p. 32.

On both sides of the issue the women use multifarious arguments—some of which we should have expected to hear only from the crustiest old hands, and some of which we had never dreamed of. Here they are, in the women's own words.

SERVICEWOMEN AGAINST WOMEN IN COMBAT

> *"In my personal opinion, women doesn't start the fight, so why should we fight? Let the men go out there and finish it."*

> *"Combat area is no area for any woman. I think men are born warriors. It's always been that way back in history. I don't feel that a woman belongs in the home, but surely they don't belong in a combat area. Nurses are different. Women doctors are different things. That's a different job than taking a gun and shooting."*

Women are the childbearers, say some, so they should be kept out of combat, to ensure future generations. "Women in combat?" responded a pregnant Air Force sergeant, a photographer. "That I disagree with. I feel a woman shouldn't be in war, in combat, due to the fact that we can reproduce and make a new population." (But later she said: "When I went to my recruiter, I overheard another recruiter talking to a male applicant quite a bit younger than I was. He asked the male would you defend your country, and the kid says, 'Man, I don't want to get shot up and die!' I said, 'Not me. You give me an M-16 and I'll be in the front line.' I don't think women should be in combat, no. But if someone asked me to, I would. Our country is worth defending.")

By nature and/or by training, others say, women are nurturers, ill-suited to hurt and destroy. An Air Force nurse who survived two tours in Vietnam—tours that included flights over Viet Cong territory, nightly bombings, and attacks by the Viet Cong on the rice paddy just across the barbed-wire fence from her hospital ward—mused: to "have to carry a gun and to shoot at somebody. You don't have a lot of women that's got that kind of personality. They can't do it, I don't think. Maybe they could. But women have always, always been the nurturer. You nurture, you take care of, that's been ingrained in you from the time you were a little bitty thing. To deliberately go out and be the hunter is a role that I think women would have trouble with . . . out in the boonies with a gun, walking around looking, on patrol and stuff."

> *"I don't think that I could—I'd probably freeze up. I'd probably run away."*
>
> *"I do not want to be there. I don't. I don't. I'm the quiet one who wants to sit back."*

The prospect of being in combat is frightening. "Women in combat? The women I've been with, we don't talk about it. The first thing that comes out of the mouth is 'Do you think I'm stupid? Do you think I want to get my butt shot off?' I'm not stupid; I'm scared. I've fired the M-16 and qualified. I've fired the forty-five pistol and qualified. The favorite thing I did was hook up to a rappelling line and go over helicopter-style flying out in the air. But I don't want to do that with somebody shooting at me. If I have to do it, that's something entirely different." "Me myself I would be scared to death," said a black specialist in nuclear/biological/chemical defense, "but if I had to go, I would go. But shoot, men are the same way. Men are scared to death of combat.

"I tell you, can't none of these guys convince me they're not scared. They sit up there and they say, 'Combat, yeah, let's go. Let's fight. Let's kill.' That's sick. I know they're just as scared as anybody else."

> *"We got cycles, right? Can't you just see us having cycles out there? Our bodies are not physically built for that type of stuff."*

Opponents argue also that women's bodies disqualify them for combat, by lack of strength, the menstrual cycle, or vulnerability to rape. "I just feel that in a war situation, a frontline situation, people do get taken as prisoners of war," a senior airman says. "If a woman was taken prisoner of war she'd go through a lot more hell than a man would. Even our own guys—I'm not saying it's military men, because men are men, but in a combat situation I think you'd have problems. I think there probably would be rapes." "There are just too many physical complications—I mean physical attractions between the male and the female," says a Marine Corps staff sergeant, worrying about similar problems. "You put them together in a foxhole, and I'm not sure we can handle that yet. I think the Army has tested it; it's worked fine in the field here, but that's in a test situation. I'm not really sure under the impact of real war if it would work out that way."

> *"I think some women can perform in combat. I have met women in the service that I wouldn't want there, because they are physically inadequate or just not emotionally suited. There are also men that are the same way. But I've seen more women that I would put in that category than men, unfortunately."*

Some women fear that they would break down emotionally under the stress of combat, for which they are ill-prepared by their upbringing. A Marine pondered, "Can I point a gun at a stranger and pull the trigger? Women can do it if they're angry, but I don't think they can do it to a stranger. Men are stronger in some ways, because they're brought up that way. If I was brought up that way, maybe—but I wasn't."

Another Marine NCO agrees: "We are still too traditional. We were raised that the woman is to be the supporting part of the family—the woman should not be confronted with the horrors of war. If I were out in battle and saw my buddy, my foxhole buddy, killed, I don't know if I'd freak out or not. I am terrified of guns. Because we have been raised the way we have been all these years, I don't feel like women are due for combat yet. Maybe after the turn of the century, but definitely not yet."

Other role conventions also show up. How, servicewomen ask, will the male react when he sees a woman killed or wounded, or even in physical danger? An Air Force command post operator says it scares her: "In combat if it came right down to it, a man would protect a woman and possibly end up getting himself killed. It's natural the way a man is brought up, to protect women. You could possibly hurt men in the field by being there."

A Marine sergeant seconds her: "Women in combat? Let's face it. It's just not practical. It's just in his head. You can be the best, you can wear all these badges and be superduper; but the man thinking of a woman behind him . . . ? It isn't like with a guy, Joe, your buddy, that can chew tobacco with you. The roles have just been there so long, women and men. We'll never see women in combat." (But she added, "If they said 'We need you out there,' I certainly would go.")

"I talked to this Warrant Officer-4 who had been around a long time and had a lot of experience," said a Marine captain struggling to understand her male colleagues' feelings. "He told me, 'Well, yeah. It's terrible to see a man get shot up in combat. But it's just worse to see a woman hurt.' 'Why?' 'I don't know. It's just worse.' You have to count feelings as real. If that's the way men are going to react, it's going to endanger the mission."

"It's bad enough to see little Johnny blown away on the five o'clock news, but to see little Jane? No."

Many women argue that, whatever their own views, American society isn't ready for women in combat—yet. "I'm not saying that we don't have the instinct to do it," protests a Marine staff sergeant. "I don't think that it's acceptable yet for women. That's not to say that I can't. That's not to say that if I were called on I wouldn't. [It's just that] I think there would be such an outcry right now, it would never blow over. When the time comes, we'll be accepted for what we can do."

Servicewomen like these generally support the combat-exclusion policy, even if they feel it limits their careers. A Navy chief in administration, for instance, thinks the restrictions that keep women off most Navy ships are quite right: "There's just no way I want to be in some firing line. I don't think we belong on battleships. I don't see how women belong on ships, period. I love the Navy to death, but not on a ship." And a captain said: "The basic mission of the Marine Corps is to seize bases, amphibious operations, and that type of thing. The American public being what it is, Congress being what it is, believing that women do not take the beach, I doubt that a woman ever will be commandant [of the Marine Corps] nor do I think she should be."

SERVICEWOMEN FOR WOMEN IN COMBAT

"There's a lot of women that feel cheated. They've given their life just like the men to the service, but they are isolated from certain duties."

> *"We have a war, they aren't holding me back here—ugh. If it's more traditional armed conflict, I'd rather go than to sit here waiting. If it's nuclear, send me. It's hard to think of my daughter growing up and sending her off to war, but I guess if you want America to survive the way we've known it, we may not have the choice."*

> *"My battalion commander on one of my OERs said that he would be happy to have me serve with him in peacetime or combat. That made me feel good that he had the confidence in me to put that in writing."*

Some servicewomen find arguments against their participation in combat mindless, discriminatory, or unrealistic. They argue for it as a duty or as a right. "I think it's bunk. If we have raised our right hand and sworn to support and defend against all enemies, for God's sake let us do it."

Listen to a black staff sergeant in the Army, for her story encapsulates arguments that we often heard. "I had that question brought up to me once by a Ranger. We were both going to a NCO leadership course. They had a class on women in the Army. Of course Rangers, they think women are like the lowest form of animals. One Ranger, he stands up and says, 'Well, I don't think women belong in the Army, period. We're gradually openin' up to lettin' 'em in the Army, but look how long it took us to let blacks in the Army. What if I was in combat and I had a woman next to me, and I got wounded, and she was on her period? What would happen?' Even some of the guys were tryin' to figure out, like, you know, what's the point?

"Boy, I tell ya, I was on the edge of my seat. I told him that was totally irrelevant. What if I was on my period while I was fightin'? What does he think I'm going to do—use some of my protection to stop his bleedin'? He says, 'No, no, women are so inferior, blah blah this.' Me and that Ranger, we was at it, like rams. Before I left that class, I tell you, I had his respect. I put myself in a bind. I said, 'I'll tell you what. We're having a PT test tomorrow, and I guarantee you that I will outscore the majority of the men in this class.' Everybody, 'Ohhhhhh, nnnooooo.' And I did. I outscored 'em in sit-ups. At my age [thirty-three] all I need is thirty-four sit-ups and about forty-one push-ups to max, but I did sixty sit-ups, fifty-five man push-ups, and I ran two miles in fourteen minutes. I killed myself doing it.

"That Ranger went to Grenada, and he made it back. Do you know he found me, and he said, 'Sergeant, you know the whole entire time I was over there, I had you in my mind.' And he's white. He said, 'I was wrong. We had some guys that jump out of airplanes, and when it come time for doing it for real, they just froze.' He said, 'I jumped out, gung ho, ready to go. I got on the ground, and bullets and fire and bombs was flying all over the place, and I froze.' He said, 'It could happen to anybody. I see what you mean. It doesn't matter.'

"I couldn't believe it. He found me to tell me that. He told me that he would have felt more secure if I was with him than some of those guys that was freezing up that time he was over there fighting."

> *"Most of your women officers are very self-confident, get-up-and-go individuals, who have to be by virtue of the fact that they're a woman in the men's Marine Corps."*
>
> *"You're going to find women in there shooting. Some of the women are going to handle it real well, and some of them aren't. You take a unit of men, and you could probably divide that unit just about in half. Half are going to perform well under those high-stress situations, and half of 'em are not. It's going to be the same thing. Half of the women will and half of 'em won't."*

Some advocates believe that women can stand the stress of combat at least as well as men. An Air Force staff sergeant says, "I'm sure there's a lot of young men that have cried in the face of death. I'm not afraid to say 'Yes, I'll go.' I'm not afraid to find myself upset by it all, or crying because of it. But I also in that same line feel confident that I could take care of myself and take care of anybody around me." So does an Army lieutenant: "I as a soldier know that there are more things that males on the other side might want to do with me physically than they would my male counterparts, but that's part of my job. That's why I learned to fire weapons. That's why I learned how to deal with sixteen different other things to try to protect myself."

A black hydraulics specialist agrees that "women in combat can make it"; she thinks "that when it comes down to a wartime situation, we're more vicious than men are! People have said, women will probably be running behind the wall; it's not true. I think we're more defenders of the homeland than anything. If it came right down to it, yeah, you can put me out there. I figure I have a lot to lose by way of family. I'll fight. If you want to live, then you'll fight too, whether you're male or female."

"Why don't you ask Joan of Arc?"

"Women are not genetically unable to serve in combat. The Israeli women have proved that. The frontier women had to fight. I imagine some of the women in Ireland could tell you a thing or two about living in a war zone. The Vietnamese women could certainly have some input. If women have to fight when they have to fight, then why shouldn't they be allowed to fight when they want to fight? Get the benefits, the advancement, of that."

Many argue that women have already proved themselves. "If we can send women into space, I don't know what insurmountable problems we would have [in combat]." "To put in a personal bitch," says an E-6 master-at-arms, "I consider myself in a combat every day, 'cause I go up against guys who don't want me there, who don't like me being there, and sometimes that's just as nerve-racking as having the enemy shoot at you. Sometimes I'm not sure who the enemy is. He's probably right there next to me." "Women are at war," said a black master sergeant. "Read your stats. Many women have died because of crime. People are getting hurt, even in their own family, by their husbands. That's war. Sometimes I don't think any war can demean a woman as much as the war she has to fight in this country to be treated as an equal."

American servicewomen cite the Soviet women of World War II and the Israeli women, but also American nurses and the American servicewomen in Vietnam. "Women served on the other side in World War II and Vietnam also," said the Army's senior woman, Brigadier General Mildred Hedberg. "Soldiers talk about confronting a tank company in Russia where the commanding officer was a woman. In Vietnam, when they were looking for identification on Viet Cong bodies they sometimes discovered a woman too."

"Let's take World War II," says an Air Force lieutenant colonel. "There were women then doing what now would be called frontline jobs. I knew some delightful little old ladies, who when they found out I was in the military, said, 'Oh, I was in the Army in World War II.' 'What did you do?' 'I drove the truck that had the communications gear and ran the radios in the back of the truck at the front lines.' I [myself] was in combat," the lieutenant colonel continues. "I didn't have a combat job, but I certainly was in combat. Many women were in the combat zone in Vietnam, and we all got combat pay."

"This male pilot says, 'You know, it would be terrible to go back to the ready room and say you shot down a woman.' I said, 'Yeah, but wouldn't that be better than saying you'd been shot down by a woman?' "

As for men's reluctance to fight next to women—the men will have to adapt. "You're going to get jokes by a lot of men, 'cause the men say, 'I might have to go protect her. I'm gonna get shot.' I says, 'Well, that's your problem. You take care of yourself, well, she'll take care of herself. There's some situations where she might be alerted to you bein' in danger before you do or vice versa. You're gonna work out there just like you would with a man.' I said, 'She ain't gonna be dressed up showin' boobies and everything and havin' that thirty-six–twenty-four–thirty-six figure all the time.' "

"Something that was really hard on me," says an Army Spec-5 who ferried supplies into El Salvador, "was how protective the guys were. 'Oh, you can't be shooting that fifty. You just be hauling ammo.' You can't let them try to protect you, because then that distracts them. Each female has got to learn that and be able to step up."

These servicewomen question the belief that men could not bond with or trust women in combat—the same argument that used to be adduced against blacks in combat. "This colonel said, 'You have a female pilot in a fighter aircraft, and in front of her is a male pilot. He won't dive under the bridge, because he just cannot believe the female pilot is going to make it, so he takes a more dangerous route. Until we can get men to believe inside of themselves that the lady is capable of doing this, that's going to be our problem.' But," our interviewee concluded, "I don't think that there are overwhelming numbers of men out there who don't think that we can do it."

Frequently servicewomen counter arguments that serving with women would impair servicemen's ability to fight by urging the creation of all-woman ships, planes, infantry units: "Something I would like to see is a prototype, one combatant ship, with nothing but women on board. A problem is twofold. You don't have enough women with experience in the rates and in command. Then you get into that separate but equal type of mentality and you don't want that. But it would be an interesting experience, on a trial basis." "They say they'll run into problems with women mixed with men—why not have a battalion of women?" "Who said there can't be a submarine with all women?"

"I realized then that I'm just as good a mechanic as he is, and I can do the same job, but if he gets killed, it's because he's a guy. And I thought it was weird. In all fairness, females should go."

"I wouldn't want to be in Korea and have a war break out and have them round me up and put me on an airplane and send me home while my friends were there. I wouldn't go."

"Don't we have freedom in this country to pick the job we want?"

Some servicewomen argue that the combat-exclusion rules discriminate on the basis of sex—against men. "It's not fair," says an Air Force tech sergeant. "It's not fair to all those guys that would have to go in my place. The guy that would have to fly the extra mission because I couldn't go." Men's lives are no less valuable than those of women. "And the death of a woman is no more tragic than the death of a man." An Air Force Academy graduate said sadly, "To think that my husband could be sent instead of me, and I could sit comfortably in the military, that just doesn't seem fair at all." She is seconded by a first lieutenant: "I would hate to say that all the girls voted and said, 'No, we don't want to go to combat,' and then we voted and said, 'Yeah, let our men go to combat.' " And a Marine master sergeant with nineteen and a half years in sums up: "Why should his service be life-endangering and hers not?"

Other servicewomen also denounce the combat-exclusion rules as discriminatory—but against women. Why should women be denied the right to risk their lives for their country? "We're just as American as everybody else." "We should have the right to go to combat if we want," asserts a black Marine motor transport driver. "I've qualified with the rifle; I've spent nights out in the field with the guys. I don't see why I shouldn't be allowed to defend my country. I love my country just as much as anybody else does. I happen to take a lot of pride in it."

A senior airman in munitions maintenance agrees: "I think the women are going to force it, because they want that equal right. They're fighting for it so strong. There are some women that are some tough broads! They're out there in the Security Police [an MOS recently reopened to women; their job is to guard the aircraft on the ground]; they're still holding 'em back from combat, but that's their job. If that's what they want to do, let 'em go do it. If they got the ambition, I'd rather have that person next to my side saving my life than somebody that doesn't want to be there. I want to defend my country too. I want to go out for those ribbons and medals of honor. Why are you holding me back from that? I give it about ten years."

Servicewomen like these believe that a combat exclusion of women on the basis of sex is impractical, immoral, and, arguably, unconstitutional. Usually they advocate some other basis of differentiation between those who should assume the risks of combat and those who should not: some standard such as parenthood, physical strength, or emotional stability—much the same standards that the military have used in time of war in accepting or rejecting men. "I hope that there will always be the kind of family clause that I understood there was during World War II: Don't take the last family member. If you take me, leave my husband to take care of my daughter. If you take him, leave me to take care of my daughter."

"Why should a married man with children have to fight while I, with no dependents, can't?" a chief warrant officer asked. "I volunteered for Vietnam and my commanding officer wouldn't release me. He said a woman's place was in the home, and since I'd seen fit to join the Navy most assuredly he was not going to send me over to Vietnam. That's the only time I wept in all this time [more than thirty years' service]. I was going to relieve a male warrant officer in Saigon, who gave my record to the Vietnam desk. They looked it over. They approved me. I was going to be the first woman warrant [officer] to ever get such an assignment. That man [I was going to replace] was married, had three children, and that CO. . . .

"Here I am single; I've never been married; my mother was dependent, but I had two brothers that would take care of her, if anything happened to me—and that man sat there and said that I may not go, because they were shooting real bullets and I might get killed. I said, 'Respectfully, sir, so what? The man that's over there could get killed and he's got a wife and children. Those children could be robbed of a father.' He wouldn't hear to it."

His attitude contrasts with that of another commanding officer, who felt that there are fates worse than war: "My boss was very funny, because he thought it would have been great for me to go to Vietnam. He saw no reason why I couldn't be a lawyer in Vietnam as well as any of the men. But he didn't think that Okinawa was a good place for me, because that was where the troops were garrisoned and all sorts of immoral things would go on, and it wasn't a good place for a lady. He had no problem with me going to war."

An Air Force lieutenant colonel says, "There are roles in the Army that I can't see myself doing. I drove a tank in Vietnam to see what it was like, but you couldn't get me to stay in one as a job. Spending hours in that metal hole bouncing around—noooo, sir. But there are other women who could do that just as well as some of the men. A blanket disqualification of women on the basis of sex does not make sense."

"Why don't they just take all the women and put us in Kansas and then have the Soviets drop a missile on us? What the heck. They're [the Soviets] going to go after the women anyways, because it's a good morale factor. You break the rear area, even if you don't get the supply line. Get the word to the front and back home that they've killed a number of women. Just poor little service-support soldiers."

Other arguments center on the risk factor. The combat-exclusion policy, which ostensibly protects servicewomen, in fact, some say, places them at risk. Such a policy may even increase their danger, for it puts them in support positions—which, the military teaches, "the Russians" (a term that in our interviewees' speech has almost displaced "the enemy") would first try to destroy. Why, they ask, are women placed in support but barred from the front? Or forced to commute back and forth to the front, without the power of self-defense?

"Oh, yes, I could be in a combat zone. I'm in Aviation," said an Army helicopter pilot. "To my knowledge this is the only combat arm open to women at this time. Apparently by the time Aviation became a branch, there were so many women that had already been trained and the schooling is very expensive, so it would be rather impractical for them to take women out. This is my personal opinion. To preclude women from being in quote unquote combat, women are pretty much limited to utility helicopters. Some women are trained in combat aircraft, like the Attack Helicopter I; they can do maintenance test flights on them, but they would never be in a combat unit. That is the policy. It's a very gray area. I could per se go toward combat, toward the front line of the infantry. But if I'm flying a utility helicopter, the difference is I don't have the capability to shoot."

An Army National Guard captain who commands a truck company says, "There is no safe place anymore. When I was in my basic course, they gave us four hours, five hours of defending your company perimeter. They gave us twice as much training in NBC [nuclear/biological/chemical] defense. An infantry lieutenant colonel came in and said, '*Now* I'm going to give you something practical. I want to teach you how to really protect yourself because they're going to hit you with biological and nuclear warfare.' "

"The battlefield is fluid and mobile," observed Brigadier General Mildred Hedberg. "We have women who could be in combat though they would be in the rear areas, in defensive positions. The enemy can parachute into the rear areas, and women are going to be there. There's nothing that says that when a woman drives an ammunition truck up front to deliver ammo, she won't be exposed to combat. A woman who commands a Lance Headquarters or Service Battery, a target located to the rear, can you say she won't be in combat?"

> *"See, I keep asking the reenlistment sergeants, could I go 11-B, which is infantry. They really train you as if you were in combat. That's the way I thought the Army would be: I look at all these war movies and I say, 'Every day we're going to be practicing something.' It's not like that, and every time I think about it it makes me want to go infantry."*

Many servicewomen, whether opposing or favoring women in combat, argue for more training in "combat skills." "I'd like to go to jump school, but they won't let me, because it's combat-related," protests a Marine lance corporal. "What I think is, if I can go to the [firing] range, why can't I jump out of a plane?" "Personally I'm not interested in getting out on the front line, the back line, any line," says a Marine lieutenant in financial management. "But I'd like to know how to defend myself, my fellow Marines, peers, family, and friends. We learn a little bit about defensive combat, but it isn't adequate. I've taken the initiative to enhance my self-defense skills." A Marine captain in communications agrees: "I fault the rule that you can't have any offensive combat training. Train us. Give us the hands-on time."

Lieutenant Colonel Ruth Woidyla (USMC, Ret.), out of the expertise gathered as Special Assistant for Women at Headquarters Marine Corps, strongly advocates "women's being defensively oriented, including being able to shoot everything, and not have the services concerned about how it might look. I think that it will be tragic if we lose women [in war] because they were not carefully and responsibly trained, so that all women in the U.S. military, no matter what their jobs are, feel confident that they can handle themselves, defend their perimeters, and manage whatever they're required to do. Military women have a responsibility to other women and children and old people and junior people that work for them. I feel very emotional about having women properly trained. But it's a political hot potato. I think that the secretaries of the services would prefer not to forward it beyond a point. I can appreciate their point of view, but from someone on the ground, I think it is not responsible behavior on their part."

> *"The senior NCOs, males, they will almost always recommend that a guy over a lady get promoted. And then they'll use the line, 'Well, because what if we go to war? She ain't goin' to war.' "*

> *"Women in combat is all equal opportunity. If I'm good at my job—and I know I am damned good at my job—I should be able to advance at the same level as anybody else."*

> *"You've got to have the sea time to make chief, and that's where it hurts women. Your chances would be a lot better if women were allowed to go on combatant ships."*

Of all the arguments against excluding women from combat, those expressed to us most frequently and most passionately address the problems of equal opportunity and status. The combat-exclusion policy, to the minds of many servicewomen, ironically leaves them at risk at the same time it denies them the career rewards offered men. Being shut out of infantry and artillery units and kept off combat ships makes it harder for officers to get command experience and any servicewoman to get operational experience—without which their chances of promotion are decreased. Besides, combat is what the military is about; most women do not *participate* in an operation but rather *support* the combat troops who conduct it. Recognizing these handicaps, the military sometimes tries to offer women substitute opportunities, as when the Navy declared duty for women outside the United States equivalent to sea duty for men. But that which the military declares to be equivalent may or may not be equal in the eyes of the promotion boards.

Sometimes the combat-exclusion policy bars women from the career training open to their male colleagues. Take the case of a Marine MP, who enlisted to prepare for a career in the Los Angeles Police Department. "I basically wanted to come in to work with K-9 dogs, and the Marine Corps will not allow females to work with the dogs, because the dogs will go out into battle. They say that since these dogs are trained to sniff out bombs besides narcotics they won't let the females work with them."

Sometimes the combat-exclusion policy banishes women from the MOS of their choice. "There were about four or five fields that I was interested in above all the rest, and all of them, I was disqualified because they were combatant situations. It really made me stop and think. That anything with a real exciting, rewarding challenge—well, that's how it seemed to me, and I'm just speaking from my own, personal opinion. It really kind of disappointed me. I felt really limited."

A staff sergeant identifies the block for enlisted career women: "Right now if maybe my goal was Command Sergeant Major of the Army, I could not be it, because I didn't have the fighting in my background." A Marine lieutenant makes a parallel observation for officers: "That's why they say there'll never be a woman Commandant. Because she's not an infantry officer, that's why. If she'd had command, which is highly doubtful—well, you just don't see women commanders. A woman is denied the chance to be a legitimate commanding officer. That's why she could never be a Commandant, or it's going to be a cold day in you-know-where before that ever happens, simply because they [the women] don't get the command time. Someone like me who wants to be a careerist, I don't think now that I'll ever get command. I can only hope that maybe I'll have a commanding officer who is professional enough to say 'Well, she's the best qualified or she's got the most time in grade, she's the most senior, I'm going to promote her vice [instead of] this other officer, even though he's a man.' I would like to see that someday."

An ambitious Navy yeoman second-class bemoaned her inability to "make those accomplishments that my male counterparts do. This program that I'm applying for, a young man who was selected last year said that the people that he'd seen that had been selected had ribbons and warfare specialties and they were air crew or they could parachute jump. A lot of those are just not available to women, so I can't compete in the same way. Even though I might be better. I resent not being able to have those opportunities."

Women with guaranteed jobs can suddenly be deprived of them. "They had closed the [career] field to women, because most of the places that people go that are in the nuclear power program are on ships, and most of those are combatant ships, and women can't go on combatant ships. They were running out of places to put the women, so they just closed it to 'em."

Or women nominally in a career field may be kept from doing its work. "I have a difficult time working in my rate," says a ship's electrician of her need to work on ships. "I may be being unfair. I may not know all the facts, okay? It's just my own perception. Of course, we have mock-ups of the gear at school, and once I was able to go on some little patrol boats and work on the gear. But a lot of the things, I've never even seen. When I came in I thought, 'Well, if I do this, I'd like to be the best. I'd like, that if some gear went down, they'd say, 'Get her; she can fix it.' I haven't even had that much of an opportunity to work on the gear."

"The combat restriction? It anchors me. Absolutely anchors me," said a first-class master-at-arms who began her career as a hospital corpsman, took a B.S. in criminal justice, and plans "twenty, thirty, forty years" in the Navy. "When it comes to competing with the guys, they have the advantage of going on a carrier, and they see more crime. The guys they work with, they go to these foreign ports, and they bring on the big dope. Carriers are notorious for murders. I'm not a ghoul, but I do enjoy that part of investigation. My people [on a submarine tender anchored at Norfolk] go home every evening at four o'clock. We go out to sea maybe four times a year for four days. On my dream sheet in Washington I have three carriers down, and if the carriers open up, I will go. The guys get sea pay—three, four, five hundred dollars extra salary that I will never see. I call it discrimination, but the government doesn't. As a corpsman I had to go through Marine training for a MASH unit. I was always taught 'There may be a time where you won't be in the front line, but you will be there' [in a combat zone]. As a master-at-arms I am taught that you are on the front lines any time you have to have a shootout. We could have a bank robbed tomorrow on the ship, because we have a big disbursing office. I may have to pull my gun out and shoot somebody. That's combat."

Lieutenant Commander Joellen Oslund (USNR) struggled for years against the restrictions imposed on her and other women by the combat-exclusion policy. The first woman Naval helicopter pilot, who earned her wings in 1974, she finally joined five other Navy women in a suit against the Navy—a suit in which, she says, "we won the battle but lost the war." The Navy then successfully sought from the Congress a new law, which broadened some opportunities for women, but "the basic combat restriction still remains, and as women become more senior, it becomes more and more of an obstacle. It's one of the reasons that I did not stay on active duty longer. I couldn't deploy, and what I was looking at was search and rescue at Naval Air Stations throughout the world. In the Navy you can't make a career of it. It's an exciting tour and very satisfying, but it's not career-enhancing. Not being allowed to go out with, quote, the real Navy, unquote—I found that too restrictive, too limiting."

Lieutenant Commander Oslund worries also about the impact of repeated shifts in interpretation of the combat-exclusion laws on servicewomen's careers. ". . . it's sad but true, that a lot of the gains that have been made are at the whims of military policymakers, and some of those privileges, if you will, that we've been granted along the way can be withdrawn. The Air Force allowed some women into career patterns which involved them manning ballistic missile silos. The Titan missile has a big silo that can house four people. The new missile, I think it's the Minuteman, only has a two-man crew. Well, the Titans are being phased out, and so the Air Force is essentially saying that women can no longer be on ballistic missile crews because they won't put them in two-man Minuteman silos. I think it's only sixty-five women, but it's everything to those sixty-five. They've invested their time in this particular career path, and now it's being closed to them."[7]

Almost to a woman the highest-ranking officers we interviewed

[7] It may only reinforce Lieutenant Commander Oslund's point about vacillation to note that six months after this exclusion, the Air Force reopened the two-person Minuteman crews to women, with the proviso—for whatever it would be worth in wartime—that both officers on such a crew must be female. Hadley, *The Straw Giant*, p. 226.

believe that women will never have full status and opportunity in the military until they are allowed to assume equal responsibility—including participation in combat. But as officers who contribute to policy decisions, of course, they must consider the efficiency of the services as well as the welfare of servicewomen. Of the possible impact of eliminating the combat exclusion, Brigadier General Gail Reals (USMC) says: "Then you go into the ratios of gain to loss, et cetera. Have we gained enough in the cause for women and what they can contribute to risk the loss over here of something that's important for the organization? I don't know. Men can come up with many of the horror stories about what would happen on the battlefield or in the combat theater, all the things that might happen that would break down unit integrity and the bonding of organizations. There is no way to fully test this short of actual combat—so I recommend extreme caution. Success in combat is paramount. We can't afford to be wrong, and thus whether or not women have full or equal status is a secondary issue to me." The stakes here are enormous, both for the military services and for the individual women whose lives may be further endangered by the decisions made.

THE FUTURE?

> *"After acknowledging that women had participated in the action against Libya and after stating that if necessary in the future women will continue to be utilized 'in a number of different aspects of those responsive actions'; and after insisting that the threat of terrorism would not lead to withdrawal of women from jobs in which they were already serving; and immediately after announcing that the Navy was going to assign women to certain ships operated by the Military Sealift Command . . . Weinberger responded to a direct question . . . with the statement that he could never support the idea of women in combat. . . . 'I think women are too valuable to be in combat.'"*
>
> —Minerva 4, *no.* 2
> *(Summer 1986), pp.* 44–45

> *"Our unit went to Grenada, but they said they didn't want any females going. But at the last minute one of the guys missed the flight so they had to grab one of the females."*

> *"It's not going to be a controversy; it's going to be a necessity."*

What do military women think *will* happen to them in the event of war? Lots of them lack enough information and experience to make a good guess. A black soldier told us about landing in Grenada: "When we got off the plane, there was no streets and I saw these big hills and cows and pigs, and I was saying, 'My God, we must be in Kansas or something.' " Although she had been on alert for weeks, it simply had not occurred to her that women would be sent on such a mission. "I never thought that females could go to combat, you know. They surprised me."

Servicewomen are confused by conflicts between the much-cited combat-exclusion policy and the evidence before their eyes. "We're in a combat unit, I think," said an Arabic specialist in Army intelligence. "You know they say we're not, but shoot, sometimes I go out there and I see all these guys in tanks. We work right along with them. So I know we're led to believe that females wouldn't deploy, but our battalion commander said, 'You *will* deploy.' But I don't know." And although the commandant has said that women could not be removed from Coast Guard vessels in less than six months, some Coast Guard women told us that in case of war they would be immediately "pulled off" their ships.

Equally muddling to servicewomen are the repeated shifts of policy. A soldier of ten years' experience, who has watched the Army move women into and out of artillery, describes the confusion caused by these shifts: "What they did was, they started this thing in '75, nontraditional skills [moving women into MOSs traditionally held by men], push push push push. And then all of a sudden they go, 'Holy shit. Look where we have all these women. We've got 'em in these frontline units.' These commanders are hollering, 'Well, I can't take these women to combat with me, and you've got these women sitting all up here in my frontline positions. My unit's only eighty percent effective, because twenty percent of the force I'm gonna have to pull back immediately before I can even send 'em out.' The Army went in one direction; now it's streaming back in the other direction. Now they're starting to close some MOSs to women, so I'm not sure what's going on right now."

She refers to the Army's reworking of policy in the early 1980s, analyzing the physical demands of and weighting the probability of direct combat for each MOS (the Direct Combat Probability Code). This analysis resulted in the closing of twenty-three additional MOSs to women, reduced after much hue and cry from servicewomen's advocates and from field commanders to thirteen (for a total of fifty-one Army MOSs now closed to women).[8] The reassignment, retraining, and uncertainties generated by these changes in policy did not raise the morale of Army women.

An Army captain, commander of a truck company in the National Guard, looks at these changes skeptically: "A mixed signal came out. They [the Army] closed units, they closed MOSs. At the same time they did physical-strength category coding, and it showed what MOSs could be held by someone who had this physical capability. That said to me, 'Ah, they're coding that now. When the time comes, they're going to be able to tell which women are going to be able physically to be in combat, because we're all going to be tested. When you need us again, you're going to have us all categorized. When the real crunch comes, you're going to know which women you're going to be able to have in combat, physically. . . .' That's just the same old story again. 'If we need you, we're going to use you. We're going to deny you all the things that go along with being able to train normally with men, being able to be assigned to the unit, of being in command of a unit, but if we need you we're going to put you in there at the last minute.' "

Other servicewomen, often in traditionally male jobs, believe that they could not and would not be removed in combat situations. "I've asked them already," said a first flight engineeer on a C-5, "what happens if I'm sitting on alert in Europe somewhere and something really happens? Does that mean that they don't have a legal crew any more because the engineer can't go? Or do they just sneak me in and don't tell anybody that the engineer is a female?" A Coast Guard lieutenant j.g.: "I was the trained CIC officer, responsible for the Combat Information Center. Along with a team of radarmen, CIC must plot all enemy and friendly forces and advise the bridge of such things as incoming missiles, detection of submarines, or even torpedoes. I'm the one that's used to working with these guys. They're used to my lingo, and, you know, we're used to working together. That was the purpose of sending us through that simulated training, so that we would get used to working

[8] Martha A. Marsden, "The Continuing Debate: Women Soldiers in the U.S. Army," in *Life in the Rank and File: Enlisted Men and Women in the Armed Forces of the United States, Australia, Canada, and the United Kingdom*, ed. David R. Segal and H. Wallace Sinaiko (Washington, D.C.: Pergamon-Brassey's, 1986), pp. 72–74.

together as a team. What would they do? They couldn't just fly me off and stick somebody else in there."

Such questions are based both on a commonsense evaluation of probabilities and on actual experience. In the fall of 1983, for instance, a Marine communications officer was one of twenty-three women stationed in Korea just fifteen miles south of the Demilitarized Zone when a Red Alert, Condition A, was called, and orders were issued to shoot first and ask questions later. "At first they talked about evacuating us [women] right away, but then when you realize they'd lose their communication officer, they'd lose their logistics officer, and they'd lose their admin officer, they thought, 'Oh, boy, you know, what are we going to do?' And so they let us stay. God, it came real close."

"Grenada? It was almost like it happened and before they knew it the females were over there. Before they could pull anybody back and stop anything, they had like 'Oh, my God!' " An Air Force pilot told us about "a girl in my squadron" who was sent to Grenada: "They came back with shrapnel in the aircraft. It wasn't like 'Hey, you know, we're going to fly into this place and pick up all these students.' They went in under fire. She was a copilot on one of the missions, and they gave her a commendation medal for it, because she flew down in Grenada. You know, that's wartime activity. I was surprised. I said, 'You were allowed to send her down there?' The first thing they said was 'Well, we didn't even think about it.' They just launched her, because she's an asset. A viable asset. A person. They don't look at her, 'Oh, she's a female and legally she can't go into combat.' This is a person. Hey. She's available. Launch. That's exactly what they do. They don't sit there and go, 'Well, she's a girl and she can't do this.' "

The combat-exclusion policy itself is constantly changing. The Secretary of Defense speaks of "Department of Defense efforts . . . to do away with occupational barriers created by combat-exclusion laws" and announces the opening to Navy women of 320 positions in ships of the Military Sealift Command. The Army anticipates "some evolutionary changes in the Direct Combat Probability Code."[9] Many of the career women among our interviewees push steadily to modify or reinterpret or eliminate the combat-exclusion policy.

[9] *Minerva: Quarterly Report on Women and the Military* 4, no. 2 (Summer 1986), pp. 26–27, 30.

Brigadier General Wilma Vaught (USAF, Ret.) foresees gradual change: "The law is quite explicit on what it prohibits, and if that's all that were prohibited, we wouldn't have much of a problem. So I think we'll see a continuing chipping away at the other restrictions that have been placed on women. We're beginning to get what we have needed for a long time to make inroads in that regard—women coming in who have technical degrees: mathematics, computer, physical science, engineering, and degrees of that nature."

And a Naval captain of more than twenty years' service ventured her "guess—just a guess," about the continuation of the combat-exclusion policy. "I see five more years. If I were to really take a poll of the people in power in the Navy today, it would probably be twenty years. But I think five to eight years, probably. Certainly within ten. Women are a valuable resource. We can no longer expect the military services are going to fill their ranks with sufficient numbers of men. They are going to have to let women come in, because women are no longer going to be satisfied with the status quo. I think the progress we've made in the last thirty years is going to continue. You talk to some of these younger women officers who have their eyes on making flag officer, and they want to know why isn't there a woman CNO [Chief of Naval Operations]. I think there will probably be more pressure from within the military than outside."

Part of the process of change, Army Brigadier General Mildred Hedberg believes, must be the education of the public—especially that segment of the public over forty—who need to learn what military women have done, are doing, and are being trained to do. "We're going to have to educate the American public. Further change is going to have to be the will of the people. The only way we're going to make those changes is to start showing military women on TV or writing about them in books. We need to show them in training and working with weapons systems, so the American public will know what to expect in war." "The American taxpayers are paying for defense systems, and I think they should have a say-so [in the combat issue]," says Colonel Woidyla. "By being so coy and not bringing it on line, I think that we are really not being up-front with the American public, and I think that we should be."

General Reals warns: "There's a difference between women being put at risk or in danger or having difficult, demanding jobs—whether it be the truck driver in a combat area or a lot of other dangerous things—than there is saying 'We're going to make a conscious decision to put women in organizations whose primary role in life is direct combat.' " Her point is vital: Even *if* or *when* they are not in the front lines, military women are at risk. As the group responsible for the Direct Combat Probability Assessment wrote: "This action will not mean that female soldiers will never be in combat, for a fluid battlefield will dictate otherwise."[10]

[10] U.S. Department of the Army, Office of the Deputy Chief of Staff for Personnel, *Women in the Army: Policy Review* (November 12, 1982, Washington, D.C.), p. 10; quoted by Marsden, "The Continuing Debate" in *Life in the Rank and File*, ed. D. R. Segal and H. W. Sinaiko, p. 74.

6. The Issues: Fraternization

"Whenever you have this imposed class system and you leave somebody outside of it, it creates hardships."

"The Marine Corps even looks at fraternization as a staff NCO *and a troop [enlisted servicemember of lower rank], maybe a staff sergeant and a corporal."*

"Not if he has anything to do with your promotion can you go out with him, because that of course is out of the question. Because that's just wrong, right?"

To most American civilians, the issue of fraternization—whether military folks of different ranks may socialize together—seems as irrelevant as whether a commoner may marry a monarch, or a cat may look at a king. But regulations exist in all of the service branches to prohibit it. Sometimes they are applied only to relationships within the same chain of command; sometimes only to officer/enlisted relationships; now and then to the relationships of enlisted people of different ranks. The whole issue nags and vexes servicewomen, who often introduced it into our interviews.[1] For fraternization policies invade their private lives. "If Captain Sam and I wanted to go fishing, I don't see why we can't go fishing on our own time. But that's still considered fraternizing. It's like you're not your own person when you're off. You're still working, even when you're off duty. And that can make life miserable."

"Let me tell you that I have a very personal problem with fraternization," said a high-achieving Army NCO, voicing a social problem common to military women better qualified than men of their rank. "I'm thirty-seven years old. I'm single. I can't date the officers. Enlisted people my rank are . . . I believe the average is seven years younger than me. The formal education level is a couple of years below me, and the informal education level is certainly below me. So the people that I'm interested in and would like to date I can't."

Consider this ambitious young woman on a fast track, eager to avoid any possible misstep, but: "Fraternization? I think it's the pits. I can understand why the military has that policy. But I don't think it should be officer/enlisted. I think it should be management/command. A senior petty officer has no business dating a junior person that works for him any more than an officer has any business dating a junior officer or an enlisted person that works within that command—there's just too many opportunities [for favoritism and injustice]. But for people that don't even work on the same coast or somebody that's in Surface and somebody that's in Aviation, I fail to see how the line can be so firmly drawn. Where I work most of my contact is with officers. I hate to say I break the rules, 'cause I'm so adamant about following the rules. I hate to have to pick and choose the ones I follow! Well, I think if you're discreet and can handle it properly, people are none the wiser. I can't see where it's wrong, but I'll support the Navy's policy; therefore I have to be as discreet as possible."

Fraternization policies, a holdover from the days when officers were considered to be gentlemen and enlisted men weren't, are still needed, the services argue, to maintain discipline and protect subordinates against seniors who play favorites. Without them management problems result and morale is lowered. A Marine staff sergeant told us about a young lieutenant, in many ways highly competent, who breached

[1] The issue obtruded itself in the same way in Professor Charles C. Moskos's study of Army women in Honduras. "Female GIs in the Field," *Society* 22, no. 6 (September/October 1985), p. 31.

the fraternization rules by showing preferential treatment to two young women, a corporal and a sergeant: "The young ladies would come in and sit up on her desk and just talk to her. You don't do that, not with an officer. If the lieutenant and her two young ladies wanted to go running, they'd be gone for two hours, two and a half hours. The entire depot knew that the three women were inseparable. Well, maybe that's not so bad, but it is, because of the effect that it had on the male Marines. The morale was very, very low."

Almost all career women and many noncareer women among our interviewees agree that seniors and subordinates within the same chain of command should not socialize. Beyond that point, which they usually regard as self-evident, most of them consider fraternization policies outmoded flimflam, unwarrantedly restricting their freedom of association.

Created long before women entered the military, the fraternization policy originally addressed social relationships between men of different ranks. Now it affects friendships between women as well. "It's so hard, 'cause she's my best friend," said an enlisted woman. "I would hate to lose her because of her being an officer and me being enlisted. If I had to make a choice between my girlfriend who's an officer and my career, I'd have to choose my career, but that would be sad. Because I can't see any harm in it." A young black soldier was offended: "If I really see someone I wouldn't mind becoming more acquainted with as a friend, go to a movie or whatever, I can't do it, if it's an officer. Even if it's a female, can't do it, because we're not supposed to be associated with each other, and if we are, it has to be kept strictly confidential. Like we're living some kind of strange life."

But the presence of women has complicated the situation and heightened feeling about it even more because the fraternization policies interfere with dating, courtship, and marriage. It's one thing to deny a servicemember a friend; it's another to deny a servicemember a lover. Protests are frequent and vigorous: "An officer married to a enlisted guy—that's a taboo. You're trying to tell somebody who not to love. Who are you to tell somebody that?"

"It's like a Pandora's box. You get into this area that is too gray, and you have these different interpretations. Some places you hear about the commanding general court-martialing someone because he's going out with

someone who's not his rank. Then you get other cases, you hear the commanding general's invited to the wedding and went."

Given the complexities and passions involved, it's not surprising that the services avoid establishing clear-cut policies, leaving their definition to the discretion—or prejudices—of individual commanding officers. As a result policies differ so drastically, both inter- and intraservice, that generalization falters. Captain Julie DiLorenzo (USN) commented in the light of her own command experience. "In the Navy the policy is 'It should not be prejudicial to good order and discipline.' It's very difficult legislating what is prejudicial to good order and discipline. We have so much faith and trust in the commanding officers, we just leave it up to them to handle the situation, and I will admit that some COs don't have the common sense God gave them, and those are the ones that explode and blow up in everybody's face. If you know that Jack and Jill are dating and Jack is Jill's immediate boss, hey, you'd better do something about it. Don't wait until they announce they're going to get married. It does raise interesting problems if one is officer and one is enlisted. To some commanding officers, that is anathema. Other commanding officers are very democratic and totally unaware that it's having a deleterious effect on the rest of the command."

How far can one trust the discretion of the CO? A lieutenant colonel described a case that "*really* torques me off. A female staff sergeant married another staff sergeant. He goes to Bootstrap; he gets commissioned. They come to my base, and she comes in my shop, in MAC [Military Airlift Command]. He, as a brand-new second lieutenant, is in the Titan missile program, in SAC [the Strategic Air Command], and they're death on fraternization. Right? There they were, two absolutely totally professional good terrific people—she makes tech sergeant, very deservedly so. If you wanted a better couple, you couldn't find one. SAC, with its new policy, comes 'Hey! One of the two of you are going to have to make a decision to get out of the USAF because we are not going to have an enlisted person married to an officer.' I mean, they really shoved it down their throat. Every day that he went to be prebriefed, he was pulled out of the audience, stood up, and told, 'You getting out? She getting out?' She just got out, in November. The Air Force allowed that to happen, caused it to happen in one way, because for about a two-year period they really pushed the Bootstrap program. Here we are, big promotion program: 'We want good people who are experienced to come into the officer corps.' Super. He does, and all of a sudden his wife is going to leave the Air Force because of it. I bad-mouth the Air Force for that."

This situation—where one partner becomes an officer after marriage, only to have the military punish her or his spouse—raises the most ire. The spouse who is forced out of the military suffers the loss not only of career but also of status—being demoted from servicemember to "dependent" or "family member," a humiliating experience. She—for in most of the stories we heard, it was the wife who left—must then take whatever jobs are open near her spouse's base or settle for separation. Contemplating such a future, an ambitious yeoman told us: "My husband is going up for LDO [limited duty officer]. I'm not sure what's going to happen if he makes it. I've actually been told that I'd have to get out, and I just said, 'Well, I'd fight that.' " Or take the case of an officer commissioned after previous enlisted service. Though her enlisted husband was about to retire, "Higher Headquarters came down specifically to my husband and asked him what his intentions were. That did disturb me. They knew my husband was an enlisted man when they accepted me for commissioning."

> *"They tell you that as long as you don't fraternize in public in uniform, it's quite all right. But back in their mind, they know. They give you a long way to go and a short time to make it in."*
>
> *"There's war stories going around, where OERs or APRs get marked in such a vein that you will never get the endorsements to get the promotions, and they're going to force you out of the system."*
>
> *"A couple in Guantanamo Bay, Cuba, did get married while she was still in. The Navy found out and they transferred him to the opposite coast. This is one of the places where the Navy hasn't quite kept up with modern thinking."*

The nebulousness of the fraternization policies leaves servicepeople groping and wary, even when officially they have broken no rules. "I don't ever volunteer that my husband's enlisted," says one young officer. "He's just in the service. People know that by his haircut. The only time we're together is at home or [when] we're both in civilian attire.

There are quite a few women [officers] that are married to enlisted guys, or guys that were enlisted and turned officer. Like my best friend—she was going out with this guy; he was enlisted. And she wouldn't tell anybody until after he was an officer, 'cause she thought it was going to hurt her career.

"Once my boss's boss asked my boss whether he knew that I was going out with an enlisted man, and my boss said, 'Sure. I have no problem, because I was enlisted once too.' *His* boss blew his top, I guess, but he never came up to talk to me about it. Yeah, in the back of my mind it gnawed on me. Like 'Oh, gee, am I going to get in trouble? Am I going to lose my commission?' I felt that I had more to lose than my boyfriend, because I just put up with four years at the Academy, and I wanted to maintain my commission."

The objections of some branches of the military to officer/enlisted marriages can cost ambitious servicewomen their promotions. "Right now nobody's saying anything officially but if you check into the females that are going for commissions, if they're married to someone enlisted, they're being turned down. When I was at Leadership School there were three females that had applied for commissions, got turned down, one of whom was the honor grad, which is the highest graduate from the leadership school, which is supposed to be the top ten percent of all your Air Force NCOs. And the girl who came in second got turned down. You can't fight it." It works both ways: ambitious husbands also get turned down because their wives are enlisted: "He has a four-point-oh average, had a general endorse him, got turned down on three different selection boards [for promotion]. His wife even put in a statement saying that she would get out of the military if he got selected. She's due to get out this summer, and he just now got selected."

A captain speculated about the impact on her career of being married to an enlisted man; her boss "spoke to the general and said, 'The two young ladies that were briefing you this morning, I did it for a purpose. I am sending their OERs forward.' And General Y said, 'If you feel that strongly about it, I'll sign [endorse] them.' We're patting ourselves on the back and chortling." But in the event, her friend got the general's endorsement and she didn't: "There's no way to track it. But I believe the difference was that I was married to an enlisted person. Period."

The sub-rosa implementation of the policies breeds suspicion and duplicity. "When I was on a ship my boss called me into his stateroom one day and said, 'The XO [executive officer] knows that your boyfriend is enlisted and he wasn't real happy about it.' Then I found out that the XO's wife was an enlisted in the Reserves. My boss told me: 'Boy, talking about double standards. Boy, doesn't that take the cake?' " Devil's food.

> *"An officer will talk to me like I have the education of a sixth-grader, simply because I'm enlisted. Usually whenever I get one that's really arrogant, like 'I graduated duh duh duh duh duh,' I just say, 'That's good, sir. I graduated with honors too.' It's really silly. But it's your ego, and after a while you get tired of having it stepped on."*

Enlisted women denounced fraternization policies for implying that officers are superior—an idea that raises democratic hackles. "It seems to me like someone thinks he or she is better than the others, and I don't like that." Here the status-conscious military collides with the democratic ideal of American society, with the orientation of recruits. As an E-4, formerly the civilian wife of an Army officer, remarked: "Sometimes I feel left out of things. I get this feeling that I'm not there. I'm invisible. Recently I've been doing an inventory of secret documents at individuals' desks. They'll be talking to each other about things that I'm interested in, but of course I'm totally left out of the conversation, and as a person, I don't like that." Rumors fly: "I talked to one person that went to OCS. He said they, like, all brainwash 'em. They say, 'Enlisted people, they're peons. They're not of your caliber.' Huh! You've got a lot of enlisted people that have had just as much education as an officer does."

Officers too have their doubts—after all, it takes two to fraternize, and the mounting numbers of officer/enlisted marriages testify to the erosion of the policy. Indeed, we heard only one committed defense of the fraternization policy, when a Marine officer, who said that were she herself attracted to an enlisted man, she would either resign her commission or break off the relationship, talked about a case notorious among our interviewees in other services. "I don't see the need to go against any policy that CMC [Commandant Marine Corps] has set, because it's futile. You're probably familiar with the case out in California, with a Marine captain and a WM [Woman Marine] lance corporal or corporal who had carried on a relationship. They number one, which is expressly forbidden, had entered into joint financial agreements. You don't buy a car with an enlisted Marine. You don't live with one in a house and decide that you're both going to buy the house. They developed a relationship. This captain was sent to a court martial and was dismissed from the Marine Corps, which is terrible for an officer."

More common among officers who talked with us was a faintly critical approach and an awareness of the hazards of the current situation. "One of the things I watch with interest is the . . . what is it called? fraternization issue," says a Coast Guard officer, whose courtship had to be carried on secretly because her husband-to-be was her superior in her chain of command. She argues that if the couple are not in the same chain of command the issue is irrelevant, and if they are, they ought to be mature enough to handle their relationship discreetly. "In a lot of respects it's much ado about nothing," unless "it enters the work space, and there it is a real problem."

Another young officer, a navigator, balanced conflicting views: "I see a need: I see why fraternization [policy] started. To get the job done, you may have differences of opinion, but you don't always have time to talk about it: you have to be able to say something and the other person do it. You have to have that kind of respect as an enlisted person for an officer. But the force—we have a boom operator [enlisted] in our squadron who has a master's degree—the enlisted forces are becoming more and more highly educated, and you have to realize who you're dealing with."

An experienced staff sergeant commented on just this shift in enlisted personnel, and the institutional response to it: "The Air Force is more people-oriented now than when I first came in. At one time certain ranks may as well have been gone: at one time enlisted were slime. Now we're on an even-keel basis. You're going to find more enlisted people running around with bachelor's, master's, that don't get a commission, because they have pride in their job. The Air Force recognized it and said, 'Hey. These people are getting an education. They know what they're doing. They're aware of their rights.' The individuals coming in now believe that the government owes them something. They know their rights, and they'll push 'em."

Where the services are headed with the antifraternization policy is arguable. The common dislike of it, the lack of sympathy for it in segments of the military and in the civilian population, and the changes in the composition of the enlisted force have already eroded the policy. There are those who love it, for it does reinforce the distinctions of rank, and rank confers both status and authority. Some senior enlisted NCOs as well as some highly placed commissioned officers argue that it strengthens the chain of command. But most of the women who talked to us neither support it nor believe that it can be sustained indefinitely as it now operates.

The situation is encapsulated in the story of a petty officer first class (who surprised us by saying that she does not plan a military career; it was unusual to hear an E-6 talk of getting out). "My husband is an officer, and it's a little tough on him. He went to the Coast Guard Academy, and they drilled into him for four years, no fraternization. He is the son of an Air Force officer—it was even when he told his folks he was marrying an enlisted person like 'Oooohhh.' So when we married, I was supposed to get out as soon as my enlistment was up. I kept saying, 'What am I going to do when I get out?' We got married three and a half years ago, and it was about a year after that that he said, 'Okay, you can stay in.' But that was it. It was kind of like I put my extra two years in, and I've decided that now I've proved my point. Next year will be my last.

"The people that we worked with were very supportive, and there are a lot, a lot of people here that are officer/enlisted. In the building I'm working in there's at least three other couples. I think the barriers are starting to come down. The problems I have had are the enlisted that I worked with. They were kind of saying 'Oh, she thinks she's high and mighty. She's marrying an officer. She thinks she's better than we are.' And many of our friends are officers. In my job yesterday we went over and inspected this friend's ship, and it's like I'm calling him 'Lieutenant X' all day and then I see him at night—it's 'Hi, John.' I don't find it difficult to go back and forth, but I'm always afraid that somebody is going to take offense.

"At this point I don't think it would interfere with my husband's career if I stayed in. There's always the one or two people who will, but I believe a majority of the Coast Guard don't hold it against him. When he was passed over [did not receive his promotion at the expected time], that was a big question in the back of my mind: was he passed over because somebody whispered in somebody's ear who whispered in somebody's ear? I will always wonder. But I believe the Coast Guard is very lenient, and I have a feeling reading the *Navy Times* that even they're getting a little softer in DOD. I don't know how far it will go ultimately, but I think it's going to start breaking down a little bit.

"My husband told me that an officer ran up to him one day and told him, 'I'm going to marry a girl who's enlisted and I saw you and your wife together in uniform. I was so excited; I had to come over and ask you about it, what kind of problems?' And my husband said, 'Well no, I don't think we're having any problems.' As a matter of fact, the officers I worked for were very supportive. They said, 'Oh, marry him if you love him. I think it's great and that you'll make a perfect couple.' I don't see it as a big problem."

7. The Issues: Feminism

"YOU'RE NOT ONE OF THOSE WOMEN'S LIBBERS, ARE YOU?"

"No! I'm not a feminist. I'm not one of those women's libbers. *Of course* I want equal pay for equal work, *but* sometimes I think they go too far. I still like to have my doors opened for me." So runs the opinion (military women, for use of) expressed so often by our interviewees that it began to sound like government issue. But by no means all military women share it.

> *"Of course I'm a supporter of* ERA*. Absolutely. Fully, unequivocally. Are you?"*

> *"The way I feel about women's rights, women could have anything they wanted if they all wanted it, because after all, this is a democracy, and*

after all, we are over fifty percent of the population. Therefore I don't feel oppressed by men. I feel maybe betrayed by women."

"I know people fancy women in the service as being out there to prove a point and into women's liberation and all that stuff. I never really was too interested in it."

Seldom did our interviewees raise the issue of feminism—as they did that of fraternization. Some were uneasy, defensive, or ambivalent when we asked about it. But our question "Where are you on the Equal Rights Amendment?" evoked wide-ranging discussions of women's rights and the women's movement.[1]

On the one hand we heard from a minority of forthright, well-informed feminists, like Brigadier General Gail Reals (USMC), who says, "I'm not a women's libber, but I believe I'm a feminist. . . . I like to have fun with it occasionally. I was the only woman in the entire senior class [at the War College] that year. [In an elective course] they asked everybody for an idol, for a model. Of course we were getting Patton and Chesty Puller, Marine Corps. I thought, 'Well, this is getting dull,' so I said Gloria Steinem. And I'll tell you, everybody woke up. They looked at me like I was a traitor. I took a lot of flak over that."

"At that point I was a member of the National Organization for Women and a group of us founded the chapter in Newport, Rhode Island," Captain Patricia Gormley (USN) told us. "There were several other active-duty women, both officer and enlisted, and some dependent wives. The people who were not military-connected for the most part had come to this through the peace movement. We didn't even know how to talk to each other. It took awhile to do some ice-breaking, because each of us had been very isolated. This is 1973, '74 or thereabouts, so freshly post-Vietnam. Feelings high, obviously. And everybody could put all that aside. We got to know each other, and just to work very positively on women's issues, getting girls' sports in the local schools and stuff like that. That was really good." A Navy E-6: "ERA? Oh, I'm all for it. I started campaigning for it when I was in the eighth grade.

[1] Although many interviewees were well informed about the amendment, others asked about its provisions: "Equality of rights under the law shall not be denied or abridged by the United States or by any state on account of sex. The Congress shall have the power to enforce, by appropriate legislation, the provisions of this Article."

I have a firm belief that everybody holds their life in their own hands. And the ERA will help me make mine better."

"ERA? Oh there's no question," an Army captain shot back. "I don't understand why they haven't passed it. I'll be damned if they say I don't have the legal right to be a full citizen. Oh, my goodness gracious. Phyllis Schlafly, I don't understand you. I have to pay taxes just like the rest of them? Ohhhh. I get so upset I can't find words."

At the other end of the spectrum, a young Air Force officer said: "I do not believe in woman's liberation. Above all I do not believe in woman's equality. My mother always said be a woman first and don't worry about the rest. The husband's the head of the household. I'm the manager of the household." And a black Spec-4 responded: "*ERA?* ERA is saying like a woman is equal to a man, and she's not, to me. And she can't do everything that a man can do. The Bible states that the man is the head. First there's God, and then there's the man, and then there's the woman. It also says that woman was made for man, and if she was made for him, then she could not possibly be head of him."

Between these extremes, military women position themselves irregularly. Loosely and very generally speaking, women in the upper ranks, of more experience, of greater age, and a higher educational level react more positively to the women's movement than other military women. But it's hard to predict where an individual servicewoman stands on any given issue.

> *"I feel that I have all of the rights that I need, because I'm getting my equal pay for my equal time. If I was a civilian I'd probably be different. If I'm doing the same job Joe Blow is doing, and he's getting a higher salary than I am, I'm going to be raising some serious hell."*

A few servicewomen doubt that problems still exist for women as a group: "I am paid on an equal basis," says a navigator on an Air Force tanker. "I guess I've been lucky. I haven't felt the prejudice that maybe some women do. I feel like things are okay as they are. As far as I've ever known, and as far as I've seen in my family [her mother is a lawyer], there isn't a need for that [ERA]. Every now and then I'll fly with a guy who I can tell doesn't think so much about women flying in the military. But on the whole I don't feel that at all." An Air Force doctor echoed these ideas: "So what if ERA gets passed? I don't know how it would change things in my life. I guess that's how I'm looking at it. I'm not having any troubles, so now I don't see what the big deal is."

Other servicewomen, recognizing the paradoxes of their situation, feel that the times and their jobs are forcing them into uncomfortable postures and role conflicts. "I think I am an extreme women's libber, even though I don't want to be," confessed an airman first class in the security police. "I don't want to be unfair to my husband. But the more I do for him, the more aggravated I get, because he's healthy to do his own things for his own self. Rather than turn to women's lib and make him fend for himself, I do a lot of things for him, to make him feel up there. See, my job makes a difference too, because I'm a female authority figure. He wants to be *the* authority figure. I guess I give in to that at home. When it comes to my job, I can't. But at home I can let him have his way."

A woman may support one feminist position but not another. A lieutenant colonel joined the Air Force explicitly to get equal pay for equal work. "There truly is a Cucamonga, and I was the editor of the *Cucamonga Times* and two other weeklies and a contributing editor to one of the dailies. I had begun to hear stories about 'Gee, if you go into the military you don't have some of the discrimination that women are having on the outside.' My boss shows up one day. He's got this young kid in tow. Doesn't know zilch about journalism. My boss parades the kid in and says, 'Teach him everything you know.' I'm making ninety dollars a week after three raises. About the third week that he was there I walked by his desk, and there is his paycheck. He made ninety-five dollars a week. I did not walk, I ran into my boss's office, and said, 'It's yours. Good-bye.' " But the experience by no means radicalized her on other women's issues: "You don't think you need to ask me where I stand on ERA? You might, you might. I think because of it we have made great strides. But I think that ERA itself is the wrong answer."

Because the military attracts more recruits from some parts of the country than others, because the young and the relatively young constitute almost all of its self-selected population, the military is not precisely a microcosm of the United States. "We tend to be conservative-type people," an Air Force public relations officer remarked. "This is a military atmosphere and we chose to live this way." Their conservatism, traditionalism, and respect for authority make them resist sharp and sudden changes (like ERA) and advocate gradualism. So the curve of opinions expressed on women's issues among the military women we interviewed skews to the right, toward the status quo.

SERVICEWOMEN TALK ABOUT THE WOMEN'S MOVEMENT

> *"I like to stay away from the word* feminism, *because it has bad connotations. It's better than* woman's lib: *I never felt like I was in bondage, so I didn't have to be liberated."*

> *"Some of the [women's] groups, I'm not sure that they really have our best interest in mind. I think women in the military on the whole are probably way ahead of their sisters. So maybe we should be helping them."*

Many servicewomen identify the women's movement with a dangerous liberalism—or even radicalism; with a brand of pacifism that condemns the military; with lesbianism; with telling other women what to do; with forcing other women into jobs they don't want; with denying other women freedom of choice—particularly the freedom to join the military; and with focusing on trivia instead of real issues.

To what extent, if any, is being in the military responsible for these suspicions?[2] Certainly military women live among men, many of whom abominate feminism—but so do women construction workers and women policemen. Certainly military women work in a hierarchical, structured world of male values, but so do women firefighters and women in many corporations. Whatever most servicepeople think about feminism, the formal efforts of the command structure are exerted against sexism, in the classes given by the Social Actions and Equal Opportunity folks, and in the discussions on women in the military in the Leadership Schools. We could not set the opinions of our interviewees down to

[2] Equally important is the question of whether the women's movement considers military women part of its constituency. The answer is beyond our scope, but among the major women's organizations only the Women's Equity Action League has established a section devoted to military women and studies of military women are noticeably absent from most women's studies conferences and publications.

brainwashing. The women are too independent. Their opinions vary too widely, and resemble too closely the opinions of many civilian women.

"ERA?" an Army chief warrant officer responded. "I'm really pissed off at some of the women that have got into it, pushing it, and they haven't experienced it, they haven't lived it. I watched TV a couple of times and watched some of these women out there. I'm goin' 'What are they talkin' about? They haven't been out here doin' these jobs. They haven't been out here livin' this life. They haven't been out here carrying hundred-pound tool boxes on their shoulder, turning wrenches.' They're a housewife somewhere, sitting behind a desk somewhere, going 'I think it's really neat to see a woman climbin' a pole.' It's almost like they're pushing it on other women, so they can sit behind their desk and go 'Now we have women doing everything.' "

Some servicewomen think the women's movement concentrates on the wrong issues. "I mean, there are real women's issues in this world. Like the way a civil court handles a rape case. Let's start attacking the issues that fundamentally affect women's safety, fundamentally affect women's personhood. I don't care if there's a chairperson of a board or if a sign reads 'People working.' That kind of thing is so damn unimportant, and I think tends to give people who basically have pretty good cards in their hands a bad press. Let's start changing people's attitudes on things where it's fundamentally important."

"The women's movement has had a tremendous impact. Without the general climate change that came about in all of society, we never would have had these changes in the military."

"That's one thing that I really don't know, the history of the women, the fight that the women had. The women in today's military have it real good, compared to ten years ago, when they were just really starting out, and no one really realizes the goals and how far we are in such a short time."

Many servicewomen see no connection between the women's movement and the gains military women have made. They know very little about their military predecessors. Few know of the sacrifices of early servicewomen. Of the court cases they brought and won to open up new assignments and MOSs, to permit servicewomen to marry and have children. Of the changes in the law they effected to give servicewomen the same pension rights as servicemen. Of their courage and perseverance in the face of active antagonism and bland indifference to their rights. Few know that 12,500 nonmedical women served in the Navy and Marines in World War I. And some military women know little about what women are doing in other services: "Do they have women in the Marines?" "You mean that Army women went to Grenada?"

After all, until recently the media have more often than not been silent about military women, and only now are writers beginning to depict them in fiction. From what materials does a youngster construct her image of the military woman? Private Benjamin and Hot Lips Houlihan? It's not surprising that most of the military women who talked to us could not recognize their debt to their military predecessors, let alone to the women's movement.

Senior military women, who have lived their own history, know better. "The status of the women in the military would not be anywhere near what it is without the external pressure and the societal changes that took place, from equal opportunity and civil rights to the issues that the women were bringing up," says General Reals. "I've always felt that women in the military were not vocal enough. I thought we were somewhat hypocritical by kind of turning up our nose about the women's movement and the quote unquote women's libbers and yet being more than willing to take the benefits. Granted, we did not have quite the same kind of freedom, but we took advantage of what had in some respects been handed to us."

The very introduction of ERA, a Navy captain remembered, precipitated dramatic changes for military women. "They had a study group set up by the Secretary of the Navy looking at ERA's introduction, the possibility that laws would be changed, and they wanted this group to study how that would affect the Marine Corps. *Most of the changes that we recommended were later incorporated into law.* Then in the case of *Owens* v. *Brown* [1978] on the seagoing limitation, a lot of these materials from the study were presented as evidence." The introduction of ERA, that is, led to the study group, which accumulated evidence later used in the critical case in which Judge Sirica ruled that women were being denied equal protection of the law. Information like this is unknown to most military women.

SERVICEWOMEN THINK ABOUT WOMEN'S ISSUES

> *"There are women [in the military] that are really on the forefront of the women's movement, particularly the enlisted women* and *the senior officer women. They're slugging it out, one by one, and in one of the most difficult environments."*

But it's necessary to distinguish between servicewomen's feelings about the women's movement and their concerns about women's issues. First, servicewomen staunchly uphold the idea of equal pay for equal work. "Where am I on ERA? Same place I've been for the last fifteen years. If I do the job, I want to get the money. All this other stuff I don't concentrate on, but if I'm going to do the job, I'm going to get paid for it." This principle in their eyes has become axiomatic, beyond question and beyond debate.

Second, a good many servicewomen base their thinking on the belief that people should be allowed to make their own choices; women can choose freely only when they have equal opportunity: "If she thinks she can do it, she should have the chance to go for it and to prove herself." "If she wants to be a construction worker," an Army E-4 who keeps flight records says, "let her be a construction worker. If she wants a sledgehammer, let her do her thing. If she's qualified to do, let her do it." "Individual merit should be the bottom line versus gender-oriented distinctions."

Third, numbers of servicewomen acknowledge the duty to share responsibility for the defense of their country and its civilian population, up to and including direct combat roles. "When I ask young women 'Why did you go to West Point?' says the Army's Brigadier General Mildred Hedberg, "nine times out of ten, 'Because I thought it was my duty and because I wanted to serve my country.' " Lieutenant Colonel Ruth Woidyla (USMC, Ret.): "Young women today want to share responsibility. There are some that would feel they should go as far as the foxhole." And almost all our interviewees believe that women should have the right to participate in combat if they want it.

Fourth, most of the military women we talked to feel a sense of responsibility to other women. Women in the highest positions have developed sophisticated systems for helping other women. Enlisted women increasingly are seeking ways to communicate with and support one another. As a Navy petty officer first class told us: "Any female who wants to go for it, I'm more than willing to help her up the ladder. And most of the senior women are like that. We do form that line and we do get the work done. The ladies very quietly get together, and they say, 'This is what we're going to do,' and it gets done. It's just something that's been passed down from mother to daughter."

> *"ERA? I still don't even know what it's all about. I don't think we should be discriminated against on the basis of sex or any other basis. I don't want to be treated as a man, but I don't want to be discriminated against."*
>
> *"Guys feel that because you're working in a male-oriented career field, well, naturally, you are for ERA. You are burning your bra. You want to be treated like a man. I'm still a lady. I like to wear dresses. I like the door to be opened for me, the chair to be pulled out. But then I can also do a man's job as good as they can. I don't think I have to change the way I am just because I'm doing that job."*

These four principles should not be obscured by servicewomen's concern for their image as women. Colonel Woidyla compiled a spectacular record in fighting for servicewomen's rights, particularly when she was Special Assistant for Women, an unenviable position ("You realize the Marine Corps is probably the last bastion of male chauvinism, and some things are done with just kicking and screaming"). Yet, she says, "I'm very traditional socially." A lot of servicewomen in their criticisms of ERA and the woman's movement are simply expressing their concern for the social niceties that reinforce their own femininity. Thus all the talk about how much they value having doors opened and chairs pulled out for them. Sometimes they see the women's movement as threatening these small courtesies, damaging their image of themselves as women. They may spend their days working on airplane engines or their nights riding patrol in a police car, but they still want to be recognized as feminine in their off-duty time. They combine worries over the trivia of social behavior with stout endorsements of equal pay, equal opportunity, and shared responsibility.

Of the more than three hundred women who talked with us, the large majority, although they know little of its history and dislike its image and its name, support the basic tenets of the women's movement.

But many distrust or repudiate its methods. Some even reject group action and legal challenges—though successful court actions stud the progress of women in the military.

SERVICEWOMEN WORK FOR THEIR RIGHTS

> *"I don't think you can get very far talking. It's what you do that counts. What you do that people see."*
>
> *"Slowly but surely the doors are opening. I don't know that we have any Susan B. Anthonys, but we definitely have women that are fighting for progress."*
>
> *"Prejudice against women is difficult for me, but I think it is as difficult for those who have been brought up differently. If I did not try to understand and find the reasons why and look at it in a rational light and not become emotional every time the issue is brought up, then I would get nowhere."*

In struggling for their rights, servicewomen encounter special problems. "Military have to be very careful about political causes. There's not an ERA group on base that I'm aware of. If there is, God, it's awfully quiet! Maybe that keeps us from being more involved and from hearing more about it than just what we read in the paper." Servicewomen are indeed restricted in their political activities. And they have their hands full in adapting to the military world. Who needs to risk being called a feminist or a woman's libber, anathema to many servicemen?

If the young woman argues for women's rights, she may be accused of lesbianism—an accusation that as a rumor may result in ostracism and as a proven fact in a discharge. "Oh, yes, oh, yes, they're frightened," says a Navy lawyer. "I would think in some circles being called a feminist would be akin to being called a lesbian."

In any world, gaining acceptance means identifying with a group. Because she may be the only woman, or one of two or three, in her unit, the new servicewoman often identifies with a group of men with whom she shares common interests—the platoon with whom the military teaches her to work as a team, the other pilots who know and care far more about her professional interests than the women in her quarters.

Black women may identify more closely with black males than with women of other ethnic backgrounds. And many military women, blazing with pride in their organizations, identify more with their services than with women in general. Identifying with women, after all, tends to separate and divide servicewomen from their world rather than integrate them into it.

Then too women recognize responsibilities to their services that present special problems. In many civilian situations, a Marine captain pointed out, men's antagonism to women's moving into nontraditional jobs is "not too critical. If the women can do the job, they can do the job. So what—it makes the men jealous? Big deal. But when you get involved in the military, there's lives depending on you. Unless you trust each other, have that trust and confidence in each other's ability, real problems can arise."

To get along in the military world at all requires a good measure of pragmatism. No one, man or woman, private or general, is going to revolutionize so large and resistant an institution quickly. Even the most determined feminists have learned to proceed with caution and discretion, both because they risk unpleasantness, unpopularity, and even their careers, and because agitation may be counterproductive. "I still think women are stepped on a bit in the Air Force, and I'd like to see that done away with. But you can't just let that one thing be your burning issue. Then people stop taking you seriously." "You're dealing with conservative people in the most conservative organization," explains a Navy captain. "[If they're known as feminists] women can't survive in an organization like that. And you go through different periods in your career where you can say more or less, and then other times you duck and pray. It's hard too because the organization will see feminism as an affront, where it doesn't exist. If most of us didn't think well of our organization, we wouldn't stay. You know, it's our life."

For all these reasons servicewomen often use action rather than words to fight for their rights. And they often reject group action in favor of individual effort. "I just live my own life," says an Army helicopter pilot. "I do what I want to. If I like it, I work hard at it. And if I don't I'll just go 'Whooo' . . . I'll blow it off and go find something else. Such as being a mechanic on helicopters. . . . I enjoyed doing it, so I did it. I didn't think of it as an ERA issue. Men told me I couldn't do it; I did it. On my own little turf right there, yeah, I had to fight my own little battles. If I wanted to turn wrenches, I had to fight to do that. If you go out and start yelling and screaming about it, you're going to get all this attention and you aren't going to get anywhere but a lot of problems. If you just keep your mouth shut and find the job that you want to do and work for it, then we'll just kind of sneak up on the men and get what we want anyway. That's how I feel ERA should happen. I feel like people like me and the other women here at the airfield, we're doing it."

"I really don't like to talk about ERA," a Coast Guard lieutenant says, "because I wish that it wasn't. I think that the changes that will come about for women can come about without ERA, and it really has to be done by the individual woman. Every career woman is always going to meet up with challenges: it's the attitudes that you have to overcome. They'll never change, because of the male ego. You don't want to get me started on the male ego! But I don't think we need ERA. I'd rather do it on my own merit."

"But that's the tragedy," says Captain Gormley, an attorney who knows the value of group action. "In many cases the same women who are not feminists and think they can do it all on their own also want to be able to do the jobs that the men are doing, think they can do better, and see no reason why they shouldn't take these things into a combat arena. [I] see it all the time. We have to start accepting the reality of the political power that gets you where you want. Not to be afraid to get it, to use it, to be comfortable with it."

As General Reals puts it, some military women in the past have been "willing to raise the issues, continue to apply the pressure, and move along. If young women in the military think it all happened by magic, it didn't. Somebody didn't wave a wand. There were women in the military, the Jeanne Holms and people like that, who were in their quiet way leading the internal crusade." As they look back, servicewomen of long experience and high rank recognize many gains, but General Holm subtitled her book *Women in the American Military* "An Unfinished Revolution."

The new generation is really the first cohort of American women for whom the military is in some degree a routine choice. They are benefiting from and consolidating the gains hard-earned by their predecessors and by the women's movement. Like all such generations, they tend to accept these gains as their natural and innate rights. But some of them too join the unfinished revolution and struggle on: "Of all the people from Fort Bragg that went into Grenada, all of the men got Bronze Stars; the women got ARCOMs—Army Commendation Medals: it's less than a Bronze Star. The women complained: 'Look. I did everything that that guy did, and I supervised him, and if they get a Bronze Star, I get a Bronze Star.' And they eventually got Bronze Stars."

8. The Issues: Families: To Have or Have Not

"Marriage and a military career? It takes a strong woman and an understanding man. I'm a strong woman, but I have to meet the right understanding man."

"The Army to me is a job. It's not a vocation. If it were to come between me and my family, I would choose my family. And I love my husband more too."

"It makes me mad that men think they can have families and kids but you [women] can't if you're in the Navy. So that's something they're going to have to get over."

The United States armed forces are becoming domesticated. "More young sailors are getting married," says Navy Rear Admiral Fran McKee. "By the time they've been in three or four years they may have several children." For the first time in history their dependents outnumber Marines. The Air Force proclaims National Military Spouse Day and declares November "The Month of the Military Family." The military services, recognizing that the single greatest determinant of whether a serviceman stays in the military is his wife, try to ease the lot of military families and keep them happy—not only with the traditional housing, schools, stores, and recreational facilities on military bases Stateside and overseas but also with sophisticated Family Support Centers. Admiral

McKee again: "The Family Service Centers—if somebody had said we would have those fifteen or twenty years ago, I would have thought they were definitely off track, because the *old* adage was that if the Navy wanted you to have a wife you would have been issued one."

As for the servicewoman . . . what of her family? Can she have one and still function in the military? What happens if she becomes pregnant? Court cases and shifts in public opinion have settled some of these questions. For long years after World War II, a woman could not remain in the service if she married, became pregnant, or accepted responsibility for a minor child, even as a stepmother. In the 1970s servicewomen fought for and won the right to have families and to receive the same military benefits for them as servicemen for their families. Pregnant soldier is no longer an oxymoron, but a fact of military life: the pregnant servicewoman may choose to stay or to leave, provided that she has not incurred a service obligation by accepting an enlistment bonus or specialized training or education and that she is not considered essential.

But incorporating 220,000 mostly young women into an organization of 2,000,000 mostly young men has raised other questions. Can serviceman husband and servicewoman wife be stationed together? What kinds of work can a pregnant soldier do? Who looks after the children when both parents are deployed, or when father or mother is a single parent? How much do a husband and family hinder a servicewoman's career? Servicewomen, like civilian women, struggle with these questions.

"Being single has been an advantage. I don't have to go home and deal with a child or husband."

Some ambitious servicewomen decide to travel further by traveling alone. "Marriage is not in my plan," said a black staff sergeant from a family of ten. "There are so many things that I want to do, I really don't have time. It's hard enough trying to get your education, to prepare myself for that next step. I have no hang-ups. If I get married, it'll come. My friends say, 'God, you're going to be too old for it.' I always kid them: 'I'm going to be rich when I get old. So if push comes to shove I'll go out and buy me a gigolo, and send him to school. If I'm too old to have kids, I'll just go and adopt a few. There's really no problem.' "

Others settle for monogamous but temporary relationships: when orders come they are free to move on to fresh woods and pastures new. "Right now I'm kind of going out with somebody that I like quite a bit. It's just a temporary thing. It's companionship at the time. You know that you both can be gone. It's not that I would like to say 'See you later.' It's just that I know what's going to happen. That way my feelings won't get hurt if I don't let it affect me and I keep up that attitude. It's not easy to do."

Still others choose to wait. So with a black soldier: "You don't hear me talking about marriage. I'm nineteen years old. I meet guys—all of them I've met, if they're my age, they are living only for today. Tomorrow's not promised, true, but why not save two dollars if you have five? They only want to go out and party and drink all the time, and see how many girls they can get wrapped around their wrists and fall in love with them. They want to ride in my car and lean back and play Mr. Cool, and I really don't have time for it."

"Oh, the military is very very good at matchmaking. Especially if they stick you in a place like Kodiak, Alaska."

Military life, if anything, increases pressures to marry. The recruit, typically somewhere between the ages of eighteen and twenty-three, enters a world populated largely by the young, and increasingly by families. She meets and works with far more men than women. Out from under the parental roof, liberated from the restrictions of the drill instructor and basic training, on their own for the first time, a good many young servicemembers decide to wed—hence the notorious "tech school marriages." Tech school, where for a few weeks to a year new servicemembers study the skills of their MOSs, immediately follows basic training. "Famous tech school marriages: think you're in love because you're away from home, you find companionship. Guys come in, it's the first time they've been away from home, they find a girl who shows a little interest. Bingo! They get married. Two months later they're divorced."

"I really shouldn't have gotten married back then," an intelligence analyst reflected. "I don't think I was ready. All it did was complicate my life. By the time I'd get home I was ready to go to bed. I wasn't ready to cook somebody's supper." "If you join the military," says an airman first class with an eight-week-old child, "put off getting married, having a family, until you are sure of what you want. It changes your priorities. To be able to do a good job and know exactly where you're going, you need to be a single person. You're thinking of only yourself. What are you going to do? What can you do for the Air Force? The job I'm in now calls for a lot of temporary duty, thirty, forty-five days, in a lot of different countries. I would find it to be a problem to leave my family for that long a period, especially my little girl. I did not join the Air Force to get married. I don't regret it. But sometimes I wish I would have waited."

"No. No children. Other women are going to hate me for this, but you've got to dedicate your life. You can't be dedicated to the Navy and children."

"Marriage is enough family right there!"

"When my child grows up and they say 'Your mamma wears combat boots,' it would not be a joke!"

Some servicewomen postpone having children, sometimes indefinitely. 'No children, just our careers, you know,' says a senior airman in munitions maintenance. 'Maybe someday we'll fit in children. It just doesn't fit the military. We move too much. It slows you down. You lose years, 'cause you're out, and get out of the swing of things. We have chemical hazards that if I was to get pregnant in my career field, I would immediately go behind a desk, so I would lose a year. I would lose skill and knowledge and I'd have to regain all that. That's a big loss."

"It took a lot of convincing of me as far as having children," said a tech sergeant in the Air Force. "I wanted a child, and I was so scared to have a child in the military. What if we did go remote? Extended TDYs [temporary duty assignments]—like last year my husband and I were in Florida for sixty-five days; the baby couldn't go. What if my husband and I are separated for a year because of assignments?"

And of course children do hamper ambitions. As a tech sergeant said of her lack of time for the education she needs to advance: "I work all day. I come home, I cook dinner, do the kids' homework with them.

They're in bed by eight, and Mommy is tired. Then I do the laundry or whatever else I may have to do. I really don't have much time for myself. It was something that I decided: I wanted a career, and I wanted children. I'm not really saying that I'm suffering for it. I love my kids. But if I had it to do all over again, I think I would have waited for children."

Many women resolve the dilemma by leaving the service. A captain has made up her mind: "Right now we're not planning to have any children. But if we would change our minds, that would be it: I'd be out of the Marine Corps. A lot of my contemporaries who have had families have gotten out. Captain X of course has a little five-month-old. I don't envy her, because she's got three jobs: she's got the Marine Corps; she's got [being] a mother and a wife."

> *"Some of us are hardcore: there's a lot of females now, whether they be married or not, with children, and they're sticking with it, and I give 'em a hand."*

But other servicewomen believe that, like their spouses and male colleagues, they are entitled to both the human relationships that families provide *and* a military career. Hormones, social pressures, and the example of the many military mothers triumph over doubts and fears. As a financial management officer put it, a bit wistfully, "I don't think it would be a problem doing both, being in the military and being a mother. It would be what my husband was doing [combining career and parenthood]." "For me there wasn't even an option when I found I was pregnant," an airman first class in the security police told us. "I was going to stay in, no matter what. I guess it was the way I was brought up. Don't depend on anybody to do for you. You've got two arms and two legs and you can go out there and do for yourself. I've always believed that. And I'll get my daughter to believe that too!"

Naturally servicewomen face the same problems as other American working women with families—the same strains and stresses of managing a household and raising children with no full-time homemaker, the frets and fatigues of doing two jobs at once, and the frustrations of the conflicting demands of two careers. Military single parents share the worries, problems, cares of civilian single parents. But military life exacerbates some of these difficulties and causes still others.

MILITARY DEMANDS VERSUS FAMILY NEEDS

"You go, 'Honey I've got duty tonight. I won't be home.' 'You just had duty the other night.' I go to work and I'm always in the cockpit with a male crew chief and a male pilot; there's me and the guys. A lot of men can't handle their wives' being the only female in the platoon."

"I'm on a tugboat. We work very long hours and different hours. I don't know when I'm going to lose my baby-sitter, when she's going to say 'I've had it. I'm tired of you bringing baby over at four o'clock, three o'clock in the morning.' "

"They feel like you're neglecting them because you're devoting this time to the military. I'm the one that's sworn in. It's my fanny that's going to go down if I get in trouble, not his."

Understanding the problems specific to servicewomen who are wives and/or mothers requires some knowledge of the military subculture. The hours are many and unpredictable. The scheduled "duty day" itself is often long: even though the hours actually spent working may not exceed those of most civilians (although they frequently do), the servicewoman must often report early for physical training, stand formation, and clean up before work. Her duty day is frequently extended without warning. Given a shortage of personnel, new people to train, or an impending inspection—frequent phenomena in the military workplace—the servicewoman may not return home from her job until fourteen hours or more after she has left it. Her gung-ho superior may suddenly decide that no one leaves until a project is complete—and the superior need fear neither the servicewoman's union nor her resignation.

Additional duties multiply. The enlisted member may regularly stand charge of quarters overnight. She may have a "war" assignment for which she practices irregularly, perhaps flying to Alaska with a box of tools and spare parts for which she is responsible. Every officer expects a number of additional assignments—voting affairs officer, equal opportunity officer, protocol officer—and social demands proliferate as her career advances. Whatever her rank, the servicewoman must respond to alerts, which sometimes come in the middle of the night.

Whether or not her job necessitates regular travel—and many do—

the servicewoman must anticipate extended periods away from home. She may be sent on a field problem—a week or two of war games in the woods. She may go to the National Training Center in the western desert for ten days of maneuvers. If she does well, she will intermittently spend a few weeks or months away at schools learning new skills. She may deploy to the Middle East for six months of temporary duty.

Every three or four years, when a new assignment sends her to a different station, the servicewoman and her family must cope with the major upheaval of moving. They may most dread the remote, usually a one-year assignment to which she is not expected to take her family, because conditions are primitive or dangerous. "Once I get unpregnant," said an Army staff sergeant, "I'll be going overseas someplace. Let's hope it's where I can take my family too. They play with pregnant women. Two months after they have the baby, they're sending them someplace. Some of them don't let you take the baby with you. If I have to, I trust my husband to take care of my baby for a year if I have to go overseas." An airman told us of her husband's worries about remotes: "Right now our daughter is eleven months old, and if one of us was to pull a remote out of a hat, how would she feel about the one that left when they got back? He's really worried about that. In a way I am too. But I feel as long as she's got one of us with her, as long as they don't say, 'Sue, you go to this one, and Jim, you go to this one, and Patty, you go to Grandma's,' I think she'll be okay."

"Which is more important, Uncle Sam or my family?"

Psychological stresses accompany these practical exigencies. The military life-style affects the whole family. Above all, the military asserts the primacy of its own demands—though, this being the United States, not without having to listen to contradiction from servicepeople. "You're a soldier (Marine, sailor, airman . . .) first," the military constantly tells the servicewoman. "The needs of the Army (Marine Corps, Navy, Air Force, Coast Guard) come first."

Servicewomen often disagree, without mincing words. "I'm not married to the service. I'm married to my husband. That's where my priorities lie, with my family." "I had a first sergeant that told me my kid comes second to the Army," fumed a black sergeant, "and I got a counseling statement [a written reprimand], 'cause I told him, 'Nobody comes before my son but God!' "

A Marine Corps captain debated with herself: "You really get into that problem of what is more important. I do have to accept the fact that I am a Marine twenty-four hours a day. I used to say 'The Marine Corps first all the time.' But it's a little bit tricky. My husband too—it's real funny how he's reacting to it. He's still a professional Marine, but I can tell that the baby is becoming more important to him than anything else. It's a challenge." "Your life does change," agrees an Air Force sergeant. "My husband and I are pretty dedicated. We're very mission-orientated. Work comes first. Going in on your day off, that meant nothing to us. Now for me it has to take a back seat—not totally, but a little bit. That's sort of hard for me. But we do have something else to think about now."

Protest as they may, servicewomen know that they must go where they are sent and do what they are told, providing as best they can for their families. "I'll tell you the one thing that really bothers me about going to Germany—I'm scared for my kids, with all the demonstrations and stuff going on over there. No matter whether I take 'em or not, I'm going to be over there three years, and my husband's going too. I have had this thing going over my mind, about leaving 'em here. You think about this. All these soldiers, dependents, and their kids in this one little country, and only so many exit points. Can you imagine the panic state they're going to be in, all trying to get out? And mine can't even . . . they're little. And most of the civilian wives that I know have three children already that they've got to handle, and I'm trying to palm my two off on 'em? When I get called at four o'clock in the morning to go to an alert, I would rest a little bit easier in my mind knowing that mine are already across the water and are safe. When that guy that outranks me says, 'Here's your weapon; go,' I don't want to be thinking about if my kids are all right."

PREGNANCY AND CHILDBIRTH

But if the service, a jealous god, taketh away, it also giveth. If the servicewoman and her family have to face special difficulties, they also reap benefits. Impelled by concern for its personnel, a desire for improved retention, and a number of court cases, the military helps its families cope.

While their situation falls far short of the ideal, American military women fare better than most of their civilian sisters in maternity leaves, guaranteed jobs after childbirth, and child-care facilities. The servicewoman may wish she had more time to recuperate and to bond with her new baby, but she can count on four weeks off *and* a job to which to return, without loss of rank, seniority, or pay. Her doctor can lengthen her disability leave. And if her job and her boss permit, she may save up leave time beforehand so that she can extend her time at home after her baby is born: "As soon as I found out I was expecting the baby, I had to stockpile my leave. I got close to sixty days, plus the thirty days of sick leave, but I only ended up getting two months off 'cause my boss wanted me back. I didn't feel real good about it. I thought the baby was a little bit too young. And I needed more time."

Servicemen's complaints about the special treatment of women's getting leave after the birth of a baby ring loud; indeed some servicewomen believe that the length of this leave, formerly six weeks, was shortened because of male complaints. Women point out that even allowing for pregnancy and leave after the birth of a baby, servicewomen lose less time from work than servicemen. "My neighbor, bless his heart, he's a real good guy, but he's always complaining about his pregnant WAVES [anachronism for Naval women], and I just say, 'Well, George, I see a lot of cases that come in on discipline [for misconduct] and they're mostly on men.' " "The men have to understand," says an Air Force tech sergeant. "They go to the hospital to have their appendix out, and they get four weeks' convalescent leave. I have a young guy that cut his hand severely; he had three weeks, and it was just his hand. I don't agree with them when they start complaining."

And an Air Force lieutenant remarked in irritation, "I would put some of my women up against five good guys. They're always there. Don't have the least problem: AWOL, sickness. So they get pregnant; they're usually right back after their four weeks. I've known guys to play football; they banged up their knees and were in the hospital for six months."

The lieutenant's point was ironically proved years ago, as Captain Patricia Gormley (USN) recalls: "When I was at the Justice School at Newport, I had my first child. They were just in the process really of changing the rules: instead of being automatically discharged, you could stay on active duty with the approval of your department. Of course you had to use your own leave, and they didn't have maternity uniforms. I didn't teach a normal schedule, because they were afraid that I would have the baby in the middle of one of the courses, so I had a lot of the short schedules. Plus we had a lot of the men out sick or injured that summer. One instructor got hurt playing football, and another broke his leg some other way. I was reasonably healthy, so I would show up at the other schools in normal clothes, very pregnant, and say, 'I'm Commander Gormley, and I'm here to teach the course in nonjudicial punishment for your surface warfare officers.' They would just look at me. 'Who is this large creature who comes in claiming to be a Naval officer and is so clearly pregnant? Somebody's playing a joke on us.' Yet they were too polite to indicate that, and they'd show me into the classroom, and I'd start teaching. I ended up teaching more hours than the other folks—which was fine. I was in very good health and did not have to leave until the baby was born, and the men seemed to be having all these disability problems."

> *"Oh, [having a baby is] so cheap! It's so cheap! $35.85 is a lot better than about $3,000."*

The servicewoman will not lose pay, even if her doctor puts her on profile (limits the kind of work she may do) because of her pregnancy. And having her baby will cost her much less than a civilian, whatever the difficulties of her pregnancy or the length of time she stays in the hospital. "While I was in Germany I became pregnant by my first husband [with whom she already had a son]. By the time I found out I was pregnant with triplets, we had split up. I went to the hospital, because I went in labor at four months. They took me to Frankfurt, Germany, in a helicopter, then back to Nuremberg, then one more time back to Frankfurt, to medevac [evacuate for medical reasons] me back to Washington. I stayed at Walter Reed from September to January. I had a choice: either keep on with the medicine and try and prevent having the babies [prematurely], have a heart attack, may not live, when I have another son that I've got to take care of—or take my chances with the babies coming out. So I took a chance on them coming out and being okay. I took me a day to make that decision. The chances of them living weren't very high anyway. But they all made it. They're sixteen months old now. One of 'em stayed in the hospital for close to seven months, and the other two were at home at about three and four months. Let the women know, when they go to a military hospital, don't let them think that they don't have to pay any bills. For one bill it was nine hundred dollars; for another bill it was seven hundred dollars; for one it was way over a thousand dollars. For an E-1 to E-4, that's quite a bit of money." A lot of money indeed for a young single parent—she was twenty-one when she talked to us. But the financial hardships that would befall a civilian mother so situated don't bear thinking about.

> *"As a matter of fact, I was pregnant, wearing orthodontic braces, and was selected Sailor of the Year. I was kind of embarrassed, standing in front of the admiral, getting my plaque. I felt a little silly, but I still was proud of myself. I've even got pictures in my daughter's album of Mommy making Sailor of the Year while pregnant with her."*

> *"My daughter has two [parachute] jumps. When I was pregnant I jumped twice. Yeah, she's got two jumps on her daddy. No, the Army didn't know I was pregnant. Not by far. I told them after that and they about had a conniption."*

Most military women work almost to the day they deliver. Often the military alters assignments to make the situation a little safer for the prospective mother, but many women take pride in having performed their regular tasks throughout their nine months. Some women protest not being allowed to do their regular jobs. "Right now I'm grounded," a helicopter pilot said. "I think that's an area that very little research has been done in, is pregnant aviators and their ability to fly. I feel I am capable of flying. At times, you know, when I'm feeling well. I think someone's put a stamp down and said that pregnancy does not correspond with flying. I just don't think there's been enough research."

A twenty-one-year-old insisted that the Army regimen improved her experience of pregnancy. "The two children that I had before I came in the service were both premature babies. I guess I just was bored and I didn't get out and do any exercise. Now I'm in really good physical shape, and I've carried the baby, no problems. I feel fantastic. I still did PT, up until they told me 'You're not doin' PT no more.' 'Cause it makes me feel relaxed. You run to be a road-guard [a servicemember who runs ahead of her unit to stop traffic while troops march through an intersection, and then runs to catch up with the unit], and if I've fallen out to do that, the sergeant says, 'No, thanks. What's the matter with you? You know you can't run.' I say, 'My goodness, I'm pregnant, not handicapped.' "

"The maternity uniform is not out yet, the BDU, battle-dress uniform, but they are coming out with it."

"The first thing the men think is if you're a female you're going to try to get over [get out of work]. No matter what. Pregnant or not. But the men tend to be really rough on pregnant women."

"Pregnancy—oh, God. I went through it here—it's like, 'You didn't have to get pregnant.' "

Pregnancy in the military is not without tears and trials. The incredible difficulties the military services have entangled themselves in to provide women with uniforms show up once again when servicewomen have babies. We read in a military newspaper on subtropical Okinawa the complaints of a woman for whom the only available maternity uniforms were made of wool. That was in 1981, but in a 1985 Stateside interview we heard: "Just thank goodness I'm getting pregnant here where I will be getting big in the summertime, because they don't have any jackets for us yet."

And pregnant women put up with all sorts of reactions. "It's interesting how certain men will treat pregnant women," says a Marine captain. "I have a girlfriend, a lawyer, and her immediate boss was very sympathetic when she had to knock off, because his wife had had a very difficult pregnancy. But the boss above him thought she was just taking advantage." And a black soldier talked about a post where "They were giving the pregnant females a hard time. They can't force the woman out of the service, but the remarks she has to accept from her superiors: 'Oh, well, she can't do nothin' because she's pregnant.' You know the tone of voice. They brought a pregnant female out to the field. The other females had to cover for her, say 'No, you cannot. . . .' An E-6 might have to go and tell her supervisor, 'Why did you tell her to dig a foxhole? You know she's pregnant.' "

And an Army E-5 cited her own experience during pregnancy: "Those parachutes I was telling about, the cargo chutes? They're two hundred fifty pounds; you're supposed to have four people carry those. Our squad leader would leave me alone to set those up for inspections. I had to haul 'em out, get 'em out of the bags, set 'em up in proper layout."

> *"You're going to fall down at home as easy as you are in a motor pool. Drop Crisco on the floor at home, you're going to slide, and if you step in grease at the motor pool, you're going to slide."*

A supervisor in an air passenger terminal, herself delivered three months earlier of a son, looked at pregnancy as a worker and as a manager: "Being pregnant in the military is really wild. Some people are totally protective and do not let you do anything. I took the place of a male supervisor on swing shift, our busiest shift. One of the airmen was pregnant while he was there, and all she did was dispatch for nine months, and all the guys, all they did was moan and groan—so unfair. That's why you get those attitudes, when the women don't do anything because of this protection. I have a young airman; she just had her baby yesterday. [Until then] she drove. She worked the counter. She processed passengers. No, she did not work any baggage. And the guys were very happy. I would never put a pregnant woman in something that might be dangerous. The guys understand that. But yet, the pregnant women do work, and the guys like that.

"I worked. I was pregnant during our ORI, our Operation Readiness Inspection last summer. I'm the NCOIC responsible for processing all the troops, giving them their briefings, getting them out to the aircraft. So I was down in the hangar for fourteen, sixteen hours a day y'know while I was pregnant. I wasn't tired. I wasn't overextended or anything. I did just fine. The guys' big thing was 'Don't have it during the ORI!' I didn't. So yes, women can function pregnant. Sure they can."

Another supervisor, a staff sergeant, described how she urges pregnant women to think about what they can do: " 'You got to decide where to draw the line, Sally Sue. What do you think you can do, and how can you benefit me? I got a mission every day.' I let them give me an opinion. And then I'll think about what I need done. I don't think a person should put in their mind, 'Oh, Sally Sue's pregnant. She's got to work behind a desk.' Bullshit. I worked down in the motor pool, and I was pregnant. I was crawling in and out from under trucks."

SUPPORT SYSTEMS

> *"Women are going to continue to have babies! That's not going to stop, whether they're in the military or not! And they should be afforded the personal help that the Air Force provides in all other factors."*
>
> *"She just had a baby. Her husband went to sea for six months, about a month ago. She works eight to eight during the day, or eight to eight at night, so it costs her about $400 to $500 a month for a baby-sitter."*

Child-care facilities are far from free, they never seem to have enough spaces for all the children who need them, and they are never open long enough (even though some stay open twelve hours a day and take babies as young as three weeks). With servicepeople subject to call at any of the twenty-four hours, child-care centers need to be open twice around the clock—but seldom are. "How do I manage being a mother and a soldier? Right now, not very well. My husband's stationed up at another post, and so I'm a geographic single parent. We have to come in sometimes like four in the morning for a road march; day care doesn't open until quarter after six. I have to find another baby-sitter until it opens. We work till eight sometimes, and the day care closes at six, so I have to find another baby-sitter for after, and I never know when we're going to work late until about three, four o'clock."

Many servicewomen rely on civilian service wives, often with children of their own, who will take in an additional child or two. Understanding military demands, they will usually pitch in at odd hours or on short notice, or keep a child overtime.

As usual, RHIP: rank has its privileges. Officers and senior noncoms can afford to hire enough help—even a full-time housekeeper. A pregnant Army helicopter pilot talked of "hiring nannies for a year . . . students who want to continue their education but don't have the money." But the nineteen-year-old sole-parent corporal, or one whose spouse is posted far away, usually must depend on makeshift networks.

Assignment abroad may complicate or ease the situation, depending on the local traditions and economy. In the Far East reliable mamasans (maids) are relatively easy to find; in Germany their equivalents are scarce and expensive.

Military parents must arrange beforehand for the emergency care of their children for periods of up to a year. "They came out with this thing where you had to make out a power of attorney for this person [the care giver] and you have to sign this paper every year saying that this person here will take care of your child while you're gone. It's a bummer."

Bummer or not, it's hard to see how the military could function without such assurance. As a staff sergeant explained, "I think it's basically because in the past there were people who didn't have arrangements until the last minute, and I was one of them. They called me one morning and said, 'We're leaving in three hours. Get ready to go.' I was frantic. Fortunately a neighbor said, 'Don't be silly. I'll take care of her.' I said, 'I can't ask you to do this.' She said, 'Don't be stupid. Bring her stuff downstairs. Sign a letter or whatever for [authorizing] medical treatment. And go.' That's why the Air Force want this done, because there were problems. Showing up for an alert with a child doesn't go over well. I did that once myself, years ago. I couldn't find anyone, and I packed her up and took her in with me. They frowned on that quite greatly."

The babies' grandmothers, aunts, even grandfathers and uncles figure largely in these arrangements, especially when they're for protracted absences—a year on a remote or three months at sea. A black intelligence analyst on her way to Okinawa planned for her son to stay "with my parents for a year. He's the first grandson and they're spoiling him to death." "I have an uncle that doesn't work, so every time I go out to sea, he comes down and watches my little boy for me." The divorcée may rely on her child's father. Thus with a keenly ambitious Air Force tech sergeant: "It works out real well. My children are nine and eleven. When I go overseas, they stay with their daddy. Of course, me and their father have a real good understanding. He's a civilian. I've been overseas several times for a year at a time, and there's no problems. It's great. I can do what I want and he can do what he wants."

Equally important to servicewomen with families as childbearing and child-care provisions are the Joint Spouse (Joint Domicile, Joint Household) programs. Although they vary slightly from service to service, all these programs are designed to station together military members married to each other, or at least assign them to the same geographical area. Their task used to be simple. But with more women entering the service, the number of servicewoman/serviceman marriages increasing, and more married women remaining on active duty, difficulties in joint assignments multiply. The programs generally try to assign couples no more than fifty miles apart, so that they can live midway and each commute twenty-five miles to work, or at worst visit each other on weekends. If they must be separated farther, the plans try to limit the separation to a year. Their technique is to link married servicemembers on the computer, so that when either spouse comes up for reassignment the other's name flashes onscreen.

How well does the plan work? Much better, of course, for intra-service than interservice couples. "Yes, being in different services did create a problem," said an Air Force tech sergeant. "Through channels I would go to CBPO [Consolidated Base Personnel Office]. I'd give the paperwork to the clerk, and he said, 'Isn't an Air Force person good enough for you? Did you have to marry someone in the Army?' And I would never hear anything about my orders. Finally I had to go see my congressman and I got my orders within two days."

"My ex-spouse was sent to Thailand right after we were married, six months. I couldn't think of it as a marriage, because of the breakup so early."

"I got an assignment overseas and my husband couldn't go; because he's a loadmaster, there's only two bases that he can go to, Dover and Travis."

The effectiveness of the Joint Spouse program differs from service to service: the Air Force claims an 85-percent success rate, and probably no other service exceeds that or does as well. A critical factor in any service is the compatibility of the spouses' MOSs. If their jobs are compatible—if one of them, for example, has a skill needed everywhere—their assignment together is easier. Otherwise they may have a hard time—like a parachute rigger married to a NAP, Non-Airborne Personnel—someone who is highly motivated but doesn't jump (as distinct from a leg, who is neither airborne nor motivated): "My husband had to go to a post where there's nobody that jumps, so there's no way I could go there. He can't come down here either. This is the closest

I could get, and now he's got assignment to Italy, and I can't go there either. We've been separated a year already. If he goes to Italy and I keep our daughter, he'll be there for two years. If he takes her, he'll be over there for three years. I'm going to try to change jobs if I have to. I'll do anything to get orders to go with him. We knew when we got married we could be split, but we've pulled our twelve months. We'd like to get back together. We need to."

Efficacy may vary also from rank to rank: some Coast Guard officers say that the program works well for them but less well for their enlisted couples. On the other hand, the higher the rank, the more difficult it becomes to assign husband and wife together: there simply aren't that many slots at any one post for Navy captains or Army colonels, or for two first shirts (sergeants in charge of personnel welfare).

The success of the plan also varies with the political skills and flexibility of the married couples. If the couple develop their own options and present a number of viable choices, or if they will accept unpopular assignments, they greatly improve their chances of being posted together. "They try not to step on each other's career. One of 'em gets transferred, the other one volunteers for assignment, and they offer options. This guy's wife got sent to Maxwell as an instructor. So he offered to go to Maxwell as a T-39 pilot; to Columbus as an instructor-pilot; or to Eglin, to fly something, or to Dobbins. He gave 'em all the options, and they sent him to Maxwell." "A lot of people cry and bitch and get out of the Army, but if you make a few phone calls, do the paperwork and do what they say, and you just have a lot of patience, it will happen. Sometimes. The majority of the time."

And some couples, especially officers, simply accept the trade-offs of separations for career advancement. "When we got married back in April of '79," a Marine Corps captain told us, "my husband had orders to Guam. How many organizations are there on Guam? Not many. They had no billet for me. So we spent our first eighteen months separated." "We've been coming and going like two ships in the night. This is the first time in almost three years that we've had a break—there's been a lull in the storm." "We both realize that I'm career-oriented, he's career-oriented, so there are going to be times when we're going to be separated."

Enlisted people too endure separations for the sake of their careers. "Before we even agreed to get married," said a hull maintenance technician's mate, "he understood that my career came first, and his too. Separations are the worst part. If it comes to a choice between accepting separation for the sake of my career or my marriage, I'd go for my career, 'cause the career is a lasting thing. The separation's going to be six months, a year. If we love each other, we should be able to make it through that. Where a year in my career may make me a chief or a senior chief or something like that. It's worth the sacrifice. We agreed to that."

But the failure of a Joint Spouse program can endanger a marriage. "I know someone right now: he's been on remote tours for years. And his wife is overseas. They hardly see one another. It has come to the point now where their career has to end or their marriage. Neither one of 'em wants to give up their career. So I guess the marriage is. . . ."

"If I have any spurs in my saddle it's over the single issue in the military. I think the single people are very much discriminated against."

The family-support programs produce side effects for single women. "Where does the Navy draw the line on trying to station husbands and wives together?" asks Captain Julie DiLorenzo. "The poor single woman, enlisted or officer, can't get to San Diego, for example. There are limited opportunities for women at major fleet concentrations anyway, because fleet activities are still very much dominated by men. But if that's where the husbands are, then that's where the wives are going to be stationed. We're only now beginning to see the magnitude of the problem. It's really getting tight. The single woman has just as much right to get stationed in San Diego or wherever as a married woman—but no one is paying attention to her. Where do you stop being 'fair' to the married woman and start being fair to the single woman?" Single people, who "have no use for a lot of the facilities that are geared toward the Navy family," can't help feeling some envy when they hear about "The Year of the Family," when they see their single-parent peers given housing allowances or permitted to live on base in comfortable apartments or houses while they themselves are required to live in a crowded barracks room, often with people they don't enjoy.

Families can also turn to the relatively new Family Support Centers. On many military bases these exist only as uncoordinated bits and pieces: a volunteer group here, the chaplain's office there, and an inadequate child-care center. The most advanced centers are state-of-the-art, staffed by professional counselors, who assist military families in every imaginable way, from certifying baby-sitters sane and nonsadistic and locating housing to marital counseling and parenting education. They provide an umbrella for the official and volunteer organizations that help families in times of stress. A single parent with four children who received no cash from the Army for a year, because she was repaying Army loans, survived by grace of a moonlighting civilian job and help from Army Community Service. "Well, when I got here I didn't have any furniture. ACS gave me three cribs. They gave me clothes. They gave me diapers. I'm stubborn but I didn't mind taking help from them, because I support them, and in turn when the kids grew out of clothes and grew out of their cribs, I gave 'em back. They gave me three brand-new high chairs. I didn't turn 'em down—they cost too much!"

MARRIAGES: MILITARY WOMAN/CIVILIAN HUSBAND

> *"My husband encouraged me. He said, 'Well, it's something that you want to do. You're doing it for all of us.' Which is true. I think if the woman decides to come in, the husband should make sure, absolutely one hundred ten–percent positive, that he wants her to be in."*

Of all military marriages, the "mixed marriage" between military woman and civilian man most challenges tradition, for the demands of a military career deny the wife flexibility: she exerts only limited control over when, where, and how long she works. She probably can't escape a geographical move every three or four years. Are the couple to reverse conventional roles, the husband holding perhaps a part-time job, supported by his wife? Or changing jobs every time she moves? Or their accepting separations by reasons of their jobs?

Former military husbands adapt more easily, because they understand the military. "My husband pushes me a lot. He says, 'If you want E-4, you've got to shine your boots up.' He helps out. I don't think I'd stay in if I didn't have him to help me." A retired serviceman in particular, with twenty years of service under his belt, knowing that he is contributing financially through his military pension, may enjoy acting as mentor and role model in the development of his wife's career. He still may be only thirty-eight or forty years old, but, as a young Coast Guard officer told us, "After twenty years of bouncing around in the service and on ships—my husband's got almost twelve years sea duty—it's a welcome change for some of these guys."

Some military/military couples even decide that the husband should leave the service and the wife remain in. "I told my husband, I says, 'You've done your time. You're going to have to get out.' He's a lot of push behind what I've decided to do." "If he hadn't married me he would have stayed in. We both wanted him to get out, 'cause if both of us had gotten deployed it was going to be a real hard time having kids. He's home at night and I know he's going to pick up the mail, water the plants, make sure that the pipes don't freeze, and when we have kids he'll be able to pick 'em up from the sitters, et cetera. He can make more money on the outside than I can. He's the smarter of us two. Oh, yeah, I'll make a career in the Army. Twenty years. Then I can go home and bake cookies and have twelve kids and a picket fence."

> *"My husband is a civilian. He's in retail management. He turned down a job in Virginia after graduation to follow his wife. As a result he had to do a lot of hitting the pavement. He had to accept a job initially just to put the money in his pocket."*

All civilian husbands, with or without military experience, face job problems. The man who can work anywhere is rare. "If he is an accountant with an established firm and he has tenure," said a tech sergeant, "and you say 'Listen, you need to quit your job because we're going to go to Alaska,' chances are that's not going to go over real well." A Marine officer cited the experience of her bunkmate from OCS: "Her husband was a photographer, free-lance. He is in North Carolina with her, and there's just not a lot of work for a free-lance who's worked in New York City before. He wasn't happy following her around, being a dependent. And they split."

The civilian husband who tries to find a new job whenever his wife is moved is almost bound at some time to face a long period of unemployment and to accept a lesser job than the one he left. "My husband works for the Auto Hobby Shop part time," a pregnant sergeant told us. "He's in between jobs." Such a husband may find himself regretting the job he left; his wife may find herself scheming to put a little money in his pocket without embarrassing him. Overseas the job-hunting husband faces a language barrier and legal restrictions. A black lieutenant told us about her husband's difficult choices: "I'm trying to get an assignment to Athens. My husband changes from day to day. Right now he's in the mind that he's going to go, 'cause he wants to travel. But he also doesn't want to end his career. We've already decided: the little one will go with me. That's going to be a tough decision for my husband."

Social pressures as well as job problems inflict stress on the civilian husband. "I know when we were first married a lot of his friends would razz him. People just don't seem to understand." Even a wife may come to resent her husband's still-unusual role: "He didn't really have anything to do in Germany, and he began playing around, so I shipped him home." A sailor said flatly of the civilian husband, "He's lost. We had one of the young lieutenants. Her husband was really an outsider, because he was Austrian, and he had no job at all, and he had that stigma of being a dependent, which even women are resenting these days."

The nonveteran civilian husband finds himself a stranger in the military world. At social functions he remains an outsider, watching his wife join easily in the conversations of the men with whom she works and with whom she shares a common language, common interests, and her days. "We met at college," began a soldier. "I was with him for five years before we decided to get married. We talked about me going to the military, and he said, 'Well, that'll be fine.' Wherever I went, he would come. When we got to my first duty station, I was working nights, weekends, pulling CQ [charge of quarters]. We only had three dispatchers; we would have to close up shop at four-thirty and go back around eight or nine, be on deck when those planes come back. He started to accuse me of messing around with everybody. I said, 'Well, look, you can't go by rumor control. Everybody's going to talk about you no matter what.' The fact was that I had to put a little bit more effort into the military than he could handle. He wanted me to get out on a hardship. Said no. We decided it would be better for both of us to split."

Civilian husbands confront daily reminders that they are outsiders. Like all spouses of military members, they are often called "dependents."

In government housing, the servicemember's name is always above the door as sponsor—in this case, the wife's name. The card that admits her husband to the post exchanges, clubs, and medical services is stamped "Dependent." "There've been people that have looked at his ID card, and said, 'Gee, aren't you kind of old to be a dependent son?' And he goes, 'Well, I'm not a dependent son. I'm a dependent husband.' "

Some couples, who think of husband and wife both as financially responsible and assess opportunities evenly, emphasize the benefits the military can confer. Her husband "doesn't really want me to get out," an Army staff sergeant with eleven years in told us, "because we've got too many years involved. He said, 'You can get a retirement check in twenty.' My husband's my dependent; but he's a very smart guy. I think it's hard for him, because I make more money, but he just says it would be senseless for me to get out and go into something where I have to work thirty years [to get a pension]."

Some civilian male spouses are sure enough of themselves to put their wives' careers first, deliberately and wholeheartedly. Their wives invariably praise them highly. "I've talked to a lot of women, and I find that my husband, Bob, is unique. He's been willing to sacrifice more than I think anybody else probably would have. I got pregnant right off when we were married . . . yes, I meant to, because he really likes children and so do I. Since the birth of our first child he has opted to work a night shift so he could be home during the day. We've had some real rough spots, because just tension gets high and you get tired of not seeing each other. Seeing the way the girls are, as compared with other people's children who are in day care, it's been well worth it. Sometimes I feel a little left out, because I don't spend as much time with them as he does. But I think it's working out real well. I've got an assignment to Germany. Bob hasn't decided whether he wants to work there; there'll be so much to see that he might benefit from just taking the girls places. But I think he's unique. If you sit back and look at it, he has sacrificed a lot."

"No, my husband is not in the Navy," Captain Louise Wilmot said. "He was enlisted in the Navy, but I met him after he had left. He was working for the *Army Times* Publishing Company when I met him. I was twenty-nine and he was thirty, and we understood what we were doing. My husband is an extraordinary man. We discussed whose career was going to take precedence, and he said, 'I know you love the Navy. I believe that you're going to go far in the Navy. It will be your Navy career that will set the pace for what we do.'

"He has moved when I have moved. He has always been able to find a job, wherever we've gone. But it's difficult for him, because he is the one who has to send out the résumés. He's the one who has to go out on the job interviews. And usually by the time we leave someplace he's reached the top, only to find himself back on the bottom when we move. I told him that he's just a better person than I'd ever make, because I don't think I could handle every three years going out and interviewing and being told 'Well, you have a very nice résumé, but we really don't have any place for you.'

"My husband has a very good idea of who he is. He doesn't have hang-ups. He's not insecure. He's just a man in his own right. For him and for me, this is the way to do it. There's no controversy between the two of us, and so sometimes we're more than a little annoyed and surprised when people ask us the rudest questions. We have had wives say to my husband, 'How can you afford to do it?' His standard reply is 'Well, I'm filthy rich and it doesn't matter.' That's the only way to handle a stranger who asks you such a personal question after they've had a couple of drinks."

MARRIAGES: MILITARY WOMAN/MILITARY HUSBAND

> *"Oftentimes women in the service will marry servicemen. Number one, it's about all we ever meet. And they understand. . . ."*
>
> *"It's easier I think than some of the guys or some of the ladies who have civilian spouses, who don't understand the terminology, who don't understand an ensign from a PFC."*
>
> *"If you marry a civilian, probably the first thing on his mind would be to get out of the military. I don't want to put myself in that kind of predicament and have to make that decision."*

Servicewomen who marry other military members generally consider themselves better off than those married to civilians. Although the possibility of separate assignments shadows their future, they can turn to the Joint Spouse program. The military husband already speaks the service language, or at least a dialect of it. And "When you marry someone who's in the Marine Corps, you've got somebody who understands why you have to spend one day out of every month babysitting a battalion, and why you have to work from zero dark thirty until whenever."

If a military husband resents his wife's absence, his own career needs, mirroring hers, soon silence his complaints. "My very first trip when he came up here," said a pilot of her pilot husband, "I was gone for ten days, and when I got back, he was fuming. He was mad that I'd take this trip. I was real tired, because when you fly across the ocean it's a nine-hour flight, and you're dragging. I was trying to explain: I'm trying to get some hours, because I want to upgrade. He really didn't understand me, until he went on his first trip. Now it's no problem. He tries to take trips when I do. And vice versa. So we can meet out in the system. On his dollar ride, which was his first trip, I met him twice in Frankfurt, which was nice."

Mutual citizenship in their closed world forms a strong bond between wife and husband. A lieutenant who worked her way up from the enlisted ranks, as did her officer husband, rejoices in their common experiences. "I couldn't imagine being married to a civilian. It's such an even flow. He understands when I need to come in and go to work at night. He understands when we have an exercise and I'm working twelve-hour shifts and I've got to be there. He understands I need this remote. He has to work his assignments, regardless of how hot or cold he is toward an assignment. Plus the flow of info. If I don't hear, usually he's heard something. We don't miss much!"

"I married the guy I loved," said a loadmaster, "and I still have him! He was the first instructor I had in the Air Force, a master sergeant at the time, and we just hit it off. Of course having the job in common helped, in understanding some of the frustrations, being able to enjoy the good things about it. Having that to talk about also; that's kind of neat. I'm glad I married another military member, now that I think about it. It's something that we take pride in. We really do, with each other's accomplishments. I think it would have been kind of weird marrying a civilian, with the image that the civilian community has about the military and where all the taxpayer money goes. Where all *our* taxpayer money goes, 'cause we all pay the taxes! All these new weapons systems we're building, and the threat of nuclear war, and all these kinds of things. I imagine that it would have been kind of awkward living with someone that had never seen it from the military point of view."

Military wives married to military husbands also compare their situations favorably to those of servicemen's civilian wives. "When Don and I PCS [make a permanent change of station], we're usually so glad to get back to work! We're ready to meet those new people. It takes so much longer for a dependent to make those connections. Especially overseas. I've seen so many divorces overseas. If they just stay in Germany out on the economy, for instance, waiting for base housing, or if they choose to live there, it's almost like isolation. Oh, geez. And the husbands sometimes that I worked with were not sympathetic at all. After a long hard day at work they go home and the wife is raising all kinds of Cain. She's been almost in isolation all day. Military to military works out tremendous."

Some couples even join the military together, because it offers them both good career opportunities. Unlike the civilian wife, the servicewoman does not have to accept whatever mangy little job presents itself near her husband's next duty station. "In 1973 we were one of the first couples to join the Air Force together," said a master sergeant. "I wanted to travel, but I was always career-oriented. I joined so I could always have a good job when I went with him." The double benefits they receive are not to be scorned. Each married spouse is entitled to a housing and a food allowance. "You each get them, y'know. So you do bring home more than you would if you married a civilian. I think monetary has a big big factor as far as military couples marrying another military."

Indeed, military women married to military men were among the happiest women who talked to us. Consider the bright young sergeant at an Air Force research base. She and her husband work in the same building and exchange shoptalk about the fascinating work each is doing: he's in optics, and she works with an engineer, creating from his plans models of the cameras he designs. No, she had never known that she had such a talent—"but I always loved to crochet and knit!" The base on which they work is singularly beautiful, set in woods and hills. At night they drive home to their condominium, with its own swimming pool; weekends they ski or camp. Her life-style delights her.

"If I was single I would stay in in a heartbeat. You know, forever."

"We had every intention of putting our twenty in, but he wants to get out now. He's got a better job. I'd like to stay in, but . . ."

"My private observation is that she makes sacrifices in her career to satisfy his, and he doesn't even have the potential that merits the sacrifice. That's something that really bothers me."

At the same time, military/military couples, like their civilian counterparts, face the problems inflicted by competition. When husband and wife work for the same employer, competition sharpens. "Why do they break up when the woman outranks the man? First of all, the male ego. The male traditionally wants to be the breadwinner. My husband was an airman first class. I was a tech sergeant. He's not the main breadwinner in the house because I make more money, even though our money went into a joint checking account. Also there's a lot of peer pressure on the male. 'Wow, that wife of yours, she's a fast-burner. Can't you keep up with her?' That does a lot to destroy a man's confidence."

Some military women, responding in the traditional way more honored in the observance than the breach, deliberately refuse to outdo their husbands. For instance—a staff sergeant has several times rejected opportunities to become an officer, mainly "because my husband has been applying for the warrant officer program and I just did not want to put my career ahead of his. In so many instances because of the jobs I've had, he has had to follow me. My chances were better, because of the type of fitness reports I'd been getting and the type of people I had worked for [a general among them]. I want to support and push him. I just could not see putting my husband behind. That's the traditional me."

"I want to be a chief warrant officer," says a Navy yeoman. "I don't really know what my husband wants to do, other than just spend his twenty years in. I'm much more ambitious than he is. Until he does retire, my career will take a back seat to his, primarily because he is in a much more specialized rate. He's an air crewman, and there are limited places where he can be stationed. I can go anywhere in the world. If we want to spend our tours together, then I have to put mine on the back burner and take lesser orders. He has told me that he doesn't particularly like that, and if I want to go do other things, he says, 'I can always get out.' I said, 'Do you really want to?' He said, 'No, not really.' I said, 'Then why are we even talking about it?' He says, 'Well, after I'm retired, if I like following you around being the military spouse. . . . If you want to go for twenty, go ahead and go for it. Go for thirty. Do it. It's not going to bother me.' "

Captain DiLorenzo worries about women's sacrifices: "The part that disturbs me is that I have seen so many couples in which she has much more career potential than he, and yet it is assumed he has the more viable career. Some of those women could write their own ticket, but they won't. They will subjugate their careers to their husbands'. When his career stagnates, it's generally too late to salvage hers. It's a shame—unless they really planned for such an eventuality. But in nine times out of ten they didn't." As a chief petty officer says, "It just kind of grates against your mind, the women's part of it."

Sometimes, instead of the woman's career, it's the marriage that gives way: "As a matter of fact we're separated right now. You always hit a point in your lives where somebody's career is going to take precedence. I felt like mine was the one that was just being put down. We were doing everything to make sure that he advanced as fast as he could and we took the duty stations that he wanted to. It ended up, he's going to stay his whole career in the Norfolk area, going back and forth from sea to shore. So I took the orders and stayed here, because of his wants and needs. But that's going to change. The big step for me was . . . I made Sailor of the Year at my command. And then went up the next step [to the next echelon] and made it there. And then went for the next step, and during that step it took four weeks of full-blown dealing with the political side of it, dealing with the Chamber of Commerce, with the Hampton area, and all the people, the news media, and you really need your spouse's support. I didn't get it. At that point I says, 'If I would have had that little bit of backing, maybe I would have gone all the way. If I could have just thought about me for that one week, maybe I'd have made Sailor of the Year up in D.C.' Oh, yes, there's a lot of competition out there. Yes, sir. I was really upset when I didn't make chief my first time up, because my husband had made it first time up. [*Laughs.*] And I knew I was just as good as he was. Yeah, there's a lot of competition."

SINGLE-PARENT FAMILIES[1]

> *"He, like, wants me to live in his shadow and his name. Till I get my identity established, I say, it'll just be me and my son. Being a single parent, it's really not easy in the military, but I've learned to deal with it, and I don't feel that I have to be married or I have to have a man."*
>
> *"It's been hard, but having a stable job has helped out. The military help a lot with the Family Services Center: they help you find a place to stay, help you learn how to manage your money, help you deal with being a single parent and having to devote all your time. Child care has been pretty good. I keep thinking, 'How would I have made it?' "*
>
> *"Single parenting in a nonconventional job doesn't work."*

Being a single parent in the military is a hard row to hoe. But it does offer job security and a range of benefits to parents who need them desperately. A thirty-four-year-old woman with eight years' service and mother of a thirteen-year-old daughter contrasted her military life with her civilian experience, running a cash register in a supermarket: "A friend just this past week said 'You have problems with your daughter sometimes. But when you think how you have come to where you are now, and what you have achieved, I would have to give you A. You've got a nice place for your daughter to stay. She's got nice things.' My daughter loves having her mother be a Marine. Every time I get promoted she brags about it: 'Oh, Mother's a corporal now! Mother's a sergeant now!' The more I achieve for myself, the more I achieve for her. I just wish I had come in sooner."

Such considerations, no doubt, have led a group of single parents to sue the military for allegedly discriminating against them by refusing to allow them to join. So far the decision has gone against the plaintiffs. Right now the military allows servicemembers who are or become single parents to stay in, but refuses to accept more, male or female—even if they are veterans. A civil service secretary at an Army post joined the Army in 1973. "I had gotten married when I was in the service. I had

[1] Single parenting in the military is by no means only a woman's problem. Indeed more military single parents are men than women—although single parenting is more frequent among military women in proportion to their numbers.

my first child in Norfolk and then I got out of the service right after she was born. I had to [because at that time the military automatically discharged any woman who became responsible for a minor child]. When my daughter was about four months old, we [my husband and I] separated and got divorced. I've worked for the government ever since I got out. Now I'd like to get back in. But you can't now. Even with the Reserves and the National Guard, which is part-time. If you're a single parent, you can't without your adopting your kids away. It's not like having a piece of paper notarized, guardianship. It's giving them away."

So attractive is the military to some single parents that they circumvent the regulation by resorting to just such clumsy and frightening stratagems. For instance: "In order to get in the Army, I had to get my son legally adopted by my mother. We had to go through the full adoption procedures. And then once I got out of AIT, I adopted him back."

> *"It's very tough on her right now, being a single parent and working and taking the daughter through puberty.* That's *tough. When we're going out and playing war in the middle of the night, what do you do with this daughter?"*

> *"I wasn't the only parent over there in Turkey without my child. There were a lot of us. We'd get together and talk about our kids. I missed my daughter outrageously. I would cry at times. But I just felt: 'I've got to be here. I'm doing this for my daughter. I might as well make the best of it.' "*

Moving around as she does, the servicewoman single parent constitutes the only fixed point on her child's horizon. Day by day the responsibility is hers alone. She deals with emergencies as best she can. "Like in the hurricane we just had, hurricane Gloria. If you live close to the base you are Alpha personnel, which means you will stay until they let you go. And a lot of people have kids that they want to get home to and they're the only parent. That's too bad. Find somebody who will take care of them."

The single parent of course remains "available for worldwide service. CMC [Commandant Marine Corps] says, 'Just because you're single and have three children, too bad, so sad, you are still subject to transfer just like any of your counterparts.' " The consequences of such policies may pain both parent and child: "Germany was really rough, 'cause we stayed in the field a lot. Baby-sitters . . . we was doin' six or seven months in the field out of the year, and I really spent a fortune. I wasn't spendin' any time with him, and he was with nobody that he could really say was his relative, nobody he loved, so I called my mom, and she said, 'Well, by all means. Bring him home.' But I was over there for three years. It was rough. He asked me was this ever gonna happen again, and I promised him no. I'm just hopin' I never have to do that again."

A captain, herself a new mother, wondered how enlisted single parents in the lower ranks cope: "It's tough. I do my best to suggest to the enlisted women that perhaps being in the military is not their best route if they're going to be single parents." A judgment call that depends on the single parent's civilian options. However, it's beyond argument that the military imposes demands that civilian life does not. If, for instance, a single parent in the military is sent to Okinawa on a one-year tour, the military will not pay to transport the child. The result? Most single parents take their children, and "pay for it themselves. Civilian jobs don't do that to you."

"A *lot of women get the comments when they become pregnant, about not being married. They [those who comment] don't have any compassion.*"

"No, *the troops don't give them a hard time. Anything, they'd be helping 'em.*"

The unwed mother, our interviewees say, may meet with anything from disapproval to friendliness and helpfulness. A black staff sergeant remarked, "I don't think there's much peer disapproval. I don't really see them being malicious. They're not very supportive. It's like all your friends before you got pregnant, they're no longer there. Everybody just goes about his several ways, because they know it's going to be a problem, and they really don't want to become part of that. So they're not very very supportive. I'm not sure they can be."

One woman who had endured pregnancy when she was unmarried reflected sadly, "They were always saying 'They should kick her out of the Army.' There were just four days that I did not work: two days in the hospital and one day off when I came back, and then I went back to work typing. All during my pregnancy I'd performed my job and I'd been staying late and did more hours in that office than the guy that was in charge. I really couldn't see why. . . . I had to eat in the mess hall, and these guys would say, while I was eating, 'They should kick her out of the Army.' All these old E-7s and stuff. It was really upsetting."

"The single mothers in the service definitely have a hard time. I know a woman that's adopted her kid and she's single and she's taken on all this responsibility for this emotionally abused kid, and yet she's not given any credit for that."

But a black twenty-three-year-old, mother of a twenty-one-month-old son, seemed completely at ease: "I have always shied away from marriage. I used to think I'd have just one [child], but I think I may have one more. I want a girl this time. Little boys are little boys. Does it worry me to think of having all the responsibility of bringing up two children and still having a career? Well, I don't plan on having another one any time real soon. By the time I have another one, my son will be able to help me a lot. So it won't be that much of a problem. Baby-sitting, maybe, but my son will always be there to kind of oversee everything, and I don't think I'll run into any problems."

Whatever the difficulties they encounter, some sole parents win out. Take a Marine on the verge of retirement: "My children are nine and eleven, a girl and a boy. In the military, everyone I've worked with has been most cooperative. I have never had a problem with someone objecting if I take the children to the doctor and those kinds of things. It could be that I've never taken advantage of it. Some people did. But I like to work, and I'm not much of a baby-sitter! I don't think I was ever meant to be a mother! But I've not had any bad problems with the kids. Sometimes when they get into trouble I think maybe it wasn't such a great idea. Other times I think I've done a pretty good job of blending being a mother and being a Marine.

"I don't even know if my kids know that I'm in the military. It's a job I go off to every morning and come home from every night, just like any other person's job, except that I do wear a uniform. They don't have any concept of my rank. Of course when I got promoted to master sergeant, I made a big deal out of it, told them what this meant to us, more money and all.

"Several months ago we went through the Quantico basic school's obstacle course in the morning and through their combat course in the afternoon. Wow! I would probably have *loved* that sort of thing had I been nineteen or twenty years old, but at age forty climbing up the side of a mountain on a rope? Laying on a little rope that's no bigger than that and going across this big culvert? Crawling through mud, going under water? That night I said to the kids, 'I've got to tell you guys what I did today.' And I drew them some diagrams of me crawling on this rope, pulling myself across this big ditch, and said, 'Now I want you to be proud of your mom!' "

The wide world of the military makes room for all sorts of families, and many kinds of women. But no more than the civilian world has it resolved the ultimate problem of the pull between family and career. Witness this stunning decision from a high-ranking woman. "Both my husband and I were selected as alternates for the top-level school. I did become a primary [choice], and after much deliberation I turned it down. Lots of reasons. But I think the most important one was that it would probably be very disruptive to the family. It was very difficult for me to make the decision, because they only have one woman a year. The school would have been good. I would have gotten to meet a lot of folks that will certainly be high ranking some day. It's a very good experience, and it's one that I would have enjoyed, I'm sure, very much. The monitor said, 'I'd like to see you go. Really I don't normally talk about making general, because that's so iffy. Who knows what the formula is for that? But you've had the experiences throughout that could certainly be grooming.' And I said, 'Oh, my goodness!' But I had to make my decision of fifteen years from now, what's really important to me? I have a one-and-a-half-year-old. I have a six-and-a-half-year-old. I have a husband. And I have the Marine Corps. I've managed to do it all and enjoyed it very much, but in the long run my family won out. It's kind of disappointing that I couldn't continue to do it all. It is. But. . . ."

9. A Different World

To move into the military is to experience culture shock, for it is a distinct world, with its own citizenry, territory, language, and ethos. All around the globe the military has established self-contained posts and bases that resemble company towns: in the United States or Germany or Japan or Saudi Arabia, it's quite possible for the servicemember never to go off base. She may come to feel so at home in this world that she fears to leave. A black Air Force staff sergeant looked toward retirement—at thirty-nine: "I have some apprehensions about getting out of the military. Me coming right out of high school, I'm somewhat institutionalized. This is all I know. I'm not sure if I actually will [get out] at twenty years. I'm hoping that I'll go ahead and get out, no matter what rank I'm at. But I have that fear."

No wonder—it's not just that civilian life is different. Women give up a lot when they leave the military—not only the material benefits and security, but also intangibles. "I love uniforms," said an Air Force lieutenant colonel. "Oh, where else can a woman get automatically recognized as something other than a secretary? I have brass on my shoulders. I don't get somebody coming up and saying 'Would you get the coffee?' " And a gunnery sergeant who left the military to follow her military husband was miserable as a civilian. "I missed my green suit. I missed just the way you feel when you're in the Marine Corps. You have so much pride. [As a civilian] I was going to school and I was progressing, but the excitement wasn't there, the camaraderie, and the stories that are told—just so much excitement involved with being in the Marine Corps. I love the type of people—even your macho Marines that I work with, because they're so unique. It's just really that sense of belonging."

In the military world, servicewomen interact mostly with other military members. If servicewomen live on base, they neighbor with their colleagues. And an Air Force officer who always chooses "to live off base, because it allows us to get civilian friends, and not strictly military talk twenty-four hours a day," nonetheless finds "that for officers, the military is a way of life, constantly. There's always something you're going to that brings you right back to the club!"

The military lingua franca baffles the civilian. Our interviewees had constantly to translate slang and spell out acronyms for us—though sometimes they didn't know *what* the letters stood for. They praise servicemembers who are *strac* (adhere strictly to military regulations—from Strategic Air Command) and *squared away* (neat, trim, and disciplined). Couples know they must avoid *PDA* (public displays of affection). They seek *separate rats* (an allowance to provide separate rations and thus avoid communal meals). Phenomena unique to the military world require their own terminology of *MOSs*, *AITs*, and XOs. Servicemembers redefine words: an *attitude* indicates sulking or balking, *counseling* means reprimanding, and *challenge* denotes problems ranging from the annoying through the insurmountable.

While military job titles are puffed to euphemism—Electronic Warfare/Signal Intelligence Morse Code Interceptor (she listens to foreign Morse Code transmissions), crew chief (she is an airplane mechanic), and cargo specialist (she is a stevedore)—conversational style is often laid back and understated. Where a college woman might describe an event in superlatives, the servicewomen we interviewed usually underplayed it: their situation is "a little bit difficult"; being deep selected for promotion BTZ (below the zone—receiving early promotion) is "a little bit unusual."

The military world is populated by *guys* (servicemen, or all servicemembers) and *females* or *ladies* (servicewomen, but most notably Women Marines). "I think where the *ladies* comes from," said a young airman obligingly trying to assuage our curiosity, "is that that's what their DI called 'em. '*LADIES!* Okay. Around the edge!' Seriously, that's where it comes from. 'All right, ladies, hit it!' "

The real key to the language is the unstated but understood premise that "The shit flows downhill." "If you don't know that, you don't know nothin'." Knowing it enables servicemembers to "Go with the flow," to "Just let it roll off."

> *"Why do they try to keep people in the military if they're not happy with it, even though you've got a contract that says 'Yes, you belong to the United States Army'? If you're not happy, then you shouldn't have to stay there."*

Paradoxically, servicemembers combine the group values taught by the military—patriotism, obedience, loyalty—with the "Do-your-own-thing" philosophy of the 1980s generation. "The mission comes first," they say; "I'm a soldier twenty-four hours a day." But they also uphold the right of individual choice; this principle underlies a great deal of their thinking about rights and wrongs, what's fair and what isn't. It shows up on all sorts of issues.

Abortion, for example. Because we tried to stay with problems significantly affected by or unique to being a woman in the American military, we asked few questions about abortion. When the subject did come up, we most often heard: "It's her affair. She's the one who has to live with it, and I'll support her in whatever she decides." "No, if a woman is known to have an abortion she doesn't have a hard time. I know one girl had two abortions, and the military knew about it, and she really didn't have any problems. When she came to talk to me, I said, 'Abortions I don't believe in unless the girl was raped. But it's up to her. I give her that choice. If you feel you can't take care of the kid, and that's what you want to do, I'm the last person to tell you not to do that, 'cause that's *your* body.' " Tolerance becomes a survival technique in a society where personal standards of speaking and behaving vary so widely.

Servicemembers assert individual freedom of choice even over matters of public policy that affect military efficiency. "The part about them forcing the military to let women in combat really should be left up to the individual herself." Often we heard suggestions that servicewomen should have a *choice* of whether or not to go into combat—and many applied the theory to males as well. In effect they argued, "If she—or he—wants to fight and is capable of it, let her . . . or him. Otherwise not." So also with arguments about fraternization. What people do in their free time, when they are out of uniform, many servicewomen said, is their affair. None of the military's business.

> *"I think at Fort Belvoir now you can't buy alcohol in uniform until four-thirty, which helps for those people who like to have a drink in the morning, stuff like that. It can ruin your career in a heartbeat, because if you're driving and you get a speeding ticket because you're drunk, you're out of the Army."*

Invitations to abuse alcohol and drugs lurk in the military world. In the past the military has done little to combat civilian efforts to sell drink and drugs to servicepeople—has even assisted with some of its own, in the form of cheap liquor and a tradition of heavy drinking. Now the services seem to be trying to change, with an outright assault on drugs through urinalyses programs (at random or by unit, without warning), and a tempering of alcohol use through such devices as the abolition of happy hours and the installation of breatholators in the clubs.

Our interviewees by and large agreed that the drug abuse program works pretty well in ridding the military of drug abusers. Usually senior NCOs and officers are dismissed from the service on the first proof (positive urinalysis) of drug use. Lower ranks are often given a second chance, with an opportunity to attend a drug rehabilitation program.

"I lost three people because of drug abuse," says a black E-7. "You walk out of the gate in Germany, and they know that you're in the military. They know you're young. They say, 'Hey, let's show you a good time.' Before you know it, they're hooked, and their careers go down the drain. You fight, but the way the Army system is now, if you are a drug abuser or an alcoholic that cannot be reformed, then you must get out. It makes you sit back and think, did the Army really have anything to do with that? If the person had been in the civilian sector, would he have been under that type pressure?" In one case she successfully intervened: "When I came to this module, I had one person that was in a lot of trouble behind drug and alcohol, and he was on his way out of the Army. He'd already been processed to be eliminated. You know, he had a family. Thirteen years in the Army, and the Army says, 'Well, you come up positive in the urinalysis test. Get out!' I says, 'You can't take that. *You* have to do this, this . . . ,' and I outlined for him what he had to do, and he did it."

Of course, some servicemembers object to the means by which the military detects drug abuse, with dogs that sniff out caches in dormitory rooms and unannounced urinalyses. The prospect of urinating before a witness traumatizes some women. One woman reported that when she returned weeping from such an ordeal, her crusty old male chief picked up the telephone and announced: "I don't care. I ain't sendin' no more females up there."

As in society at large, alcohol abuse is more widely tolerated. Too many servicemembers seek release in liquor, and little beyond their own common sense salvages them, unless their addiction severely impairs their job performance. "For the first three or four months [in Japan] it was like all we did was go out and party," said a Marine corporal. "I was going to work with a serious hangover. . . . I said, 'I don't need this.' So I stopped drinking. Cut and dry. When I got back here I started again. I just needed a drink one night, so I just went out, me and my roommate. I got pretty loaded. I still don't drink as much as I did when I first got over there. Get bored, you go on the town, you go to the club." And an Army E-4 spoke of her own bout when she was separated from her three-month-old son for almost six months: "Alcoholism? I had a slight problem with that when I was in Germany, before my family got there. I was depressed. I got off duty at five and went over to the NCO Club and I would stay there till it closed. I could go to the Class Six store ten o'clock in the morning if it was open and buy something if I wanted to. Which lot of people did. I was quite bad, but I stopped myself. Now I don't drink. Once in a while I'll go out to a party, but I know when to stop now. I mean, I put my hand into a window before, all because of alcohol."

"In the Army, you know, there's only two types of women: either you are homosexual or you have a reputation for sleeping with everyone in your company, male type. It's sad, because that's not the way it is."

"I don't hear about lesbianism as much anymore as I used to, say maybe four or five years ago. It's hard—I was raised as a tomboy, so sometimes I tend to get a little sporty or whatnot and I say, 'Well, m'gosh, I hope I'm not acting not feminine enough.' "

Few of our interviewees commented on lesbianism, except to deplore the way it has smudged the image of military women. Their reluctance is understandable.[1] The military regulations against homosexuality, male or female, are strictly enforced: proof of lesbianism results in discharge from the service. "It's not a case-by-case review, it's out." Yet the suspicion of lesbianism is rumored about military women all too freely, both by the public in the old "slut-or-lesbian" myth and by servicemen—sometimes out of generalized animosity, sometimes out of pique at a refusal of sexual favors. An officer recalled her experience "trying to fit in, to be one of the boys. I felt, 'Gee, if I go to the club with them and have beer, maybe we can get some work done and maybe I can get some things officially in concrete.' That's the way the system normally works. But people are always looking when you're unmarried, trying to find out what type of social interactions you have. A lot of the men when they can't figure out where you fit in just kind of classify you as 'Well, you go to the club with us for beer and popcorn and watch the strippers or the dancers, so what kind of . . . not what kind of officer are you, but what kind of woman are you?' Oh, yes, they were suggesting that I was a lesbian." And a black senior airman said,

[1] "The true incidence of lesbianism (or male homosexuality) in the military is unknown. Even raising the issue brings on vertigo. . . ." Charles C. Moskos, "Female GIs in the Field," *Society* 22, no. 6 (September/October 1985), p. 31. See also Helen Rogan's discussion of lesbians in *Mixed Company: Women in the Modern Army* (Boston: Beacon Press, 1981), pp. 96–97, 151–159.

"I was called a lesbian, 'cause when I first came here, I lift weights, I do a lot of sports. I went to the movies with one guy, and afterward he said, "Aren't you gonna go to bed with me?' I said, 'You don't even know me! What is this?' He goes, 'Yeah, right. Yeah, So-and-so said you a dyke.' I said, 'The only reason he said that is 'cause I didn't go to bed with *him*.' " We heard enough such stories to make us realize that in a predominantly male world the charge of lesbianism is a tempting means to express resentment of women's presence. The widespread male hatred and fear of homosexuality is reinforced by the military code.

Because whatever lesbianism exists in the military is necessarily secret, literally no one, in the service or out, knows its extent. Our interviewees report that they hear about the expulsion from the military of male homosexuals more frequently than of lesbians, but whether because of greater incidence or greater discretion, who can say? Men after all outnumber women ten to one in the military population. A black E-7 says that "The hearsay is always there. As a drill sergeant you see a lot of females say, 'I don't want to sleep in the room with this one because this and this and this is going on.' Or they would come to you and say, "Hey, I'm a homosexual and I wanta get outta the Army.' A lot of times you don't know whether that's true or not, because they just want out."

Problems with lesbianism tend "to recur, every five years, every six years," observed a public affairs officer of long experience. "Back in the '73 to '78 time frame on the enlisted in basic training they had a big problem, and they drummed out ten or twelve female drill sergeants and thirty or forty recruits. There were enough people coming into the military at that point that they could afford to just—'Out!' That happened again, and they drummed out another thirty or forty, and then there have been pockets here and there. Where I've seen it or known about it, it's mostly been at the recruiting point. I even heard a story at that point in time that there were two or three women who had been in for years who were actually recruiting lesbians, like a training system, and infiltrating them at various bases. I didn't believe that, but I'll be damned if it didn't work out that way. There were some higher-ups within the military that knew this was going on and allowed it to happen, or at least this was what I was told. You could shut your eyes to it, because the women that are running this group are also getting a lot of good recruits, and that's at that time what we needed. But something broke, and that was the end of that. Other than hearing things like that, I don't know that it's that big of a problem or that big of a deal." The officer's knowledge of these incidents came from her public affairs responsibilities.

Experienced servicewomen agreed that usually lesbianism does not interfere with efficiency or professionalism, with the way the women do their work. A woman of long service in Social Actions said that she has met several lesbians, each of whom has a good record as a servicemember. Nor does she believe them to be seducing other women. As a black NCO said, "Personally all I know is what I've heard. It's there, I guess, you know. Oh, no. I've never seen it affect a woman's work. No. No. No. No. No."

Clearly our interviewees were bothered far more about the stigma of lesbianism than about any actuality in their experience.

"I work together with my platoon. They know what I'm thinking sometimes. They know how I'm going to react. They know what I want when I don't even say it. I almost feel like I'm married to them."

"See when you're working with people so closely every single day, it's like they become brothers and sisters to a certain extent. They really do."

"The military in a way has been the father I never really had."

Close friendships develop within the military. "Our motor pool's just like one family. Our motor sergeant used to say, 'Everybody go home,' and we said, 'Well, aren't you goin' home?' It's like nobody would leave until he left. Sometimes we'll be marchin' back, and we'll clown around with each other, and our sergeant will say, 'Everybody that's clownin' around owes me. Who owes me?' I'll raise my hand. Last time it was me and this other girl that was jokin' with each other. He says, 'Okay, get on down and do push-ups.' We got down, and everybody got down. Uh-huh. Times like that, it's great. We're a family. We'll do for each other."

"In time of crisis or trauma, these people really come through and are there twenty-four hours a day," said a lieutenant commander, the widowed mother of three small children. "Without asking they have anticipated your needs. They fill them for you. They are ready to give more in any way, shape or form, because being in the military they know what you've gone through. The wives of the squadron that my husband had belonged to knew that something could happen at any time, so they appreciated what I was going through. But also the Naval officers, the aviators as well as his associates on board the ship that he was killed on, certainly can appreciate what my husband was trying to do, what his goals were, what his commitment was."

"We develop a close relationship in our office," says a black Navy chief. "I just stood there some time and shake my head, how close we are. When it's time to leave, everybody's crying and carrying on, like you're losing your sister." Farewells are frequent in this floating world. Friends are constantly leaving. (Enemies leave too; repeatedly women console themselves by remembering that either they or their antagonist will soon be rotated.) But friends also return. "No matter how many years go by, someday somehow you always cross paths with another person you've served with, and it's like welcoming home family members. The more you cross paths and serve together, that bond gets a little tighter. I would think the change would disrupt the solidity of the organization, but in the military it seems to add to it."

The military woman expects to spend considerable time in other countries. She usually looks forward to these overseas experiences, which nonetheless demand adaptability and strength of character. For the environments around the bases can be as raunchy as a Reginald Marsh painting. It's quite an experience to walk out the front gate of Osan Air Base in Korea into a warren of bars, clubs, corn-dog stands, and stores overflowing with souvenirs, cheap satin lingerie, and T-shirts stamped with English obscenities. Merchants hover with their carts or tout bargains in front of their stores, and beggars plead. If the servicewoman joins a group seeking amusement in a bar, she is apt to find herself jostled and cursed by the Korean "businesswomen," who see her as a rival.

A Marine captain recalled trying to avert the dangers for her young troops. "As a lieutenant I was the OIC of the Women Marine Barracks on Okinawa. Some of them were seventeen. For some it was the first time anywhere after boot camp. It was a mixture—people from different stratas, of different ages and experiences. The really young ones, never been anywhere before—you had to watch 'em carefully. We had one girl: meritorious material [capable of being promoted early], sharp, but in with the wrong crowd. I kept talking to her, trying to tell her 'Hey, you can't do this.' They were running the street, spending all their time down on B and C Street [Bar and Club Street, the American designation for a notorious street in Kadena on Okinawa]. Over in Japan, if you ever got caught with drugs, they would lock you up for the rest of your natural life. But boy, what finally got her attention was she got caught. She was at a party where they were using drugs, and they busted 'em. Of course, the Japanese according to the [Status of Forces] agreement have jurisdiction. We worked it out that we got her off the island. But first I made arrangements for her and a couple of others that were starting to stray to go down and see the jail. That changed the two that were starting to walk down that path's mind. This other girl was scared. She knew that she could have been left on Okinawa for the rest of her life. It was a shame. They're so young and impressionable that you lose 'em."

A black NCO shared these worries: "The Army definitely needs to—I feel—look at their policies on young people going overseas or so far away from home at an early age. It's just unbearable. It is sickening." To the young troop, being overseas can prove a Kafkaesque experience—even on base. The feeling that nothing counts, that the currency is "funny money" and the human relationships temporary, can be disorienting. An Army staff sergeant told us about being sent straight from basic training to "big, big Seoul. My drill sergeants had me scared to death. All the stories they told me: I would probably be raped within the first week I was there. When I landed I was put in a placement center, where they told me I couldn't go where my orders said, 'Because you're a female, and they don't have any facilities.' For three days I sat there with nowhere to go. People made advances to me, both Korean and the Army guys, or other services, whoever was there."

For some servicewomen, especially those in nontraditional jobs, the military life often proves dirty—a real hardship for the squeaky-clean generation—and sometimes dangerous. Almost everyone, female or male, enlisted or officer, complains about going to the field, with its sweaty work and makeshift plumbing. The military, we sometimes think, must rejoice that an exercise so clearly necessary also gives a natural vent to servicemembers' gripes.

And some women regularly take risks as part of their jobs. MPs, for instance, have a fund of "war stories": "I wasn't only female, but I was brand spanking new in the Army. I didn't know how to handle myself. So they said, 'Well, we're going to see if she can take it.' They pushed me indoors in the middle of a fight, and I caught my stitches and I got my eyes blackened. Once I went down for the count, and they had to drag me out of there, but I went in swinging from then on. In Germany I was in the middle of all the terrorist stuff. When General X got ambushed, I was designated as a decoy to get Mrs. X back up to her residence; she sat in the front seat and I sat in the back where she normally sat, so that if there was another attempt, I was her second-chance best. Brave? You know I didn't even think about it. I was so excited about sitting in the back of that big old limo! And the adrenaline was pumping so hard. Nervousness was there: if something happens am I going to take the appropriate action?"

Another MP, this one a Marine: "One time I walked into a barracks, and all you see is blood and glass everywhere. We go on down the hall and see a couple of guys go out the fire escape; one of them went through the glass door. The biggest guy got my partner trapped in a corner, and the only thing that I had was a flashlight, so I started using that on him. He got a little upset that I was using that. He picked my partner up, threw him down a flight of steps, and then he turned around and hit me. He sat down and he said, "Don't hit me anymore." [*Chuckles.*] I was like "Okay" with the blood coming out of my lip. He goes, "You're a female." I go, "Yes, I am," and he started apologizing all the way downstairs. When we got him in the handcuffs, he was apologizing."

Sometimes adventure comes in the heat of the desert. "I was TDY in Saudi Arabia, ninety-six days. Right, ninety-six days in Saudi Arabia is a very long time. Saudi Arabia was a challenge. Women were not allowed to drive. Women were not allowed to ride in the front of the bus. The Saudis explained it as protection of women, okay? The women walk behind the men, and you don't touch, at all. You put your hand out and you lose it. I felt like they mistreated the Saudi women, but when they went shopping, the Saudi women would just point to what they want and they got it. So I don't understand.

"To go downtown, we couldn't go unaccompanied. The American guys were nice about taking us. Most of the time I waited to go downtown with the guys that wanted to walk. Because being crowded in the back of the bus in that cave, can't get out, was the most uneasy feeling. The bus was so packed the guys couldn't get to the front to tell the driver to open the door, so they'd jump off the bus while you were still on there. They had a buzzer back there that you ring to let the driver know you want to get out, but he never opened the door. You'd beat on the paneling, and then he'd open the door and you'd get out and go 'Whew!'

"Downtown I had to have a blouse that came past the buttocks. You couldn't show curvature in Saudi Arabia. They didn't enforce covering the head, but I was suggested, y'know, by being black, to cover my head, because the Saudis mistake me for a Saudi female, which caused you to get spit at. I got spit at a couple of times, well, okay, three times. That was the hardest thing, just being spit at and not being able to say anything, y'know. I don't know if it was my clothes or my attitude. I didn't stand there and argue about it!"

Sometimes adventure comes in the company of cold, sleeplessness, and danger. "I was the boarding officer and arresting officer for a Swedish vessel that had eight Colombians and an American master. The captain wouldn't allow me to enter the cargo hold, where the marijuana was, but he allowed me to walk around the rest of the vessel all I wanted, so I went down into the engine room and there were two holes in the forward wall, or bulkhead, of the engine room. If I shined my flashlight through the hole, I could see the bales of marijuana and I could smell it. If I was to put the flashlight through the hole, I would have gone beyond the consent of the master of the vessel, but shining the light through the hole was not.

"I had taken Spanish in high school, so I was talking to the Colombians [who must have been pretty dazed at being captured by a Coast Guard woman of Chinese descent], reading them their rights in Spanish, and making them acknowledge and sign and all these things. We transferred them to the cutter, and they were kept in custody there. I had to stay with the Swedish vessel because of chain of custody. I had two other men with me, so we took turns staying up. It was a very rugged week. A storm had come through. I tried to keep my engines going, but they had died twice, and I couldn't revive them, so I had to be towed, and then they transfer-towed to another vessel, out of Portsmouth, to drag us in. Out of that came a Coast Guard achievement medal."

Parachute riggers as part of their job must jump "out of perfectly good airplanes. It's an excellent feeling. There's no problem in the world. You can have a million things wrong with you on the ground, but once you get out of that plane, it's you and God. You almost hold your breath, because you're afraid if you breathe, you'll break it, you know, you'll lose that. . . . I had a collision over in Italy. We went MASSTAC out of both doors—Mass Tactical. They just kind of push from the back, and everybody goes. But the guy that went out this side—you're supposed to alternate each door, but it ended up we went out pretty much the same time. So we met in the back of the plane because of the air blast, and his chute opened all around me. I couldn't see the sky. I couldn't see the ground. But I was surprised I wasn't more scared. I had my hand on the reserve. I was waiting to pull it, as soon as his chute got away from me, you know. But his chute opened up, and mine was fine. I came down, landed great. It made my heart beat a little faster while I was up there." But most of all she loves night jumps: "I guess I'm a little romantic on things like that, but. . . . My last night jump was in Italy, and I could see all the lights in the towns nearby, and it was Christmas. Just teeny little lights. It was pitch black. Oh, it was beautiful."

This military world full of young people is also full of parties and fun. An Air Force officer merrily told us a "war story" of her well-spent youth. "I get to my new base, and I find out that I'm chief of administration for the base. That's a lieutenant colonel's slot! I am a brand-new first lieutenant, eighteen months in the service. I got forty people working for me. On top of this what the general really wants me to do is be his protocol officer. I was really turned off by this whole protocol thing from the female aspect, and I don't care what you want, General. Female protocol officers, the use thereof, I was not thrilled by. However, it got to be real interesting.

"The general has a reception one night, and he's telling one of the local hotshot judges, 'You know, people in the Air Force these days just don't face life with the sense that they used to back in my days. They're not there in the forefront challenging things and having a good time, working hard and playing hard.' He turned around to me and he winked. Well, with two drinks, I thought, 'All right, you want to challenge me. You want us to do wild and wonderful things.' I took his staff car. The front doors [of the club] were two double glass doors with a canopy thing over the top, and you could just get the car in between, and I blocked the doors. I went in the back door, took the keys into the women's rest room, hid them up in the towel dispenser, and I walked into the main dining room and got onto the microphone, started calling the general: 'Sir, general officers, with all due respect, ought to park their cars properly like everyone else. I hear tell that your car is improperly parked.' Well, while we're going through all this routine, the cops had come by and put a ticket on it. Monday morning he called me into his office. I had worried the rest of the weekend. 'Oh, am I going to be in bad trouble! This is the court martial coming.' Walk in, he pulls me to attention in front of his desk. I salute him, say 'Good morning, sir,' with as much professionalism as I could muster. He says, 'I only have one thing to say to you, Lieutenant.' He hands the ticket out to me, and he says, 'Fix it!' "

A Marine captain recalled a birthday party in Korea. Her platoon was "a really close-knit, a tight group. They had a good time at my expense on my birthday. They . . . I don't know how to put it gracefully. When they'd go out on liberty at night in town, they'd. . . . VD is a horrible disease over there, and they try to get the troops to avoid it, so they give 'em prophylactics. The fact is they're given their liberty card and a pack of prophylactics. So what these guys did. . . . I went to the shower at four-thirty A.M., went to the staff meeting at five, and then I was going to go back and brush my teeth, then go to my office tent. And I got back there, and they'd taken this long roll of brown paper that said 'Happy Birthday, Lieutenant,' and strung it at the end of my tent, and made all these animals out of the prophylactics like balloons. They made dogs and giraffes. They filled my tent with 'em. We had tent inspections, and I thought 'When the CO sees those in here, he's going to start wondering what's going on.' They had the animals hung all over.

"They had gotten the MPs to take 'em out in town and they pooled their money, and they got me a birthday cake from a Korean bakery. The entire formation—we had six hundred people out there. My platoon decides that they're going to call me forward, you know, like 'Lieutenant X, report forward.' So I reported up to the gunny. They gave me this cake, and they all sang 'Happy Birthday' to me. Then they bombarded us with water balloons, made out of the same type of paraphernalia. They were having a real good time. Well, we cut the cake up, so everybody got a taste, and it was horrible. It was like sourdough bread, covered with this gritty . . . it looked like chocolate icing. It had plastic flowers stuck on it. I know they really went out of their way to get that cake. But even my biggest chowhounds couldn't choke that stuff down."

SEPARATING

> *"The military is restricting. I guess that's it. What I really miss is the freedom."*
>
> *"It will be ten years by the time I finish up this enlistment, which is a big chunk. Then I'll resign. No bones about it. There's too much out there, too many opportunities. It's time to get out there and shake some of the cobwebs that I've built up."*

Despite all these joys and "challenges," relatively few women—or men—make military service a career. Some of those who choose for one reason or another to leave active (full-time) duty join the Reserves for part-time service—subject to recall to active duty. In this way they return to civilian life but keep one foot in the military.

Many servicepeople, of course, never intended to serve more than one term. Having finished the promised stint, having completed the desired training or education, they simply resume their interrupted civilian lives or choose civilian rather than military jobs.

Occasionally their separations are involuntary. "Sure I get in trouble every now and then," said an E-4. "Since I've been in I've had one Article 15 in my record, which I was disrespectful to an officer. They got it so that I'm ineligible to reenlist. Only way I can reenlist is get a waiver." But proportionally fewer women than men are separated for disciplinary reasons. In a few MOSs, military women (and men) must leave because the military does not have enough slots for all the lawyers and nurses who would like to remain. Some women are forced out by the fraternization policy.

And women are sometimes booted out for reasons that others judge unfair. A Marine officer told us with distress about a staff sergeant with eight years of service: "They said she didn't have any learning or growth potential. She is really smart. She goes to college, takes like two or three classes each semester. And still she got canned, because she stuck up for one of her men. I was glad she did, but she got the worst end of the stick. She got put into a different section, and she really didn't have a job. It was kind of demoralizing. I had respect for her and admiration, sticking up for her troop and telling it like it was. She could not have said anything and let the guy take all the yucky stuff. She is a hard worker. She's done a lot of things and helped a lot of people. She hasn't got much recognition or anything for it. Women, it's a hard time. I think she would have been treated differently if she'd been a man."

Women who are separated from the military against their will lose not only their careers but also their status: their sergeant's stripes, their officer's bars or stars. Particularly if they are married to servicemen, they feel keenly the demotion within the military world from servicemember to dependent. A woman forced to resign her officer's commission in 1971 because she was pregnant told us of her struggles to find jobs as she moved with her officer husband from one assignment to another; she had both professional training and military experience as a major department head, but time and again she could find nothing appropriate or challenging. Moreover: "The transition from the military woman to the military spouse was and is to this day the most difficult transition I've ever made. I say that unequivocally, publicly. You went from a status of a full person to having the rights of a child. You had no rights. Anything that you did was dependent on your husband or your husband's commander. The traffic ticket that I got went to my husband."

The major problems that we have already examined—the hardships of combining family and military life, the complications caused by military policies against fraternization, the rigors of living in a man's world, the denial to women of full citizenship and full opportunity—probably account for most separations among women who might otherwise pursue a military career. Beyond these, what qualities in military life disillusion and disappoint the potential career woman?

"I would like a little more control than I have in the Navy over what I do with my life."

"You know, civilian world, if you get ready to tell somebody to bug off, you do it. Not here."

"Sometimes it's not for me. I mean, everybody here, it's like hardcore stuff. Tryin' to be a man. A woman tryin' to be a man. Can't do it. I'm too feminine."

Some people simply dislike all that the military demands apart from one's job. An Army bandsman: "Our secondary mission is security—we're to help the MPs in time of war. So we'll be going on field training exercises with the MPs, and whew! That's no fun. No, my life here doesn't center around music. It's around buffing [floors]. See that buffer out there? That's what we do. It's around soldierization." A Coast Guard woman wanted no part of ships: "They needed some nonrates to go on a big white—a ship, the *Gallatin*. I was, like, to the point where, 'If you've got to cut me orders anywhere, cut me orders home. I will accept a discharge.' I felt like my whole world was going to cave in, because a ship is nowhere for a woman. It's like a hundred fifty guys and there's like only maybe three or four women on the ship, and you'll be out for like three or four months on the water. I'm not a perfect swimmer. I wouldn't have lasted one day on that ship."

Military life does indeed impose demands unknown in most civilian jobs. When servicewomen talk about being "a Marine twenty-four hours a day" or having "raised my hand, taken the oath, and signed on the dotted line," they imply more than just being on call twenty-four hours a day, or having to put the needs of the military before their private interests and responsibilities. They can be called to account for all sorts of matters that most civilians consider their own private affairs: their hairdos and their jewelry and the color of their nail polish; the condition of their barracks room or of the lawn outside their base housing. Fraternization policies limit their choices of friends and lovers. Certainly they don't have the freedom to choose a homosexual life-style. They must take orders. And above all, as they say over and over, they can't quit.

Some women get discouraged about promotions: they may be slow, and they depend on the availability of slots, and often much more on time in service and time in rank than on merit. "Promotions are badly backed up in the Coast Guard. The deep selection [early promotion] process is a joke. You can have somebody sitting on their tail ashore in an administrative office while you're afloat being graded harder than they are—although the boards do take that into account, the degree of difficulty of the job—getting paid essentially the same, maybe a hundred dollars, a hundred fifty dollars a month more; having no time to yourself, no nothing. And you're going to get promoted the same time. In fact, if he's an Academy graduate, he'll be automatically on the list ahead of you. In essence you're closed off from even bothering to put forth superior performance. It's great if you want to stay mediocre your whole life. But if you try to go anywhere, if you're setting your sights on something, it's incredibly slow."

"It's been the hardest decision I've made in my life, the decision to resign," said a thirty-three-year-old lieutenant commander with an impressive track record. "I've dedicated ten years of my life to the Navy, ten very enjoyable years. The Navy has been very good to me, and I in turn have been very good to it. They had only great things to offer me out of here. But I'm to a point in my life now where what they had to give me back didn't outweigh the personal sacrifices I was making—you know, the twelve-hour days. I'm not averse to long hours, as long as you're rewarded commensurate with the effort that you expend.

"If you take just that one group of people who all came into the Navy in the same year group, you'll find significant differences between their contributions. No matter how hard you work and how good you are, you're going to be promoted along with these people. So you can beat your head against the wall for the rest of your life and sacrifice all these things, and people who produce significantly less are going to be promoted just the same as you are. There's really no deep selections and advancements below the zone. The Navy doesn't really want performers necessarily.

"It's actually been in the last year that we've had a female promoted to commander in my community [intelligence], so it will be on into the nineties before we have anyone selected for captain and years beyond that before we even have anyone eligible for flag selection [admiral]. Someday it's completely possible that one of the three flag billets in our community will be filled by a woman. There isn't a great big difference between what women can do in my community and what men can do. I'm not knocking my head against the wall because I'm not allowed to do what my male counterparts are allowed to do. I guess my problem was that I'm not being allowed to advance as quickly and to the level that I think I am capable of."

Thus ambitious women begin to look around for other career options. "I'm still thinking about whether I want to stay in the Air Force," says a black first lieutenant. "I'm still doing it one tour at a time. One of the problems I have is my personal feeling of not being used to the utmost of my potential. The military has its way of controlling. It's just like a child. At this stage you're . . . I don't want to say seen and not heard, but it's something along that line. Oftentimes I feel stifled."

"In the military it's easy to lose your power of creative thinking, to learn to function within the parameters and to do that well. You can become a chief master sergeant or a colonel and run the base. But because they're so good about setting the rules, you really don't have to think too terribly much."

Some women complain that the military organization breeds narrow-mindedness and nit-picking. "Success in an entity like this is frequently more on presentation of data than on the quality of the data and the thought processes behind it." With some supervisors "You don't do anything but what that person wants, and there is no room for original thinking, except that which fits this tiny little area over here. I don't know whether that's because it's the only way to get things through the bureaucracy . . . there is something to that. There are other senior officers, fortunately, who are simply a little bit more commonsense about it."

Even the fulfillment of ambition presents its own hazards. "Jobs in any military organization get worse as you get senior. The actual control you have over events is less. It's not just eroded by the chain of command; it's eroded by the environment. People in the civilian community think 'Oh, you can just tell people what to do.' Yeah, when you're on a ship and you're performing a mission, they're going to do it. The administrative environment doesn't work that way. You have to get people to see your perception and tie into your program, if you're going to be successful."

"Everything was green. The buildings were green and the cars were green and the uniforms were green and the plates were green. If it wasn't green it was brown. There were no flowers. No colors. No anything. Plus the patients. My patients could not respond. At all. My patients couldn't talk to me."

Nurses who see combat duty constitute a special case. For some of them—particularly those who join because the country is at war—its horrors define the military experience. A World War II veteran still remembers the destruction she saw: "Professionally I think one gains a great deal. It's just the philosophical problem that I have, because I saw such terrible, terrible human waste."

"I was a hippie, twenty years old," says a Vietnam veteran, once an Army lieutenant. "I thought the war was wrong. Didn't like Nixon; thought he was a very nasty man. Going in seemed like the thing to do. I had nothing against the military at that point. I worked in a neurosurgical ward. Intensive-care ward. A lot of patients were . . . okay, probably seventy-five percent of them were head injuries. The other twenty-five percent were back injuries. So they were either unconscious or paralyzed. At times probably half of them didn't recover. Half of them died. More than that, really, if you counted the ones who shipped out, who died back in the States or Japan.

"All of my friends there, men and women, felt like my family. They'd do anything. But we didn't talk about what was going on. These people are dying all the time. And if they weren't dying, they were . . . I have a very vivid image of just a row of dead bodies. . . . Dead brains, live bodies, really what it is. No, we didn't talk about them. What could we say? We would talk politics a lot. Most everybody that worked there was antiwar. They were young and they were taking care of nice healthy nineteen-year-old men who were dead.

"There's a little phrase that I use, which is 'Death and DEROS [date of expected return from overseas],' and that to me feels like what I dealt with for a year. It still feels like all of my patients died and all of my friends left, and I never saw them again."

HOW THE MILITARY CHANGES WOMEN

> *"I was telling my friend just the other day, 'I used to feel like a little kid all the time. I feel like I'm grown up now.' Like I can handle things on my own. That's what I like about the Army. It gave me that."*
>
> *"I'm an achiever and didn't know it."*

Most of the women who talked to us, whether or not they plan to stay in, value their military experience. "I feel very fortunate that I was strong enough when I was seventeen, eighteen years old to actually consider the service, because today I would still be a hairdresser, standing on my feet in a small town of twelve hundred people," said a Marine Corps gunnery sergeant who has earned both a bachelor's and a master's degree in the service. And an Air Force tech sergeant: "I feel better than a lot of people back home, because they haven't done anything for themselves. *They never left home.*"

For most women, the critical difference is the confidence they've gained. "The Air Force has helped me realize that I'm capable of doing a hell of a lot more than what I knew I could." "I don't think I ever was as stupid as at one time I thought I was," says a captain with prior enlisted service. "I was real hesitant when I first came in. Now I make decisions every day and I don't sit back and say, 'Is that right? Is that wrong?' Press on. What's the next problem? I don't think I would ever achieve that had I not been in the Air Force. And then just being happy."

A captain credits the military with having taught her the rules men play by. "In the military, like no place else that I've ever seen, the rules are hard and fast, and there's never a question of whether you're going to play with a girl or a boy. It's made me able to get more for myself if I want to. I feel like any woman who's been a military officer is five steps ahead of her civilian counterpart."

Brigadier General Gail Reals (USMC) points to the paradoxes of military service: "You think you're being so controlled, especially in recruit training, you think you've really been led around, and it has the reverse effect. You become much more self-confident." Or, as a resigning officer put it, "People say that if you want security, go to the military. It's done the opposite for me. I am more independent, because I'm more confident. I would never have thought of doing risky things like going into business for myself, adopting kids. I would never have said, 'I'm going to go out and make a million dollars.' "

A chief petty officer especially values working with different kinds of people. "If I'd stayed in South Dakota, I would never know half the things that I know now. Dealing with the foreign people up in Iceland and over in Scotland and London. I'd met one black person before in my life."

Sometimes the newfound knowledge is tinged with skepticism. "I just realized that you can't trust people in general, especially in the military, because a lot of people are just out to punch their ticket. I'm not saying everybody. I'm just saying I've become more wary until I know what they're about."

"Maybe in a way my attitude toward men has changed since I've been in the Corps," said a young captain. "Sometimes I resent them. To me their moral standards are so low. They don't set their goals high enough. They don't look for tomorrow. I don't think they're that hard of a worker. There's always that ten percent that are really good guys. The other ninety percent just wreck it for 'em. You really don't need men anymore, except to have kids. If you're thinking of marriage, you need a guy to have a strong social unit. But when you're single you don't need one. You can make your own paycheck and you sure as hell can fight. Maybe men are luxuries now."

> *"When I went over to Korea, when I saw how they lived, I was never so glad to be an American. God bless America, land that I love! You know? To heck with this white, black, green garbage. I love America."*
>
> —A BLACK ARMY BANDSMAN

Often her military service deepens a woman's patriotism. She associates with people for whom service to country is a paramount virtue. She reads the service newspapers and when she is abroad listens to or watches the Armed Forces Network. Living overseas gives her a new look at her own country. "I nearly got thrown out of high school for not saying the pledge of allegiance," a yeoman told us. "I said, 'I'll do anything you want me to do for the country, but I am not going to sit here and talk to a flag.' But when I went through Pass and Review in boot camp, when you're finally finished and you march by the reviewing official and they play the national anthem, the chill that I got . . . I'll pledge allegiance to the flag. Just in that one month my whole attitude changed."

As an Air Force staff sergeant said, "To be honest with you, I came into the service mainly to get an education and to support my daughter. The idea of wanting to help to keep my country the way it is has come over the years. I've lived in Spain and Turkey. As a child in Spain, I remember the death cart, as we called it, rattling past our house; half hour later, machine gun fire, and then the cart would rattle back by, and it would not be empty. In Turkey you couldn't speak out against certain things. Occasionally a story would hit *The Stars and Stripes* [the newspaper of the U.S. military] or the Turkish press about this person saying something the government disagreed with: they were going to have a small jail term. If you would call three or four years small. I realized that this country could be the same way, if we weren't here to try and protect it."

HOW WOMEN CHANGE THE MILITARY

> *"The greatest change that has come about in the United States forces in the time that I've been in the military service has been the extensive use of women. . . . The United States has taken a male institution and turned it into a coed institution."*
>
> —GENERAL JOHN A. VESSEY, JR.
> (Washington Post, *February 3, 1984)*

> *"The men are in an environment that was made for them. We're in an environment that was made for them. So what it is, either it's going to change, or else we just get used to it. But I think it's going to change."*

One of the things all those nice girls are doing in the military is changing it. The United States Armed Forces are unique in the number of women they enroll.[2] Brigadier General Wilma Vaught (USAF, Ret.) commented: "The first thing that strikes you as you work in the NATO environment where I have is sheer pure numbers. Percentagewise and in just gross numbers, the United States has an incredible number of women in the armed forces, far in excess of what anyone else has. . . .

"Fundamentally the problems are not that much different as you go from country to country, but we have women doing far more things than almost any other country. There are some more innovative things being done [in other countries] in the sense of experiments or trials. Particularly in the Scandinavian countries you find less concern about how men and women solve some of these problems, and so women are

[2] John G. Kester, "The Reasons to Draft," in *The All-Volunteer Force After a Decade*, ed. William Bowman, Roger Little, and G. Thomas Sicilia (Washington, D.C.: Pergamon-Brassey's, 1986), pp. 301–302.

permitted to do some things that we're still struggling with.[3] But you walk away from looking at NATO knowing that there is no question but what we are just further ahead, when you look at the practicality of what women are really doing."

Even the USSR and Israel, whose use of women in combat in time of war seized the popular imagination, don't enroll women in their peacetime military in anything like the numbers or the varieties of jobs that women have claimed in the United States military. Israeli women are now confined to noncombat jobs.[4]

Yet women cannot afford to forget that American society has time and again summoned them to work when it wanted them, in the military or in industry, and ordered them home again when it didn't—often without so much as a return ticket. A recent upsurge in servicewomen's numbers came with the end of the draft (1973); in this emergency, women saved the all-volunteer force.[5] As a shrewd and experienced woman among our interviewees observed, "I think that's why they opened up for women in the military. They weren't getting enough men, because the men were going, 'Oh, wow, you know, Smith down the street here, man, he had his balls blown off in Vietnam, so I'm not goin' into the Army because they're gonna send me to Vietnam.' Well, then the Army's goin', 'Oh, shit, we don't have enough men comin' into the military. Okay. We'll let some more women in. We'll let 'em go into some of these other jobs.' I really believe if the draft had stayed and we were getting men into the military, women would still be on the same thing that they were doin' in 1966 when I came in, and they told me then that I can be a cook or clerical or medical.

"The men gave us the opportunity, because they wanted to sit back somewhere else. In '67 and '68 there was a couple of guys that were

[3] "After a successful four-year trial of women in Navy combat roles . . . , Denmark has begun to test women soldiers in Army and Air Force combat positions. Fifty women are using guns in tank and armored-infantry companies and in front-line ranks in field artillery and air-defense batteries. In the Air Force, 77 women work in missile squadrons and defense units but will not fly fighters or fire missiles." *Minerva* 5, no. 2 (Summer 1987), p. 21.

[4] Martin Binkin and Shirley J. Bach, *Women and the Military* (Washington, D.C.: Brookings Institution, 1977), pp. 9, 13.

[5] In Bowman, Little, and Sicilia, eds., *The All-Volunteer Force After a Decade*, see John D. Johnston, "Commentary," p. 106; Martin Binkin and Mark J. Eitelberg, "Women and Minorities in the All-Volunteer Force," p. 89; and Kester, "The Reasons to Draft," p. 301.

clerks at the time, that other men would say, 'Well, you know, you guys are sittin' back here takin' these women's jobs, instead of bein' an 11-Bangbang with the rest of us,' which is an infantry troop. The ones here were goin', 'Once I stay a clerk, I don't have to go into combat.' "

But most of our interviewees believe in an expanding future for women in the military. Military women, they say, have changed the forces by making a place for themselves. The military organizations have huffed and puffed their way through the more minor problems (real or perceived) of incorporating women. Masculine energies have been expended, through tortured conferences, on what kind of jewelry women may wear with their uniforms, whether black women may wear cornrows, and the permissible depth of shade of nail polish. A pilot hilariously described a meeting where "They called us in and briefed us, just the women, on our underwear requirement. [*Giggles.*] We had to wear cotton bras, and we couldn't wear just T-shirts: we had to wear bras. I started laughing and said, 'What are you going to do? Have open-ranks inspection?' An NCOIC that was sitting there sort of went 'KKKKKkkk,' started laughing. The commander didn't think that it was funny. They were really worried about all these little things. All these colonels sitting in the office talking about what kind of underwear we wear. [*Cracks up.*] In all seriousness, they sit here with long faces—oh, geez. They really put this on the staff meeting thing—What are we gonna do about the women's underwear? Oh, dear."

And the annals of difficulties with women's uniforms, ranging from absurdity to safety hazards (like men's combat boots for women on runs and forced marches), are still being written. Although we never asked a question about uniforms, we heard a lot about them! Women leaped to their feet to demonstrate that flight suits ought to have drop seats and that Coast Guard pants were designed by a retarded male recluse in a remote Western desert who *might* have seen pictures of women, but probably had only read descriptions.

Despite glitches like these, the military women we interviewed chalk up real advances: notably, the strides toward equal opportunity represented by opening more MOSs to women; eliminating discrimination against married women and mothers; and instituting the Joint Spouse, Equal Opportunity, and Family Service programs. A Navy petty officer showed us how much some of these programs still depend on individual servicewomen: "I make sure all my girls know their rights, the grievance procedures. I like people to know that they have choices. But I think it's good too when you get a lot of the old people to go to these classes. For the past year and a half we never had any officers or chiefs attend, and I said, 'It's not fair. It's not right. It's against the reg. . . . You're supposed to have 'em.' So now . . . it's a compromise. We have lieutenant commanders and below go. I guess they just got tired of hearing me bitch. Master chief said it was like a thorn in his side: 'Every month we do these workshops, and here you come saying "This person didn't go." ' I'd raise the devil if they didn't show up. And I taught the workshop. I said, 'We can make it interesting and all get involved and get done about one, or we can sit here till four-thirty. How do you want to do it?' "

Although the record of military women's rising numbers and careers is clear and easy to read and the increasing acceptance and respect for them are apparent, their full impact on attitudes within the military world seems quite literally incalculable. How can anyone disentangle what military women have done from the changes wrought by societal pressures over the last forty years? Yet common sense tells us that coeducational institutions differ from single-sex institutions, that organizations with both male and female employees differ from places where men work alone. And those branches of the military that exclude women or severely limit their functions differ from those in which women and men work side by side.

Some speak of a *civilizing* effect. The female drill sergeant instructs her male trainees that they *must*, minimally, be wearing shorts before they can speak to her. The presence of women in the office, in the field, in the coed barracks and quarters raises the consciousness of the males about their dress and their language. Perhaps *normalizing* or *liberalizing* is a more accurate word. Women and men working together maintain a balance that checks the extremes of strutting masculinity and simpering femininity. As servicemen become accustomed to servicewomen as co-workers or supervisors, they gradually begin to think of them as colleagues instead of merely as mothers, wives, or sex objects. In military/military marriages, husbands learn how to accept their spouses not only as mates but also as workers. The young serviceman who passionately repudiated the idea of military women may find himself defending equally passionately the rights and status of the servicewoman he marries.

Other relationships change attitudes too. The conscientious military supervisor acknowledges a duty to encourage and guide his personnel, female or male. Recognition turns to advocacy: the male lieutenant wants the merits of his efficient female yeoman rewarded. Or the commanding officer of an aircraft carrier begins to wonder why he cannot request for his ship the outstandingly competent female lieutenant he worked with on a tanker.

Servicewomen themselves have effected many changes. They have fought through the courts to improve their status and opportunities. Women in senior positions have developed sophisticated political skills, working within the military, through the DACOWITS, and through the Congress. Their efforts have been backed by thousands of military women, proving repeatedly that they can do the job.

One of them is an electrician's mate who works and lives on a Navy repair ship: "A lot of guys can't deal with the idea of being on a ship with a woman, but all they've been on is a carrier with a thousand other men. If you went to interview some of the men on board these ships with women, I think you'd get positive responses from at least three-quarters of them. I'm the only woman in my shop, and I think they treat me great. You've got to go in there with a positive attitude and be willing to take the punches and roll with 'em, just like everybody else has to. I was a little nervous at first. There was a lot of silence for a couple of weeks. But after they got to know me and I got to know them, as individuals and working partners, I find it very easy to work with my male friends. I have very polite people that I work with."

An Army staff sergeant wound down her interview with "I'm gonna have to be goin' here. But I just wanta make one statement. Let me think. When I went to Hawaii, we had a sergeant major there. He had some bad experiences with women. And he said I was the new troublemaker. He just knew it. I was farm-raised, bred, and I was raised with a bunch of boys. When that sergeant major saw me liftin' the tents just as fast as the guys were and you're talking two, two-fifty, pickin' up a tent, camouflagin', diggin' trenches, he had to come up to me and apologize. He said, 'I never expected any woman to do somethin' like what you did. I thought, you know, that you were gonna give us another bad name for the office, bein' a female and stuff like that.' And I says, 'Sergeant Major, whatever you need, let me know. I'll try and do it.' "

If high-ranking women of long military experience have a regret, it is that, particularly in the switchover from separate women's corps, they have accepted men's ways of doing things rather than persuading men to adopt the superior methods women had developed. Navy Captain Julie DiLorenzo commented: "Hindsight being what it is, I think I should have insisted that in a few more areas we should have required the men to do things the way the women were doing them, rather than just accepting the fact that because men were doing it, it was the best way. I am very disturbed that in too many people's minds equality means lowering ourselves to the men's standards rather than raising men to ours." Every servicewoman faces the same dilemma in microcosm: How much does she adapt to the conversation and behavior of the overwhelmingly male military population, and how much does she try to modify them? The trick evidently is to be "outspoken, yet know when to tone things down."

The pragmatic military woman knows better than to try to reform the system wholesale. But repeatedly, pushed too far, she tells someone off, takes a stand, fights for her turf, wins her point. "They've got a few rules that need to be broken here that they're not too sure about, and I'm planning on breaking those," observed one of the first women in an extremely traditional male unit. "I'm going to pop a few of their bubbles. You bet. 'Cause there's nothing that irritates me worse than to see a bunch of men sitting around a table discussing something about a female when the female isn't there. They're going to have to get over it."

In one closed MOS after another, some military women press for change, asking "Why not?" A senior airman is just "waiting for more advances, like when women fly jets, because I want to be the first. I figure by the time I become a pilot and get trained, they'll let women fly jets by then. I would say it will take me about five years, going to part-time night school to get my degree. It shouldn't be any more than ten years before they get to that, I don't think."

Day by week by year servicewomen change the American military. *And* the way servicemen think about what women are and can do. These new attitudes seep out into the population at large. If military women owe some of their gains to the women's movement, so also civilian women owe part of their progress to the accomplishments of military women.

THE LAST WORD

The military, servicewomen agree, is no Garden of Eden (except perhaps that Eve is just as likely to be blamed as she always was). None of our interviewees found it without fault. None found it without benefit (though some came close). Let the servicewomen end this book, as they began it.

An electrician's mate of Korean descent: "This is not the best way of life. There are better ways to make career. I would not recommend it to my daughter. Because lot of people still consider military as a low life. I can put up with it. But it is in some aspect; it is low life. The military is not easy. You have to make a lot of sacrifices and you're always going to run into people not as always nice. There are some cruel people out there, but I got to cope with it. I handle it in my own way. I know what I'll be able to get from the military, from the Navy. But it wasn't all that easy. No.

"If someone does come in, she should know what she wants. Have a plan. And try to give your best shot to work that out. Don't join the Navy out of the blues and just wander around. A lot of females do. I might have been one of them. That first couple of years, changing my rate, didn't know what I really wanted to do. I woke up one day."

"Military women have their problems," says a black NCO in the Air Force, "but yet still this is the most equal area that a woman can go into and be treated equally, as far as promotion and as far as pay. Master sergeant, whether I'm female or not, it's the same thing, as far as pay is concerned, as far as benefits. There are some things that they still need to do. Like I'm trying to find out why our clothing allowance is less than men's!

"The military has been truly a rewarding experience that's going to be the basis of whatever I do in the future. No way around that. They have trained me. They have given me an opportunity to meet new people and learn from them. On the other hand, there's nothing that you can do to stop things like discrimination. You can try to control it, of course, but that's a reality. Any woman coming in today, I would tell her that 'You will in your career be discriminated against. But don't let that be the thing that determines your future. It's just like realizing that a stop sign exists at a corner. Okay. You know it's there. It might detain you for a few minutes. But if you're patient, and you're willing to work around it, you still will succeed in your course, wherever you're going. You just have to stop for the stop sign every now and then.' "

"Say, 'Hey, the regulation says you have to let me do this,' " another servicewoman advises. "Not 'I'm asking a favor,' but 'I have the right. And you're going to do it not because I'm going to scream and holler, but because you're required to do it.' "

Captain Louise Wilmot (USN) talked about the future of women in the military. "We're in a very conservative time. But today's radical idea is tomorrow's conservative idea; I see conservative groups espousing ideas which a couple of years ago were considered the absolute most liberal kinds of ideas, because they've come around to be convinced it's the only way to solve the problem. A mobilization plan [to draft doctors and nurses in the event of an emergency] was briefed to the Defense Advisory Committee on Women in the Service a year ago. This one woman truly came out of her chair. She was horrified at the thought that here she is, a very conservative Republican, listening to another very conservative Republican, and the administration is saying 'We will draft women. They will be nurses and doctors, because we do not have enough medical people to take care of injuries if we had to have any kind of conflict.' I think today drafting medical personnel is perfectly acceptable.

"And [in] some surveys done by the Ford Foundation asking young people whether or not they would object to women in combat, almost forty-five percent said they had no problem with it. Now I don't think they went on to ask the other question: Would you volunteer to do this? But I don't think men would volunteer to go in combat either.

"So I think that women have made a lot of gains. There are more gains to be made. For the Navy, the last step is to decide to put women on ships and to fully integrate women in the Navy, and that's not a secret. We've known that that is the final step for many, many years. The view [at the top] is that it's not going to be the Navy that takes the steps. *It's got to be society as a whole agreeing* that the Navy is going to do this. But I think that that's the next thing that needs to be done for women. Yes, right—and increase their numbers. Because with the increase in numbers comes pressure to do everything else."

Servicewomen are doing their jobs, serving their country, and working for new opportunities. The country owes it to them to recognize their achievements, to try to understand their problems, and to give them a fair chance. What these women may look forward to—whether they have equal opportunity, whether they go into combat—depends largely on the decisions taken by the society that the military serves. However narrowly, the United States still clings to the principles of civilian regulation and review of the military. Not by chance have the most marked advances for servicewomen followed the changes in public ideology of the 1960s and 1970s. Military managers, knowing where the money comes from, watch the Congress and public opinion. As far as they can make it out, they learn the lesson of the writing on the wall.

Chronology

This is a partial list of major steps in the recent history of women in the armed forces. Each step represents a point in a gradual process of change and adaptation to pressures and circumstances. Because each service handled these changes in its own way, the implementation of policy changes varied from branch to branch and over time. These complexities can be understood only by careful study of Martin Binkin and Shirley J. Bach, *Women and the Military* (Washington, D.C.: Brookings Institution, 1977), and Jeanne Holm, *Women in the Military: An Unfinished Revolution* (Novato, Calif.: Presidio Press, 1982).

1948

The Women's Armed Services Act established a permanent place for women in the DOD services.

1967

Congress enacted Public Law 90-130, which eased previous restrictions on career opportunities for female officers, allowing them to hold permanent grade up to colonel and naval captain and to be appointed general or admiral; removed the difference between men's and women's eligibility for retirement benefits; and removed the 2-percent ceiling on female enlisted personnel.

1969

The Air Force ROTC was opened to women.

1970

The services opened many more MOSs to women.

1972

The Army and Navy ROTCs were opened to women.
ERA cleared Congress, arousing DOD concern about its utilization of women.
The USS *Sanctuary* (hospital ship) was recommissioned with an integrated crew.
Women constituted 1.9 percent of all military personnel.

1973

The end of the draft introduced the All-Volunteer Force (AVF).
The Supreme Court forced the services to provide the same family benefits to servicewomen as to servicemen (*Frontiero* v. *Richardson*).

1975

DOD (facing substantial litigation) discontinued the practice of automatic discharge for pregnant women or women with dependent children (and the need for a waiver of the regulation).

The Coast Guard Academy admitted its first class of women cadets; Public Law 94-106 required the DOD services to admit women to their academies in 1976.
The services required weapons training for women.

1976

The Second Circuit Court held the Marine Corps regulation requiring discharge of pregnant Marines unconstitutional (*Crawford* v. *Cushman*).
The DOD service academies admitted the first women cadets.
Women constituted 5 percent of all military personnel.

1977

The Coast Guard assigned the first servicewomen to sea duty as permanent crew.

1978

The Coast Guard removed all assignment restrictions based on sex.
Judge John J. Sirica held the blanket exclusion of women from serving on Navy ships unconstitutional (*Owens* v. *Brown*). The Navy asked for and got a congressional modification of existing law and began assigning women to duty on noncombat vessels.
The Army, Navy, and Air Force abolished the WAC, WAVES, and WAF and integrated their servicewomen.
Women were gradually permitted to command organizations composed of both men and women.

1980

Congress passed the Defense Officer Personnel Management Act (DOPMA), integrating women into men's promotion lists.

1985

The services began denying women the opportunity to resign because of pregnancy *if* they were essential or had incurred a service obligation.

1986

The Army opened 10,000 additional support positions for assignment to women; the Navy reclassified support ships (store ships, ammunition ships, and oilers) as "other combatant," thereby increasing the number of ships prohibited to women; the Air Force opened 1,645 additional positions to women.

1987

DOD services project these strengths at the close of fiscal year 1987:

	ENLISTED	OFFICERS
Army	71,000 or 10.5 percent	12,000 or 10 percent
Navy	46,500 or 8.8 percent	7,500 or 10 percent
Air Force	62,800 or 12.4 percent	12,500 or 11 percent
Marine Corps	9,800 or 5.3 percent	664 or 3 percent

The Coast Guard does not have a projected goal for females.

Sources for Women in the American Military

Some of the history of women in the American military, short as it is, has already been lost. The women who served as Yeomen (F) and Marines and members of the Coast Guard in World War I have left few traces: literature on them barely exists. Except for Mattie E. Treadwell's valuable *The Women's Army Corps* (Washington, D.C.: Office of the Chief of Military History, Department of the Army, 1954), the WACS, WAVES, and SPARS of World War II and their successors were similarly almost entirely ignored by scholars until the groundbreaking publication in 1977 of Martin Binkin and Shirley J. Bach's *Women and the Military* (Washington, D.C.: Brookings Institution), followed in 1982 by Jeanne Holm's *Women in the Military: An Unfin-*

ished Revolution (Novato, Calif.: Presidio Press). These two institutional histories set an admirable standard of thoroughness and excellence. They have been supplemented by Judith Hicks Stiehm's *Bring Me Men and Women: Mandated Change at the U.S. Air Force Academy* (Berkeley: University of California Press, 1981); June A. Willenz's *Women Veterans: America's Forgotten Heroines* (New York: Continuum Publishing Company, 1983); Betty C. Morden's *The Women's Army Corps, 1945–1978* (Washington, D.C.: Office of the Chief of Military History, Department of the Army, 1983); and Sally van Wagenen Keil's *Those Wonderful Women in Their Flying Machines: The Unknown Heroines of World War II* (New York: Rawson-Wade, 1979), a book enlivened by the personal reminiscences of some of the WASPs.

Primary sources on women in the military consist largely of multitudinous statistical studies and surveys, conducted most often at the request of the military; military documents; spotty newspaper reports; a handful of oral histories of top-ranking military women in Navy and Marine archives and at the Schlesinger Library at Radcliffe College; and ephemera. Women's place in the military world has been discussed in Patricia J. Thomas's *The Role of Women in the Military: Australia, Canada, the United Kingdom, and the United States* (San Diego, Calif.: U.S. Naval Personnel Research and Development Center, 1978). Nancy H. Loring has edited a helpful set of papers on policy issues, women and military readiness, and trends in the utilization of military women, *Women in the United States Armed Forces: Progress and Barriers in the 1980s* (Chicago: Inter-University Seminar on Armed Forces and Society, 1984). A useful collection of sociological studies and policy discussions has been pulled together by William Bowman, Roger Little, and G. Thomas Sicilia, who edited *The All-Volunteer Force After a Decade: Retrospect and Prospect* (Washington, D.C.: Pergamon-Brassey's, 1986). *Life in the Rank and File: Enlisted Men and Women in the Armed Forces of the United States, Australia, Canada, and the United Kingdom*, edited by David R. Segal and H. Wallace Sinaiko (Washington, D.C.: Pergamon-Brassey's, 1986), incorporates historical, sociological, and statistical materials.

All too few military women have published their experiences: a few World War I nurses, who held semimilitary status; Joy Bright Hancock in her *Lady in the Navy: A Personal Reminiscence* (Annapolis, Md.: The Naval Institute Press, 1972); and Louanne Johnson in her witty *Making Waves: A Woman in This Man's Navy* (New York: St. Martin's Press, 1986) are worthy exceptions. Helen Rogan pioneered efforts to explore the nature of military women's experiences in *Mixed Company: Women in the Modern Army* (Boston: Beacon Press, 1981), living with a group of women in basic training and interviewing women in the first class at West Point, women who remembered the Women's Army Corps, and Army nurses who had been imprisoned in the Philippines in World War II. Michael L. Rustad based *Women in Khaki: The American Enlisted Woman* (New York: Praeger Publishers, 1982) on information from Army women on a base in Germany. Vietnam has evoked several books of personal experiences. Al Santoli included some women's experiences when he edited *Everything We Had: An Oral History of the Vietnam War by Thirty-three American Soldiers Who Fought It* (New York: Random House, 1981) and *To Bear Any Burden: The Vietnam War and Its Aftermath in the Words of Americans and Southeast Asians* (New York: E. P. Dutton, 1985). Shelley Saywell wrote a chapter on American nurses in *Women in War: First-Hand Accounts from World War II to El Salvador* (New York: The Viking Press, 1985). Lynda Van Devanter movingly related her own story in *Home Before Morning: The Story of an Army Nurse in Vietnam* (New York: Beaufort Books, 1983). Keith Walker's *A Piece of My Heart: The Stories of Twenty-six American Women Who Served in Vietnam* (Novato, Calif.: Presidio Press, 1985) and Kathryn Marshall's perceptive *In the Combat Zone: An Oral History of American Women in Vietnam* (Boston: Little, Brown, 1987) have recorded the memories of both civilian and military women. Now fiction about the experiences of military women is beginning to appear: Patricia L. Walsh's *Forever Sad the Heart* (New York: Avon Books, 1982) and Jeanne Westin's *Love and Glory: A Novel* (New York: Simon & Schuster, 1985) are two examples.

Nancy Goldman has edited a book exploring the women-in-combat controversy: *Female Soldiers: Combatants or Noncombatants? Historical and Contemporary Perspectives* (Westport, Conn.: Greenwood Press, 1982). The women's movement has been divided on the questions of whether women should join the military and whether women should fight. Although, for example, during the Carter administration the National Organization for Women filed a brief with the United States Supreme Court in favor of including women in any future draft registration, most feminist publications have strongly opposed women's participation in the military. This position has been elaborated by Cynthia Enloe in *Does Khaki Become You? The Militarization of Women's Lives* (Boston: South End Press, 1983) and summarized by Birgit Brock-Utne in *Educating for Peace: A Feminist Perspective* (Elmsford, N.Y.: Pergamon Press, 1985). Still, to a startling degree feminist writers have ignored the presence of American women in the military: for example *Behind the Lines: Gender and the Two World Wars*, edited by Margaret Randolph Higonnet, Jane Jenson, Sonya Michel, and Margaret Collins Weitz (New Haven, Conn.: Yale University Press, 1987), does not mention them, although one of its chapters focuses on British women's military services in World War I and other chapters discuss American civilian women in World War II.

Two other books remark briefly but tellingly on the status and roles of women in the American military: Admiral Elmo R. Zumwalt, Jr.'s, *On Watch: A Memoir* (New York: Quadrangle/The New York Times Book Company, 1976), and Arthur T. Hadley's *The Straw Giant: Triumph and Failure: America's Armed Forces* (New York: Random House, 1986).

Two journals are indispensable: *Armed Forces and Society* and *Minerva: Quarterly Report on Women and the Military*. And the Women and the Military Project of the Women's Equity Action League (805 15th Street NW, Suite 822, Washington, D.C. 20005; 202-638-1961) is an invaluable source of accurate and extensive information.